Wynfield's War

Praise for
Wynfield's War

These new adventures of Marina Neary's gothic anti-hero take us from the horrors of a Crimean field hospital to the intrigues of mid-Victorian London, meanwhile providing intimate glimpses into the lives of Florence Nightingale, Lord Lucan of Light Brigade infamy, and other famous personages of the time. Intensively researched, with unsparing attention to grim detail, *Wynfield's War* is a fascinating and frequently disturbing read.

> — Eileen Kernaghan, author of *Wild Talent:*
> *A Novel of the Supernatural*

Neary's new work of historical fiction will delight her readers who were captivated by her first novel, *Wynfield's Kingdom.* Her latest work, *Wynfield's War,* transports her maturing hero into the depths of depravity and British military incompetence during the mid-1850s Crimean War. With the familiar words of Tennyson's *The Charge of the Light Brigade* sounding out its rhythmic "*...cannon to the right of them, cannon to the left...*" and the surprising personage of "saintly" Florence Nightingale, Wynfield witnesses a string of British and Russian military blunders that brilliantly pulls the reader along. Neary skillfully marries history and emotion with her masterful use of words to paint a compelling narrative that is sure to tantalize and titillate both old and new followers of her artistic writing. *Wynfield's War* is a worthy addition to any novel-lovers book shelf."

> — Cathal Liam, author of *Fear Not The Storm:*
> *The Story of Tom Cullen, An Irish Revolutionary*

A fascinating look behind the military curtain--a story of men and women who look beyond the tenets of a waning empire toward a modern world just beginning to reveal itself.

> — Meghan Walsh, editor of *The Recorder*

Wynfield's War
by
Marina Julia Neary

Fireship Press
www.FireshipPress.com

Wynfield's War - Copyright © 2010 by Marina Julia Neary

ISBN: 978-1-61179- 066-5

BISAC Subject Headings:
FIC014000   FICTION / Historical
FIC032000   FICTION / War & Military
FIC002000   FICTION / Action & Adventure

Address all correspondence to:
Fireship Press, LLC
P.O. Box 68412
Tucson, AZ 85737

Or visit our website at:
www.FireshipPress.com

1.0

Contents

Part 3
Rough Meat and Excellent Champagne
Summer, 1854

Part 6
A Nightingale Among Vultures
Scutari
November, 1854

Dedication

I dedicate this work to my husband and superb character actor Walter Lawrence Neary in recognition of his blood-chilling portrayal of Lord Lucan in the 2009 theatrical production of "Lady with a Lamp". You were born to play British villains, my darling. Thank you for being my crew-mate through yet another Neo-Victorian odyssey.

Part 1
Light in the Tower
Selimiye Barracks, Scutari, Turkey
November, 1854

Chapter 1
The Barber of Liverpool

Timothy Bennett had not felt such elation since the day he stuck the shaving blade snatched from his father's barbershop into the pulsating belly of a rat. Timmy was twelve years old then, bursting with innate boyish wonder and determination to grasp all the mysteries of the universe. Creatures long dead, much like broken mechanisms, held very little interest to him. There is no sport in taking apart a clock inside which all the gears have long ceased moving.

A decade later, he was standing in the middle of a surgical tent in the Crimea where his intellectual pursuits had led him. Instead of a dull barber's blade, he was holding a real surgical saw, just like the ones he had seen in medical catalogues and at trade shows. (Oh, how he sighed over those shiny treasures arrayed so elegantly in their wooden cases lined with velvet!) The squirming rat was replaced with a twenty-four year old Private Seamus Martin, whose hand he was about to amputate. The patient was sufficiently sedated, even though his eyelids were still twitching, and an occasional spasmodic rattle would escape from his parched lips. Through his delirium, the soldier seemed to be protesting the impending procedure. He was already strapped in to the table, his left hand on the chopping board, his swollen purple fingers that still had some sensation left in them, wiggling weakly. When a brick of wood was placed between his teeth, he nearly choked on his own saliva. That brick already bore bite marks from dozens of other patients who had been strapped to the same table. More than half of them were taken away wrapped in sackcloth.

The young surgeon, however, forbade himself to take those deaths as personal defeats. The drafty tent transformed into a theater, and he, Timothy Bennett, became the star of his own opera, *The Barber of Liverpool*. In a sonorous tenor that still lapsed into prepubescent descant, he kept spouting orders to his two nurses assisting him.

The younger one, Rebecca Prior, was a pink-faced blonde with bulging cornflower eyes, an upturned nose with flaring nostrils and swollen lips that she kept licking nervously. One could tell that her hair had not been washed in ages, although clumsy attempts had clearly been made to curl it. A few random ringlets sprouted from the crown, falling on top of her greasy flaxen strings. Who could blame the girl for wanting to look spiffy for her surgical debut, even within the constraints of the nurse's uniform? Rebecca's responsibility was to hand out the appropriate instruments. Her more experienced mates would agree that sporting a ruffled blouse was probably not the wisest choice. At least, she had enough common sense to roll up the sleeves.

Her companion was a lean brunette in her mid-thirties, inconspicuously beautiful, with a Spartan posture and a purely symbolic bosom. Her presence disquieted Timothy. He had a most burdensome feeling that she was there not so much to assist him but rather to evaluate him. The elongated lines of her neck, nose, and forehead communicated an air of superiority.

Florence Nightingale! That name seemed to be on everybody's lips these days. This insufferable shrew, this power-hungry spinster, whose temper no sane man with the exception of Sidney Herbert would tolerate, came here to lay down her law—in other words, to steal the glory from the surgeons. She had already tried to chide him, Timothy Bennett, the most revered surgeon in the entire hospital corps, about his method for cauterizing wounds. Now she was trying to point out to him the exact place on the patient's wrist for applying the tourniquet. Having hung the lamp above the surgical table, she opened the amputation manual that Timothy new by heart. As if by accident, he elbowed the book off the table. Without a word, the nurse picked it up, opened in the same spot, and laid it out on the table next to the patient's head.

"Five minutes," she said, tapping the yellow page. "If you follow my instructions, it should take you no more than five minutes to saw through the bone."

My instructions...

"What did you say, Miss Nightingale?" Timothy inquired, squinting. "I'm a bit hard of hearing these days. All those moans in the hospital corps wore out my eardrums."

"In that case, I will speak louder," she replied imperturbably.

"I assure you," Timothy said, unbuttoning the cuffs of his sleeves, "your narration won't be necessary. My eyes and hands are perfectly intact. Private Martin isn't my first patient."

"You mean, not your first victim?"

Timothy inhaled, raised his eyebrows, and remained frozen in that pose for a few seconds.

"What's the matter, Mr. Bennett?" she asked. "Did you hear something disagreeable? Are you ears playing tricks on you again?"

Timothy felt the corners of his mouth twitching, stretching into a mad grin against his will. No doubt, this woman was jesting. It must have been her method of easing her own anxiety.

"Hand me the curving knife, Miss Prior," he demanded, his eyes still on Florence Nightingale.

Having heard her name, the younger nurse shuddered and began rummaging through the surgical kit. There were five knives of different sizes, and she was not sure which one Mr. Bennett needed.

"I'm sorry," she sniffled at last. "So dreadfully sorry..."

Rebecca bowed her head, inviting the well-earned wrath, but Timothy had no time to chastise her. He yanked the kit from the girl's hands, pulled out one of the thinner knives, and held it to the light, admiring the sharpness of the edge.

"Tighten the tourniquet, Miss Nightingale!"

Just as he was ready to put the knife to use, Florence placed her fingers on the patient's forehead, brushing the hair back, then leaned close to him and whispered something, even though he probably could not hear her.

Her last gesture struck Timothy as an act of conspiracy. The brazen nurse dare to whisper into the patient's ear in the presence of the surgeon, the man with the knife!

Struggling to retain control over his breathing, Timothy flattened Private Martin's hand against the board, using the entire weight of his underdeveloped body, and made the first incision.

The patient's back arched, and the table shook.

"The saw!" Timothy shouted when he was done with the knife.

A second later he heard a gasp behind his back followed by gurgling sound. The novice nurse vomited into her apron and fell to her knees. The smell of half-digested gruel filled the tent, blending in with the smells of blood and pus. The content of the surgical kit spilled on the floor.

"Get out," Timothy ordered through his teeth without turning around.

Rebecca exited the tent on her fours, leaving Timothy alone with Florence. The expression of the older nurse's face remained unchanged. Not a drop of sweat appeared on her forehead. It seemed that this woman was incapable of perspiring at all. In the matter of seconds, she located the retractor and the saw. Having made sure that all four major arteries in the patient's arm were still tied, she nodded, giving the surgeon a sign to proceed—not that Timothy needed her permission.

The sawing took even less than the predicted five minutes. It was not Timothy's custom to rush through a procedure of this sort, but this time he was anxious to free himself from that woman's company, from her suffocating, paralyzing gaze.

As soon as his job was done, he tossed the saw aside and dashed out of the tent for a gasp of air. Just at the entrance, he tripped over Rebecca's foot. The girl was still sitting on the ground, still wearing her vomit-stained apron. At the sight of Mr. Bennett, she tucked her foot under her petticoats fearfully and crawled away, straight into a pile of soiled linens.

Now was a perfect opportunity for him to explode.

"This is preposterous!" he shouted, throwing his bloodied arms up.

"I'm sorry..." Rebecca mumbled her litany, rubbing the bridge of her nose. "So very dreadfully sorry..."

"It isn't my forgiveness that you should be begging. Apologize to Private Martin, who had to witness your tantrum from the comfort of the surgical table!"

The girl lifted her head and sniffled, inhaling the secretions from her nose.

"'Tis that... 'Tis that I never seen so much blood b'fore."

Timothy could not help chuckling at this last declaration. What did she expect—a parish outing, a tea ceremony, perhaps? So much for being a butcher's daughter!

At that moment, Florence emerged from the tent. She rushed to Rebecca and pulled her to her feet by the ties of her apron.

"Now, Miss Prior, look Mr. Bennett in the eye and promise him in a steady voice that this shall never be repeated."

"You can bet your sweet life it won't!" Timothy exclaimed. "Miss Prior, you are not to come near the surgical tent ever again. Do you hear me? You'll be on the first ship back to England, where you can resume rationing gruel at a workhouse!"

"It won't be necessary," Florence interrupted him hastily. "If I send every skittish nurse home, I won't have any hands left. There's a fitting occupation for everyone. I shall put Miss Prior in charge of sanitizing the instruments and boiling the laundry. Young lady, start with your soiled linens. Remember to soak the blood out with cold water before boiling."

The hapless girl nodded, pulled her head into her shoulders, picked up the heap of linens, and dragged them into the laundering tent, dropping a few pieces on the way. When Rebecca was out of sight, Florence lifted her chin and took a step towards Timothy.

"I marvel at the pliancy of your conscience. Taking your personal embarrassment out on a creature like Becky Prior—how convenient!"

"Miss Nightingale, I don't have the faintest..."

"Oh, come now! We both know why you lashed out at Rebecca. Naturally, you are infuriated by your own mistake."

"What mistake?"

"The loss of Private Martin's hand," she replied, gesturing towards the tent. "Had you followed my instructions for cleaning and dressing the wound, the infection would not have spread, and gangrene would not have developed. There would have been no need for such... terminal surgical measures."

Timothy felt the idiotic grin returning to his face. So the woman kept on jesting!

"I shan't continue this conversation with you, Miss Nightingale."

"Very well, then you shall have it with your superiors!" she replied, raising her voice. "I'm certain that Dr. Grant will have something to say regarding this matter."

By God, she was not jesting! She was threatening him quite earnestly. A part of him was curious to hear the rest of her tirade, to see the extent of her audacity.

"Your imaginary crown won't tarnish," she continued, "if you would heed my advice from time to time. Young man..."

"It's Mr. Bennett to you!" Timothy shouted. "I address you by your surname, so please, extend the same courtesy to me. I would be most grateful if you did not project your unused maternal sentiments onto me."

Her fatigued shrug indicated that she had heard those accusations before.

"Rest assured, Mr. Bennett, the good Lord spared me such sentiments," she replied, untying her apron and blotting her hands with it. "I've been endowed with more practical talents, such as speaking candidly, especially in the face of blatant malpractice and negligence. Crippled soldiers are of no use to England."

Timothy began walking around her in circles, leaning into her and pulling back, rising on his tiptoes and crouching, examining every eyelet on her collar. She remained standing with her arms folded, looking upward.

"Miss Nightingale," he said suddenly with a sinister softness, "I worry about your well-being. The whites of your eyes are turning quite scarlet. So much righteous anger will do you no good. You recall that you've already suffered one emotional collapse. And do not let chloroform go to your brain."

Chapter 2
The Quack of Southwark

"You better start reading my letters, Sidney," Florence muttered to herself, watching the surgeon's scrawny frame disappear inside the barracks that had been serving as a hospital. "What sort of people have you sent here? The nurses dread the sight of blood, and the surgeons like it a bit too much. How am I to create a respectable medical establishment?"

Feeling a sudden numbness in the ankles, Florence sat down on an empty wooden box that once contained provisions. She attempted scribbling in her notebook, but the pencil kept slipping out of her fingers. With indifference, she examined her hands and noticed pools of blood under her fingernails where the vessels had burst while she was holding down Private Martin. The hapless Irishman was still lying on the surgical table inside the tent, and he was likely going to spend the night there. There were no more surgeries planned for that day, and after what he had endured under Timothy Bennett's saw, it would be inhumane to jostle him around.

Sensing the drop in the temperature, Florence thought it would be a sound idea to fetch a blanket for Private Martin. If only she could find one that was not crawling with lice. At least the chief of medical staff, who initially was not thrilled about her arrival, had finally agreed to have a separate tent built for surgeries. Before then amputations were performed in the hallways of the barracks, on blood-soaked straw mattresses, in plain sight of other patients.

Suddenly, the sound of a man's cough distracted Florence. She closed her notebook and smiled. Every day she heard hundreds of coughs, but that one had a distinctive low-pitched undertone that reminded her of a bear's growl. It could only belong to Thomas Grant, a physician from Southwark. He was the one greeted her at the shore upon her arrival and showed her the hospital. After nightfall, his ursine side emerged. A beast and a scholar at once, he fascinated her.

"Did I miss a mutiny?" he asked, rubbing his gloved hands.

"Some of our colleagues take too much pleasure in their profession," Florence replied, setting her notebook aside, for it became clear that she was not going to do much writing that night.

"Dare I guess: Timmy Bennett delivering another tirade?

"A perfect tyrant at age twenty-two! Imagine, being so young?"

The last question was articulated with a hint of universal envy.

"What would I know about such things? I've been forty-nine my entire life."

"Rest assured, Dr. Grant, at this pace, I'm not far behind you."

They both went inside the tent to check on the patient. When Tom lifted the towel covering the stump and saw the result of Mr. Bennett's masterwork, his gray eyebrows contracted.

"Damn that scrawny butcher! He took the whole hand."

"Did you not instruct him to do so?"

"I certainly did not! He either misheard my orders or blatantly disobeyed them. Tell me, Miss Nightingale: has Timmy ever played deaf with you?"

Florence stepped back and rubbed her temples.

"Incredible," she whispered. "People come here because they have failed at everything else. I'm still waiting for dressing gauze to be delivered. Soon I will have to tear strips from the hem of my skirt to bandage wounds. I waste too much time writing letters that make no difference at all. I honestly don't know how much longer I can hold down the fort."

"For what it's worth, I have an audience with Lord Cardigan next week," Tom attempted to console her. "I have no idea why he summoned me, meager and nameless as I am, but I'll be sure to plead on your behalf. Imagine: I shall travel across the sea all the way to Balaclava Harbor on the next transport vessel just to rendezvous with his Lordship's yacht."

That name solicited a spiteful smirk from Florence.

"Cardigan, you say? I wouldn't let my hopes soar. He won't release any of his men to bring provisions and medicine of which there is plenty along the coast. He deems the endeavor exceedingly perilous. Naturally, it is safer to let his soldier starve and die of wounds."

"At least I'll see the interior of his infamous yacht," Tom continued in a deliberately mysterious, tantalizing tone. "If I'm lucky, I'll catch a whiff of his brandy. It's been a long time since I smelled quality spirits."

The last statement was intended as a joke, a damn hilarious one too, but Florence did not respond to it as she usually would. Breaking her own rules, she leaned against the surgical table. It was an act of blasphemy for which she would give any other nurse hell. Under no circumstances was one allowed to use medical equipment as furniture, but for an instant Florence forgot where she was. The chloroform-soaked towel that Timothy left behind continued to release the substance into the air. Florence had already inhaled enough of it during the surgery. The ground beneath her feet turned into a rocking ocean of mud. Another second and she would fall into the sticky black waves.

Tom, in turn, broke his own rule of not touching nurses and squeezed her shoulders.

"When was the last time you slept?" he asked.

She caught his hand before he had a chance to pull it back.

"Good God," she mumbled, frowning. "Have you been laying hot bricks?"

"No—cold corpses," he replied nonchalantly. "Forty in a day! The chaplain was out of breath, poor devil. We wrapped them all in sailcloth and laid them in rows, based on ascending rank. Tomorrow will be a perfect day for a mass burial—cold and clear."

Florence shook her head, chasing away that high-pitched ringing that periodically muffled the external sounds. She relied on Dr. Grant's voice to keep her awake and was determined not to lose trail of what promised to be a most stimulating cerebral exchange, the kind she had been denied since her last visit with Sidney Herbert. Having to simplify her speech in her present surrounding, constantly having to shorten her sentences and choose Anglo-Saxon equivalents to Latin terms proved to be a draining chore. She was exerting too much effort making sure she was being understood. And there was the enigmatic, erudite Dr. Grant, talking about the weather!

"How can you predict such things?" she asked, as the muddy ocean beneath her feet gradually began to harden.

"I simply look at the stars. Their clarity tells a great deal about the atmospheric fluctuations."

Beginning to feel the effects of the chloroform himself, Tom led Florence out of the tent. They sat on the empty provision box in an impermissible proximity to each other. The knowledge that the calluses on their fingertips were of the same texture awakened intoxicating camaraderie. Who would forbid them to retreat into their private intellectual oasis?

"Thank you, Dr. Grant," she concluded, when the ringing in her ears subsided.

"For the lesson in meteorology?"

"No, for not ruining a perfectly scientific moment with poetic drivel. You had an opportunity, to spout something utterly nauseating about cosmos, and infinity—yet you withstood the temptation. For that I am grateful."

"I assure you that such thoughts never crossed my mind," Tom lied. "In turn, I am grateful for not having a mass burial in rainy weather with water destroying freshly dug graves. I looked up, and the stars told me what I needed to know."

His last words drowned in a stifled yawn. Two deadly fatigued individuals should avoid making direct eye contact if they wish to remain awake. Tom and Florence were discovering the sedative effect of studying each other's quivering eyelids.

Florence sorely needed to find a topic that would anger her enough to sustain her alertness.

"Did you know I was once courted by a poet?" she began with a mixture of amusement and embarrassment. "Richard Milnes, Baron Houghton."

As a matter of fact, Tom knew about Florence's infamous engagement, as he had begun following her endeavors long before her assignment to the Crimea. Her name appeared in the press during the Poor Laws reforms in the 1840s. From his bear's den in Southwark, he had been observing the bewildering odyssey of this rebellious girl who claimed to have heard the voice of God, the voice that instructed her to denounce her roots in the name of science and charity. Certainly, she was not the first girl to have made such declarations, but she was one of the few to have silenced her detractors. Gradually, Tom became her passive, invisible supporter. Fate had presented him with several opportunities to meet Florence, but he never pursued them. Now the two of them were sitting on the same provisions box.

At last, he could study her face closely. She looked enviably fresh for being in her thirty-fifth year. This woman never dabbed her face with cubes of frozen milk to smooth out the tiny lines around her eyes and mouth, yet any twenty-year old socialite would give half of her estate for such pristine skin. That narrow face with a straight nose, high forehead, and wide eyes held a certain nonchalant allure, undeniably feminine in nature, despite her habit of referring to herself as "man of action." She flexed her wrists and snapped her knuckles in the same manner that Tom's former colleagues from Cambridge did. It was not inconceivable that certain men should find themselves enchanted by her. So yes, Tom knew all about Richard Milne and a few other victims. Still, he was curious to hear the story from Florence directly.

"A baron?" he asked, imitating envy.

"A sentimental dolt!" she blurted out impatiently. "And a clumsy liar too... How he swore he wouldn't interfere with my practice! He even donated a sum to the hospital. Yet I knew it was only to cajole me into marriage. Had he attained his goal, all his false interest in my work would dissipate. Ah, he's married now."

Florence was fully awake now. The resurrected vexation scattered her drowsiness.

"That does not prevent him from writing to me on occasion," she added boastfully and flirtatiously.

"Poor Richard!" Tom cried with mock pity.

"Poor Florence! Those self-proclaimed connoisseurs of the female soul know nothing about the female body. The man kissed as if he were afraid of poisoning me. Is it such a crime on my part to desire a skillful, well-executed kiss that isn't followed by a poetic couplet?"

She touched her lips and then glanced at her fingertips, as if expecting to see traces of blood.

"I endorse your righteous indignation!" Tom replied, drumming on his knee. "Abstinence is next to idleness. Together, they cause insomnia and fits of hysteria. Like men, women need physical work and physical pleasure."

"Amen! I attempted to communicate those simple medical facts to my dear Mama, and she howled that she had never heard such obscenities from a lady."

Florence removed the net covering her hair and pulled out the pins out of the bun one by one—a ritual she usually performed in the privacy of her room. The wind quickly diffused the strands into a ragged black veil. Tom marveled how such a savage mane could be tied in a knot the size of a fist.

"According to Mama," continued Florence, laying out her pins on the palm of her hand, "the sole purpose of my endeavors was to humiliate the family. In her eyes it was all a spectacle, a prolonged adolescent rebellion. A spoiled privileged girl experimenting with charity, poking beggars and orphans, dirtying her hands only to enrage her mother... What can be said in my defense? That's the kind of unfeeling ogress I am. I have a turnip in place of a heart."

"A turnip in place of a heart," Tom echoed pensively. "Why, that is poetry in its own right. Is that your expression?"

"No, that's what Richard stated in his last letter to me. He does not recover from rejection quickly."

Now Tom knew the real reason why Florence left her suitor. The baron proved to be a dull, inhibited lover, and she simply would not tolerate it. His alleged lack of interest in her work served as a mere excuse. Indeed, poor Richard... And poor Florence! Her staunch Christian convictions projected onto the wounded in her care. In intimate matters, she was less inclined to self-sacrifice.

Suddenly, the expression of unappeasable annoyance on her face gave way to that of adoration and unabashed nostalgia.

"And then there was Sidney Herbert," she continued, "a divine man in every way—but married."

"You saw that as an obstacle?" Tom asked incredulously.

"I didn't—but he did. Amusingly, years ago, when Sidney was free, he had an affair with a married woman. But now he won't betray his own wife, even though she disappoints him, and temptation is so near."

Florence inhaled regally and arched her neck with an air of self-complacency and superiority. Alas, she could not hold that pose for long. A few seconds later her posture collapsed.

"Believe it or not, it was his initiative to send me to the Crimea," she lamented, her arms dangling. "He thought it would be prudent to put some distance between us. His wife was relieved, I'm certain. Sidney had joked about marrying me, should he suddenly become widowed. It's a hellishly awkward situation, and there will be no relief as long as all three of us are alive. One of us must die, or..."

"Or you could find yourself a new lover," Tom suggested, savoring the delicious and mutually disarming indecency of this conversation. "That would be a far more peaceful and pleasant solution."

"I wish it were so easy," she whispered under her breath. "I was impossible to impress in the past, but after meeting Sidney... How should I put it in scientific terms? Having tasted of morphine, how can one return to opium? I just know I shall die alone, a victim of my own fantastic standards."

Tom nearly choked at the injustice of it all. This woman, sublime in her candor, has been deprived of carnal tenderness for God knows how long. This slender, strong, well-proportioned body that could produce handsome, sturdy offspring has been starving. This long pliant neck has been without kisses. Sidney Herbert, the Secretary of War, who could have almost any other woman in the kingdom, enticed Florence for the sake of his own male vanity and then, after her company became burdensome, dispatched her to the war zone. In a matter of seconds Tom's otherwise sluggish imagination painted a most vibrant and gut-wrenching picture of seduction. The blood-curdling audacity of Sidney Herbert! Did he not know that women like Florence were intended not for soldiers and poets but for scientists and explorers? Had Tom only been younger, richer, worthier, neither Richard nor Sidney would have even entered the picture.

The sudden surge of indignation brought on another coughing fit. Tom should not have allowed himself to become so agitated, not while he needed to conserve every bit of strength.

Florence rubbed her eyes, embarrassed by her own weakness.

"Forgive me, Dr. Grant," she resumed. "It is awfully rude of me to burden you with my complaints. You need not hear any of this."

"I'm accustomed to hearing all sorts of confessions from my patients," Tom reassured her, marveling at how steady his voice sounded in spite of the fire between his inflamed lungs. "They mistake me for the chaplain. Earlier that night one of the lads from Donegal caught me by the waistcoat and sang a mournful ditty from his native village—in Gaelic. But Miss Nightingale, how I wish I could lift your spirits. I know! I have a perfect book for you."

"Oh, what's the title?" she asked wearily.

"England on Her Deathbed."

"And the author?"

"Yours truly," he replied, bowing.

Florence recoiled, looked at him steadfastly, and shook her head, even though the revelation did not astonish her one bit.

"Where can I procure this masterpiece?"

"Oh, it hasn't been completed it. I'll be sure to give you the final version before sending it to the printer. Imagine decades of medical journals, depicting everything from epidemics to opium addiction. There you'll find the most peculiar deaths of various English citizens, including my own daughter."

"You had a daughter?" she asked skeptically, almost spitefully.

"And a son—though neither one of them was mine by blood," Tom replied hastily. "Ah, it's long story. Those two entered my life after I had vowed not to pursue conventional fatherhood. Undoubtedly, you've heard about gang wars on Jacob's Island?"

"Now that's a hell cauldron!"

"Well, those two children emerged from it, mutilated in body and soul. The girl must have lost one third of her blood, and the boy's face was slashed up. At first, I treated them as patients. By then my medical license had been revoked—my former employer had seen to that. Fortunately, one does not need a license to operate on casualties of gang wars. So, I patched them up the best I could; and for the next fifteen years I reared them as my children. Although, if you ask the boy, he'll probably tell you that I am the most tyrannical exploiter to have ever walked the English soil. He and I did not part on an amicable note. During our last encounter, he tried to choke me to death. The girl's death had rendered him mad. He began ranting about being a lord, a long-lost heir of some baron, and having a thousand pounds as pocket change. Then he tried killing himself by guzzling what I assume was morphine. I did what I could to stop him, and that seemed to infuriate him. Before I knew it, his hands were around my throat. That is about standard gratitude for a father to receive from his son. I tell you... While the girl was alive, they were like two halves of the Iron Maiden—that was how they referred to themselves jocosely. Grinnin' Wyn and Diana the Wolf-Cub... Partners in crime and misery who became lovers..."

"How those children entered your life or how they kept each other amused is immaterial to me," Florence interrupted him. "I only care to know how they departed. Down with those lyrical digressions. What was the cause of the girl's death? What was it: cholera, diphtheria?"

She squeezed his hand impatiently, demandingly. How could Tom refrain from chuckling? When was the last time he saw such raw hunger in a woman's eyes? Florence was not going to let him evade the answer. Her nails dug deeper into his wrist.

"I fear you'll have to wait until the book is finished," he said. "The suspense will give you a reason to continue our friendly dialogue. I trade my knowledge for your company."

She released his hand as abruptly as she seized it. "That is unpardonable cruelty, taunting me in this manner!"

"Come now. I promised you would be the first one to read it. Until then, you'll have to muster all your patience."

"In that case," she declared, folding her arms defiantly, "prepare to hear more unsavory confessions from me. By the end of this campaign, you will be so satiated with my company that you will shove your unfinished manuscript into my hands just to be rid of me. Let's see whose patience runs out first."

"I accept the challenge."

They looked at each for a few seconds, and burst out laughing. Tom's laughter immediately turned into a coughing fit.

"Something must be done about this beastly growl," Florence said, resuming her stern, commanding tone. "That chamomile extract I gave you? Drink it. I spotted that flask on your nightstand. It wasn't even opened. And fetch another pillow for your upper back. It will help you breathe. And open the window, even though it's cold."

Suddenly, they realized that they have had an observer. It was the butcher boy from Liverpool, Timothy Bennett.

"It pains me to interrupt your intellectual tryst," he began, "but Miss Nightingale, you better attend to Private Martin. Soon he will be waving his stump and screaming out your name."

Disregarding Timothy's presence, Tom took Florence by the elbow and whispered to her:

"You better rest. I'll send for someone to watch the patients."

"Now, remember my instructions," she replied. "This is no joking matter. You're one cough away from pneumonia."

Having thrown one last glance at Tom, Florence departed.

"There she goes," Timothy chanted out pompously behind her back. "The Joan of Arc of English medicine!"

"Mr. Bennett," Tom began sternly, "I wish you would show more courtesy to your female colleagues."

The last word sent shivers of indignation throughout Timothy's lithe frame.

"You mean—my female subordinates? As far as I recall, surgeons still rank somewhat above nurses, who in turn rank only somewhat above common whores."

"Well, since you raised the question of hierarchy, I am forced to remind you that I am still your superior. But, hierarchy aside, I implore you, as a fellow-gentleman."

Another wave of shivers engulfed Timothy.

"You still classify yourself a gentleman? Thomas Grant, the Famished Bear!"

"Bravo!" Tom applauded. "I see you've done your detective work."

With the righteousness of an avenger angel, Timothy pointed his freckled finger at the exhausted, smirking doctor.

"I know why you lost your medical license: you nearly killed a young patient, Lord Middleton's nephew. So you spent the last two decades in Southwark trading opium, sleeping between two circus girls and sheltering criminals in your home.

Timothy's sparkled triumphantly as he listed all of Dr. Grant's crimes. He spouted them out on one breath, making sure that he did not forget any.

"Yes, very well-researched..." Tom nodded. "Some of those events took place before you were even born. Your interest in ancient history is commendable."

Such nonchalant response to the accusations on the doctor's behalf bewildered Timothy. His index finger twitched and turned limp.

"What, you have nothing to say in your defense?" he demanded, shaking his head incredulously. "For God's sake, have you no instinct for self-preservation?"

"If I had any such instinct left, would I have sailed to Crimea?"

16

"Oh, I see where this is leading!" the young butcher concluded, cocking his index finger again. "It's all perfectly logical. After indulging in every perversion under the sun, the Famished Bear resorts to a life of asceticism. He has no instincts! He has transcended them!"

Timothy jumped up on the wooden box and opened his arms, as if embracing the chilly Crimean night.

"Can't you admit being envious of my colorful and adventurous past?" Tom asked in a patronizing tone. "Don't despair, my young friend. You too will have a reputation some day. I need not defend myself before anyone. It may disappoint you, but all my misdemeanors are common knowledge. I have no secrets. I have no shame. However, I still have an obligation to my patients, which brings me to the subject of Private Martin, whose hand you amputated earlier. I had specifically instructed you to remove the index finger above the joint. How do you explain your improvisation?"

"The hand was gangrenous!" Timothy screamed, jumping down from his pedestal. "Another day—and we'd have to amputate up to the elbow. Two days—up to the shoulder. Three days—and he'd be dead."

"Mr. Bennett, your youthful imagination paints all sorts of Shakespearean catastrophes. I examined the patient this morning. The hand was perfectly salvageable. You crippled a man for no reason. It was my decision to make—not yours."

"You are not fit to make such decisions; and I shall make sure that everyone knows it! You'll go back to trading opium and helping slum whores get rid of their unwanted offspring."

Tom rubbed his chin defiantly.

"I've been alive for half a century," he said, looking the young butcher in the eye. "Over the course of that time, many wars have been waged against me. Yet I'm still alive, which cannot be said for my adversaries. It is God's will that I should remain in this world and in this profession. You may want to consider that, Mr. Bennett, before your next attempt to remove me from your path."

Chapter 3
The Angel of the Heavy Brigade

Before awarding himself the luxury to collapse for the night Tom needed to attend to one more matter. He had heard of a young officer from the Heavy Brigade who came to the hospital along with the wounded soldiers under his command. After the Battle of Balaclava, he could have remained with Sir James Scarlett at the post inland where the lodging was cleaner and the food more abundant, yet he volunteered to accompany his men across the sea to Scutari on a sick transport ship and see that they received proper care. According to the rumors, he possessed some basic medical knowledge and jumped at the opportunity to exercise it. The superficial wound in the left arm that he sustained in Balaclava did not hinder him. It was his altruistic whim to share the filth and hunger with his men.

What was the young officer's surname? Kensington, Huntington... Tom could not remember. He only knew that this man was his direct link to the higher-ups. Tom had a list of sorely needed medications and supplies that he intended to present to the officer, who in turn would present it to his direct superior. Sir James, notorious for his impractical compassion, would be more likely to respond than anyone else.

As Tom was walking down the hallway of the hospital, the wounded would rise on their mattresses and reach out for him, grabbing his trousers, mumbling feverishly, imploring, demanding, and cursing. Contrary to his usual custom, he ignored their pleas and kept on walking, stepping over the bandaged legs, pushing away the hands. His eyes were fixed on the door behind which the Heavy Brigade was lodging.

That hovel seemed like an oasis of optimism. The men were jovial, though not to the point of obscenity. Unlike their comrades-at-arms in the next room who squeamishly avoided physical contact with each other, the men of the Heavy Brigade clustered together, trading jokes, handshakes and side punches. A deck of cards was being passed around along with a dish of snuff. Those must have been consolation gifts from their patron officer, the so-called Lord Kensington or Huntington. Tom marveled at how gingerly, how reverently the men sampled the tobacco. He felt a vague pang of remorse, as if he had interrupted some sacred ritual.

His gaze fell upon a dragoon's uniform hung on a three-legged chair, the only piece of furniture in the room. Judging from the size of the overcoat, one could tell it was tailored for someone with a very narrow waist, a tall child rather than a fully-grown man. Having surveyed the room, Tom quickly identified the one to whom the overcoat belonged—a dark-haired, alarmingly slender youngster. Adorned with a necklace of gauze, bloodied and clean mixed together, he was tending to several patients at once. Tom could not ignore the beatific expressions on their faces. What those bloodshot eyes exuded went beyond mere camaraderie or gratitude. The soldiers gravitated to their commander like lepers to Christ. Tom winced at his own comparison, though it seemed fairly accurate. As for the officer himself, he appeared oblivious to everyone's adoration. He had dozens of limbs to bandage, all mangled to various degrees, and rather limited resources.

The young officer turned his head, looking for a clean strip of gauze, and on his cheek, illuminated by the Turkish lamp Tom perceived a dark crooked scar, the same scar on which he had looked for fifteen years. There could be no mistake. Tom recognized his unpardonably amateurish work, his first and last experience with the scalpel and needle. The blizzard of 1839, the noise in the cellar, the blood on the snow, the smell of laudanum concoction, the scalding heat of boiled surgical instruments in his hands... It all came back to him, fifteen years condensed into one second. He wavered and dropped his medical bag.

Having heard the noise, the officer turned around.

"At last, you're here, good doctor!" he exclaimed. "I was about to begin experimenting with stitches. What a frightening thought. And I've never as much as sewn a button on my uniform."

He was standing under the dangling lamp, grinning, his face fully exposed and illuminated.

A hoarse cry escaped from Tom's parched throat. "Wyn!"

The young officer chuckled and arched his raven eyebrow. "Win? Why, indeed! That is our intention—to win this war. Isn't it so, gentlemen?"

Dirty fists and bloodied stumps sprung up in the air, followed by a howl.

Tom trembled and subsided to one knee, covering his mouth.

"Dear God..." he mumbled through his fingers. "My child... Is this a dream?"

He stretched both hands forth, opening and closing his fists. The young officer looked as if he was about to recoil but at the last moment, he stepped towards his visitor.

"Yes, it is a dream, most certainly. Doctor, you are sleepwalking. You must've been on your feet for the past twenty hours."

Tom dropped his hands and burst into weak mad laughter.

"Listen to him jest! You haven't changed your ways, Wynfield."

The officer's scarred face assumed a colder expression. "I fear you are confusing me with someone else," he declared tersely and folded his arms, "which is not an astonishing effect of fatigue. I don't believe we have met before. My name is Jeremy Griffin Helmsley, Lord Hungerton. And these gentlemen are my heroes. I assume you came here to help me relieve their sufferings."

"I'm at your service, Your Lordship," Tom mumbled, staring at the dangling lamp that suddenly blazed up brighter and enlarged, occupying his entire spectrum.

"Gentlemen, vacate a mattress for him at once!" the officer ordered. "The good doctor is delirious."

Those were the last words Tom heard before he sprawled on the dirty floor amidst broken crutches and torn shoes. The voices of the wounded soldiers faded into one collective hum. That was the sound of souls in the Purgatory. Dozens of dirty, callused hands slipped under Tom, lifted him, and lowered under a shapeless lumpy mattress.

Chapter 4
Cockney and Blarney
Fraternize in Misery

Ill fortune had been haunting Rebecca Prior since her arrival at the barracks in Scutari. Each day brought a new disaster, each more embarrassing than the one before. Last Wednesday she went on an errand to fetch the provisions and forgot to put on the woolen cloak with the sign "Scutari Hospital," the same cloak that distinguished her from other hangers-on. As she was returning at dusk, dragging an enormous bag of wheat flower, three lightly wounded soldiers ambushed her outside the hospital walls. By the time she had a chance explain to the gentlemen that she was one of Miss Nightingale's nurses, it was too late. Beastly cravings made the soldiers deaf to her indistinct squeaks. They wrinkled her skirt and tore her last good pair of pantaloons to shreds. What was even worse, they accidentally ripped the sack that they used as a mattress. When Rebecca finally stood up, she was all covered in flour. Ground wheat was everywhere: all over her blouse, in her hair, on the tip of her nose. When Rebecca began crying, tiny dough balls formed on her cheeks, which the soldiers found entertaining as hell. One of them laughed so heartily, that he literally popped a few stitches on his wound in the shoulder.

Of all the assaults of this nature that she had endured, this was, beyond doubt, the most humiliating one. Even her father's mates from the butchery displayed more gallantry. At least, they never jumped at her three at a time. Now the entire hospital corps would know that Rebecca Prior could not be trusted with a task as simple as delivering provisions. No wonder she was demoted to being a laundress. Still, even in that meager role she did not show particular competence. The washing did not help much. The sheets came out of the cauldron almost as dirty as they went in. The bloodstains faded, but the fabric itself turned yellowish-gray. Even after three rinses, the smell still lingered. Miss Nightingale would not be pleased. Perhaps, she should have stayed in England and gone to the workhouse with the rest of her family. God knows, there were fewer maggots in the gruel.

Drowning in delicious self-pity, Rebecca did not realize that she was dropping towels and sheets, leaving a gray trail.

On her way to the nurses' tower, she saw a ragged figure wavering outside the surgical tent. When the figure moved towards her, Rebecca gasped and dropped the linens, preparing for another assault.

She saw that the man's arm was in a sling. It was the wretched Irishman the sight of whom caused her vomit a few hours earlier. He was still under the effects of anesthesia.

"What are you doing out of bed?

"I grew bored starin' upward," the Irishman replied. "I see a deep shadow movin' 'cross the ceilin'. I see hell's gate openin' up to suck me in. I'm not ready to go yet. The idiot chaplain hasn't stopped by to absolve me."

She pinched the sleeve of his shirt with her two fingers and tried to lead him back into the tent.

"You shouldn't be walking. You've lost too much blood."

"When I'm on me feet, I don't think 'bout the missin' hand," he replied, not moving from his spot. "And then I try to light a cigar... And I remember I've no tobacco. Blimey! Someone emptied me pockets."

Rebecca released his sleeve and bowed, mumbling:

"I regret your loss, Mr. Martin."

"The tobacco?"

"No, your hand!"

Martin's clumsy attempt at a joke did not amuse Rebecca.

"This is no great loss, not fer England," he objected, examining his stump. "Even b'fore this happened I was useless. Me dead Ma will testify to that. Now, with only one hand left, I'm half the thief."

He laughed like a madman, spouting frothy saliva, which caused the nurse to draw back.

"Sweet Rebecca, don't flee," he implored a second later. "You needn't fear me."

"I don't fear you," she said, lifting her head hesitantly. "I fear *for* you. The sedatives make you rant."

She approached him again, with renewed decisiveness, and took him by the elbow this time, determined to drive him back under the covers. The touch of the girl's plump pink hands melted Martin's resistance. He allowed her to push him back inside the tent.

"Those drugs didn't do a bloody thin' save blur me eyesight," he continued commenting on the state of the army medicine. "I recall the lantern danglin' 'bove me head, fadin' out and blazin' up again. I recall seein' yer face, green and twisted, and hearin' yer scream, that very scream I m'self was denied, as I lay there, strapped to the table, me hand on the choppin' board and a block of wood 'tween me teeth. 'Twas yer first time, eh?"

"And last..." She lowered her eyes with embarrassment. "Mr. Bennett says I'm not to enter the surgical tent again."

The sound of the surgeon's name galvanized the Irishman.

"That butcher exiled you? Surely, he wants to fill the tent wi' his own kind. Lucky is 'e that I'm crippled. Wouldn't I love to take 'im by the throat... Put me both thumbs right there."

Martin pointed to the hollow under his Adam's apple and then remembered that doing away with his enemy in this manner would be problematic, considering that he only one hand.

"There's many a man I'd like to strangle," he continued, "not just the surgeon. All of 'em... Don't yer know, that clown, Lord Card'gan, is drinkin' 'himself stupid on 'is yacht. Not a hair on 'is bloody head was harmed; but the man trembles b'fore Lord Lucan, and Lucan trembles b'fore Lord Raglan. In short, we've got a chain of tremblin' cowards, murderers they be!"

"Be careful, Mr. Martin, saying such things," Rebecca whispered, looking around fearfully.

The Irishman shook his head and winked, dismissing her fears.

"But yer see, love, I'm not the only one sayin' such thins. Yer ought to hear the lads in the tent. If I be shot for speakin' my mind, they may as well shoot the entire Light Brigade—well, whatev'r is left of it... There's a mut'ny brewin'. Unluck'ly, I won't partake in it. I'm sailn' home soon. 'Tis costly to feed a useless cripple. Every breadcrumb is accounted for, yer know. They promise me twenty pounds fer the damages. P'haps I'll change me trade. I'll buy a hook for me stump and a parrot for me shoulder and frighten 'em children by the docks. I already know plenty of robber songs. Now I'll learn a few pirate songs."

He lifted an invisible wine goblet to the sky, stomped his foot and belted out:

> *Fifteen men on a dead man's chest*
> *Yo ho ho and a bottle of rum*
> *Drink and the devil had done for the rest*
> *Yo ho ho and a bottle of rum.*

Very few sounds in nature can compare in ugliness to the notes that emerged from Private Martin's parched throat. They prompted Rebecca to cover her ears and shake her head. Although her stomach was completely empty after the last vomiting fit, she felt the familiar pangs of nausea returning.

Seeing the suffering that his singing inflicted upon the young nurse, Martin became silent, his good hand still frozen in the air. In what other manner could he show the profundity of his devotion?

"Until then, Rebecca," he concluded with a hint of gallantry. "I shall remain your most loyal vassal."

With his good hand, he seized Rebecca's plump wrist and, before she could free it, applied his salivating lips to it. If he had only seen that mixture of bewilderment, terror, and disgust on in Rebecca's eyes, he would have reconsidered the kiss.

In Martin's defense, his face was not nearly as ugly as his singing. Had it not been so filthy and twisted with agony, Rebecca would have noticed the clean, boyish lines of his profile. Under different circumstances, she would not be so opposed to allowing him a kiss, and not just on her hand but on more privileged parts of the body.

Rebecca let out a mousy squeal and pulled her wrist out of Martin's dirty fingers, causing him to lose his balance and collapse into her lap. Blood began sipping through the gauze around his stump.

"Mr. Martin, you're bleeding!" Rebecca shrieked, not caring if she was rousing the entire hospital. "Your wound... What am I to do? Miss Nightingale! Someone, come, help me!"

A few seconds later she heard footsteps, but they did not belong to Miss Nightingale. It was a nervous, hasty gait, like the scurrying of a rat. The curtain of the tent pulled over, and Rebecca saw the face of the dreaded surgeon, Mr. Bennett.

"Do you want gangrene to spread, eh," Timothy hissed, grabbing Martin by the scruff of his neck and pulling him out from Rebecca's lap. "One amputation wasn't enough for you? Perhaps, you want me to repeat the procedure?"

"Oh, wouldn't yer love that—choppin' up yer victims inch by inch!" the Irishman shouted cockily, on the verge of spitting his tormentor in the face.

Timothy tried to wrestle the wayward patient back onto the operating table. The forces were clearly uneven, as Martin was broader in the shoulders and considerably stronger, even with one hand missing. Timothy did not succeed at once. Sensing his physical inferiority, he squeezed and wrought Martin's stump, using pain his ally. It was the only way he could defeat the Irishman.

"If you don't stop ranting," Timothy whispered into Martin's ear, "I'll cut off your tongue too."

The Irishman remained on the table, with his knees bent and his eyes rolled back. Crouching on the floor, covering her head with her hands, Rebecca did not hear the soldier's guttural moan, nor did she see the devouring glare that Timothy threw at her before he exited the tent.

Chapter 5
Apparition

When Tom regained his senses, it was already two in the morning. An air of shallow anxious slumber enveloped the hospital. An occasional moan, a cough, or a curse from the hallway would interrupt the lull.

Tom could not remember the cause of his fainting, but he did remember why he came into the room in the first place.

"Did this happen? Did I truly faint in front of my own patients?" Tom asked himself, stifling back the humiliation from his weakness. "What will they think of me now?"

There was no sense in rousing them at that point. Sleep would be more wholesome for them than his medical intervention.

Leaning against the wall, Tom began making his way towards the door and suddenly tripped over the legs of one of the soldiers. Damnation! In addition to feebleness, he also had clumsiness to boast about. "Forgive me," Tom muttered, his embarrassment escalating.

The body did not as much as twitch. Tom peered into the soldier's face, at the sightless eyes and the breathless mouth framed by red tufts of the mustache and the beard. Astoundingly, this was the patient who looked the strongest only a few hours ago. That was the last man Tom would have expected to die in the middle of the night.

The rest of the soldiers appeared to be alive. After just two months in the Crimea, Tom had learned to distinguish the dead from the living without even touching them—a skill unfathomable to an outsider. They all had the same parched gray skin. The red-bearded soldier was no longer Tom's responsibility. Doctors only handled the living, and the chaplain handled the dead. Poor Rev. Bryce! Every day he had more corpses coming into his care. They were coming faster than he could identify, absolve, and properly bury them.

Suddenly, Tom realized that he could not find his medical bag. He remembered dropping it just before he lost consciousness. Perhaps, the soldiers went through its content while he was sleeping. For a doctor, losing the medical bag is like losing the gun for the soldier. What did it matter? One more embarrassment for the night... Another personal item he could not find was his scarf, his fine tartan scarf made of Scottish wool bought in the late 1820s, and the last proof that he had once lived like a doctor. The soldiers must have claimed it too. This anonymous borrowing of each other's possessions was not uncommon. At least, he still had his gloves and his socks.

Tom's need for fresh air was stronger than his aversion to cold. He feared that if he remained inside that room, he would faint again.

He made his way down the corridor, navigating around the bodies. Right by the entrance he saw Rev. Bryce, a comely youth from Cheshire. The chaplain was providing spiritual guidance to a blonde nurse. Judging from his sympathetic nods, Rev. Bryce understood the girl's indistinct whimper, as St. Francis could understand the language of birds and animals.

"I am pleased that you chose to confide in me, Miss Prior," Tom heard the chaplain say. "You must not worry Miss Nightingale. Bring all your sorrows before the Lord. He never gives more than one can bear."

At a closer look, Tom realized that the chaplain was asleep, even though his eyes remained open, and his lips kept moving, releasing fairly coherent statements. The sight did not astonish Tom. He had seen plenty of doctors and surgeons work in this somnambulist state. That is what happens when one spends four hours in bed, and the remaining twenty on the feet.

Obeying the force of habit, Tom saluted the chaplain, expecting no response, and walked outside the barrack.

He leaned against the stone wall, rubbing his neck with his

gloved hands for warmth. In all honesty, he could not blame the soldiers for stealing his scarf. Even outside, he was still short of breath. The cold wind did not have the desired refreshing effect on him. On the contrary, it irritated his lungs, increasing the tightness in his chest. What started off as a common cold was progressing into something more bothersome. Tom was still hoping that the malady would go away on its own.

In those moments, the universe appeared to him as a giant tomb. There was a time when Tom would have scoffed at this bombastic analogy that was worthy of a first-year philosophy student at Cambridge. However, now it struck him as accurate. What sense was there in digging graves when everyone was born into one? How thick was the line separating the living and the dead? Food for thought, food for worms... Sleepwalking chaplains, blind generals... Everything mixed into one chaotic twirling mass.

A faint smell of tobacco brought by the wind distracted Tom from his cosmic musings. He turned his head in the direction from which the wind was coming and saw a young officer no farther than ten yards away. He was standing in the same pose as Tom, with his back against the wall, his gaunt scarred face turned to the moon. A chewed up cigar was dangling from his pale stiff mouth. He stood in the middle of the cosmic grave, the angel of the Heavy Brigade, Lord Hungerton, a terrifying prankster once known in Southwark as Grinnin' Wyn. Nothing had changed, except that he had traded his pilot coat for an officer's uniform. The same tilt of the head and the same habit of chewing his cigars to pulp.

At once, all those memories that Tom had been repressing, all the sentiments he had been forbidding himself to feel for the past six months, avalanched upon him. How did he manage to keep his footing and not to collapse under their colossal charge? How did he bring himself to approach the young officer?

"You still smoke the same cheap tobacco," Tom began.

"Best medicine on earth," the officer replied without changing his pose. "Some physicians would probably argue with me."

"I could have smelled you across the sea," Tom continued. "My eyes and my ears deceive me on occasion, but not my nose."

"How very observant... Watch this, good doctor."

The officer stuffed what remained of his cigar into his mouth, chewed it up, sucking out the juice, spat out the remains on the ground and ran the tip of his tongue over his front teeth, producing a squeaking sound that could cause one's blood to curdle. Tom had seen that ritual before. The boy had certainly perfected it over the years.

"At least now you do not deny knowing me like you did a few hours ago," Tom said. "I suppose that alone is considerable progress."

"What exactly did you expect—a filial embrace?"

"Oh no, I wouldn't subject myself to such risk. The last time we saw each other, your hands were clutching my throat. But tell me: what compelled you to act as if we were complete strangers?"

The officer glanced at Tom for the first time. "But we *are* strangers, good doctor." He spoke rapidly through his teeth, his gray eyes exuding a strange light that froze and incinerated at the same time. "Commit that fact to your memory somehow. My men have witnessed enough gut-wrenching scenes, and I was not about to subject them to another one. While you were groveling at my feet, clawing the air and mumbling, I was ready to die of embarrassment. Do you have any idea how hideous and pitiable you looked?"

"Of course I knew! After all, that was my sole purpose—to humiliate you. I barged into your room after midnight to make a spectacle before your men and turn you into a laughing stock. What other meaning can my life have? What are fathers for?"

"You are *not* my father!" the officer exclaimed, his whole body tensing with belligerence. "Don't even jest like that."

"Don't jest, you say? Listen to yourself! Where's your sense of humor? Personally, I find it quite amusing that we chose the same destination for our exile. Ah, my dear Wyn..."

"My name is Lord Hungerton! And I'm not here in exile or on a pilgrimage of penitence. I'm here on a tour of duty."

"So I've heard," Tom replied, nodding. "Quite impressive, I must remark! Of all your pranks, this one must be the most brilliant. I can conceive of you stealing revolvers from a factory, but stealing an entire nobility title?"

The officer separated himself from the wall and began flexing his fists.

"Did it ever occur to you that, perhaps, this title is one thing I did not steal but rather was stolen *from* me—among other things? This revelation must grieve you to no end, good doctor. I am no longer an orphan whom you disfigured and enslaved. I am a soldier, a hero! I have a new commander, who has grand hopes for me and treats me like he would his own son. And there is an excellent chance that I will marry the most beautiful woman in London—that is if God wills to keep me alive until the end of the campaign."

Tom did not hear much past the absurd accusations throw his way. Did he catch the words correctly? Did the boy really say "disfigured and enslaved"?

The creature that was brought back to life, this apparition in red uniform could not possibly be his son. What became of the wayward idealistic child who worshipped Hugo, who proclaimed Cromwell as his hero, and who would rather die than embark on a campaign to benefit the English crown? Wynfield would never dress in red on his own accord. That went against all laws of Nature. Clearly, the boy had been bewitched. But by whom? The body had been resurrected, but the soul had been lost, which confirmed Tom's theory of the world being one bottomless grave.

"I am unspeakably happy for you," he said at last. "Lord Hungerton..."

"I am glad we have reached an understanding," the officer replied, somewhat disappointed that the conflict was not escalating. "I could easily denounce you for the torments to which you have subjected me in my adolescence. My commander would bury you alive. However, this is no place to settle scores. You are not the only piece of scum aborted by the medical community. They would have to imprison half of the medical corps. I hope you find the company of like-minded creatures enjoyable. You can trade secrets on human vivisection. This is why I am here, to watch over my men, to make sure that England's finest patriots are not turned into laboratory rats."

The officer could have continued his tirade for another ten minutes, but Tom deprived him of this satisfaction. He glanced up at the moon, breathed on his gloves to trap some heat in the fabric and went back inside the hospital without a word of farewell, as if the encounter had not taken place at all.

I'll be damned if I understand any of it. It's another enigma for my weary brain. So the boy was not joking when he told me he was a lord. It was not a delirious rant after all. He had sensed it all along, and so had I. All those talks we've had about the Parliament and peerage, they were not in vain. I'd seen the signs but not taken them to heart. How slowly his wounds healed. Only aristocrats bleed for that long. Baron Hungerton... Who would've thought? Isn't that every street thief's dream? He falls asleep on the floor of a prison cell and wakes up in a palace! No matter. He's still Grinnin' Wyn to me. Quite a destination he chose for himself, I must say. He could have stayed in London, gorging on oysters and guzzling champagne, yet he is here, in this God-forsaken corner, sharing room with common soldiers. And all that talk of marriage? I suppose, he's fully recovered from Diana's death. In April, he was ready to follow her into her grave, and now he is planning a wedding. Six months is a respectable mourning period. Is this how long it takes for modern young men to get back into the saddle? But then again, what do I know?

Chapter 6
The Anatomy of Aesthetics

The fenced-off area behind the barracks served as both kitchen and laundry. In the center, above a giant fire pit, two cauldrons were suspended side by side. One served for cooking stew and another one for boiling bloodied sheets. Often both cauldrons were in use, and the fumes from each blended, filling the yard with salty moisture.

At six o'clock in the morning, Tom was already sitting at the long wooden table underneath a sailcloth awning where doctors and nurses took their meals. His breakfast consisted of tepid weak tea that did not differ in taste from puddle water and a slice of stale toast. By the time Tom removed the moldy crust, there was not much left to eat. The discovery did not distress him, as he had no appetite at any rate. Not far from him Rev. Bryce, far less picky about food, was chewing his ration monotonously. The glasses on his nose mimicked the circular movements of his jaw. The young chaplain had a gift for managing multiple tasks at once. His ability to chew and hum an Anglican hymn without choking deserved a round of applause. To brighten his meager meal, he provided his own musical accompaniment. Tom recognized one of his favorite melodies by Henry Purcell, "Rejoice in the Lord Most High!"

He took this opportunity to consult the chaplain on a metaphysical matter.

"Rev. Bryce, may I have a word with you?"

"Certainly, Dr. Grant," the chaplain replied in his usual ethereal drone. "I am pleased that you have chosen to confide in me."

"How much do you know about demonic possession?" Tom asked, moving closer to his godly advisor. "A certain young man whose fate is of considerable importance to me is displaying disturbingly uncharacteristic behavior. I've known him for fifteen years, over the course of which he demonstrated on more than one occasion his utmost disregard for authority. Now he is an officer, who speaks of loyalty to his commander and service to his country. I am convinced that there is a malevolent entity in his head that is making him utter such things."

"Bring all your sorrows to the Lord..."

"What an original advice, Reverend! Could you provide a bit more detail? It is not often that I seek aid from a man of God. The formulaic secular science that I have been advocating for most of my life is of no help to me now. Clearly, there are forces at work that cannot be expressed in simple mathematical equations. Rev. Bryce, are you listening?"

"The Lord never gives more than one can bear."

Tom clapped his hands in front of the chaplain's nose. The young man's eyelids did not twitch under the foggy glasses. Reeling from side to side, he continued humming the hymn.

"For Christ's sake, Edwin, wake up!"

This exclamation constituted a double offense. First, Tom took the name of the Lord in vain, which was blasphemy. Second, he addressed a clergyman by his given name, which was a crude violation of etiquette.

"Ah, let the poor fellow sleep," he heard a woman's voice behind his back.

He turned around and saw Florence Nightingale, his companion of last evening. She was sporting a fresh, monstrously unflattering blouse with a lace collar that resembled a murdered doily. Her hair had been rinsed with abrasive industrial soap—Tom was well acquainted with the smell. The same cleaning substance was used for everything, from dishes, to laundry. Seeing the red blotches of irritation on her forehead, Tom thought that this woman took the "cleanliness next to holiness" motto a little too seriously. There was no reason to subject her lustrous hair to such tortures. Last night he saw that hair in savage disarray, the slender throat exposed, the Spartan back arched in yearning, as she spoke to him of carnal love. Was it all a dream or a midnight hallucination? Daylight returned her to him as a semi-nun.

"What sort of advice where you seeking from Rev. Bryce?" she asked.

"Someone had abducted my boy," Tom replied wearily, picking up breadcrumbs with the tip of his finger, "and I don't even know who it is."

Florence rubbed her temple, trying to reconstruct the conversation from the previous night. "I assume you are referring to your adopted son, a former patient who had tried to choke you?"

"Yes, the one and only Grinnin' Wyn, the terror of Bermondsey."

"I thought you told me he was dead or on the run."

"Oh, he was, for a while; but now he's returned—sort'a... His wanton little soul had been sequestered and mangled. I wish I knew the bastard who had done it to him. My boy, my precious, wicked, troublesome boy, became some general's flunkey. Would you believe it?"

"Dr. Grant, I'm afraid you aren't making any sense."

This ranting unsettled Florence. She recalled one of her patients, who in the final stages of delirium kept calling out for his lost dog.

Battling a burdensome premonition, she sat down next to Tom and placed her fingers on his temples. A crease appeared between her eyebrows.

"Your temperature has risen," she said, looking him in the eye.

"Oh, has it?" Tom asked, faking surprise. "I didn't notice."

"I have touched many foreheads in my life to know that this is no ordinary cold." Her fingers slipped behind his ears, then under his chin. "Can you feel the swollen lumps? Do they not hinder your swallowing?"

As she continued palpating his neck, the crease on her forehead deepened.

"Will you reveal your secret, Miss Nightingale?" Tom asked suddenly. "How on earth do you manage to stay so beautiful in such dire conditions?"

"Heredity," she replied without hesitation. "All women in my family have the same bone structure. Lean, elongated faces retain a youthful appearance, whereas round, fleshy faces have a tendency to droop and wrinkle with time. It is a simple anatomic principle; but do not change the subject. Last night you sent me back into the tower to rest. What about yourself? What were you doing while I was sleeping?"

"I was composing a petition for Lord Cardigan." Tom delivered this half-truth without stuttering. Indeed, he had dedicated at least two minutes of his time to his upcoming audience. "I took care no to leave anything out. Let us pray that His Lordship has the patience to sit through my entire speech."

"You are making me very angry," Florence said, pulling her hands away. "Provoking me, testing the limits of my composure…"

"Come now," he chuckled tenderly. "You cannot allow yourself to become angry with every wayward patient."

"You are not a mere patient," she whispered, wringing his wrist. "First and foremost you are a doctor, one of the few competent ones. What shall become of the soldiers in your care if you join them?"

There was no need for Florence to whisper, for they had no audience. The cook and the chaplain did not count.

"You wish to reclaim your medical bag, don't you?" she asked suddenly in an icy voice. "Surely, your find your professional activity significantly hampered by the absence of your tools."

This poorly concealed anger made Florence irresistible. For that very reason Tom continued provoking her. He did not mind at all that her fingernails were digging into his veins. His was the privilege of witnessing the dark side of the moon, the vulnerable, passionate side of Florence that she did not disclose to anyone else. He cajoled her into scolding him and actually applying physical force.

Tom knew better than anyone that this behavior violated more than one article of the professional code by which they both were bound, but it nurtured his masculine vanity that had not been indulged in ages. How could he deny himself such pleasure, at the age of fifty, in the middle of a war? Few things delighted him anymore. Of all the jokes that Fate had played on him, this was by far the cruelest. On the verge of complete bodily and spiritual crumbling, he met a woman who corresponded to his ideals, even those that he did not dare to vocalize—a reserved, erudite, articulate brunette with impeccably proportionate features. Her eyes were positioned a perfect distance from one another, and the tip of her nose tilted under a perfect angle. Having taken a drawing class as

38

part of his anatomy curriculum in Cambridge three decades ago, Tom could appreciate the structure of a woman's face. Her Venetian profile, the trademark of Renaissance paintings, reined in his fantasies. The physician and the aesthete in him bowed before this woman. If only he could be a little younger, a little richer and not quite so decrepit. Yes, heavens were mocking him. The least he could do was mock in return.

"You have quarantined my medical kit, Miss Nightingale?" he asked in the same tender, taunting tone.

"I certainly have. It is in a safe place, and you may have it, after you sleep for four hours."

"Why, Miss Nightingale, this is overt blackmail, not to mention, direct violation of medical hierarchy."

"What choice do I have? You will not respond to any other method of persuasion. I swear, at times you resemble a child who locks his jaw and shakes his head from side to side, refusing to swallow a bitter-tasting remedy. What will you do, Dr. Grant—denounce me to the chief of medical staff? I fear he will take my side."

She grabbed his other wrist and pulled him to his feet. Tom marveled at her strength. This woman could take on any male patient, no matter how resistant. Such admirable forearm arm muscles he had only seen on tightrope dancers.

"Follow me," she ordered.

"Where are you taking me?" he asked, not really caring about an answer, for he was willing to follow her anywhere.

"A place where nobody will trouble you," she replied and led him up the stairwell into the nurses' tower.

A few minutes later Tom found himself in a tiny room with a low ceiling and a single window overlooking the yard. The interior consisted of a narrow bed, a portable stove and a nightstand. Judging from the puritanical simplicity and the fanatical tidiness, Tom concluded that it was Florence's room, the sanctuary from which she wrote her manifestoes home to England. Many nights, while passing in front of the barracks after dusk, Tom would see light in her window, even when the rest of the hospital was dark—a gravedigger's lantern in a cemetery.

"This bed is for me?" he asked, somewhat intimidated by the whiteness of the sheets. "It would grieve me to mar it."

"Just be sure to remove your shoes," she said drily. "You may leave your clothes on except for the coat."

Obediently, Tom slipped under the tartan blanket. This sudden contact with clean fabric struck him as heavenly. When was the last time he lay on a mattress that did not smell like rotting straw? When was the last time he slept in a horizontal position with an actual pillow under his head instead of his fist?

Tom had not realized the extent of his fatigue until he stretched out on his back, and the pressure was alleviated from the joints and his spine. The capillaries in his fingers and toes suddenly began pulsating, lamenting the abuse to which they had been subjected, like factory workers protest under the windows of the foreman's house. Now Tom feared that he would never find the strength to stand up again. His body was gearing up to teach him a lesson. The springs in the mattress, like hundreds of magnets, held his limbs down.

With a corner of his eye Tom spotted a stack of letters on the nightstand. Apparently, that was Florence's correspondence with her two infamous gentlemen friends, Sir Sidney Herbert and Baron Houghton. The theory was confirmed when Florence blushed and hastily hid the letters inside the top drawer. Tom did not know whether to be amused or offended by this frantic precautionary measure. Did she think even for a moment that he would browse through her letters in her absence?

As much as he wanted to follow her with his glance while she moved around the room, he discovered that he could keep his eyelids unsealed. He could neither move nor speak. He could only listen to the sound of bubbles rising in a kettle and inhale the smell of valerian root extract. A pair of hands unbuttoned his shirt and placed a hot towel on his chest.

"I will lock the door from the outside," he heard her say. "Should anybody knock, do not answer. I am the only one with the key. In four hours, I will return to release you. Thus you will be free to continue wrecking your health."

Chapter 7
The Noble Yachtsman

Nothing could soothe Lord Cardigan that evening. Not the three rounds of chess he played with his cabin boy. Not the fragrant hot bath administered by the most skillful courtesan. Not even the seven-course supper prepared by his French chef. Nothing could stop the tremor in his hands, and now Lieutenant General James Thomas Brudenell, 7th Earl of Cardigan felt more like a prisoner than the rightful owner of his luxury yacht *The Dryad*. After all the usual diversion methods failed, his lordship had nothing left to do but retreat into his stateroom and crouch in his armchair with a bottle of brandy, twitching from every creak of the door. Those onslaughts of tremor started in late October, shortly after the Battle of Balaclava during which the Light Brigade was lost.

Rocking back and forth, he became nostalgic for the past summer spent in the savagely picturesque bay at Devna, across from the cholera-ridden Varna, in a quaint cottage built by a stream. It was there that he nursed his chronic bronchitis, devouring seasonal fruit by the basket and sending daily messages to the men of the Light Brigade.

Those boorish ingrates of the 11th Hussars did not appreciate the effort he put into turning them into the most dashing, flamboyant, and fashionable unit in the British army. He invested his own fortune into hiring top-notch tailors to sew their uniforms. They actually had the audacity to complain when he forbade the serving of porter that was the drink of choice among the officers. How could they not understand that porter was a plebeian potion?

Oh, and then they dared to criticize him for choosing to travel to the Crimea separately from his brigade! Did they not understand that he could not leave Europe without a proper farewell? No, they could not possibly appreciate the splendor of the dinner party that he gave in Paris. Could he refuse to be entertained by Napoleon III and his wife Princess Eugenie? That would be an insult to the French government, an unforgivable faux pas that would permanently underline the alliance between the two countries. It was his quest to champion the elegant traditions of the aristocratic class against otherwise reformist sentiment of the era.

In addition, how could his men hold his brief tour of Athens against him? It only lasted three days. His overexerted body needed an opportunity to grow accustomed to the new climate. Above all, he needed the solitude to muster all his willpower for the upcoming encounter with his loathed brother-in-law, Lord Lucan. That alone warranted a lengthy therapeutic vacation. Did anyone comprehend the magnitude of his responsibilities? Certainly not the men in his command! They christened him "the Noble Yachtsman" in jest.

"Outrageous," Cardigan mumbled between sips of brandy. "Unspeakable!"

The cabin boy opened the door, and a tall, morose man around fifty crossed the threshold of the stateroom. His posture communicated great unease and reluctance.

Cardigan secured the brandy bottle on a sturdy card table between the portraits of his former wife Elizabeth Tollemache Johnstone and his principal mistress Adeline de Horsey, stood up and opened his arms with extravagant familiarity.

"Ah, Ted!"

"Tom," the visitor corrected him coldly.

"No, my name is Jim," Cardigan dragged out slowly, as if addressing an idiot.

"I am aware of that—your Lordship," the man replied, struggling to maintain dignity and diplomacy but at the same time mimicking Cardigan's condescending tone. "*I* am Tom." He tapped his chest. "Thomas Henry Grant, doctor of medicine and philosophy. Reporting for duty, Your Lordship."

To reinforce his words, the man turned out his shoulders, even though one could see with a naked eye that he was struggling to keep his back straight. Even insignificant physical exertion caused him pain.

Cardigan circled his guest a few times.

"Well, Thomas Henry Grant, do you know why you were summoned here?"

"I dare not fathom, Your Lordship."

"So tell me: how do you like your occupation?"

"I am honored to serve my country," Tom replied, trying to conceal his reluctance.

"Bah!" Cardigan rolled his eyes. "I would've expected a more original answer from you. All this pompous mockery... 'Honored to serve my country!' At any rate, your service won't continue much longer."

"Why is that, Your Lordship?" Tom asked in a low voice, still staring before himself.

"I've been corresponding with a certain Mr. Bennett. He was kind enough to inform me about your past practices."

No longer able to maintain his stoic posture, Tom let his shoulders droop and scratched the back of his head.

"What exactly has Mr. Bennett told you?"

"Oh, only good things." Cardigan flicked his wrist casually. "Your fondness for Bohemian women, your selective adherence to the law, your intimate knowledge of narcotics. Clearly, a man like you does not belong in the military hospital."

"It grieves me infinitely to hear that, Your Lordship. If only I could persuade you to rethink your decision..."

Cardigan stamped his foot impatiently.

"Let me finish! A man like you should not squander his time, talent and knowledge on the sort of tasks you've been performing for the past month. He should serve his country on a higher level."

"Exactly, how high?" Tom asked fearfully.

"How much do you know about sedatives?" Cardigan inquired in a businesslike manner.

"Enough," Tom replied tersely after a second of deliberation; it was the truth.

That was precisely the answer that Cardigan had hoped to hear.

"I have a family member in dire need of sedation," he began in a mysterious voice, dragging out the vowels, "deep sedation."

"I am afraid, I do not understand," Tom mumbled, even though he knew where the conversation was going.

This feigned bewilderment irritated Cardigan.

"You know perfectly well of whom I speak! Lord Lucan, my brother-in-law! The fault is all his, you know."

"What fault?"

"The Charge of the Light Brigade, naturally!" Cardigan exclaimed vindictively. "My dear brother-in-law botched the campaign. It is his choleric temper and incompetent leadership that cost us so many soldiers. He sent us in the wrong direction. Of course, he'll attempt to put all blame on me, coward that he is. He's always hated me. Lord Raglan has demanded a private audience with him. It won't astonish me if poor old George is court-martialed."

Cardigan was pacing around the stateroom, spraying brandy-flavored saliva. Tom remained on the same spot; his head drooping lower and lower.

"So, how does my pharmaceutical expertise fit into your vengeance plan?" he asked. "Am I expected to poison Lord Lucan?"

"Of course, not! I want him alive, to watch him reap his shame in full. I want him debilitated, unable to lead another Englishman to his death." Cardigan stopped pacing and lifted his index finger, having been struck by a brilliant idea. "Better yet: instead of a sedative, give him a hallucinogenic. Turn him into a raving lunatic!"

He rubbed his hands in evil delight and then threw his arm around Tom's neck, practically hanging on him.

"Yes, yes... Humiliate him before his subordinates and superiors, his mistresses and his bastard offspring. I know where he stores his wine bottles."

Nauseated by the small of brandy and caviar on the general's breath, Tom slipped out of his grip.

"Your Lordship, I do not believe that you are in the condition to plan such intricate retaliation. Perhaps, we could continue our audience at a better time, when your mind is a bit more lucid."

Cardigan twitched, as if he had heard the most bizarre, most insulting accusation of his life.

"You think I am drunk? I'm perfectly sober! You haven't seen me drunk, my friend. I only took a few sips of brandy to warm up. Would you like some? Perhaps, that will place us on the same altitude. In no time, you shall be thinking and behaving like Cardigan!"

"Oh, joy..." Tom mumbled.

His hands still trembling, Cardigan took his bottle from the card table and poured a drink for his guest.

"Do you see, Tom? I pour my own brandy with my own hands for you. Tell me, Tom. When you were in Southwark, did you think you would ever find yourself on the most splendid yacht, in the presence of England's greatest general? I'm almost envious of you. To rise so high in such a short segment of time..."

With his back turned to the door, Cardigan did not see another visitor who appeared at the threshold. Unlike owner of the yacht, who sported wool sweaters in a home setting, the visitor was wearing a general's uniform, complete with a sword and a revolver at his side. When his eyes met with Tom's, he pressed his finger to the lips, demanding silence. Not that Tom had any intention of opening his mouth. Having compared the man's features to those on a photograph he saw in a newspaper, Tom realized that he was in the presence of George Charles Bingham, 3rd Earl of Lucan.

Good heavens... Everyone knew about the ongoing conflict between the two men, who never concealed their hatred of each other. At fifty-four, Lord Lucan looked at least a decade younger than his age. One could envy his slender, muscular figure, smooth skin and impeccable health. Those were the only advantages that he could boast about before his brother-in-law. The Binghams never had as much wealth as the Brudenells did. Anne Brudenell, Lord Cardigan's younger sister, took a step down when she married Lord Lucan. Her new husband could not provide the level of comfort to which she was accustomed living under her father's roof. Allegedly, the marriage started off as one of love, although outsiders had trouble believing it. The Countess was not without a tyrannical streak herself. Shortly after the birth of the youngest son, the spouses separated informally. They saw each other several times a year to consult on the matters concerning their children. Usually the meetings took place on neutral territory, in one of the fashionable salons in London that the Countess frequented.

45

Lord Cardigan viewed his younger sister as a victim of the circumstances and would have gladly challenged Lucan to a duel. Thirty years earlier, he had fought another young man who, in his opinion, insulted one of his sisters. Luckily, the Duke of Wellington intervened in time and prevented a physical altercation between the two brothers-in-law. Now they were on the same yacht.

Enamored with the sound of his own voice, Cardigan continued rambling. When he finally turned around and saw his brother-in-law standing at the door, he shuddered and dropped the glass with brandy that he had poured for Tom.

"What are you doing on my yacht, George?"

"I was about to ask you the same question, James?" Lucan responded, entering the stateroom. He was still limping slightly from the wound he sustained at Balaclava. The limp did not detract from his menace but rather enhanced it. "How long do you think you could hide from the world?"

"I am not hiding," Cardigan objected, tucking a strand of hair behind his ear. "I am recovering."

"I see..." Lucan mumbled and pointed at Tom disdainfully. "What is *this*?"

"This?" Cardigan leaped for joy, eager to make the introduction. "This is my new chum, Thomas Henry Grant."

The drunken earl pushed Tom forward and hid behind him. The broad, slouched back of a physician made a convenient shelter.

"Ah, the pioneer of human vivisection!" Lucan exclaimed cheerfully, separating his words with claps. "Cambridge is famous for producing mad scientists."

Tom eased his way into the conversation with an introductory cough.

"Lord Lucan, forgive my intrusion, but I would like to contest those allegations. I have never cut a living being without an explicit consent."

Lucan huffed dismissively.

"Good doctor, your wild experiments are none of my concern. I have more important issues to ponder than a few dismembered orphans." He began moving towards his brother-in-law slowly and menacingly. "James, you know well that you and I have a lengthy discussion ahead of us. I'd like the pleasure of your brotherly company for the next four or five hours. So get rid of the evil genius."

"The evil genius is treating my injuries."

Cardigan grabbed his shoulder and made a grimace of pain. Independently of each other, the gesture and the grimace would have been convincing, but not the way that Cardigan timed them. Such blatant insult to his intelligence unnerved Lucan.

"Ah, those the injuries you sustained while riding back from the front lines, as the men in your command rode to their *deaths*? You can show those injuries to Lord Raglan during our audience tomorrow. Anything to prove your valiance!"

"My presence was not requested," Cardigan whimpered, as blood rushed to the whites of his eyes. "It is not my custom to go where I am not invited. I have no doubt that you will relate your version of the story coherently."

"But I want you to be by my side, Jimmy," Lucan cooed with mock affection. "You are my right hand, the one that doesn't always follow the commands of the brain. I've grown to find your stupidity endearing. It adds excitement to the dull military routine. I never quite know what my darling Jim will pull on the battlefield. This mystery is what keeps me in the saddle; and at this moment I am relying on your brotherly love to do what is asked of you. Do not make me employ my status as your superior."

Having realized the futility of arguing, Cardigan attempted to employ humor. "But George, if we stand side by side, the thin ice beneath our feet will surely crack."

"The ice has already cracked, my dearest. I'm already up to my chin in water. And as I go under, it would be comforting to know that you too are drowning, not far from me."

Sensing that it was his turn to bring some comic relief, Tom pointed at the revolver showing from under Lucan's belt.

"Is that a Model Adams?" he asked. "Excellent choice! You know, my son used to extract those guns from the factory in London. He's dead now; but when he was alive, he was quite a metal scavenger. You should've seen the oddities he brought home from the streets.

Cardigan let out an exaggeratedly enthusiastic laugh in support of Tom's joke. Lucan moved in rapidly, gazing straight through the doctor.

"You think this haggard mass of bones and chest hair can protect you, James? Quite a bodyguard you've found! A sickly bear with red eyes... Will he dare to raise his claw in your defense, against me? This is why you invited him here, didn't you? So you wouldn't have to be alone, with me..."

Lucan leaped forward, pulled his brother-in-law by the front of his shirt, and knocked down with one punch to the jaw. His mouth agape, Cardigan reached his hand out towards Tom, begging for protection, but Lucan stepped on his wrist.

"Watch this, good doctor," he said to Tom, who was staring downward, his breathing quickening. "After all, what else can you do? Here's an intimate moment in English history, something for you to discuss in the surgical tent with your butcher colleagues."

Having kicked his victim in the stomach a view times, Lucan drew back abruptly.

"There's no sport battering a drunk," he concluded, dusting off his uniform in disgust. "Good doctor, do your duty. My brother-in-law will need a few cold compresses. Thus, he won't need to fake his injuries for the audience tomorrow. His pain will look more authentic."

Lucan turned on his heels and left, fetching the half-empty bottle of brandy on his way out.

"Oh, not my good brandy..." Cardigan moaned, stretching his bruised hand.

When they were left alone, Tom shook up and helped the battered earl to his chair.

"Now you see that he is perfectly insane," Cardigan lamented, gesturing towards the entrance through which his terror had walked out a few moments ago.

"All I see is that you and your brother-in-law have much to sort out," Tom replied, examining his new patient's bruises.

"Tom, I can't reason with the man," Cardigan continued, seizing his caretaker by the hand. "He won't respond to logic; but he will respond to your concoction. It's our only hope."

Tom straightened out and backed away from Cardigan.

"On another thought, I must confess that my knowledge of the apothecary field has been over-praised," he said with exaggerated self-deprecation. "I do not know that much about sedatives after all. Perhaps, you should recruit someone more experienced. It sounds like an awfully important mission, and I would hate to botch it."

"You are a pitiable liar!" the earl howled, pointing his finger vindictively.

"This is precisely why I am a doctor and not a politician," Tom replied, resuming his sincere tone. "Honestly, Your Lordship, I should not partake in this plot."

"Leave the plotting to me," Cardigan reassured him with a wink. "Your duty is to mix the potion."

It was becoming increasingly difficult for Tom to care for his new patient.

"My Lord," he said through his teeth, "you put me in a most unenviable position."

"But then, whose position is enviable, do tell? You know any men who sleep well at night?"

"The chaplain!" Tom answered with unflinching certainty after a few seconds of deliberation. "He dumps the corpses in a mass grave, blurts out a prayer, and snores away the night—a job well-done."

The declaration made Cardigan roll his eyes spitefully as he always did when commoners were mentioned.

"I was referring to men of importance, men whose names are recorded in history tomes. Tom, as much as I detest resorting to such bluntness, you have no choice. You aren't leaving my yacht pretending that his conversation had not taken place."

"My Lord, as much as *I* detest resorting to such bluntness, you have no power over me," Tom declared sternly and defiantly. "This ragged old puppet's strings have been cut long ago. I do not fear for my own life. As for my loved ones, they're all dead."

An all-knowing grin stretched the earl's glistening face.

"Ah-huh, that is not entirely true," he dragged out, waving his index finger. "Mr. Bennett told me that you've been growing quite chummy with a certain nurse."

"You mean, Florence Nightingale?" Tom asked with a shrug. "She means nothing to me. A conceited spinster... I am not saying that she is entirely useless. A pair of hands... But there's nothing about her to capture my fancy. As a rule, I do not pursue women over the age of thirty."

"Ah, Tom, my poor Tom..." Cardigan shook his sweaty disheveled head reproachfully. "One day, I'll teach you to lie with a straight face. Until then, don't make any attempts. You are in love with Florence Nightingale! And why wouldn't you be? She is an exceptional woman. And you are an exceptional man."

Tom pretended not to notice the set of hairy knuckles pushing into his chest. Lord Cardigan was approaching that state of intoxication where the remains of his high-brow demeanor that he advocated in a sober state would retreated. He was no longer controlling the movements of his hands.

"I can't compete with Sidney Herbert," Tom muttered, recollecting the conversation he had with Florence last evening in front of the surgical table. "By God, the man is the Secretary of War."

The earl sensed that the mention of the nurse's name altered the direction of the doctor's thoughts, so he jumped at the chance to exploit the only viable affection in Tom's heart.

"And Florence can't compete with Sidney Herbert's wife," Cardigan continued. "It's hopeless. I'm privy to the situation. Sidney is another close chum of mine. He shall never divorce or betray Elizabeth. For that I can vouch. In the meantime, our saintly Florence, the Lady with the Lamp, has nothing left to do except pray secretly for her rival's death and grow mad little by little. Ah, the demon voices in her weary little head... It would be a crime to leave her in such a perilous state. She needs somebody seasoned, witty and commanding to distract her from her unhealthy fantasies—someone like you."

The hairy knuckles burrowed deeper into Tom's chest.

"Why, Lord Cardigan," he mumbled with embarrassment, "I don't think I've received so many compliments from another man in my entire life."

"But wait: I have more than mere compliments to offer."

"What exactly did you have in mind, my lord?" Tom asked with growing unrest.

"How about ten thousand pounds as a modest appetizer?"

Cardigan gave his prospective ally a few moments to digest the proposal and count the zeros.

"The sum may seem fantastic to you now," he continued, "as you haven't adopted my habits yet; but you shall learn to burn through money with breathtaking elegance. And if you do not care for money, I shall find other ways to compensate you. Imagine having a splendid laboratory in Westminster, and all the leisure and comfort in the world for your intellectual endeavors. Imagine being surrounded by dazzling minds. You will not need to seek them—they shall seek you. A few words from me—and all the young medical prodigies of England shall flock to you; and Florence shall be by your side all the while. I shall advocate for that stubborn girl. You two can become the golden couple of the English medicine. Now tell me that all this is not worth a small flask of potion?"

Suddenly, Tom wavered, clutching his chest with one hand and leaned on the back of Cardigan's armchair with another.

"Forgive me, your Lordship," he moaned under his breath. "I have been unwell for a few days. There's an infectious cough in the hospital corps. If you don't believe me..."

No, this time Cardigan believed him.

"Dear friend, you must preserve your strength," he said, hastily vacating the armchair and ushering Tom into it. "This isn't the time to fall to pieces. We have much work ahead of us."

Chapter 8
Centurions and Gladiators

Having descended the gangway of *The Dryad*, Lord Lucan spotted in the twilight the solitary silhouette of a young officer. Apparently, he had been waiting on the shore for quite some time. He fidgeted on the spot, drawing circles in the sand with the tip of his boot, his hands hidden in the pockets of his uniform. Every now and then, he would glance up at the darkening sky.

"Lord Hungerton!" the earl called out jovially, raising the brandy bottle that he had carried off as a trophy.

The young man turned his disheveled, dark-haired head and rushed towards his commander, nearly knocking him down. "How was the audience, Lord Lucan?" he asked, panting anxiously.

"Bah, the usual," the earl muttered, with a dismissive flicker of a wrist. "Where is a good comedic playwright when you need one?"

"My lord, why didn't you allow me to accompany you?" the officer asked imploringly. "How I wished I could stand there by your side. For that reason alone, I left the hospital to catch the first transport out of Scutari. I knew this encounter between you and Cardigan was imminent. My men needed me at the hospital, but you needed me even more sorely."

Lord Lucan pouted with mock endearment. "Ah, it's hellishly sweet of you to worry—but completely unnecessary. I am perfectly capable of weathering minor family storms."

The young man averted his eyes. "Am I not your family now?"

"You certain are, in the best sense of the word. Although we are not tied by blood or any legal alliances, you are the child of my heart, and you have been for the past six months. I adopted you when I found you by the docks in Rotherhithe. The Almighty had sent me a treasure, a hero. That is precisely why I wish to keep you secluded from the ugly side of my family. Tonight my dear brother-in-law overstepped all conceivable boundaries. He even recruited some vivisectionist as his bodyguard. Is that wild enough? He knew I was coming. But, guess who won?" The earl shook the half-empty bottle above his head, stirring the content. "Now," he continued, squinting with an air of conspiracy, "who loves you like a father loves his firstborn?"

"You do, my lord," the young officer replied with a timid smile.

"And who has molded you into the finest soldier you can be?"

"You have, my lord."

"And who has impeccable judgment?"

"You do, my lord."

"And who makes his enemies tremble before him?"

"You do, my lord."

"And who will emerge heroic from this war?"

"You do, my lord."

With every response, the young man's intonation communicated more and more servility. As Lucan's eyes grew narrower, the young officer's eyes grew wider. He stood before his commander completely defenseless, struck with filial adoration. The wind from the harbor blew his dark hair.

Lucan laughed approvingly and self-complacently. Then, in a perfectly controlled sweeping motion, he wrapped his arm around his ward's neck and made him drink from Cardigan's bottle.

"There, drink up, dear boy," he whispered. "No need to occupy your sleepless little head with such trifles. I have full control over everything."

The young officer drank obediently without posing for a breath until Lucan pulled the bottle away.

"Enough, impudent pup! That ought to keep you warm. We have a long ride to the outpost."

The young man wiped the drops of brandy from his lips and mumbled hesitantly:

"To tell you the truth, I intended to return to Scutari."

"All right, this must stop," Lucan declared, squeezing his upper arm. "This ludicrous charity, this extravagant altruism must come to an end right this instant. Do you hear me? This frantic sailing back and forth across the sea between the outpost and the hospital puts needless strain on your body. Besides, you have not recovered fully from the wound."

"It's but a scratch," the young officer objected. "I've had worse. It's nothing, truly."

"Let me be the judge of that! I've seen even the most insignificant of wounds become infected. Those transport ships are filthy!"

"But the soldiers, my lord..."

"The Heavies?" the earl inquired spitefully.

"I promised to return to them. They expect me."

"That is because you instilled the idea in them. They whine and pine for you because you have been hovering over them every night, blotting their scratches and listening to their tales. It is your own fault, my dear fellow. You placed yourself in this needlessly obliging position. The men have a host of perfectly capable doctors and nurses. Centurions do not patch up gladiators. It is that simple. I do not want you catching cholera or some other infections disease and bringing it to the rest of us. Recall how our own General Scarlett suffered? You must be alive and well to marry my beautiful daughter, no?"

The earl tightened his arm around his future son-in-law's neck and began ruffling his hair.

"I didn't hear you, Lord Hungerton. Are we preparing for a wedding or not?"

"Yes, yes, my lord," the young man replied and hid his blushing face on his commander's shoulder. "God, this brandy is strong..."

"You have forgotten the art of drinking, dear boy. You've been deprived of fine spirits for too long. That will change when you return to the outpost with me tonight. Tell me: do you love my daughter?"

"More than life itself... May the Devil strike me down if I'm lying!"

"Then write to her!"

"I've tried, my lord. Upon my soul, I've tried."

"If you are lost for words, I will gladly assist you. I have written many a love letter in my life. Relate to her the details of the battle. Do not hide your heroism. You have plenty to boast about, dear boy. But first you must promise to me as your future father-in-law, not to mention, your commander, that you will not set your foot in that filthy hospital again. It is overrun by butchers and crooks that go by names like Thomas Henry Grant."

Having heard that name, the young officer let out a muffled gasp and leaned forward, as if someone had stabbed him in the back.

"What's the matter, dear boy?" Lucan asked, rushing to break his fall. "Too much brandy at once?"

"Yes, my lord," the young man whispered, laboring to steady his breathing. "That's precisely what it is—too much brandy on the empty stomach. How right you are. I must never set my foot there."

Silently, they mounted their horses and headed towards the outpost where the remains of the British cavalry were congregating.

The young officer wavered in his saddle, arching backwards and then leaning over the horse's head, burying his face in the mane. His bony shoulders twitched in fits of drunken laughter. Luckily, the stallion had been trained to tolerate its master antics and was determined to deliver him to his destination.

As for Lord Lucan, he was regretting his decision to share the stolen brandy with Lord Hungerton, whose ability to handle fine spirits he clearly overestimated. Hopefully, the boy would sober up by the time they reached the outpost. A proper supper and a hot bath would restore his senses. He needed to be reminded of his superior standing, as he as was beginning to look, behave and smell like common soldiers. The wretched creature had been drinking the same muddy tea and using the same harsh soap as his subordinates.

Before the Balaclava harbor disappeared out of his view, the earl threw one last glance at his brother-in-law's floating palace. If human eyes could exude fire, the gallant yacht would be incinerated in a matter of seconds.

Part 2
The Swans of Laleham

Six Months Earlier

Laleham Park, Middlesex,
Lord Lucan's Estate
Spring, 1854

Chapter 1
Lady Lucan's Bedroom
Turns Into a Laboratory

Dr. Richard Ferrars, the designated physician of the Bingham clan at Laleham, was in no danger of growing bored or idle. The residents of the estate always provided him with new challenges, new medical mysteries to solve. A paradise for an inquisitive, Cambridge-groomed mind!

Countess Lucan, the matriarch of the clan, has been his most devoted patient since his arrival in 1849, making sure that the young graduate's skills would not become rusty. The noble lady seemed afflicted with one or another fatal illness that produced no overt symptoms. She would summon Dr. Ferrars to her bedroom in the middle of the night, for that was the invariable time of the alleged attacks. He would listen to hear heartbeat and find no irregularities, palpate her forehead and feel no fever. Nevertheless, the lady insisted on the imminence of her demise. Having a physician by her side would not suffice, and she would also summon an attorney to revise her will; and what use was an attorney without a jewelry appraiser. Since the price of precious metals and gems kept fluctuating, Lady Lucan's heirlooms needed to be reevaluated. Within an hour, her bedroom would turn into a meeting hall. The lady would lay in bed, panting, with Dr. Ferrars holding her wrist, Attorney Kent standing at her feet with a copy of freshly revised will, and Mr. Bloom, the local jeweler, spreading her diamond necklaces against candlelight.

It took Dr. Ferrars some time to understand why a robust woman in her forties, a mother of four children, would want three men in her bedroom in the middle of the night. One day he stumbled across a certain pamphlet written by a former schoolmate. The content of the pamphlet floored the Cambridge clique as both absurd and obscene. It provided Dr. Ferrars with invaluable insight into Lady Lucan's condition. Suddenly, he identified the cause of her tantrums.   The wretched creature was deprived of male company! The young doctor was aware of the falling out that the Countess had with her husband. The two were separated, though not officially divorced. Lord Lucan spent most of his time at his Irish estate, busy with evictions. Once or twice a year he would make obligatory and much dreaded trips to Laleham to see his to youngest children. The Countess found her husband's company insufferable and would purposely plan her excursions to London around the time of his visits to avoid crossing paths with him.

The sight of the withering, neglected woman awakened masculine compassion in the doctor. One day he let the Countess know that she no longer needed to rouse the other two gentlemen in the middle of the night and that he, Richard Ferrars, would personally see to her comfort and satisfaction. Christian charity and the Hippocratic Oath dictated his actions. The proposal was delivered with such reverence and flawless tact, that no woman, however fastidious, could resist.

The Countess was so tickled by the selfless initiative of the handsome doctor that she added an extra three hundred pounds to his yearly salary. The money came out of her personal allowance. Lord Lucan knew nothing of the raise. He would most likely consider it extravagant.

As one may have anticipated, the onslaughts of the mysterious malady stopped at once. The Countess became jovial and compliant. She did not altogether cease terrorizing her children and her servants—that practice brought her too much pleasure—but the frequency and the intensity of her fits lessened considerably.

Undoubtedly, Dr. Ferrars was a gift to the Laleham estate. Gradually, he migrated into Lady Lucan's bedroom. He spent more time there than in his own quarters. Being a serious young man, he did not spend a penny on frivolous pleasures. Instead, he bought a collection of books that were not widely available even to the members of the medical community. He took particular interest in the field that at the time was still in its embryonic state.

Some doctors referred to it as moral physiology and others called it psychology. The connection between body and mind fascinated him.

Between therapy sessions with Lady Lucan, Dr. Ferrars would read to her excerpts from the works of the French physiologist Pierre Cabanis, who had explored the properties of the nervous system. Cabanis' essay *"On the Relations Between the Physical and Moral Aspects of Man"* was a first attempt at psychological analysis. Dr. Ferrars explained to his patient how the mind could trick the body into experiencing certain symptoms. The monstrous illness from which she was suffering prior to his intervention could be called melancholy of the womb.

"Just think what this discovery could mean for other women," he said to the countess.

Lady Lucan considered it a great honor to be included in Dr. Ferrars' scientific studies. She volunteered her bedroom for a laboratory and her own self for a specimen. Together they tested the principles of hypnosis.

"Devotion is an increasingly rare virtue and therefore must be encouraged and rewarded," she said one day. "As you know, Lord Lucan, the perpetrator of my illness, is due for another visit in April. My absence will coincide with a conference of physiologists in Greenwich. The event was not widely publicized, and the vacancies were limited, but I have made the arrangements for you to attend. The fee has already been paid and the hotel room has been reserved. All you need to bring is your handsome, enthusiastic self."

Dr. Ferrars exhaled and raised his eyes to the ceiling, for he had been waiting for that news. Ah, his efforts were not expended in vain after all! He had been catering to her wishes, and she finally reciprocated.

"I only ask one thing of you," she continued. "Promise you do not forget your benefactress when you attain fame and fortune. When you organize your findings in a tome, I insist that you dedicate it to Anne Brudenell, Countess of Lucan. Ah, what a thrill! As a young girl, I did not even dream that in the twilight of my years I would become a muse for a medical genius. Dear Richard, please promise me..."

Yes, yes... Dr. Ferrars kept nodding without paying attention to the chatter of the Countess. His mind was already at the convention. He began preparing his introductory speech. He would need to review his notes and practice the skill of public speaking. Had the Countess asked him for his head on a platter, he would have consented.

"Should Lord Lucan not return from his Crimean campaign," the Countess continued, "should the Almighty see it fit to make me a free woman again..."

"As you wish, my lady..."

"This could all be yours, my dear Richard. For God's sake, look at me!"

"I am looking at you, my lady," the doctor mumbled, still staring upward. "Your heavenly face is forever before my eyes."

Chapter 2
Dr. Ferrars' Career Changes Direction

The second week of April, Lord Lucan arrived at Laleham. This time he did not come alone. Sprawled across the seat of the carriage was an unconscious young man with a gash on his forehead. The gash itself was not terribly wide and it had already started closing. The young man's listlessness indicated that there was considerable internal damage.

"Look what I found by the docks," Lucan said with a mixture of curiosity and superficial pity, as if the creature in question was a mauled pup. "Imagine this, Dr. Ferrars? We landed in Rotherhithe after a hellishly choppy voyage, and there he was, hanging off the edge of the pier, his hand practically touching the water. My original intention was to pass by, for I was falling off my feet from exhaustion. Then a thought occurred to me that he was a bit too well dressed for a drunken sailor; so I returned, flipped him on his back, rummaged through his pockets and found a stack of visiting cards. I couldn't believe my eyes! The wretched creature turned out to be Baron Hungerton! That name probably doesn't mean anything to you, Dr. Ferrars. You're much too young to remember the explosive scandal of 1829, but I remember it quite well. What a stroke of luck! Lying at my feet was the golden child of anarchy, a humorous souvenir from King William's era. Perhaps, old age is making me sentimental. It would be a sin to let the boy drown. He was muttering something in the coach, but then he fell silent. At any rate, he's in your hands now."

The prospect of touching blood energized Dr. Ferrars. It had been a long time since he worked with an open wound. How refreshing it was to care for someone with an easily identifiable injury.

The servants carried the patient upstairs into the guest room and situated him out on the bed. Lord Lucan held on to the dirty waistcoat of his foundling. In addition to the visiting cards, there were some other papers in the pockets that Lord Lucan wanted to examine. Perhaps, there were secret documents, letters from foreign ministers. The examination left him disappointed. He found no secret correspondence, just a few letters in French and excerpts of what he presumed to be works of fiction. They were signed with the initials V.H. Without a second thought, the earl crumbled the letters and tossed them in the trash basket.

He felt a vague thirst for brandy, but he could not muster the energy to fetch the glass, so he drank directly from the carafe, staining the front of his shirt. Decidedly, he was growing much too old for such long trips. Next time he would ask his children to visit him at Castlebar instead.

For the next half hour, he sat with his chin pushing into the tabletop and his arms dangling, staring at the half-empty carafe. Then Dr. Ferrars came in to report on the patient.

"How is our foundling?" Lucan asked without changing his pose.

"Quite fragile, I'm afraid," Dr. Ferrars replied. "I gave him half a glass of warm water with mint extract and honey to help fight the nausea. He won't be able to eat or drink much for the next few days. It is an elaborate injury, combining repeated blows to the head, an overpowering combination of narcotics and severe emotional turmoil. Think of one's memory as an elaborately painted ceramic plate. Imagine this plate shattered, half of the pieces lost and the other half reassembled oddly so that there is very little left of the original design."

"Dr. Ferrars, I am not a hopeless idiot!" Lucan interrupted him. "Down with these poetic allegories! You can use scientific terms with me."

"I fear there are no exact scientific terms to describe Lord Hungerton's condition—at least, not yet. I base my theories on Pierre Cabanis' writings and my own observations. I take particular interest in patients who have suffered head injuries of various degrees. One thing is certain: Lord Hungerton suffers from more than mere memory loss. His entire perception of reality has been altered. He keeps referring to a girl with knives, to whom he was intimately attached and who, apparently has since died. The amount of anger he harbors is astounding. All of it seems to be directed onto one man, a certain physician by the name of Thomas Grant. It is him that Lord Hungerton blames for all his misfortunes, including the death of the girl with knives."

"How peculiar," Lucan mumbled, straightening up and leaning against the back of his chair. "Do continue!"

"I must reiterate that my conclusions are little more than educated speculations. What Lord Hungerton remembers may not be what had really happened. This Thomas Grant may very well be an innocent man—if he indeed exists—but not in Lord Hungerton's mind. It is not uncommon for patients to project all their sentiments onto one person, real or fictitious. One thing is certain: your young guest is very confused and very vulnerable."

Lucan squinted and rubbed his chin pensively.

"Vulnerable, you say?"

"Exceedingly so—to external influences! At present, his brain is like clay. It can be molded into anything. Do not be deceived by his skittish, erratic demeanor. The man wants to trust, desperately. He will cling to anything that appears like a solid rock. Under appropriate circumstances, he can be turned into a most devoted ally or a merciless killer. That is precisely where the danger lies."

"And my advantage," Lucan murmured under his breath.

Then he raised his eyes at the young physician.

"Thank you for such an informative report. You are dismissed."

Dr. Ferrars bowed drily.

"Good night, my lord. I shall check on the patient one last time before I depart tomorrow morning."

He was prepared to leave, but Lucan waved his hands in the air, like a shepherd rounding up his sheep, letting him know that the conversation was not over.

"Wait now! Where exactly do you think you are going?"

"The conference in Greenwich, my lord."

"I don't recall making any arrangements."

"Her ladyship made them. It is for the advancement of my expertise."

"Is that how she articulates it? She finds a euphemism for everything, doesn't she? Blast that woman... At any rate, Dr. Ferrars, you can forget all about the conference. You are not going to Greenwich."

"I am not?"

"No. You are going to a much better place—the picturesque Crimean Peninsula!"

Dr. Ferrars glanced at the half-empty brandy carafe, then into Lucan's red eyes.

"My lord, it is very late."

"Not at all—only half past midnight! Lady Lucan has kept you up later than that. So go and start packing your things. Or rather, don't pack. Long distances are better traveled light. Whatever you cannot bring with you will be given to you upon arrival. Stop looking at me like that. This is my first campaign, and everything has to be perfect. I am trying to build a clique of exceptional men, and you are one of them. It's an honor! Understand?"

Dr. Ferrars began perspiring behind his ears.

"My lord, according to our contract..."

"You are to cater to my needs, regardless of the location," Lucan stated, hitting the tabletop with his index finger. "Failing to do so will result in the immediate termination of the contract. Honestly, I will be surprised if you procure another favorable situation. There are thousands of doctors in England, in no way inferior to you. Cambridge and Oxford spit out new graduates every year. I give you until morning to consider my terms."

Dr. Ferrars saw plainly that his master was exhausted and drunk. Compliance is the best policy with drunken men. It was one of the principles that Dr. Ferrars learned through the course of his studies in physiology.

"Forgive me, my lord," he said. "How selfish it is of me to trouble you with my obstinacy at such a late hour."

Chapter 3
Call of the Lions

The mint and honey solution given by Dr. Ferrars helped re-store Wynfield to his senses. This state of partial consciousness was worse than a complete swoon. He was alert enough to feel pain yet too weak and drowsy to control his muscles. The sheets suffocated him but gave him no warmth. Having finally freed himself from the linen prison, he slipped onto the carpeted floor and surveyed his environment. His first impression of the room was that it had neither corners, nor walls, nor boundaries. He was sitting in the middle of an oasis of light falling from the fireplace. Like the rest of the objects in the room, the frame of the fireplace dissolved into darkness. Wynfield could only make out the lions' heads on the mantelpiece and the spiraling bars of the grate.

His felt his lips move, but he could not judge the intensity of the sound escaping from them. Was he whispering or screaming? The only sound that he heard distinctly was the ticking of an unseen clock. Every shift of the arrow resonated like a blow against his eardrums.

A new gust of chill engulfed his body, throwing it into a fit of involuntary tremor. In an attempt to abate the clattering of his teeth, Wynfield squeezed his jaw.

Suddenly, his dissipated gaze fell on the two carved lions on the mantelpiece. He could have sworn that the two beasts opened their jaws in tandem, summoning him. The bars of the grate parted, and the glimmering coals blazed up again.

The bloodied bandage around his head partially undone, Wynfield gathered all his strength, pulled himself up on his knees and crawled towards fireplace. Having stretched his hands forward over the flames, he watched in stupor how his fingertips were turning red. There was no pain, only mild tingling, not at all unpleasant.

Suddenly, he began losing balance and leaned forward. Another second—and he would fall into the flames. At that moment, he felt on his shoulders the grip of tiny swift hands that pulled him away from the fireplace and heard a high, sonorous voice.

"By God, what sort of medicine did Dr. Ferrars prescribe to you?"

Wynfield fell backwards with his head landing on someone's knobby knee. Streams of silk cascaded down both sides of his face. The warm hands began patting him on the forehead, fixing the bandage. With great effort, he unsealed his inflamed eyelids and through the fog saw the face of a young girl with wide gray eyes and ash curls tied back by a green ribbon.

"You've been ranting wildly, Lord Hungerton," she continued animatedly.

"You heard..." Wynfield muttered.

"Certainly—on the opposite end of the hall!" she affirmed with an impish giggle. "You kept repeating 'No! This isn't how it ends...' I don't think I'll fall back to sleep tonight after what I just heard. Do promise to tell me your story once you recover. By the way, my name is Lavinia."

There was only one other Lavinia that Wynfield knew—the hapless daughter of Titus Andronicus. For some reason, Shakespearean apocrypha remained clear in his jumbled memory. Having forgotten most events of the first twenty-five years of his life, he still remembered the name of the heroine from his favorite play and her gory fate.

"What lovely hands," he mumbled, examining the veins on her wrists. "It would be a shame to chop them off."

"My poor friend," she replied, in no hurry to pull her hands away. "Papa must have another conversation with Dr. Ferrars. You have a pool of blood under your skull. Did you know that? I overheard their conversation in Papa's study. Sadly, I am quite ignorant in such matters."

When she smiled, her upper lip curled, her eyes narrowed, and the tip of her nose tilted upward. Wynfield was looking at a completely different face now. He never thought that a smile could alter one's features to such extent. Foggy as his consciousness was, he could not help catching a hint of affectation in her voice and smile. Such joviality struck him as unnatural. The nervous abruptness of her movements and the moisture glistening in the corners of her eyes betrayed the fact that she had been crying. The girl, to her credit, was too proud and well mannered to flaunt her vulnerability, though not mature enough to hide it completely.

To distract herself from her private sorrow, the girl began making fuss over the wounded guest. She pulled the pillows from his bed and placed them under his back. It amazed Wynfield that she managed to move so swiftly without becoming entangled in the folds or tripping over the hem of her gown. He had never seen such elaborate sleeping apparel. It must have taken at least ten yards of white silk to construct her nightgown, and another twelve for the penoir. The pleated train resembled the tail of a white peacock.

Wynfield's vision began to blur again. The girl's figure turned into a wavering shaft of light. She dove into the shadow and reappeared a few seconds later with a chess box.

"The game is said to have medicinal properties," she began, unfolding the board and arranging the figures. "When my brother George fell of a horse and he sustained a head injury similar to yours, Dr. Ferrars recommended chess to help him regain control of his mind. We played in his room for hours. I defeated him repeatedly. Now, do you prefer white or black?"

Wynfield shook his bandaged head grievously.

"My lady, I'm afraid, I won't make a worthy adversary."

"Did you forget the rules of the game?"

"I don't believe I ever learned them."

"Why, that shall be remedied," she declared, rubbing her palms eagerly. "I shall teach you."

"Your patience will wear off very soon, I must warn you. At present, my mind is like a bottomless jar. Have you played Castilian poker?"

"Alas, I haven't."

"That too shall be remedied. You see, I am so anxious to repay you for your kindness, and no better token comes to mind. You shall find a deck of cards in the pocket of my waistcoat. I must introduce you to the favorite pastime of Spanish sailors. As soon I as remember the rules..."

Now it was Lavinia's turn to shake her head.

"Mama does not allow us to play cards."

"Why not?"

"According to Mama, it is an unfit occupation for a young lady whose hand has not yet been claimed."

"Forgive me," Wynfield sighed bitterly. "I haven't been in your house for a day, and I am already undermining your chances of marrying well. I wreck things before I even touch them. One steadfast glance will suffice to turn a fortress into a pile of ashes. Ah, there I go ranting again."

"Perhaps, the chess game can wait," Lavinia concluded and began folding the board. "The little ivory horses won't run away from us; but you must not speak of yourself in such apocalyptic terms. My father happens to hold a completely a different opinion of you."

"Your father?"

"Yes, Lord Lucan—the man who saved your life. He employs one of the best physicians in England. Dr. Ferrars is a miracle-worker. He cured my mother of a disease so terrible that it did not even have a name. Papa is very pleased to have found you. He fosters grand plans for you."

Grand plans! Where had Wynfield heard that before?

Suddenly, he noticed that he was no longer trembling. The chills retreated, giving way to another extreme. His cheeks and the palms of his hands started burning. The heat began spreading onto the rest of his body.

"Dr. Ferrars says it is not unusual after a concussion," Lavinia remarked, having recognized the symptoms from which her brother had suffered after his injury. "I'll ask him to see you in the morning before his departure. Until then, you mustn't be alone. I'll stay here for the rest of the night."

Lavinia crawled into the enormous rocking chair, like a squirrel would into a nest, wrapped herself in the folds of her gown and immediately turned her face away from her guest, to his great relief. Wynfield suspected that he would not be able to fall asleep under her gaze.

Feeling his body temperature finally stabilizing, he sprawled on the pillows and let his eyelids fuse.

Chapter 4
One Hundred Yards Away from the Laleham Abbey

Having learned about Lavinia's heroic deed, Lord Lucan felt a pang of paternal guilt for having come home empty-handed. How forgetful, now inattentive had he been! His youngest daughter had just saved the wounded guest from the fire and stayed up all night tending to him, and her own father did not have as much as a pretty trinket for her. He should have brought her one of those bronze bracelets with Celtic knots that the artisans in the vicinity of Castlebar produced in abundance, or a tartan sash, or an Aran shawl. Naturally, Lavinia's mother, the grumpy ogress, would never allow her unmarried daughter to wear such boorish ornaments before potential suitors, but Lavinia had a fondness for all things Celtic. Besides, indulging his daughter's vulgar tastes against his wife's will gave Lord Lucan unspeakable pleasure. He could not affect her choice of husband, but he could make her look like a wild Irish wench. Pity Lavinia had no freckles. The porcelain quality of her skin was maddening.

Lord Lucan did not blame Lavinia for not having given him a greeting kiss. He accepted her cold demeanor with all possible humility when she met him in the morning for their traditional stroll through the estate. They walked in silence side by side along the banks of the river towards the Laleham Abbey.

"What's the matter?" Lucan inquired at last with a grim smirk. "Are you not pleased to see your father?"

"Of course, I'm pleased, my lord," Lavinia replied reluctantly through her teeth.

This affected formality made Lucan chuckle.

"My lord!" he chanted, mocking her. "Is this my punishment for coming without a present? Now, be honest. What exactly has your mother been saying about me in my absence?"

Lavinia folded her lips and whistled vacantly. "Oh, nothing out of the ordinary."

Suddenly, Lucan slipped his arm around his daughter. It was a slow, deliberate, menacing move, more like a trap than an embrace. Lavinia struggled not to cringe, unaccustomed to physical contact with him. Sensing her resistance, Lucan squeezes her shoulders even tighter. It entertained him to make his daughter uneasy. At least, disgust was an emotion.

"I commiserate, my child," he said with blood-chilling softness, leaning to her ear. "There comes a time in a young woman's life when having two living parents becomes burdensome, especially if they loathe one another. Well, I may have some encouraging news. There's an excellent chance that this burden will soon be lifted."

"What are you saying, my lord?"

"You know well what I'm saying," Lucan replied nonchalantly. "I'm sailing to the Crimea—a place from which not many Englishmen return. If I do not return, it will make your mother very happy."

Lavinia froze and interrupted him in a trembling voice. "No, Papa..."

The sudden change in tone amused Lucan. He grabbed his chest with an air of theatrical shock. "Papa, eh? What happened to 'my lord'? In truth, Lavinia, my death won't be any great loss for you. Right now, you see me twice a year. If you cease seeing me altogether, what difference will it make?"

Lavinia blinked and opened her eyes widely. "You can't leave me at the mercy of that... Venomous woman! She'll marry me off to the first fat ugly man."

Lavinia squeezed her eyelids again and shivered, causing Lucan's amusement to escalate. With a burst of malicious laughter, he released his daughter.

"Why, this is the silliest thing I've heard! Who'll want to marry you? We have no money—all thanks to me. I must be the poorest earl in England, the laughing stock of the Parliament!"

He pounded himself in the chest proudly. Lavinia glanced at him with a mixture of disbelief and relief.

"Dear girl," the poorest earl continued, "you've been on the market for a year now. Your mother drags you to balls and receptions. So far, we've seen many admirers but not too many buyers—an avalanche of compliments, and not a single proposal. What does that tell you?"

He lowered his voice, as if he were telling his daughter a terrible secret.

"My darling child, those fat ugly rich men that you so dread marry equally fat ugly rich women. Beautiful paupers do not interest them. When your mother fails to sell you at a desirable price, she'll abdicate. That much I promise. Then you'll be free to marry a starving poet or a mad scientist—for love. Believe it or not, your mother and I loved each other once. I know, now it sounds like a tasteless joke, but... I do want you to experience this impractical feeling."

Lucan wagged his hand dismissively and threw his arm around Lavinia again. This time she did not resist him but clung to his chest.

"Don't go, Papa," she whispered. "If only I could dissuade you..."

"You cannot dissuade me," Lucan declared categorically. "I've already signed a contract with Lord Raglan. However, there's something you can do to increase my chances of returning home safely."

Lavinia lifted her head from his chest and wiped her tears.

"I'm listening, Papa. I'll do anything."

"Our wounded guest upstairs..."

"Lord Hungerton?"

"Yes. I'm taking him to the Crimea with me. He doesn't know it yet. I haven't told him. As soon as he recovers from his head injury, I'll hand him over to Captain Scarlett for training. Intuition tells me that he'll make an excellent ally; and I need loyal people. Do you understand?"

"Of course," Lavinia replied, nodding feverishly. "And what is my contribution?

"It's all very simple! See that in my absence our young patient wants for nothing. Give him the pleasure of your company. Indulge his every whim—within reason. Make him want to return to England and to this house. Understood?"

The girl frowned, trying to digest her father's words.

"If the task proves to be disagreeable to you," Lucan said with a hint of concern, "I'll gladly delegate it to your sister Augusta. You see, I've always loved you more."

"Papa," Lavinia interrupted him. "Augusta is married."

The statement astonished Lord Lucan.

"Married, you say? Our Augusta? Since when?"

"Since last year. Her husband might object to this sort of initiative, even for the benefit of the crown."

Both father and daughter blushed and winced.

"Oh, dear..." Lucan mumbled at last. "Where have my wits been? Ah, no matter! I only needed an excuse to tell you that I loved you more. You believe me, don't you?"

Of course, Lavinia did not believe him for a moment. She knew perfectly well that her father had made similar declarations to her sister when he needed a favor from her. Still, Lavinia chose not to sabotage his attempt at saving face. Exchanging white lies was the accepted custom in the family.

"Of course, I believe you, Papa," she said. "And I in turn favor you over Mama. May that remain our little secret?"

"Now, be honest," Lucan resumed in a more serious tone. "Do you find our guest repulsive?"

"Not in the least."

"I understand that Lord Hungerton is not the sort of man to which you're accustomed. I'm not privy to the particulars of his story, but I know that the first twenty-five years of his life were quite turbulent."

"Was he raised by wolves?" asked Lavinia, trying to make a joke.

"Worse—sailors and longshoremen. The horrors! I cannot vouch for his manners, his grasp of our etiquette. He does not look or speak like one of us; yet, he is one of us. At any rate, I needed to warn you. Should anything crude come out of his mouth, do not be offended."

"Consider it done, Papa!" Lavinia exclaimed eagerly. "I shall see to Lord Hungerton's comfort."

"And I shall see to yours. Now, when is your mother returning from London?"

"In another week."

"I shall find a way to detain her in the city. She won't disturb you. Dear girl, this is your contribution to England's history. Do you hear me?"

The earl took his daughter by the chin and attempted to make eye contact with her. Hesitantly, Lavinia gave herself permission to savor that illusion of communion with her father and significance to her country.

At that moment, the bells of the Laleham Abbey began tolling, like a chorus of indignant voices scolding Lavinia, awakening her to reality.

"I heard you, Papa," she replied, averting her eyes.

Chapter 5
Wynfield's First Attempt at a Coherent Conversation with a Woman

His perception of time and space still being tentative, Wynfield had grown to derive peculiar enjoyment out of his foggy state. There was a certain liberty in allowing one's brain to absorb the images and sounds without digesting them. Wynfield did not feel obliged to make sense of what was happening, having surrendered himself to the guidance and guardianship of Lavinia Bingham. The same tiny hands that had pulled him out of the fire were now leading him through the English Elysium that was Laleham, inhabited by deer and wild birds that were never sited in the city. If God had willed to bereave Wynfield of memory and toss him into another dimension, Lord Lucan's estate was not the most terrible holding place, and his youngest daughter was not the worst company.

Lavinia timed their strolls for early mornings. Wynfield could not go out when the sun stood high, as bright daylight would immediately trigger severe vertigo. He could not even wear a hat to protect his eyes, as the brim would put pressure against the wound and hinder it's healing.

They spent their afternoons migrating from one room of the house to another. Peculiarly, they never ran into the hired help, which led Wynfield to conclude that Lord Lucan's servants were invisible. The table set itself. The food and wine appeared and vanished. The porcelain bathtub filled with hot water on its own. Only once Wynfield caught a brief glimpse of a dark, slender figure at the end of the hall. It was the family physician, Dr. Ferrars on his way out of the library. He had an air of contempt, indignation, and suspicion about him.

Wynfield established his own way of keeping track of time. He knew another day had arrived because Lavinia was wearing a new dress. What he did not know was that Lavinia would change her wardrobe up to four times a day. The women of her station subjected themselves to this compulsion. Undoubtedly, the world would end if they sat to dinner in the same dress they wore for the morning walk. Close to thirty dresses had twirled before Wynfield's eyes. It seemed to him that he had already spent a month at Laleham while in reality a mere week had elapsed.

Lavinia had not forgotten her mission to teach the guest how to play chess. Every evening she would take out her father's set, but Wynfield's mind would stumble and abdicate after the first few moves. He would stare at the board for a few minutes until the white and black squares would begin dancing before his eyes. Without a drop of frustration, Lavinia would round up the figures and resume story telling, an activity that did not require Wynfield's active participation. She kept relating the history of her father's neoclassical estate, describing in great detail the original pattern on the marble floors, the Doric porch with pillars, the semi-circular staircase, and a cupola. Wynfield could only remember that Laleham House was built for the second Earl of Lucan in 1805 by the architect to the Prince Regent, J.B. Papworth, who ended up altering the original design in subsequent decades.

Somehow, his bandaged head would inevitably find its way into Lavinia's lap. As his ability to maintain balance for longer stretches of time began returning, he would lean on her shoulder instead. He sensed that such closeness was, if not impolite, inhumane. Bearing the weight of his bony body must have been a burden for Lavinia. One must be a saint to tolerate the presence of such a crude, disfigured creature as himself, who could not even complete a sentence without falling into incoherent rant.

The girl did not appear to object to the physical contact. On the contrary, she was the one initiating it. She would draw Wynfield closer, cradle and rock him, as if trying to dull her own pain, leaving him with a disturbing yet strangely endearing impression of being a hideous plush toy in the hands of a sad child. From time to time her chest would suddenly inflate and collapse in a spasmodic sigh that sounded too much like a sob.

Wynfield knew that once he had been quite the humorist and possessed the gift to make others laugh. If only he could resurrect this gift for a moment to help Lavinia out of her spleen. If only he could remember one joke! At the same time, he was not certain that this girl would understand his jokes. God knows, he did not wish to make her worse.

One evening, halfway through the bottle of burgundy Wynfield suddenly discovered that his sense of taste and smell returning. The wine was no longer mere red liquid that he kept pouring down his thrown mindlessly.

The taste was not entirely unfamiliar to him. He could have sworn that he had drunk this wine before. Suddenly, the outline of a Georgian mansion in Westminster appeared before his eyes. He saw a shady gallery covered with nautical paintings and the face of his mysterious host, an aging man dressed like a vicar. He also remembered the wolfish glance of the girl with the knives, the smirk of her bloodless lips, heard her malicious, tantalizing chuckle.

Along with his sense of taste, an entirely different hunger returned. Suddenly, his bone marrow came to life and began demanding what it had been denied. His carnal memory remained intact and perfectly lucid. Wynfield was accustomed to having his desires satisfied immediately. Restraint was one virtue he had not exercised in years. The girl with the knives, that savage imp, utterly bereft of shame, never declined any of his proposals, however extraordinary, and even pitched a few of her own. Intuition told Wynfield that most women would not consent to half of those delightful atrocities that he enjoyed with his former mistress, at least not without extensive cajoling.

Those thoughts developed in his head over the course of mere seconds, before he could order himself to cool his ardor. The only woman by his side at that moment was Lavinia Bingham, a lord's daughter. She was sheltering him in her bare arms, stroking his hair, delivering lectures on neoclassical architecture. Wynfield made every effort to follow her narration, if only to keep his thoughts in a safe harbor.

Examining the interior of the room, he caught a glimpse of their reflection in the glass cabinet and suddenly realized the distressing contrast between himself and his exquisite companion. His forehead was a giant bruise, like a puddle of spilled ink, with a red wound right below the hairline. A knotty dark scar adorned his right cheek. A smaller scar was hiding in the left corner of his mouth, forming one line with a permanent crease.

Wynfield knew that he still smelled like cheap tobacco, even though he had not smoked a single cigar since his arrival and Laleham and spent countless hours in the bathtub.

Lavinia herself was either unaware of the contrast between them or unperturbed by it. There is a limit to how much a woman, no matter how well mannered, can conceal her disgust. Could Wynfield allow the possibility be that disgust was not the pre-dominant sentiment burdening Lavinia at the moment?

The girl's fingers, growing warmer and swifter, slipped from his forehead down his mangled cheek. Their strokes became longer, deeper, and more deliberate. They communicated more curiosity than pity. Lavinia yearned not to efface the evidence of his former grapples with the devil but to learn about them.

This girl had probably never heard a true horror story or seen a deep scar up close. The concepts of disfigurement and suffering must have been rather vague to such a sheltered creature. She simply had not encountered enough tangible ugliness in her life to develop an aversion to it or even understand its origin.

Wynfield felt strange gratitude for her ignorance. At the same time, those palpations had a disquieting effect on him. When it became nearly impossible for him to bear her caresses passively, he suddenly covered her hand with his.

"Lady Bingham..."

"Lord Hungerton," she replied unperturbedly.

He did not peel her fingers away from his face but merely halted their frantic movement.

"My lady, I am sure you have a thousand questions for me. I hope that one day I will be able to satisfy your curiosity."

"Do not fear," she said, slipping her hand from under his. "I shall not interrogate you about the origins of all your scars."

"I couldn't remember at any rate."

"Oh, there will be more scars," Lavinia declared with assurance. "Prepare to have yourself marked up."

It was a first semblance of a coherent conversation. At last! Encouraged by this sudden clarity of thought and his ability to finish sentences, Wynfield labored to lift his head and look Lavinia in the eye.

"What makes you so optimistic, Lady Bingham?"

"My father's intuition! It never fails him. He wouldn't waste his time grooming some careless officer who would get himself killed in the first battle."

"He expects me to survive in the Crimea?"

"And sweep up all the medals!"

"And I haven't fired a single shot in my life," Wynfield murmured, his bewilderment escalating. "Your father is aware of that fact, isn't he?"

"Ah, any fool can fire shots! This isn't why my father wants you for his campaign. There's an air of immortality about you."

The pomposity of the last statement made Wynfield laugh.

"Immortality! Is that what they call it these days?"

He returned his head to Lavinia's shoulder, this time taking particular care not to cause her any physical discomfort. By then, he had enough strength in his arms to be able to prop himself.

Lavinia sensed that her enigmatic guest was no longer leaning on her for support but rather extending a gesture of affection. After a week of tending to him, she learned to interpret the responses of his body. Feeling his muscles stiffen through the sleeve of his shirt, she became aware of the power and vigor that he had once possessed and that were now returning to him. The wounded sparrow had been endowed with an eagle's might.

"You have nine lives," she continued with a slight tremor in her voice, "and you haven't even used up half of them."

She turned her head slightly, and their glances intersected for the first time. They discovered to their mutual surprise that they had the same eye color and almost identical slant of the eyelids. It seemed as if Nature had dipped the brush in the same pot of paint.

Neither of them dared to vocalize the discovery, let alone suggest any symbolism behind it. Although, Wynfield was tempted to make a joke that Nature gave them the same eyes to weep over the same tragedies. In the end he decided to keep the joke to himself, as he knew it was not his wittiest one, and his companion would probably not appreciate the pitiful remnants of his humor.

Lavinia was the first one to look away. She picked up a black pawn from her father's chess set and began polishing it with her thumb.

"Apparently, God takes particular pleasure in shattering my body and memory only to reassemble me again and then repeat the ritual," Wynfield concluded. "I feel like an alchemy experiment that is botched time after time."

His memory appeared to him as a twisted tunnel. On one end of it stood the Girl with Knives, whose cold pale skin smelled like cinders. On the opposite end stood the Girl with Pawns, whose skin had the ability to flush and smelled like lilac water. Both had a similar curve of the chin, but that was the only thing they shared in common. Blessedly, there was no danger in confusing the past and the present.

The sun had set hours ago. A breeze from the river brought the scent of cherry blossom through the open window and extinguished the candles at once. The bedroom sunk into a cool, fragrant darkness.

Lavinia heard a faint chuckle right by her ear, and a second later the cracked lips of her new friend brushed her neck. Was it an accidental brush or a deliberate kiss?

The pawn slipped out of Lavinia's hand and rolled on the floor.

"Do you have ghosts, Lady Bingham?" Wynfield asked.

Darkness made him more decisive, as it softened the contrast between him and Lavinia. He felt a little less wretched and monstrous.

She neither responded nor recoiled. Having interpreted Lavinia's silence as encouragement, he plunged unceremoniously into the familiar ritual that he had performed with another woman. This ritual existed independently from any oath Wynfield may have given in the past. It was hellishly pleasurable and for that reason alone worthy of repetition. Perhaps, it could help dissipate Lavinia's melancholy. He had completely forgotten about his promise to teach her how to play Castilian poker.

Lavinia reciprocated with a tentative twitch of her lips, which instilled in Wynfield a suspicion that this girl had not exchanged many kisses in her life. Perhaps, by lavishing all his fantasies and caresses on her at once he risked to induce stupor. Struggling to curb his ardor, he detached from her mouth and resorted to light, superficial strokes, similar to the ones she bestowed on him.

"You must mistake me for someone else," she said suddenly. "I suspect that these kisses aren't intended for me."

Wynfield released her and let his hands fall. Lavinia's observation was more sobering and disarming than outward rejection.

"My amorous repertoire is quite limited," he confessed. "Forgive me, Lady Bingham. You see, I've only loved one woman."

"And you still love her. It's quite apparent."

They moved away from each other and for a few seconds stared in opposite directions, but the silence could not last long.

"Ah, how tempting, how convenient it is to idolize those who are dead," Lavinia resumed. "They can no longer disappoint you."

"You speak from experience?"

"Yes, experience—if one could call it that."

She rose to her feet, closed the window, and lit the candles again.

"He was a bishop's son—a rotten boy!" she continued. "His lineage required a certain dose of perversity. I still keep his letters in which he described, in meticulous detail, all the carnal atrocities that we were going to commit together."

"I suppose," Wynfield began with timid mischief, "it would be presumptuous of me to ask for a sample of his... prose?"

"By all means!"

Lavinia unlocked the bottom drawer of her desk and extracted a stack of wrinkled letters. She perused through them, pulled out a few and handed them over to her guest.

Such casual willingness on the girl's part to share her secrets with him astonished Wynfield. For a minute or so he simply marveled at the superhumanly elegant cursive. As he began reading the content, a contemptuous smirk appeared on his face. Suddenly, he poked his finger in the middle of the page and bursts out laughing, completely bewildering Lavinia.

"Ah, I can see," he said, "that the fellow has a vivid imagination and an inflated opinion of himself but no practical experience or knowledge of anatomy. For instance, this particular maneuver is highly over-praised, this one is anatomically impossible, and this one is possible but not recommendable. I would not subject a woman I loved to such ordeal."

"What are you saying?" Lavinia asked, squinting.

Wynfield folded the letter reverently and fanned himself.

"I am saying, Lady Bingham, that you mustn't think yourself deprived. Had your friend lived to perform all those maneuvers, you would have been left disappointed and slightly disgusted."

"How easily you disparage another man's initiative!" Lavinia exclaimed, trying to mask her embarrassment as indignation. "And what do you have to show for yourself? Since you are such a master..."

"I never claimed to be a master." Wynfield raised both palms in the air, defending himself jokingly. "I told you, I have only loved one woman."

"Oh, but you have done enough with her—enough to place you above me and my hapless, deceased pen-mate."

"Lady Bingham, what is your preferred method of expression?" Wynfield asked. "Is it verbal or written?

Lavinia pulled the letter from his hands and tossed it aside.

"Since I have a stack of letters already, a practical demonstration would not be out of order. Prove to me that you are not a mere braggart. Show to me what your previous mistress had seen."

With an air of defiant determination, Lavinia resumed her place on the floor next to Wynfield.

"I would be delighted," he replied with a chivalrous bow, "but I am afraid that your noble father might object."

"My father sees me twice a year. Nevertheless, he appointed me to oversee your recovery. He left clear medical instructions but no prohibitions of any sort. His austerity projects onto his soldiers and servants but not his children. There are unquestionable rewards of having an aloof father. I live under the shroud of his apathy. He is so permissive that I have no desire to rebel. Many girls in my circle would kill to be in my place."

"As many men would kill to be in *my* place right now. It will give the pups at the Parliament yet another reason to hate me and covet my head on a stick. Right you are! There will be more scars, more reasons to boast."

Lavinia watched him as he pulled a few pillows from the sofa and arranged them on the floor, just like she did for him on the night when they first met, the night when she pulled him away from the burning furnace.

Still keeping the girl at arm's length, Wynfield reached over and pulled the ribbon out of her hair. Seeing the strip of green satin land drizzle on the floor, Lavinia made herself a promise that she would never wear it again. Such an adornment was more suitable for a child or a doll.

Without breaking eye contact, Wynfield diffused her curls, examining their texture and the way the light became tangled in them. Hers was the sort of hair that blanched easily in the sun. Ash-brown at the roots, it acquired a wheat hint towards the ends, keeping the memories of the previous summer. A pattern of light freckles, like a dusting of pollen, was visible on her cheekbones and the tip of her nose. No, Lavinia certainly was no doll and no fairy. She was a tangible woman who walked on earth—a very pleasant patch of earth, one would remark.

With a light tap on the arm, Wynfield he tipped her over on her back and hovered over her for some time, peering into her flushed face. He had never seen her from that angle. Now it was his turn to explore her, and he was doing so with the same intent fascination that she lavished upon him a few hours earlier. When his hand began sliding along her leg, stroking it through the dress, the girl suddenly froze. Her knees twitched and locked together under the petticoats, and her bare arms crossed over her chest.

"What's the matter, Lady Bingham?" Wynfield asked unperturbedly. "Are you cold? If you have changed your mind about a practical demonstration, perhaps we can revisit the idea of a letter? I must warn you that my handwriting is quite crude. You may not be able to discern my prose."

Lavinia shook her head.

"No... No more letters."

"I suspected that there wouldn't be. Nevertheless, I am relieved to hear that directly from you."

"And no more ghosts," Lavinia added hastily, "for either one of us. This is my only condition. This room will not become a place for conjugal visits with our respective deceased idols."

Wynfield realized that by having ridiculed the nameless bishop's son, he placed himself in a perilous position. He had no choice but to exercise utmost diplomacy, even at the expense of his own pleasure, to make certain that Lavinia would not be disappointed. Suddenly, he became aware of another daunting task—he would need to brave his way through the obstacle course of countless hooks and buttons on Lavinia's dress. Accessing her body was not a matter of pulling out a few pins. Whoever designed the wardrobe for women of Lavinia's class clearly aimed to complicate the lives of potential lovers.

Then an idea occurred to him. Instead of struggling with Lavinia's dress and risking embarrassing himself with his clumsiness, Wynfield removed his own vest and undid the top three buttons of his shirt. All the while, he was kneeling, letting Lavinia know that he would not be taking any further steps without her explicit encouragement. He was willing to remain in that pose for many an hour, not making any sudden moves, having already accepted the fact that his wishes would not be fulfilled that night.

The girl rose on the pillows and glanced under his collar. The smoothness of his narrow chest had a peculiar, reassuring affect on her. His body looked younger than his face. It was the face that had taken all the beating. In every other way he could pass for an adolescent.

Wynfield's face did not twitch when Lavinia's hand undid the remaining buttons on his shirt and rested in the hollow above his collarbone. Careful not to laugh, he allowed her to explore his ribcage and locate his heartbeat.

With every stroke, Wynfield became more and more aware of the magnitude of his task. Those caresses were not of a grown woman but of a curious child who had but a very nebulous idea of what desire might mean. Some time would pass before they would become equals.

"My friend," he heard her whisper. "My only friend..."

Wynfield suspected that this phrase was probably not intended for his ears, so he did not respond to it.

With all of Lavinia's ignorance, there was an undeniable quest to impress and to please, which filled Wynfield with vague remorse for his prior selfishness.

The girl began tugging at the bodice and the tapered sleeves of her dress, trying to free her shoulders. Truth be told, her knowledge of all the hooks and buttons was not much better than that of her lover, for it was her maid's responsibility to fasten and unfasten them. Wynfield heard the sound of threads tearing and buttons jingling against the floor, as he tried to help her with the stubborn dress.

"Let them perish," Lavinia murmured between nervous laughs. "One day I shall toss all my gowns and petticoats into the furnace."

Having finally fought his way through a layer of green muslin, Wynfield discovered a peculiar structure of plates and stiff fabric tied in the back by a satin string run through metal eyelets. It must have been some punitive device, a distant cousin of the chastity belt, a buskin for the waist.

"Does it hurt you?" he asked. "Does it stifle you?"

"I don't notice it," Lavinia replied. "I began wearing it at the age of eight. Mama says it helps to keep the posture."

Wynfield felt the whalebones through the fabric and frowned with an air of skepticism.

"Lady Bingham, if you intend on burning articles of clothing, this atrocity should be the first thing to go into the furnace."

"Undo the lacing," she requested quietly and tersely, turning her back to him.

Wynfield sighed, brushed Lavinia's curls aside, and pulled the string. There were more distressing revelations in store for him. A decade of meticulous binding had stunted the development of Lavinia's torso. Involuntarily, Wynfield compared the outline of her figure to that of his previous mistress. Fragile as Diana was, her ribcage did not curve so steeply inward, and her waist did not look like a chisel scooped it out. There were several inches of flesh missing. Was there any room for the lungs and the liver? So that was the price of a fashionable silhouette!

Lavinia could not see Wynfield shake his head, but she felt the tension and tremor in his hands.

If I ever have a daughter, I will never subject her to such violence. Perhaps, twenty years from now these torture devices will be extinct.

He exhaled sorrowfully and pressed his forehead against Lavinia's bare back.

It was not his place to vocalize his indignation over the customs of her circle. If she could accept his scarred face, he could accept her deformed rib cage. Neither one could brag about having an immaculate childhood. Barbarism made its way into all social circles. At least, the two of them could examine, appraise, and eventually laugh off their injuries, whether they took ten seconds or ten years to inflict.

Freed from her contraption of whalebone and cloth, Lavinia turned around and locked her arms around his neck before he had a chance to take a proper look at the rest of her body.

"I did not foresee any of this," she confessed, pulling him down on the pillows next to her. "I imagined it would be an ordinary spring, like any other. There were no signs of any sort. And I always look for signs."

It took some time for them to get accustomed to the idea that they were embracing, half-naked. For Lavinia, this process of carnal acquaintance was reminiscent of the first tentative immersion into the cold, murky water of the Thames. She was standing in the same place where the bishop's son, the author of the infamous letters, drowned two weeks prior. The current was strong, and the bottom slippery. The loose sand beneath her feet stirred up, tickling her ankles. Lavinia struggled to keep her balance until she fell backwards, mimicking the pose of Ophelia and the Lady of Shallot. Miraculously, she did not drown that day, even though she made no effort to stay afloat. The same river that swallowed William pushed her up to the surface. Perhaps, the deity dwelling on the bottom was not looking to snatch another soul. Lavinia could have lain thus infinitely, rocking on the water, had the servants not found her. She remembered their hoarse shrieks, the frantic waving of arms and the splashes around her. They pulled her out of the water, laid her out on the sand, and covered her with their coats. She heard her name being called repeatedly but did not respond, remaining in the same pose, with her arms tossed apart and her eyes fixed on the tin sky.

The heat of a man's body had the same entrancing effect on her as dark water. At last, Lavinia could resume her meditative experiment that she had begun on the banks of the Thames and which was so crudely interrupted by the arrival of the servants. Now the doors were locked, the servants were asleep, and both her parents were absent. Nothing could ruin the tryst that the higher forces—Lavinia presumed them to be benevolent—had plotted for her meticulously and inconspicuously. She never would have been able to arrange such an adventure for herself. The arrival of Lord Hungerton in her father's estate constituted nothing less than an indulgent, conspiratorial wink of Fate.

Chapter 6
The Conversation Becomes Progressively More Coherent

That night presented Wynfield with a string of pleasant revelations. In the end, Lavinia gave him more than he had initially dared to expect. She broke her own rule of not resurrecting any ghosts—one would have expected this change of heart—and gave Wynfield her explicit permission to love her as he had loved "that first woman." Once the initial vertigo-inducing shock of being in bed with a man had subsided, female rivalry began stirring, diffusing the remains of shame. In order to defeat her invisible, deceased rival, Lavinia needed to learn and master all her ruses. She imagined that by mimicking the caresses that her new friend had received with his first mistress, she would be mocking the memory of her predecessor of whom she, essentially, knew nothing. This intangible, imaginary enemy struck Lavinia as more threatening than any of the girls she had encountered in the dancing halls and drawing rooms of London. A sudden need to blaspheme overwhelmed her, and she could not identify its origin. From which source was this sweet, scorching venom pouring? Lust and possessiveness awakened simultaneously, each fueling the other.

This chemical tempest in her body did not frighten Lavinia. On the contrary, she welcomed it. Preparing for an earnest battle with a ghost, she pressed against her new lover, pouring extravagant absurdities in his ear, which resulted in the hasty removal of their remaining clothes.

Wynfield had to applaud the stoic manner in which Lavinia

took the inevitable pain. She managed to stifle the cry, apparently considering it demeaning, although he would have almost preferred for her to cry out. Instead, he sensed her inner panic and resistance. The bout lasted only a few seconds, but it was enough for Wynfield to regret his haste. The girl clearly overestimated her readiness for full-fledged carnal intimacy. He took something he was not certain was intended for him, and there was no way to give it back. Contrary to all his chivalrous intentions, he put himself in the role of a violator. Splendid! That was precisely the sort of sin that his soul was lacking. Even though Wynfield could not recall the particularities of his previous crimes, he was fairly certain that he was a thief and, possibly, a murderer. Now he was a violator of virgins too! The devil was cheering, no doubt.

Wynfield came close to cursing himself through his teeth, but that would only enhance the monstrous awkwardness of the situation. He froze over Lavinia, their bodies still being joined. He knew he could not continue looking down at her, but he could not decide whether to blink or to avert his eyes.

To his unspeakable relief, Lavinia recovered almost instantly. The girl had her own reasons for embarrassment. She realized how foolish she looked having invited a man into her bed and then made him witness her terror. Now he would think her skittish and infantile. No, that could not be allowed; so she raked her fingers through the hair on his temples, letting him know that her consent had not been revoked and she still wanted him for a lover.

"Fortunately, the toll at the gates of Eden is only paid once," she whispered. "It is done already. The gold coin was dropped. I fear that the gates are flung open. We may as well enter."

They both chuckled, and a second later their lips fused again in what could now pass for a conscious, reciprocal kiss. The girl had no qualms about laughing in bed—always an encouraging sign! The lump in Wynfield's throat melted, and he could breathe freely once again. He was not a criminal after all, and Lavinia was not a casualty. Clumsy and frantic as their first copulation was, the girl clearly derived at least some pleasure from it. She may not have stepped on the grounds of Eden yet, but she had already seen its walls from a distance. She knew that it existed and that it beckoned her.

As for Wynfield himself, his wretched shaken brain was not ready for such exertion, as it had not yet regained its ability to process the sensations of the body or modulate the ferocity of emotions. When the tingling in his spine reached its peak, his tenderness for Lavinia turned into unbridled idolatry. Having fully realized the irrevocability of what they had done, he reverted to chaste caresses that would be suitable even for a virgin, fervent superficial kisses in which gratitude mixed with apology. He slipped his hot hands under her back and elevated her from the pillows, as if preparing to toss her on some invisible pedestal.

The half-closed wound on his forehead began secreting pink fluid that mixed with sweat. He must have uttered some wild oaths that Lavinia did not expect to hear, because she suddenly became rigid, squeezed his head, and attempted to look him in the eye, as if questioning his sanity.

"What was that, Lord Hungerton?" she inquired. "Do repeat."

Wynfield failed to deliver a satisfactory response, as he could not vouch for what he blurted out a few seconds ago. Seeing his embarrassment, Lavinia laughed again, released his head, and allowed him to collapse on top of her. How little it takes for a woman to defeat a man!

Having witnessed her new lover in a state of such weakness, Lavinia could now make better sense of the stories that her older brother had shared with her. Replaying George's cautious, nebulous narrative about his university days, she celebrated her initiation into the ranks of versed women.

Fortunately for Wynfield, Lavinia had no intention of enslaving him, as she had not yet developed hostility towards men. The desire to punish the entire opposite sex for some universal offense was still foreign to her. The bachelors to whom she had been introduced in the parlors of London had not given her any reason for hatred. The obliging setting did not allow for overt display of unattractive masculine traits. The gentlemen abode by the same protocol of behavior—formal, dull, utterly non-threatening. Their demeanor followed the same predetermined formula of rehearsed phrases, mechanical nods, and smiles. Those men simply did not arouse Lavinia's curiosity enough to make her speculate about their lives outside the parlor walls. It did not concern her whether they went to a church or to a brothel after the reception.

Suddenly, she recalled her private conversation with her father on the road to Laleham Abbey and the earl's sardonic warning about the "boy who was raised by longshoremen." If Lord Hungerton harbored any crude or brutal tendencies, then she had not experienced them firsthand. Thus far, she had only tasted of his carnal generosity. She remarked that he lacked the trademark pomposity and arrogance of the men from her circle. One could only congratulate her on such excellent choice of a first lover.

Bathing in self-complacency, Lavinia had no regrets about her headlong plunge into intimacy with Lord Hungerton and already made up her mind about pursuing the tryst, wherever it would lead.

Tempting as oblivion appeared, Lavinia kept reminding herself of the sobering fact that Lord Hungerton could not belong to her entirely, at least not yet, even if there were no female rivals in sight for her. He was not merely her lover—he was first and foremost her father's subordinate. It would be prudent to curtail this perilous attachment in light of the inevitable, possibly permanent separation, but she Lavinia already permitted herself not to exert willpower, at least for one night. That night she would not give up the bliss of falling asleep with her nose buried in the ridge of his ribcage, the part of his body that she found particularly beautiful.

Their strokes were growing slower, lighter.

"How strange..." she said suddenly, her eyes already closed. "For an instant I forgot that I was in a war camp."

"In God's name, Lavinia, what are you mumbling?" he asked, fighting drowsiness.

It was his first time addressing her by her given name.

"Ah, whatever comes to mind," she replied, no longer being selective about her words. "It's a luxury not granted to me often. Forgive me if I slip into obscenities."

"I am dying to hear them."

It was a gallant lie. In reality, Wynfield did not want to hear any family sagas, as his current attention span would not allow him to appreciate them. Still, he did not wish to offend Lavinia, so he made an effort to feign interest.

"You see, my older siblings were mere consequences of careless conjugal life," she continued. "My birth had a purpose—to reconcile my parents. And I failed at my mission, quite miserably."

"Who put such atrocities into your head?"

"My dear Mama—who else? She had hoped that a pretty and obedient child would change her husband's heart and persuade him to return to his family. Now my parents employ me to injure one another. I am both a weapon and a hostage of their war. Naturally, nobody outside the family knows it. Such matters are not discussed in places I frequent. I know my complaints are childish. I'm hardly the only girl whose parents are at war. There must be a secret club of miserable daughters to which I have not been invited yet."

Lavinia slipped out of his embrace and sat up on the bed, regretting her frankness.

"Ah, I mustn't be saying such things to you. My father is your future commander. You must respect him."

"Your father has shown me superhuman kindness. Nothing you say has any bearing on my loyalty to him."

"I don't want you to see him as some sort of tyrant."

"All I see is an unhappy man, whose private misery infects others. Why won't your parents divorce? It's becoming a fashionable practice. Your own uncle, Lord Cardigan, was divorced?"

"Twice—unless my memory fails me."

"You see? Search no further for an inspiring example."

"I'm afraid my parents aren't quite as fashionable as Uncle James. No, they won't divorce until I am married. They would hate to ruin my already meager chances of making a suitable match. Truthfully, I cannot boast an avalanche of proposals. The Binghams aren't the wealthiest family. My father's Irish estates bring us no money."

She spoke tersely and hastily through her teeth, accompanying her tirade with flippant gestures.

Wynfield was looking for a tactful, gentle way to end this conversation. He drew Lavinia to his bare chest.

"I have a somewhat brilliant idea," he said. "Please, don't be in a hurry to reject it. According to the visiting cards in the pocket of my waistcoat, I am a baron—for what it's worth. You could become the next Lady Hungerton."

This proposal did not solicit the response he expected. Lavinia cast an irate glance at him and moved away.

"Grand!" she exclaimed, picking up a small pillow between them and tossing it. "You'll marry me out of pity?"

"Precisely!" he responded with mock earnestness. "What I did to you a moment ago was pure Christian charity. In the best Anglican traditions! The Archbishop of Canterbury himself would approve. If I continue at this rate, I will soon become a saint."

His gift for jokes was returning to him slowly.

"In earnest," Wynfield continued, "if your father can offer me an officer's title out of the blue, why can't I offer you my heart? This will certainly alleviate the burden on your parents to keep up the appearances. They will be free to part ways and seek happiness elsewhere. A stellar resolution! Now, what is the proper chess term for this?"

"Checkmate."

Chapter 7
A Woman's Intuition
Saves a Man's Life

Wynfield awoke to the sound of the bedroom door slamming.

"What in God's name happened here?" a furious male voice demanded. "I leave my house for two weeks and return to *this*!"

It was the first time that Wynfield heard his new patron speak. If only he could remember his early life, it would be passing before his eyes just about then. There was no point in him raising his head, since it was going to be chopped off at any rate. Yes, he was about to join the ranks of other careless lovers who got caught by their mistresses' fathers. Wynfield saw a pair of military boots just a few inches away from his face and smelled the shining cream and freshly cut grass. The splendid red uniform and the revolver in the leather holster made for perfect execution attire.

When Lucan turned away, Wynfield threw a timid glance at the crease in his bed and discovered that Lavinia was gone. The girl, who had slept the entire week by his side, must have sensed that it would be prudent for her to spend that particular night in her own bed. She slipped from under Wynfield's arm so quietly and swiftly that he did not notice. As a result, it appeared that the execution was postponed for a while.

Wynfield took a second to thank heavens silently and sat up on the bed.

"Good day, Lord Lucan..."

Not quite knowing the proper way of saluting his superiors, he touched his temple and tried to give his face a stern expression. Luckily, the earl was not even looking at his clumsy guest. He was preoccupied with a far more important task—picking up the pawns from the floor.

"This rotten girl!" he kept on raging. "She took out my chess set, my prized set from India! Would you believe it? I had specifically forbidden her to touch it. Now I'll never collect the pieces. I leave her in charge for a few days, and she turns the house topsy-turvy!"

"My Lord, please do not be angry with Lavinia," Wynfield implored. "I am the one to blame. I was the one who wished to see the chess set, and Lavinia was kind enough to show it to me."

Lucan's anger subsides at once. He straightened out his jacket, embarrassed by his own outburst.

"You seem well. Hurry! Captain Scarlett is waiting. You have five minutes to make yourself decent."

"Where are we going?"

"To the training camp, my young dolt! Have you forgotten our arrangement?"

"Of course not, my lord," Wynfield responded under his breath. "How could I?"

"There's tea and bread downstairs. Forgive me for the meager breakfast. You better grow accustomed to gastronomic disappointments."

"Tea and bread will suit me perfectly fine, my lord."

"That's comforting to hear. To be honest, you did not strike me as someone who would demand poached salmon and lemon scones in the morning. I counted your ribs while pulling you out of the water. That reminds me—your uniform!"

Lucan tossed at him a red coat, identical to his own.

"Try it on!"

"Thank you, my lord," Wynfield replied, stroking the wool and the shiny buttons.

He had never seen a military uniform up close, and now he could not believe that he was about to put one on.

"If it's too loose, just pull the belt in tighter. The idiot tailor has two left hands, I swear! We'll be the ugliest-looking soldiers on the field, but you'll just have to endure the embarrassment. I can't be bothered with such trifles. After all, it's a war, not a parade. In a time of peace I never would've allowed one of my officers to be seen in such atrociously tailored uniforms."

"I'm an officer?" Wynfield asked.

The question irritated the earl.

"Of course, you are an officer! What did you think I was going to make you—a drummer boy? Honestly, Lord Hungerton, sometimes I wonder whether you are purposely provoking me, testing my composure. This isn't a good time for such games, young man. Get dressed!"

Lucan exited as abruptly as he entered. After the door slammed, Wynfield lingered on the bed for a few minutes. As his hand was rummaging mindlessly through the sheets, it came across a sharp object; it was Lavinia's earring.

Wynfield held the sapphire pendant to the light, recollecting the events of the last evening. Pity, their acquaintance was cut short; and he was just beginning to diffuse Lavinia's inhibitions. Last night she did not have a single episode of panic. At last, Wynfield allowed himself to consider his own pleasure. They kissed in the bathtub until the water cooled, and then continued the lovemaking on the floor, in a nest made of pillows. It was almost heavenly, and he had every right to be proud. Lavinia's body finally gave him the response for which he had been waiting and working. The combined efforts of the entire week, all that caressing, cajoling, meticulous diplomacy, and self-restraint were beginning to pay off. When he felt Lavinia stiffen in his arms, he knew it was not another fit of skittishness. It was a considerable triumph for them both, certainly worthy of celebration and repetition. Another few nights in that key and he would succeed at persuading her that remorse was not a mandatory consequence of pleasure.

In spite of Lavinia's verbal bravado, there were quite a few fences to break. If she married an indifferent man, who would not be disturbed by her inhibition, she would continue squeezing her knees, covering her breasts and turning her head sideways, hoping that the kiss will be planted on her cheek and not her lips. What a waste of beauty and raw carnal potential that would be! Wynfield winced at this disheartening thought and he thanked fate for granting him the privilege of becoming Lavinia's first lover. It became his quest to nurture healthy hedonism in this compliant, benevolent child. She deserved to know the secrets of her own nervous system. If she would have him for a husband—and he assumed she was earnest about her consent—he would make certain that she was never bored in flesh or spirit. She would be the most entertained wife in England.

Then he heard Lucan calling him from the ground floor.

"Damn you, Lord Hungerton! Have you fallen back to sleep?"

Wynfield jumped up and pulled the red coat over his shirt hastily. Through the open window he could hear the stomping of horses' hooves and terse male voices.

On his way down the hall, Wynfield stopped by Lavinia's bedroom in hopes to catch her before his departure. He tapped on the closed door gently and called her name, but no sound came from inside. He waited a few seconds, then sighed and hid the sapphire earring in his pocket.

Chapter 8
Lord Lucan's Front Yard Turns Into a Training Camp

There was no time left for breakfast, so Wynfield dashed by the kitchen straight into the courtyard, where Lord Lucan was waiting for him in the company of a stocky, red-faced, white-haired gentleman in his mid-fifties.

"At last!" the earl exclaimed, throwing his arms up. "Is this how long it usually takes you to get dressed, Lord Hungerton? Were you powdering your nose? Those prissy habits must be broken at once!"

Wynfield muttered an apology, avoiding eye contact with the earl.

"Meet your direct commander," Lucan continued, gesturing at his silent companion. "Sir James Yorke Scarlett, the head of the Heavy Cavalry Brigade."

The red-faced general stepped forward and saluted his new subordinate. His facial expression did not change. The white mustache did not twitch. Scarlett's reserved yet unmistakably benevolent demeanor alleviated some of Wynfield's unease. As he later found out, Sir James was one of the best-loved generals in the British army. Modest, sensible and unassuming, in contrast to his own superiors, he won the loyalty of his soldiers. He had brought along Colonel Beatson and Lt. Alexander Elliott. Both officers had spent many years in India serving in the Bengal Light Cavalry were they earned stellar reputations. Lord Raglan, who looked down upon "Indian" officers as inferior, rejected both. Luckily, the commander of the Heavy Brigade recognized their achievements and made them his advisors.

"Scarlett," Lucan continued, "I present to you Lord Jeremy Griffin Helmsley, Baron Hungerton, whom I have appointed officer in the 5th Dragoon Guards."

Wynfield mimicked Scarlett's gesture, feeling the remains of his apprehension evaporating.

Naturally, Lucan could not allow this moment of silent fraternizing last too long. He did not like ceremonies in which he played the role of a host. He snapped his fingers, and one of the stable boys brought forth a three-year old black stallion that looked like a mixture of Arabic and Spanish.

"Here is your horse, Lord Hungerton," he said, shoving the reigns into Wynfield's hand.

Having felt a stranger's grasp, the stallion huffed and recoiled. Wynfield wrapped his reigns around his wrist and for a second he feared that his shoulder would come out of his socket.

"What's the matter?" Lucan inquired smugly. "Don't tell me you're afraid of animals."

"On the contrary," Wynfield replied under his breath. "They are afraid of me."

The veins on his wrist bulged, and his entire arm was vibrating with tension. The stable boys found the scene comical, yet they did not dare to laugh in the presence of Lord Lucan. He alone was allowed to concoct comical scenarios and laugh at them.

Scarlett, an expert horseman, who had trained many soldiers, thought it would not be altogether inappropriate to intervene and instruct the young Lord Hungerton.

"Slip your left foot in the stirrup," he began slowly and imperturbably. "Then give yourself a push with your right foot, as if you were leaping forward."

Lucan did not let him finish.

"Try to mount the horse before it takes off, unless you enjoy being dragged on the ground by the foot. This is the same horse that threw my son. If you can master this beast, you can master anything."

God be my witness, I will not be humiliated today.

That was the thought that passed through Wynfield's head as

he placed his foot in the stirrup. Ten seconds later he was gallop-ing down the alley, choking with laughter, with Scarlett's advisors on either side. Beatson and Elliott were riding very closely to him, shouting instructions, but Wynfield could not make out their voices through the crackling of gravel under the horses' hooves.

Watching the three riders disappear at the end of the alley, Scarlett spoke to his commander.

"Lord Lucan, if Lord Hungerton breaks his neck, I will not be able to take him to the Crimea with me."

"Rest assured," the earl replied. "The boy is made of steel. It will take more than a tumble from the saddle to break his neck."

Chapter 9
Moving Targets

How did I live without a horse for all these years? Wynfield questioned himself, watching the stallion graze along the banks of the river. His two companions kept smirking to one another complacently, grateful that the first riding lesson did not end in broken bones and knocked-out teeth.

Colonel Beatson unstrapped a wooden case from his saddle.

"Onto our next lesson," he said, opening the case before Wynfield. "I only hope that you are as good a marksman as you are a rider."

The case contained a revolver along with cleaning and repairing tools. Wynfield took out the gun, inspected it in the light, and twirled it around his index finger, which made Elliott cringe.

"You've never seen model Adams before, have you?" he asked, slightly mortified by such juvenile handling of weapon.

Not every soldier was fortunate enough to have a revolver of this model in his possession. The army did not hand them out indiscriminately. Only officers have the means to purchase them privately. Scarlett went through the trouble of procuring one of his new subordinate.

"Colonel, do we have the targets ready?" Elliott asked his comrade.

"We certainly do!" Beatson replied and threw his arms open. "Take your pick, Lord Hungerton. Laleham Park is filled with moving targets: deer, swans, quails, rabbits."

Hardened as the two soldiers were by the years of service, they had enough paternal benevolence and sense of humor to enjoy the sight of a child delighting in his new toys. Beatson stayed behind to watch the horses and start a campfire, while his comrade took the young officer into the depths of Laleham Park for a first lesson in marksmanship. For the next hour and a half, the Colonel listened to the rhapsody of gunshots and jubilant cries coming from the woods.

Around noon, the two men emerged, perspiring and laughing, dragging a bag filled with small pheasants and a doe's carcass.

While Wynfield was busy sorting the hunt, Elliott approached Beatson and confided in him.

"Between us, Colonel, I don't believe the young fellow had ever taken a life before, not even that of an animal."

"What leads you to such conclusions?"

"Colonel, you should've seen the young fellow's eyes as he brought down that doe. I perceived something akin to pity and remorse. This may prove to be an obstacle on the battlefield. Do you think it would be wise to warn Scarlett?"

"I don't think it's necessary. I've never met a man who would cling to such remorse. Tell me rather: does he have a steady hand and a good eye?"

"Why, look at the content of the bag. He shot most of those birds."

"Then nothing else matters."

The birds were promptly beheaded, plucked, and gutted. Beatson, an expert in battlefield cookery, carried a box with salt, pepper, and curry mix, which he rubbed into the bluish skin of the birds. Then he picked up a few oak branches and carved out some skewers with his pocketknife. Within ten minutes, the pheasants were roasting over the coals.

Wynfield watched the demonstration in amazement.

"Enjoy the aroma of freshly hunted fowl whilst you can," Beatson advised him. "God knows what sort of food will be given to us in the Crimea. Remember this feast as you eat rats and worms."

Elliott pulled a half-empty whiskey flask from his breast pocket and shook it in the air tantalizingly.

"Have a sip, Lord Hungerton," he said, offering the flask to Wynfield. "You have earned it."

"Gentlemen, I do hope that you will tell me all about your Indian adventures one day," Wynfield said, accepting the flask. "Is it true that eight-armed, elephant-headed gods walk the streets?"

His two mentors did not know where to be insulted or amused. They remembered Lord Lucan mentioning that the young officer did not receive traditional schooling and had noticeable gaps in his knowledge of foreign cultures.

"Young man, your ignorance is endearing," Beatson said at last. "A part of me is almost hesitant to scatter it. The reality is far more prosaic than the myth, I assure you."

"Wait until you taste of those Turkish herbs," Elliott intervened with a wink. "The Crimea has elaborate flora as you will soon discover. Once you taste of hashish, dear friend, you will never return to old-fashioned tobacco. I predict that after the war it will become the vice of choice in the most stylish gentlemen's clubs in London."

At that moment, they heard the rattle of hooves and Lord Lucan accompanied by Sir James Scarlett and Dr. Ferrars.

"The smell attracted them," Elliott remarked with a chuckle. "Gentlemen, claim your lunch before the earl steals it from you. He certainly looks famished."

Military-style eating freed the generals from the necessity to use utensils. They could unleash their inner savages and rip the smoked flesh of the bird from the bone with their teeth. Lord Lucan welcomed this opportunity. He preferred white meat, so he had already visually claimed the pheasant's breast for himself. Seeing the predatory fire in his commander's eyes, Sir James decided that it would be more prudent for him to curb his own appetite.

Chapter 10
Certain Principles of Unarmed Combat

Dr. Ferrars declined the invitation to join his master for lunch. He dismounted from his horse and retreated to the banks of the river, clutching his lower chest as if fighting nausea.

While the generals were feasting, Wynfield slipped away furtively and followed the physician.

"You have been terribly quiet as of late," Wynfield began, subsiding on the sand next to the doctor. "I don't believe we have exchanged a word since the day of my arrival."

The physician picked up a wet branch and plunged it into the sand.

"Sometimes silence is the only way of refraining from rudeness," he replied in a trembling voice, his eyebrows arching and falling like two wrestling caterpillars.

"You can be as rude with me as you wish," Wynfield allowed graciously. "My skin is quite thick. Besides, you helped save my life."

"I was merely fulfilling my duty and Lord Lucan's orders. I don't have the luxury of angering him."

Wynfield glanced over his shoulder to make sure that they had no witnesses and moved closer to the physician.

"Lord Lucan doesn't need to know of our conversation. He is preoccupied with things that are far more important. If I have in any way offended you, I would like an opportunity to apologize. We are about to embark on a rather trying campaign, and I would hate to bring enemies from England."

Dr. Ferrars pulled the branch out of the sand and threw it into the stream.

"In earnest, Lord Hungerton, can a man apologize for ruining another man's career?"

"Lord, have mercy," Wynfield whispered. "When did I do that?"

"When you first arrived at the estate. Don't you know? I was planning to leave for Greenwich the next morning, to attend a conference that could prove crucial to my professional growth, but Lord Lucan detained me here instead, to care for you. Now he wants me to accompany him to the Crimea. Now I must leave behind my lady-friend, the only being I care for in this rotten, God-forsaken world."

Dr. Ferrars' tone betrayed internal abdication. He knew perfectly well that Lord Hungerton could not be blamed for the sudden change in his plans. He surveyed the patch of sand on which he was sitting, searching for another stick to take his wrath, but there were no more sticks in his immediate surrounding. So he began cracking empty mollusk shells, creating a sound that could induce toothache.

"What is your lady-friend's name?" Wynfield asked in the most cautious, diplomatic, unassuming manner.

Dr. Ferrars hesitated for a second, but the desire to talk about his mistress proved to be stronger than his sense of discretion.

"Her name is deceivingly common—Anne. Many English-women bear it."

"A common name, indeed," Wynfield agreed. "Wait now... Isn't Lord Lucan's wife also Anne?"

"She certainly is," Dr. Ferrars sighed.

A completely idiotic, all-betraying smile appeared under his neatly trimmed mustache. Wynfield in turn covered his mouth with a fist to stifle a chuckle. The sheltered young doctor was no good at keeping secrets. He spent too many years in isolation from society and did not know how to lie convincingly.

"Your lady-friend," Wynfield continued questioning him, "what is she like?"

"Oh, she's different with everyone," Dr. Ferrars dragged out dreamily, forgetting his shells. He lit a cigar and tossed his head back. "With others she can be abrupt, despotic and plain insufferable at times; but with me she's jovial, tender, uninhibited. It is amazing how little it takes to turn a cackling witch into a muse—just a bit of genuine interest. I believe I have found the key to women's minds. Astonishingly, they are not that different from our own. I was looking forward to sharing my findings at the conference—but that never transpired. Now Lord Lucan is forcing me to go to the Crimea. If I refuse, he will see that I never practice medicine again."

"I could plead with him," Wynfield suggested.

"Don't dare!" Dr. Ferrars seized his patient's elbow, his eyes bulging in terror. "If he finds out that I complained to you, it will anger him even more. The man is capable of unspeakable atrocities. He can easily arrange to have my license revoked, and his reprimand may not end there. He can crush a life with one snap of his fingers. Understand? You and I are both his prisoners."

"Ah, you are exaggerating," Wynfield attempted to object. "I find it difficult to believe."

"Oh, you'll believe it soon enough. I've known Lord Lucan for five years. Blessedly, I've been spared the daily interactions with him. He spent all his time in Ireland; but now, I'll be spending every waking hour with him. Imagine a war camp, with cholera and gangrene... I've read about those diseases, but I've never seen anyone afflicted by them. Lord Hungerton, you may think me a coward, but I am not expected to be brave. It is not my profession. I am not a soldier. Nor am I a field doctor. This terrible man is preparing a terrible death for me. Perhaps, I deserve it."

The doctor dropped the cigar into the wet sand, squeezed his head and began choking. Wynfield slapped his companion on the back a few times.

"Dr. Ferrars... Richard? Look up at me."

The physician succumbed to uncontrollable tremor. Wynfield pulled him to his feet by the collar, turned towards himself, grabbed him by the shoulders, and shook him.

"Richard, be a man! Collect yourself at once."

The physician whined indistinctly. Wynfield glanced up at the clouds, and, after a few seconds of reflection, gave Dr. Ferrars a sobering punch in the jaw.

"Forgive me, Richard," he said, wiping his knuckles. "You left me no other choice. This is a proven method for settling male hysteria."

The noise from the blow and the muffled groan distracted the generals from their lunch. Lucan, Scarlett, and the two advisors leaped to their feet and rushed to the scene of the skirmish.

"What is all this?" the earl asked, pointing squeamishly at the man curled up on the sand.

Panting, Dr. Ferrars spat out a clot of blood—during the fall he bit his lower lip—and addressed the earl in a perfectly steady voice:

"Lord Hungerton was demonstrating certain principles of unarmed combat."

Lucan glanced at Sir James, then at Wynfield.

"In other words, Lord Hungerton took upon himself the liberty of training others, without seeking my explicit permission?"

"Something of the sort," Wynfield replied innocently. "Is it prohibited? One cannot be overly prepared."

Lucan squinted and tapped his mouth with his index finger, commanding silence.

"Gentlemen, can anyone you tell me what Lord Hungerton has just done?"

Sir James chose to remain silent. Beatson and Elliot thought it would be wise to follow their commander's example. The silence pleased Lucan.

"Gentlemen," he continued, "I will tell you what Lord Hungerton has done. He has usurped the initiative. Can someone tell me what the prospective consequence for such behavior on the battlefield?"

"I'm eager to learn, my lord!" Wynfield spouted, turning his shoulders out.

Lucan's eyes kept growing narrower, until they turned into two grey slits. Suddenly, he detached his finger from his lips and raised it to the sky.

"The consequence for such behavior is immediate promotion!"

Sir James and his advisors swallowed simultaneously, while their facial expressions remained unchanged.

"Take a good look, gentlemen," Lucan went on, pacing before them as he usually did during his speeches. "This is an example of dedication and camaraderie. Lord Hungerton did not wait for my orders but stepped forward on his own accord, and that is much to my liking. On battlefield, I would have promoted him from Second to First Lieutenant. But, since we are not on battlefield yet, I will limit the reward to a few words of praise. Well done, Lord Hungerton!"

The two of Scarlett's advisors moved closer to their immediate commander. Only thirty seconds ago they were fairly confident that Lord Lucan would court-martial Lord Hungerton for insubordination.

Wynfield never thought that punching a man in the jaw would merit an elevation in the rank. Apparently, he had much to learn about the English army.

Chapter 11
A Physiologist on the Ambush

Towards the evening, the left side of Dr. Ferrars' face swelled up and his lower lip became discolored. He kept palpating his jaw with his fingertips to make sure it was not broken. He remained silent for the rest of the day, as it hurt to speak, and saliva kept flooding his mouth, forcing him to swallow every ten seconds. He could swear that one of his wisdom teeth felt a bit loose. It suddenly occurred to Dr. Ferrars that he had never been struck before in his life. Neither his parents nor his countless tutors had ever raised their hands on him. Then his own patient, whose wounded head he had bandaged, initiated him into the world of physical violence; and Lord Hungerton did not even intend to cause any lasting harm. The punch was meant to merely cut his onslaught of panic. Dr. Ferrars could not help being grateful for this unorthodox favor. Lord Hungerton pushed the coddled bookworm over the hurdle that separated him from his archetypically masculine brothers. Having received his first injury, Dr. Ferrars felt a little more prepared for his trip to the Crimea.

The plan was to depart the first thing in the morning and head to London to fetch another group of officers that was due to sail on the same ship. Elliott and Beatson had already stamped out the coals from the campfire and joined Sir James Scarlett at the guest room of the house.

Dr. Ferrars surveyed the river's banks along which he had strolled for five years. Was he ever destined to return to this place?

Perhaps, it was God's will that he should pass the impending trials. Perhaps, he needed to taste of the battle to be worthy of Anne.

An obscenely optimistic thought zoomed through his mind. What if the earl should die, and he, Richard Ferrars, should live? Oh, he would return victorious, heroic, and Anne, a new widow, a free woman, would flutter into his arms!

He had to slap himself on the swollen side of the face in order to come down to earth. It was a bit early to dream so high.

"Richard, collect yourself at once..." he mumbled the same words that Lord Hungerton had addressed to him a few hours earlier. That phrase would become his litany for the next few months.

After the punching incident, Dr. Ferrars started regarding the brain-damaged young baron if not as a potential friend than at least as a buffer between himself and Lord Lucan. Being on civil terms with Lord Hungerton would considerably increase his chances of survival.

In the meantime, the earl and his newly recruited officer were standing under a tall oak tree, conversing. Unable to hear their words, Dr. Ferrars had to rely on their body language to determine the subject of their discussion. The earl was doing most of the talking, holding a bottle with one hand, and slapping himself in the chest with another. Lord Hungerton was mostly nodding his bandaged head. Suddenly, they both laughed and shared a jovial handshake. Dr. Ferrars concluded it was time for him to return to the house. It was, quite possible, his last night at the Laleham estate.

Chapter 12
Memory of Trees

A few sips of Colonel Elliott's whiskey made Wynfield brave enough to finally ask the question that had been lodged in his throat for the past ten hours.

"Lord Lucan, do you suppose, I could see your daughter just one more time before our departure?"

"Not a chance, I'm afraid. Her mother came to fetch her early in the morning." The earl wagged his gloved hand negligently. "Fortunately, our paths did not cross. Vexatious, extravagant witch! She pulled the sleepy girl out of her bed by the locks and stuffed her into the carriage."

"I'm very sorry to hear that," Wynfield replied, his shoulders slouching.

"Why are you so eager to see Lavinia at any rate?" the earl asked, perplexed and annoyed by the fact that the conversation took such a frivolous turn. "Do you have something terribly important to tell her?"

"For one, I would like to thank her for her patience and kindness. After all, my arrival disrupted her leisure, and she bore the inconvenience with utmost graciousness."

"Wait now," Lucan whispered and squint with uncharacteristic mischief. "You aren't in love with her, are you?"

Wynfield averted his eyes and scratched the ground with the tip of his boot, as if digging his own grave.

"Bah!" Lucan shouted and opened his arms. "You rotten bastard! You love my daughter more than you've loved anything on earth. Say it!"

He locked his arm around Wynfield's neck and gave it a hearty, persuasive squeeze.

"Say it, you cur! You love her!"

To say "yes" would be a slight exaggeration, but to say "no" would be unforgivable blasphemy. Lord Lucan was waiting for an answer, and he clearly would not retreat until he received it.

"Yes, my lord," Wynfield whispered at last, abdicating. "I've had the audacity to take fancy to Lavinia."

"And you honestly believe that a ragged scarecrow like yourself, who reeks of seaweed and tobacco, is worthy of my daughter, the most beautiful girl in the fashionable society?"

"If you wish to hang me on that tree, I will not protest, as it befits a scarecrow."

"I will not hang you," Lucan replied, releasing Wynfield, "not before you are given a chance to demonstrate your abilities on the battlefield. If you disappoint me—then I will hang you. If you serve up to my expectations—I will give you Lavinia in marriage. Does this arrangement strike you as fair?"

"My lord, it is not my place to appraise your fairness. My body and mind belong to England. The part of my heart reserved for a woman belongs to your daughter, and nobody else."

The earl threw his arm around Wynfield again, this time with more benevolence.

"Why, you are far more polite and articulate than I had thought. You certainly know how to talk to superiors, don't you? Tell me the truth: whom have you served in the past?"

"My lord, before you I've never had a worthy commander whom I would be eager to follow."

"What about Dr. Grant?"

A seizure ran across Wynfield's face. He touched the old scar on his cheek as if it were a fresh wound.

"What's the matter?" Lucan inquired. "Does the memory distress you?"

"It infuriates me," Wynfield whispered and examined at his

hands, surprised that they were not stained with blood. "I could kill the man if I saw him."

Then he glanced up at his new patron, who at that moment seemed like the embodiment of fatherly concern and compassion.

"My dear boy," said the earl, drawing Wynfield closer to him, "you need not continue. Clearly, I have inadvertently stepped upon a sore spot."

"I could kill the man if I saw him!" Wynfield exclaimed. "He imprisoned me and kept me as a slave. When I disobeyed him, he cut my face with a broken bottle. I remember his basement littered with bottles... They looked liked corpses piled up on top of each other. I didn't fear for my own life. If I disobeyed him again, he would take out the rage on the innocent girl."

"The girl?"

"Yes, his other victim. She was considerably younger than me and completely helpless. I needed to protect her. She's dead now, because of him. That means nothing can stop me from killing the bastard."

This sudden avalanche of aggression from the boy left Lord Lucan perplexed. In all honesty, that was a bit more than he expected to hear. He marveled at this sudden change in Wynfield's demeanor. Only ten minutes ago, this boy was galloping through the park, laughing, joking with the officers, delighting in his new horse and his new revolver, and now he was trembling and clenching his fists. The earl remembered Dr. Ferrars' warning to take the patient's confessions with a grain of salt. Still it was an excellent opportunity for the earl to step in and provide the much-needed comfort for his young friend in a moment of vulnerability.

"I do not know the particularities of your ordeal," he said to Wynfield. "You can confide in me without reservation. I myself am no stranger to family strife, although my misadventures are nothing compared to yours. On the battlefield, I am your commander, but in private I am your friend. My rank obliges me to treat you sternly before others. Do not be deceived by my public demeanor. There is no concern or suspicion that you cannot share with me. Do you hear me?"

Wynfield exhaled and nodded weakly.

"Yes, my lord..."

His right knee began to twitch. In a matter of just a few seconds, his overwhelming rage gave way to overwhelming drowsiness. The ache around the gash on his forehead reminded him that he was still recovering. Weighed down by the exertions of the day, he collapsed under the oak with his back against the trunk.

Chapter 13
Road to London

"What has your father been telling you in my absence?"

"Nothing out of the ordinary."

That was the exchange taking place between Lady Lucan and Lavinia, as the coach was taking them away to London. The countess savored the chance to sink her claws into her daughter. She needed to wait until they were alone inside a rather tight box on wheels. There was no chance of the girl escaping. As soon as Laleham Park disappeared from view, Anne plunged into the most cherished of maternal privileges. How she had missed those heartfelt dialogues with her darling child during her stay in London! A day was considered a waste if Anne did not manage to make her daughter cry at least once. Under normal circumstances, Lavinia's eyes would already be tearing up right about now, but this time something was amiss. The girl stared at the embroidery on the cushion, her head wavering from side to side from each bump in the road.

"You know that your father purposely separated me from Dr. Ferrars, the only physician who understood the nature of my illness and was capable of treating it," Anne continued in a solemn, mysterious voice, convinced of the malicious intentions of her husband. "Should I die, his lordship will be very pleased. You know, he has been plotting my demise all along, don't you?"

"Imagine that..."

Lavinia was barely moving her lips. Her eyes resembled those of a fish that had been lying without water for several minutes.

"It is a very clever and subtle and all the more cruel plot!" Anne declared. "No doubt he had consulted a true hater of women. Your father is not intelligent enough to concoct something of this sort on his own."

"My dear girl, I do not believe you truly understand the magnitude of your father's hatred for me and his desire to see me in a coffin. As I was ascending the second storey to fetch you, I heard a man's cough coming from the guest room, a hoarse, crude cough that could not emerge from a gentleman's breast. I can't fathom of a more vulgar, disagreeable sound. Who in God's name was he? And what was he doing under our roof in my absence? Dare I hope that your father introduced you to the man properly? Of course, he did not! His lordship turned what once was our lovely home into an infirmary or a shelter for truants. It was his subtle—or perhaps, blatant—insult to my good taste. He knows how I detest having strangers in the house. Their scent infuriates me. He knew I would be passing through the corridor, so he purposely planted that filthy vagabond in my way. Lavinia! Are you listening to me?"

"Yes, Mama..."

Having realized her failure to make her daughter cry, Anne began to cry herself. It was her crown trick, one to which she did not resort frequently before Lavinia.

"No, I don't believe you are listening," she whimpered. "Do you care in the least that conspiracy has been launched against your own mother? And where is your earring? Do not dare telling me that you lost it. I simply won't listen to it. Your father is bitter—understandably so; but you, dear child, how do you explain your hatred towards me? Did I not carry you under my heart? No doubt, that abominable man persuaded you to take his side! You have allied with him to drive me to madness, haven't you?"

Lavinia did not respond. The countess sniffled in silence for another few minutes, toying demonstratively with her handkerchief and her smelling salts, panting and rolling her eyes back, displaying all the signs of her famous cardiac fit. Suddenly, she heard Lavinia's voice that was just as vacant as her stare.

"It was heavenly."

"What was heavenly?" the countess asked, blotting her nose.

"Having both of you away... There comes a time in a young woman's life when having two living parents becomes burdensome."

Part 3
Rough Meat and Excellent Champagne
Summer, 1854

Chapter 1
The Intricacies of Equestrian Pedagogy
(Scutari, May 1854)

Fanny Duberly broke her rule of not sniffling before witnesses. Watching her favorite stallion go mad and perish in the Mediterranean heat brought her more grief than all her miscarriages combined. When the carcass of the graceful Pegasus that had carried her across the parks of her native Wiltshire was dumped overboard, she fainted. Although blessed with a strong stomach and a lucid head, she was equally cursed with a soft heart. She had prepared herself to witness the endless suffering of men, but not that of horses, the most graceful, and noble of God's creatures.

Born Frances Isabella Locke, she accompanied her husband Captain Henry Duberly, the paymaster to 8th Royal Irish Hussars, on his voyage to the Crimean. Fanny was not by any means the only woman aboard a military ship sailing for the East. Many of the officers brought their wives, mothers, and brides along.

Gregarious, daring, and witty, Fanny kindled a string of flirtatious friendships with her husband's comrades. Her station could be compared to that of Lady Marion among the Merry Men. Her antics solicited benevolent chuckles from Captain Duberly, who had cultivated immunity against jealousy early in the marriage. He was not above healthy masculine vanity, which is incompatible with possessiveness. He derived too much pleasure from the envious glances of his comrades to keep his trophy of a spouse hidden from them. The young captain did not mind sharing his wife with others during the day. In the evening, he demonstratively led her into his stateroom, making it clear to the world that this gorgeous Amazon belonged to him.

She carried around a sturdy, leather-bound journal, which she was planning to keep meticulous account of her forthcoming adventures in order to dazzle her English audience later on. So far, the journey was not taking the turn that Fanny had originally expected. She needed some time to digest the astonishments she experienced before committing them to her journal.

Fanny remembered the jubilant embarkation, with cases of wine, baskets filled with fruit and flowers being carried into the staterooms. She was standing on the deck shoulder to shoulder with Lady Errol, with a garland of forget-me-nots about her neck, tossing petals into the muddy water, as the sail ship moored off. Was it a dream or a joke?

Oh, Fanny had suspected that the impending journey to the Crimea would be somewhat different from a hunting expedition to which she was accustomed. As a matter of fact, she was looking forward to a diet of salted pork and the romanticism of sleeping in a tent. The other reason for the journey, one she could not openly publicize, was to meet Captain Lewis Edward Nolan, who shared her passion for horses and turned it into his vehicle to international fame. Fanny idolized this handsome, fervent Irishman who had lived in Milan and Austria. Nolan was entrusted with the pleasurable and enviable task of selecting and purchasing horses specifically for the Crimean campaign. Having traveled Turkey, Syria, and Lebanon, he delivered three hundred animals to Varna, Bulgaria. His book "The Training of Cavalry Remount Horses: A New System" became the Bible of equestrian pedagogy.

Fanny imagined how furious Captain Nolan would be if he chanced to see those magnificent creatures martyred below the decks of the ships that were transporting the British cavalry across the Black Sea. Descending into the holds was like descending into Hades. No proper arrangements were made for the horses. They were crammed in foul mangers, with their men at their heads, holding them by the reigns. With every tilt of the ship the horses would be tossed. They would fall on top of each other, threatening to crush their men who were trying to pacify them. This nightmare went on for two months, for that was how long it took for an English sail ship to reach the East.

Fanny's grief over the loss of her stallion and her growing disgust fueled her wit. She embarked on a mission to capture and publicize the ugliest, most comical, moments in the campaign. She knew that the high society home in England, the same society that condemned her for her allegedly masculine behavior, would devour army gossip and scandals. Yes, she still was a woman enough to gossip. Nature blessed her with a sharp eye to spot everything grotesque and an equally sharp tongue to relate it to the world. The chronic conflict between Lucan and Cardigan would provide excellent food for a military satire. The two brothers-in-law engaged in a game of exchanging venomous letters and denouncing each other to Lord Raglan, the Commander-in-Chief. Like infantile tattle-tales, they would squeal on each other. Lucan accused Cardigan of insubordination and demanded disciplinary action from the Commander-in-Chief. As for Raglan himself, he preferred to look past Cardigan's violations of hierarchy. He would not stoop to serving as a moderator of the battle between the two brothers-in-law.

One peculiarity of Lucan's that Fanny remarked immediately was his intense aversion for simple, wholesome human happiness of others. He gladly tolerated and even encouraged fornication with the nameless native women, yet for some reason frowned upon soldiers bringing their lawful wives on the campaign. Obviously, the sight of someone else's marital bliss scorched his eyes. He actually made every effort to stop her, Mrs. Duberly, from accompanying her husband! The fuming earl sent his aide-de-camp demanding that she disembark from the transport ship, even though she had explicit permission from the Admiralty and the Horse Guards. Fortunately, Lord Raglan, who had become immune to Lucan's tantrums, reassured Fanny in his letter that he had no intention of interfering with her.

Shortly after their landing in Scutari, Fanny requested a private audience with Raglan to thank him for his patronage. To her unspeakable delight, he consented. For the first time she had the chance to contemplate the face of the aging one-armed hero. Fanny put on her most elegant dress and asked Lady Errol's servant to arrange her hair in the most flattering fashion. Weeks of seasickness and grief for her lost stallion had left Fanny's complexion drained. It took an impressive amount of oil and powder to restore the former glow to her skin. In the end, the efforts paid off. When Fanny crossed the threshold of Raglan's quarters, his droopy eyelids trembled, and the pale face beamed with nostalgia for his youth.

Mrs. Duberly could not resist remarking that he looked more like a Venetian cardinal than a British general.

"There is an ecclesiastic docility about your countenance," Fanny commented reverently. "My lord, I believe that you made a grave mistake in regards to your vocation."

"Half a century is not too long for living a lie, Mrs. Duberly," Raglan chuckled and stroked the empty sleeve of his uniform. "After such a segment of time, any lie may start appearing as a truth."

Before leaving his quarters, Fanny, enchanted and almost enamored, turned around, and asked him the question that had been weighing on her for weeks.

"Do you still have the ring, my lord?"

Raglan lifted his graying eyebrows.

"What ring, Mrs. Duberly?"

"The one that was removed from the finger after the amputation at the Battle of Waterloo. Is it still in your possession? Nothing would please me better than to see it."

The Commander-in-Chief reached into the pocket of his uniform and a second later presented a ring with an enormous ruby.

"It is yours, dear Frances. Take it as a souvenir from an era before your birth. I pray it brings fortune to you and Captain Duberly."

Fanny's first reaction was to refuse the ring. She clasped her hands and began babbling indistinctly about not being worthy of such a gift. Raglan did not repeat his offer but simply continued to hold the relic in the palm of his hand before Fanny. She babbled a bit more, then suddenly silenced, snatched the ring, and put it on her right thumb. Having marveled at her new adornment, she threw her arms around Raglan and, abandoning all rules of propriety, gave him a kiss on the cheek, awfully close to his mouth.

On her way out of Raglan's quarters, Fanny, entranced by the sparkling of the ruby on her thumb, nearly slammed into the stiff breast of another general. She gasped apologetically, lifted her head, and then gasped again, this time in terror. Towering before her was her enemy, Lord Lucan. He was fortified on both sides—a nervous fair-haired physician on his left and a dark-haired, menacing lieutenant on his right.

"How do you do, Mrs. Duberly?" the earl asked with a mocking bow.

"I couldn't be better, Your Lordship," Fanny replied, rubbing the ruby, as if it were an amulet that could keep her knees from giving in. "Thus far the Crimea has been most hospitable."

"Yes, it is an excellent riding country. It is a shame that your horse perished, truly. You would have enjoyed riding it here. I hope that my men never learn the pain of such bereavement."

Lord Lucan became silent, giving his companions a chance to laugh at his clever comment. The physician, growing even more restless, pulled a watch from his pocket and began winding it frantically. As for the dark-haired lieutenant, he crossed his arms, and drew closer to his commander, communicating solidarity. A ruthless, condescending grin cut across his pale-scarred face. Fanny, who maintained her ability to appreciate beautiful things under the direst of circumstances, noticed the exquisite shape and depth of the young lieutenant's eyes. The melancholy in them conflicted with the sardonic brutality of his smile. They seemed to exist apart from the rest of his face that seemed like a mask of bewilderment, sorrow, and unresolved rage.

Suddenly, to her great unease, Fanny realized that there is no cruelty she could not forgive this man, because he had the eyes of her dead stallion.

Chapter 2
Wartime Logic
(Varna, Bulgaria—June, 1854)

Wynfield did not attempt to make sense of what was happening around him since he sailed from England. His duty was not to understand or even to mask his ignorance but to follow orders. Except, there were no orders coming to speak of. Initially Wynfield imagined he would be immediately sent to Varna, since he supposedly belonged to the Heavy Brigade. At least, that was what he had been told back at Laleham Park. According to the terms of his contract, he was a Second Lieutenant in the Heavy Brigade, reporting directly to Sir James Scarlett. It seemed only logical that Wynfield should keep close to his immediate commander. Then why did he remain in Kulali outside Scutari with Lord Lucan, one hundred and fifty miles away from the rest of the troops? He watched the regiments of the British cavalry being moved across the Black Sea, tossed from one port to another, and thrown from Turkey to Bulgaria. Apparently, civilian logic did not apply in a time of war.

Wynfield tried to take solace in the thought that those who organized this elaborate military manipulation knew what they were doing. There must have been some brilliant, meticulously designed plan behind this seemingly chaotic rotation of pawns across the chessboard, a plan that his tattered brain could not appreciate. No doubt, the generals were throwing handfuls of troops from one site to another to confuse the enemy. The Allies were purposely positioning themselves as idiots to mislead the Russians and make them abandon caution. In addition, those outbreaks of cholera and dysentery were staged, no doubt. All those reports of soldiers dying of dehydration must have been fabricated. Some small prey animals feign injuries to lure the predators away from their nests. Wynfield concluded that that was precisely the tactic that the Allies were using.

Dr. Ferrars, on another hand, was not heartbroken to be apart from the troops, for he had heard about the outbreaks in Varna being particularly fierce. Just like Wynfield, he was Lord Lucan's unofficial prisoner, but unlike Wynfield, Dr. Ferrars did not even attempt to feed his illusions about the competence of the army leaders. He had no trouble believing that the rumors about the devastating outbreaks were true. The French and the British landed in the savage town without taking any sanitary measures. It took no more than a week for the epidemic to blossom. Whatever it took to delay his immersion into his duties as battlefield physician, Richard Ferrars regarded as a blessing. In his heart, he still nurtured a hope that the whole campaign would be cancelled, and he would return to England without having marred his hands.

No such luck. One day in early June, Lord de Ros, amicably eccentric and persuasive quartermaster-general, visited Lord Lucan on a diplomatic mission. They spent a few hours conversing behind the closed doors. Lord de Ros managed to smooth the earl's ruffled feathers and convince him that his clashes with Cardigan were mere miscommunications, and that he, Lord Lucan, was still in charge of the cavalry. De Ros' promises had the desired effect, and the next day the earl sailed to Varna in the company of his aides and his two favorite hostages, Dr. Ferrars and Lord Hungerton.

They landed on June 15th only to discover that most of the regiments of the cavalry had already been moved due to the epidemic that had left the town and the bay in a state of excruciating chaos. Sir James and the Heavy Brigade fled nine miles away from the city, while the Light Brigade joined Cardigan at Devna. The Noble Yachtsman continued residing in the bucolic cottage, thriving on a diet of "rough meat and excellent champagne" and issuing bizarre orders, such as forbidding the night patrols to wear cloaks on the grounds of it being effeminate. Once again, Lord Lucan was chasing his own troops, fuming from the conviction that this ordeal was arranged exclusively to humiliate him.

After a few days of raging and tormenting his aides, the earl took quarters in a half-empty barrack and attempted to usurp power over the regiments within his reach. The 4th Light Dragoons were among the misfortunate ones who were not moved in time and therefore had to bear the burden of Lucan's enthusiasm.

Wynfield's bewilderment reached its pinnacle during the review for the Turkish Commander-in-Chief. Several regiments of the Light Brigade were summoned on the parade grounds. This was Lucan's first contact with his troops, his first chance at handling them, so naturally the earl could not wait to demonstrate his brilliance before his Turkish ally. However, as soon as he opened his mouth, a stream of archaisms poured forth, driving the 5th Dragoon Guards into utter confusion. Neither the officers nor their men understood knew what on earth Lucan wanted of them. As it turned out, in the seventeen years of his military idleness the words of the command and the entire drill had changed. He had simply been shelved for too long. Anthony Bacon, Lucan's old rival, chuckled maliciously:

"Imagine a cavalry commander from the Thirty Years' War rising from the dead to command modern troops!"

Not being one to run in shame or admit to personal failure, Lord Lucan demanded instead that the troops revert to the old drill, for he would not bend to the new traditions. His declaration sent a wave of rumbling through the lines of officers, who now were presented with a daunting task of retraining their men because of Lucan's whim.

Wynfield, who watched the parade without blinking, became even more convinced that Lord Lucan was indeed an exceptional leader. In order to prevent his troops from growing bored and complacent, the earl introduced new challenges into their routine. What a brilliant idea! Not to mention, the very fact that Lord Lucan was willing to sacrifice his own popularity for a greater cause testified to his selflessness. He did what needed to be done in order to keep the English soldiers alert and on their toes, even if it meant enduring their hatred.

When Lucan summoned him later that evening, Wynfield rushed into his commander's room, impatient to express his deepened admiration.

The earl was in the middle of taking a bath. His broad shoulders, reddened from the steam, towered above the foamy surface. The cigar in his hand resembled a royal staff. Even without his magnificent coat, Lord Lucan looked intimidating.

"Well, won't you join me, Lord Hungerton?" he asked, or rather ordered.

Sharing bathwater with one's superiors must have been one of the sacraments in the military. Bizarre as Lord Lucan's invitation struck him, Wynfield complied. In a matter of seconds, his uniform ended up in a pile on the floor.

"My daughter is one fortunate woman," Lucan remarked, making a subtle appreciative gesture with his cigar.

"I am glad that you approve, my lord."

Wynfield jumped into the bathtub across from his commander, forcing the foamy water to run over the edge. The splash extinguished Lucan's cigar.

"Producing sturdy offspring," the earl began, squinting, "is one way you can thank me for my kindness. I expect a grandson before the end of the next year. You hear that, my dearest Hungerton?"

"I hear you perfectly, my lord," Wynfield replied, unperturbed. "I do not intend on disappointing you."

"You still have much to learn about wartime camaraderie," the earl continued. "It is fortunate that you have spent this time with me instead of Scarlett. He would do nothing to facilitate your social acclimatization. You are so savage, skittish, and puritanical. Ah, I do not like what this war is doing to me. It is turning me into a ranting old man."

"We cannot have that!" Wynfield intervened.

"Incredible, isn't it? I know I have managed to preserve my body remarkably well. Many men younger than me would kill to have my figure, my teeth, and my hair. If you place me next to my brother-in-law, who is about my age, the difference in our appearances would be astounding. Decades of drinking and whoring did their dirty work on poor Jimmy. His face looks like a dried mushroom. There is nothing he will not do to undermine my indisputable physical superiority. Dear boy, if I told you that I was almost thirty years older than you, would you believe me?"

"It would be quite a strain on my imagination," Wynfield responded. "To me you don't look a day over thirty... five..."

"Why, thank you! Still, every now and then I am reminded of my age. What you saw today on the parade ground is a sign of the decline our glory. Whose idea was it to change the drill and violate the golden tradition? Some irreverent young idiots came and eliminated the commands that I had been taught. Ah, listen to me! I sound like a cranky old sot."

"You sound like a rightfully indignant general," Wynfield objected, lifting his fist out of the foam. "If you make it your quest to restore grandeur to the British military, I will be the first one to cheer you on. The subsequent generations of soldiers will thank you, for certain. I promise to educate my sons, however many God gives me, in the ways of their grandfather. They will march to the same commands as you did in your early youth. Will that alleviate your worry?"

Chapter 3
Lord Lucan Discovers
Balkan Treasures

After an entire month in Varna, Dr. Ferrars was yet to employ his skills as a doctor, even in the middle of an epidemic. Somehow, he had managed to avoid situations that would require him rolling up his sleeves. That is not to say that he was sitting in utter idleness. Lord Lucan gave him an assignment that was almost as bad as caring for the cholera-stricken soldiers.

One July evening Dr. Ferrars escorted into the earl's quarters two adolescent sisters from Varna. They went by the names of Viktoria and Elisaveta. Both were sporting traditional town attire: narrow half-length skirts of plaid wool and fitted black vests over embroidered blouses. Strings of red and blue beads adorned their pliant swarthy necks. The girls brought woven baskets filled with ripe strawberries and the same rare damascene roses that yield fragrant oil, one of the costliest luxury items in Europe.

At the sight of the guests, Lord Lucan beamed, inhaled languishingly, and rubbed his hands, as if gourmet dinner had been served.

"You gave my cigar case to their father?" he inquired of Dr. Ferrars without getting up from his chair.

"I certainly did," the physician muttered, smoothing his mustache nervously.

"And is he clear about the terms of our exchange?"

"My lord, I'm afraid that their father does not speak much English."

This declaration made the earl roll his eyes in contempt. The laziness, the dimwittedness, and the sheer inhospitality of the natives were revolting! One would think that the men of Varna would make at least some effort to learn the language of their guests. Those Balkan savages did not expect British officers to learn their barbaric prattle, did they?

"My dear Lord Hungerton," the earl continued, turning to Wynfield, who lay sprawled on the bed in the corner, sipping rum, "it occurred to me that we never had an opportunity to celebrate your birthday. It falls somewhere in the middle of June, doesn't it? I've seen your natal affidavit before we left England. I hope it is not too late for me to present you with a modest gift."

"Strawberries and roses?" Wynfield asked with a noticeable tremor in his voice. "My Lord Lucan, how obscenely kind of you... To have such lush delicacies delivered straight to the tent by two charming young ladies..."

The earl shook his head categorically, forbidding any further expression of gratitude.

"Alas, I cannot exercise generosity to the fullest in such confining conditions. I promise you, my dearest Hungerton, that we will celebrate your quarter-centennial properly upon our return to England. For now, we will have to enjoy the gifts of the Balkans to the fullest. It is nothing extravagant, but nonetheless..."

The first theory that came to Wynfield's mind was that Lord Lucan was testing his loyalty to Lavinia. The earl summoned the girls on purpose to see how little it would take for his future son-in-law to succumb to carnal temptations.

"My lord," Wynfield said, "I hope that the young ladies will have adequate escort back to town. It is getting quite dark."

"How humorous you are!" the earl laughed sonorously. "Feigning innocence in such a manner—clever indeed! For an instant, you had me perplexed in earnest. You can't honestly believe that these beauties were mere mules for berries and flowers? No, they will be sharing our luxurious quarters with us tonight. Their father knows not to expect them until the next morning."

Wynfield threw a timid, quizzical glance at Dr. Ferrars, who in turn coughed and tugged at his mustache once again, confirming his suspicion.

"My lord, I wouldn't dare," Wynfield mumbled. "This... This arrangement transcends all boundaries of my audacity."

"I don't blame you for hesitating," Lucan reassured him. "Naturally, you are worried about catching some disease, especially so close to your wedding. As if cholera wasn't enough! Syphilis is never a welcome guest in the marital bed. I applaud your dutiful consideration for my daughter. I wouldn't expect any less of you, but allow me to scatter your fears, dear boy. Tonight's entertainment will have no unpleasant consequences for either one of us. These two savage young ladies are virgins. Dr. Ferrars will testify to that."

The physician glanced up and whistled, slapping the side of his leg, practically melting from embarrassment.

"And when I heard that they were named after two great English queens, I knew it was fate!" Lucan concluded complacently. "How often does one encounter two sisters bearing such names? Tonight will be our tribute to the crown! Why do you say, Lord Hungerton?"

For the first time, Wynfield allowed himself to take a close look at his two female guests. They were paler than the Turkish women he saw on the streets of Skutari but darker than Londoners. The hue of their skin was neither olive nor gold but peculiar dusty pink, like the petals of the roses in their baskets. He also remarked the difference in the body language. English girls would avert their eyes coyly, even when assuming most provocative poses. As for the Balkan girls, they stared brazenly in the eyes of their male hosts, while their bodies remained rigid. Viktoria had her hands locked behind her back and her chin elevated slightly, like a martyr preparing to ascend the scaffold. It was difficult to determine whether her attitude was of defiance or of subservience. Her younger sister Elisaveta had her arms crossed over her breasts, though she seemed more willing to reveal them.

Lucan glanced at his pocket watch and then peered into the older girl's face, which made her bare toes wiggle.

"Viktoria, darlin'," he droned tenderly, beckoning her with one hand and tapping his knee with another.

The girl remained standing in the spot, her knees locked. Realizing that he was dealing with a frightened kitten, the earl applied every effort to harness his impatience and avoid abrupt movements.

"Come here, child," he beckoned again, assuming she would understand his gesture.

She made a tiny step forward, struggling to keep her footing. If she continued moving at this pace, it would take her the whole night just to cross the floor.

The earl rose from his chair and swept up the girl in his embrace, freeing her from the necessity to walk. Viktoria did not wrap her arms around his neck as he expected she would. Her hands dangled down, one of them still squeezing the handle of the basket. Stroking her back and whispering words of consolation into her ear, the earl carried her upstairs.

As soon as the sound of Lucan's footsteps faded, Dr. Ferrars covered his mouth, as if he were about to vomit, and stormed out of the room, leaving Wynfield alone with Elisaveta.

The girl shook up like a sparrow after a bath in a puddle and fluttered towards her new English gentlemen-friend, landing in his lap. Her fresh, delicately sculpted face beamed with mischievous eagerness. One could tell that she was relieved to be appointed to the younger of the two officers. Before assuming her duties, she threw a brief anxious glance at the door through which her older sister was carried a few moments ago.

For the next minute, she and Wynfield sat facing each other, exchanging chuckles, nods and winks.

"His Lordship wasn't joking when he said he had a surprise for me," Wynfield muttered, knowing that Elisaveta did not understand him. "What am I to do with you, little one?"

Considering it his duty to ease the girl's fears, he gestured at the door and pressed both fists to his heart.

"Lord Lucan," he continued, "is not a terrible man. He will not harm your sister. And you in turn have nothing to fear from me. I will take nothing you aren't prepared to give. Whatever you were instructed to do, you may forget it."

The Balkan girl watched him with her gooseberry-green eyes, trying to guess the meaning of his words. She thought he was promising her gifts. Her swarthy warm hands began rubbing his upper arms and shoulders. She must have expected that her caresses would cause gold coins to pour from his pockets.

Wynfield's vision began to blur. Through the filter of recently consumed rum, the girl appeared older. She looked like a child while standing, but when she was sitting on his knees their difference in height seemed less obvious. Her insinuating strokes began stirring the familiar tension below the buckle of his belt.

When he untied the woven string at the collar of the girl's embroidered blouse, he noticed between her small breasts a shining cross with a slanted bar on the bottom. Having never seen this symbol of Orthodox creed before, Wynfield held it in his hand for a few seconds, examining it in candlelight, then tossed it over the girl's shoulder.

"We'll put on a little show for the earl," he whispered conspiratorially. "He does not need to know the particulars."

He crinkled the collar and the sleeves of her blouse to create an impression of slight disarray. Then he partially unbraided Elisaveta's hair and ruffled his. This bizarre behavior startled the girl even more than an overt advance would. Was that how British men initiated intercourse with their women? Having assumed it was time for her to fulfill her obligations, the girl leaned forward.

Suddenly, Wynfield stopped grinning, covered her mouth with his hand and shook his head. His attempts to communicate his intentions were only exacerbating her confusion. Finally, he found her shiny cross amidst the red beads and shifted it back in its proper place under the blouse.

Having finally understood what the young officer wanted of her—or rather what he did not want—Elisaveta blinked and exhaled through his fingers with a mixture of astonishment, relief and gratitude. Was it possible? Was he truly allowing her to walk away from her obligations?

She kissed him in the crease between his eyebrows and tightened her embrace, causing him to fall on his back.

"Hush, little one..." He laughed, feeling her tears on his neck.

When Lucan came out of his bedroom at two o'clock in the morning, yawning and stretching like a lion after a nap, he discovered an iconic military post-coital scene. Wynfield was sprawled across the bed with one leg hanging down. The shiny buckle of his belt was glistening on the floor. The Balkan girl, her braids undone and blouse wrinkled, was lying on his naked chest, depositing strawberries into his mouth.

The knowledge that he presented such an exquisite gift to his subordinate and future son-in-law filled Lord Lucan with a profound sense of satisfaction.

"Three cheers for the father who raised such fine daughters!"

he declared. "I must send him my pocket watch as well. Dr. Ferrars will escort the ladies back home. There is no need for them to stay here for the night. I simply can't fall asleep with another creature fidgeting by my side."

A few seconds later Viktoria stumbled in, her disheveled head hung, leaning against the wall for support, clutching the collar of her blouse, her knees still locked. Clearly, the girl was still in denial of her defloration.

Elisaveta lifted her head from Wynfield's chest and addressed her sister in Bulgarian.

"Shoo, off you go, both of you," Lord Lucan scolded them, irritated by the fact that they dared to speak their barbaric language in his presence.

Before departing, Elisaveta coughed into her fist, unobtrusively reminding the officer that he was forgetting something.

"Of course!" Wynfield exclaimed. "I can't let you leave without a kiss. God knows when I'll see you next."

He dipped the tip of his tongue into rum and then licked her lips until they parted. A thorough, invasive, unquestionably adult kiss followed. Now the girl knew the quintessential taste of an English officer. That was as much as Wynfield was willing to take on his conscience that day.

Chapter 4
Lord Hungerton Reflects on the Benefits of British Imperialism

"I told you he was a monster," Dr. Ferrars hissed to Wynfield.

The physician had just returned from his errand of taking the girls back to their father's house. It was about four o'clock in the morning. In another two hours, the soldiers were expected to rise.

"Of whom are you speaking?" Wynfield asked, rubbing his eyes.

"Oh, don't play a fool, Lord Hungerton! You know well of whom I speak."

"As a matter of fact, I do not have a faintest idea. After all, are we not at war? There is a monster hiding behind every bush."

The young physician shook his head in grievous disbelief and a hint of disgust.

"By God, Lord Hungerton..." His voice broke. "Upon our first encounter, I thought..."

"Yes, Dr. Ferrars?" Wynfield gasped in mock anticipation. "You thought what? Do continue. I am dying to hear your epiphany."

"I see now that my judgment of character failed me, which is a considerable shock, given my otherwise reliable intuition."

"Please, hurry, Dr. Ferrars. I am drifting in and out of sleep. After the evening I've had..."

"Lord Hungerton, I have mistaken you for a man of at least some fundamental moral principles."

Wynfield made a sympathetic pout.

"Ah, you mean a man who doesn't fornicate with his employer's wife—that type of man?"

Dr. Ferrars shot both index fingers forward, as if they were artillery guns.

"Now *that* is entirely different!"

"Is it?"

"Beyond doubt!"

"In that case, enlighten me! I do not understand all the intricacies of sexual indiscretions."

"You need me to explain to you the difference between adultery and rape? A mature woman, regardless of her marital status, can dispose of her body in accordance with her desires. She gives and withdraws her favors. There is no element of exploitation or violence. Those girls were both under the age of fifteen. That... that beast whom you serve... He purchased them like a pair of hunting hounds!"

"So, he made an honest deal with their father," Wynfield blurted out with a shrug. "He did not gag and abduct them in the middle of the night; and you, Dr. Ferrars, delivered them here. You played your part in this dirty, exploitative transaction, so you aren't exactly in the position to condemn others. Lamb's bleating does not sound so convincing rolling off your lips. In earnest, your indignation mystifies me."

Wynfield lit a cigar and stretched on the wrinkled sheets. Dr. Ferrars continued standing over him, trembling.

"Forgive me if my heart does not break for those girls," Wynfield continued nonchalantly, toying with the rose that Elisaveta had left on his pillow. "They think themselves quite fortunate. I doubt that our behavior is more atrocious than that of Bulgarian men. You honestly believe that those drunken village idiots treat their women with gallantry? Our arrival is the best thing that has happened to this country in centuries. Fifteen-twenty years from now, when those girls are wrinkled hags, they will be telling their countless grandchildren about a regiment of dashing English cavalrymen gracing their rotten little town."

Wynfield laughed and nudged Dr. Ferrars in the knee with the tip of his boot.

"Lighten up, Richard! You can let your eyebrows resume their natural position. Have a sense of humor, in God's name. I didn't touch the girl—not below the waist. She entered my room as a virgin, and she left as one. Lord Lucan gave her to me for the evening. He did not give me explicit orders to deflower her. As it happened, my whim was to have her lay on top of me and feed me strawberries. One day in the near future she will give her hymen to one of the village idiots who speak her language. The night she spent on the naked chest of a British officer will be just an intoxicating memory."

He burst out laughing again and dipped his fingers into the basket.

"I wouldn't advise you to be so greedy with Balkan gifts," Dr. Ferrars warned him in an icy voice. "Make no mistake, I am ecstatic to see you reap the benefits of British Imperialism, but the mixture of rum and strawberries will give you severe indigestion, and I will need to hover over you all night, holding you by the scruff of your neck as you vomit over and over."

"On the contrary," Wynfield objected, his mouth filled with red pulp, "fruit acid is rumored to reduce one's chances of contracting cholera. Lord Cardigan devours fresh fruit by the basket, and he is in perfect health, which cannot be said for poor Sir James, whose diet consists of salted pork and biscuits. However, it is rude and selfish to me to eat all the strawberries by myself. It just occurred to me that I have not offered you any. Dear Richard, please accept my apologies."

He lifted the basket with two fingers and held it before the physician, red juice smeared all over his grinning face.

"Go on, Richard, have a few whilst they are in season. They are obscenely delicious. Imagine being kissed by Calypso."

Dr. Ferrars locked his hands and drew a few steps back.

"Lord Hungerton, a few months ago you were gracious enough to restore me to my senses with a hearty punch in the jaw, a punch I sorely needed at that moment. I fear that soon I may be obliged to return the favor. You are a decent man—I am not yet ready to relinquish that belief. However, you've been spending too much time in Lord Lucan's company. I know how toxic that man's spirit can be."

Chapter 5
Effects of the Balkan Sun

Since no concrete orders were coming from the Commander-in-Chief, and Lord Lucan hated to see his subordinates bored, he entrusted Wynfield with the task of teaching the soldiers the old drill. He spent his days in the scorching sun, with a notebook filled with Lucan's scribbles, trying to stir reverence for the old ways in the soldiers. Fortunately, the men of the cavalry had taken to him and exercised subordination even though he was not their direct commander.

Another responsibility that Wynfield assumed was helping nurse the horses back to health. The only activity that Lord Lucan forbade him was helping those affected by cholera.

Then, on June 25th came the news that the Turks freed Silistria with some help from the so-called "Indian" officers. Lord Raglan immediately ordered a reconnaissance to the banks of Danube to find out the location of the Russian Army. Wynfield secretly wished to join the 8th Hussars on the expedition, but the man in charge of the enterprise was none other but Lord Cardigan. Raglan appointed him without consulting Lucan. Wynfield feared to imagine what reaction he would receive from his commander if he dared to utter Lord Cardigan's name. So, he had nothing left to do but stifle a sigh of disappointment and resume his drill duty, which in the end, turned out for the best. He did not miss out on anything except for a heatstroke and dehydration.

The expedition, nicknamed "Sore Back Reconnaissance,"

proved to be a disaster, one of many that were to follow. It lasted for over two weeks, over the course of which the men did not change their clothes once. Cardigan, anxious to display took close to two hundred men with him, no tents and no food except for the famous salted pork, the very sight of which would bring on violent nausea.

The horses suffered more than men. Heat, exhaustion, and lack of water rendered half of them ill and unfit for any work, which was an unforgivable loss for the Light Brigade. Mrs. Duberly made sure to mourn the horses in her journal.

Cardigan, in no way disheartened by the toll of the reconnaissance, fled to an oasis in Yeni-Bazaar, almost thirty miles away from Devna, taking most of the Light Brigade with him. The plummeting morale of his troops, who spent their days burying comrades and horses, did not keep Cardigan from drilling them twice a week. The diet of "tough meat and excellent champagne" upheld His Lordship's energy and spirits. The vibes of helpless rage that his brother-in-law was sending his way from Varna did not ruin his appetite.

Those were the times during which Wynfield, even with all his immeasurable his devotion to Lord Lucan, preferred to avoid his company. The earl withdrew into his study, engaged in the ritual of writing and crumbling one letter after another. In the meanwhile, the troops at Varna did not complain about spending their days with Lord Hungerton. He seemed like a younger, warmer, more vivacious version of Scarlett. Wynfield would have found this comparison undeservedly flattering. He still had not given up hope of reuniting with his real commander. As for Scarlett himself, he had moved upcountry shortly after Lucan's disastrous review. Varna and its vicinity were turning into a circus, a boxing rink where wills and vanities collided into each other, and Scarlett wanted no part of it.

One evening, when Wynfield returned to his quarters, he found his shirts folded and his spare boots shined. The bed that he had usually left unmade had been covered with a blanket. Examining the polished ashtray, which had been emptied for the first time, he felt arms slipping around his waist. He turned around and saw the young Balkan girl whom Lord Lucan had presented as a gift. This time Elisaveta came on her own accord, unescorted and empty-handed. She was standing before Wynfield with her hair loosened and practically undressed. Apart from her beads and the cross she wearing nothing except for a semi-transparent blouse that fell above her knees, leaving her smooth muscular calves exposed.

She stood up on her tiptoes and bounced with an air of flirtatious impatience, her movements being not unlike those of a spaniel at the sight of its master.

"What a surprise," Wynfield mumbled, inhaling the scent of roses and strawberries. "Little one, you are out of your mind."

The heat exuding from her breasts saturated the beads of her necklace. It was an example of flesh bringing stone to life.

"You are positively mad," Wynfield repeated, giving her a reproachful squeeze, and nodded at the map above his bed. "You know I cannot take you with me. My commander won't allow it. Why did you come here? Go! Leave at once. I released you before. I took pity on you. Now you take pity on me. I am not made of steel."

Elisaveta tilted her head and brought her mouth very close to his, letting him know that she wished to repeated the kiss they demonstrated before Lord Lucan.

Out came the bottle of rum. Wynfield and Elisaveta both took sips of the burning liquid and tumbled into bed. Their clothes mingled on the floor, the red wool of his overcoat and the cream linen of her blouse.

"I will not do this," he murmured, while his body was engaged in an act that contradicted his words. "I will burn in hell for this. Ah, what's the use? I'll burn at any rate, if not for this transgression then for another. Forgive me my ranting, little one..."

Thus began their clandestine, unsanctioned wartime marriage. This practice, as Wynfield found out, was not uncommon in the army. Depending on how much effort they were willing to expend on rudimentary courtship, the officers would frequently start temporary but exclusive affairs with local women. As a rule, those women, aware of their dispensability, did not allow themselves to sulk or burden their lovers with frivolous demands and complaints. For the privilege of bedding dashing British officers, they would feed, water and scrub their horses, nurse the victims of cholera and later dig graves for them. All those chores were performed to the sounds of Bulgarian folk songs. The Balkan women employed an open-throat singing technique that allowed their voices to carry over great distances.

Elisaveta's voice, still developing, lacked that distinctive Balkan edge. Her approach to delivering a melody resembled that of

Celtic and Saxon women. One would imagine that the girl was experimenting with a different ethnicity. Instead of throwing all her strength into projection, she took care to connect the notes smoothly. In her repertoire, there were several lullabies that sounded almost Irish. Lord Lucan himself swore that he had heard something similar on the streets of Castlebar.

To Wynfield's welcome surprise, the feeling of guilt did not overwhelm him to the point of him breaking off the tryst. The pleasure tuned out the remorse. Under the guidance of Lord Lucan, he had already begun mastering the art of rationalizing his actions. He kept telling himself that even blatant exploitation could be handled with basic human decency and even gallantry. Wynfield made sure that Elisaveta's whims were indulged. Since he could not express his appreciation through gifts or compliments, he did it through energetic and lengthy foreplay.

It was a refreshing, unprecedented experience for Wynfield— non-obliging carnal relations with a girl without inner demons. Even if Elisaveta had any dark secrets, she could not share them with him at any rate, because the two could not communicate verbally.

Wynfield kept repeating to himself that the Balkan girl was not a threat to his English bride. Lavinia remained untouchable. He was not yet prepared to admit that he and Elisaveta shared anything more than a sensual friendship. One thing, however, he could not deny: he had clearly overestimated his willpower. Neither the fatigue from training the soldiers in the Balkan heat, nor the chronic malnutrition, nor even the general atmosphere of anxiety and uncertainty that hovered over the camp could dull the hunger of his flesh; and by indulging his body with this girl, who seemed unsuitable for anything else, he was endangering his heart. The inevitability of their parting was something he chose not to ponder. He was growing more preoccupied with Elisaveta's wellbeing than with the state of the campaign.

One time when she came down with a cough and a slight fever, he situated her on his bed and spent the evening changing wet towels on her forehead, in spite of her weak protestations. Unnoticeably to him, the roles reversed, as he was tending to her now. The sight of her pliant, agile body, the same body that he employed for his gratification every night, in the throes of even a minor malady drove Wynfield to such anguish that it did not even occur for him to call Dr. Ferrars for assistance. He had completely forgotten that they had an excellent physician at their disposal, one that had been idle for months and would have welcomed an opportunity to help a live patient.

The same night he had a dream that he and Elisaveta were riding side by side along the sore of the Black Sea. He was wearing civilian clothes, and Elisaveta, dressed in a dark-blue riding gown, was speaking English with the same languishing high-class inflection as Lavinia. The images of the two women merged into one.

Wynfield woke up with an ache between his ribs. Elisaveta's fever had broken overnight, but he himself was perspiring and panting. Was his shaken brain, overheated in the sun, playing pranks on him again? He had not had a nightmare or even a vivid dream in ages.

Lucan's aide-de-camps began nudging one another, whispering and chuckling.

"Lord Hungerton is done for..."

"Watch his face when we set sail!"

Those words were uttered without any malice. The aide-de-camps, among which was none other but Lucan's oldest son Charles George, were generally fond of Lord Hungerton. Even though, according to logic, the young Lord Bingham appeared to have good reasons to resent and mistrust his father's new protégé, hostility did not take root in his heart. On the contrary, the good-natured young heir welcomed his future brother-in-law, who would share with him the burden of the earl's erratic behavior. They took turns serving as Lucan's scapegoats. In private, they addressed each other by their given names, Georgie and Jerry.

"He will make a fine husband for my sister," Lord Bingham said. "If he dotes like that on this Balkan wench, I can only imagine how he will worship Lavinia."

In the very beginning of the affair, Wynfield kept Elisaveta hidden from the eyes of his comrades. Eventually, he began allowing her to enter the room that was used for dining, gaming, and staff meetings. Elisaveta would serve food and pour rum for Lord Lucan and his men while they played poker. She would watch the game standing behind Wynfield's back or sitting on his knee, enveloped in a cloud of corrosive tobacco. Her presence made him lose miserably, much to the delight of Lucan's aide-de-camps, who would sweep up the coins. By the end of the night she would fall asleep on his shoulder, obliging him to carry her into the bedroom. However, as soon as her head would touch the pillow, she would awake immediately. Her gooseberry-green eyes would open wide like those of a doll. Her lips, stained with strawberry-juice, would first fold into a pensive pout and then suddenly stretch into a smile.

Observing the elaborate mimicry of Elisaveta's childish face, Wynfield could not refrain from laughing.

"Why must you do this?" he would ask, aching with tenderness. "You know I cannot keep you."

Chapter 6
Lord Lucan Reflects on the Drawbacks of British Imperialism

One evening in August, as Lord Lucan and his aides congregated around the poker table, Dr. Ferrars, contrary to his custom, intruded on the game.

"I do not know how to deliver the news," he began. "Lord Hungerton, I am afraid you will never see Elisaveta again."

"Has she grown bored with me already?" Wynfield asked self-deprecatingly. "Perhaps, she found a richer, more influential officer. Ah, that is well by me. I will not hold that against her."

Dr. Ferrars did not allow him to finish.

"She's dead, gentlemen!"

The declaration did not have any terrifying effect on Wynfield at first. He stopped shuffling cards and looked up at Dr. Ferrars reproachfully. Can one make such poor jokes so late in the evening? Elisaveta could not possibly be dead. She was in his bed only two nights ago. It was not unlike her to leave Lord Lucan's quarters for several days to visit her family back in town. She always returned.

The earl, on another hand, had no trouble believing the news.

"How did she die?" he inquired with moderate interest. "Did cholera catch up with her at last?"

Dr. Ferrars shook his head.

"No, my lord, her death was not of any natural causes. She was murdered, stoned by the men from her own neighborhood."

"Imagine that," the earl huffed and rolled his eyes. "What else is to be expected from those savages? Well, don't end your narration here. Did you see her body?"

Dr. Ferrars winced in disbelief. Did the earl truly expect him to give the gruesome details of the murder? Did he want to know how many blows to head it took to break the skull and whether her eyes had been knocked out?

"There are certain times, when words fail me, my lord," the physician said, having regained partial control of his speech. "I fear that you will need to employ your imagination. I do not wish to bore you with medical jargon."

"This was intended as a message," Lucan concluded, "not so much for us—but for their women, particularly those who aspire to rise above their surrounding. Ah, what a shame... I'll have to refill my own rum."

With a shallow sigh of resignation, the earl reached out for the bottle.

The rattle of a chair being turned upside down caused him to spill a few drops of his precious rum. Lucan lifted his head and saw Lord Hungerton trying to load his revolver with his trembling hands.

"Young man, where exactly are you going?" the earl inquired.

"To make those bastards pay!"

The revolver slipped out of Wynfield's hands and fell on the floor, scattering the bullets. Unable to subdue the tremor in his fingers, he buried them in his hair and squeezed his temples. For a few seconds he stood thus, panting, shifting his mad gaze from one corner to another.

The earl found his protégé's outburst most distasteful.

"My dear Hungerton," he said, "we are not here to steal bread from Bulgarian police—if they even have one at all. Those men committed a crime, however heinous, on their own soil towards their own countrywoman. This is not our place to intervene."

Wynfield got down on the floor and began gathering the bullets frantically.

"I am just as furious and distraught as you are," Lucan continued, shuffling the cards. "Years of service have taught me restraint. We are in no position to antagonize the natives. They already blame us for the outbreak of cholera. Those men are savages, no question about it. Still, it is not our duty to civilize them. I do not wish to wake up in the middle of the night with the roof of my quarters on fire."

Having gathered the bullets, Wynfield rose to his feet and made another attempt to load the revolver. Such persistence aggravated his commander even more.

"Lord Hungerton, you are making me nervous," Lucan said. "You are in no condition to handle loaded weapons. Besides, there aren't enough bullets for all the men in Varna. You don't intend on executing all of them, do you?"

Lucan's bewilderment was genuine. He truly did not understand why this young officer, who had a fiancée waiting for him in England, took the death of some Balkan as a personal insult.

"A woman I..." Wynfield stammered, not daring to say the word "loved." "A woman of whom I was fond is dead, murdered by her own kind; but even if I didn't care for her in particular, her death wouldn't be any less infuriating. If I witness atrocities committed against a woman, regardless of her origin or connection to me, I simply cannot avert my eyes. To me there is no such thing as foreign women."

Having finally succeeded at loading the revolver, he dashed towards the door.

"Stand still!" Lucan shouted. "Make one more step, and I will have you court-martialed for insubordination!"

Wynfield froze in the doorway, his back turned to Lucan, hand still holding the revolver.

"A fine time you chose for flaunting your chivalry!" the earl continued scolding him. "You mean to tell me that you develop this ludicrous puppyish attachment to every woman you bed? Had I know you would be such a sentimental, thin-skinned fool I never would've introduced you to that wretched girl. I had erroneously assumed that you were a mature man with a healthy, philosophical outlook on such matters. You took what was meant as an innocent, disposable birthday present and turned it into some quixotic quest! How am I supposed to give you presents after this?"

As the earl carried on his tirade, Wynfield's breathing slowed, and his head drooped lower.

"Dr. Ferrars," Lucan said at last, "take Lord Hungerton into his room, and see that he does not shoot anyone, including himself.

Give him some sedative, whatever you have in your possession."

The physician nodded, welcoming the opportunity to leave the company of his loathsome commander. Cautiously, he approached Wynfield and took him by the shoulders.

"Lord Hungerton, relinquish your weapon," he spoke in a soothing, nonjudgmental voice. "I assure you that those men will pay for their deed."

"Utter nonsense!" Lucan exclaimed irately. "You cannot make such outlandish promises. Mind your business, doctor. You neither make nor enforce laws. Your duty is to mix opium cocktails."

The physician gave the earl one of his life-or-death glances that he did not squander lightly.

"Oh, yes, there will be justice!" Lucan declared with exaggerated enthusiasm, when it finally dawned on him what Dr. Ferrars was trying to accomplish. "Tomorrow we will join forces with Lord Cardigan and charge against the wicked men of Varna! Never again will they harm one of their women."

Lucan ranted some more, but fortunately, his words flew past Wynfield's ears. By then the Dr. Ferrars had succeeded at recovering the loaded revolver from him.

"There, Lord Hungerton. You will have your weapon back tomorrow. You have no need for it tonight."

Instead of leading his patient back into his bedroom, Dr. Ferrars took him outside, fearing that the sight of the unmade bed in which Wynfield had spent so many nights with Elisaveta will provoke another outburst.

"Here is your opportunity to gloat," Wynfield said lowly, when the two of them were alone. "A girl of thirteen is dead because of me. I exploited her, put her in harm's way, and then failed to protect her. Now you can return that punch. Go on."

"Indeed," Dr. Ferrars replied. "This is precisely what I went to Cambridge for—to delight in the sufferings of others. For that and nothing else, I took the Hippocratic Oath. I spent years studying anatomy and physiology—all for the gratification of saying 'I told you so!' I sit in the ambush, waiting for another man to sin, just so that I may condemn him. What can be sweeter?"

"I am sorry, Richard. I did not intend to insult you."

"Naturally, you did not. Neither did you intend for Elisaveta to have her skull crashed by her own people. She had her fervent little mind set on being an Englishman's mistress. She must have suspected that the men from her neighborhood would not build a monument in her honor."

"Richard, you mean to imply that the girl brought this upon herself?"

"She pranced over the gaping bear trap. She knew the customs of her people better than we did. Lord Lucan was right in the sense that we cannot counter certain expressions of barbarism that has been flourishing here for centuries. Nor can we claim that such atrocities do not take place in our own country. If it hadn't been you, it would've been some other English soldier, who, in all likelihood, would have treated her with far less consideration. Lord Hungerton, I saw you hover over the girl whilst she was ill. Believe me, I empathize with you; but do not expect the same empathy from Lord Lucan or others who are molded from the same clay. Their marriages are meant to fortify political alliances, and their affairs are meant to indulge the body. Love may be found in their vocabularies but not in their hearts. Sanctioned or adulterous, to them love is a frivolity, a consolation prize for insignificant weaklings—like me."

"Richard, you are not a weakling."

"I certainly am—in Lord Lucan's eyes—but so is most of the humanity. At any rate, I am not here to discuss your commander. I am merely trying to convince you not to blame yourself for Elisaveta's death."

"I wish I could say with assurance that it was only Elisaveta," Wynfield sighed. "Somehow I fear that hers is not the first innocent life that ended before its time with my intervention. It is some sort of curse."

"I'm afraid that curses and evil eyes are not within my spectrum of expertise," Dr. Ferrars abdicated. "I have enough trouble making sense of the natural, let alone supernatural. Perhaps, you need to consult Reverend Bryce instead."

"No, not just yet," Wynfield whispered, rubbing his temples. "I must attempt to remember my sins before I confess them. I do not want to waste clergy's time on mere speculations." Then he glanced at the doctor. "By the way, Richard, you may begin addressing me by my given name as well. I have been meaning to tell you that for quite some time."

Dr. Ferrars smiled, genuinely flattered by this extension of camaraderie.

"I better not provoke fate in this manner, Lord Hungerton," he said, stepping back with a slight bow. "It will not be to Lord Lucan's liking—us becoming exceedingly chummy. He will imagine that we are conspiring against him. His Lordship is already convinced that Raglan favors Cardigan over him. It would be wiser to postpone familiarities until after the war."

Relief for Wynfield's moral sufferings came in the form of a physical ailment. The very same night he began running a fever and lost his voice. His throat became inflamed, making it impossible for him to swallow anything besides water. Lord Lucan did not care, as long as it was not cholera. He ordered Dr. Ferrars to quarantine the patient and let him recover in solitude.

"That vexatious Balkan wench," Lucan growled. "She simply couldn't depart from this earth without a farewell present. Infecting my men like that... It wouldn't astonish me if she had brought the disease to us on purpose. And that idiot of a boy! If not for the fever, I would've thought that he faked his illness, to just to buy himself some time to mourn his harlot. On the other hand, perhaps, he simply grew weary of drilling my men in the sun. At any rate, no more presents for him."

The earl had not been in the highest of spirits for weeks. Prolonged inactivity had driven him to the bottom of apathy. He had abandoned all concern for his scattered cavalry and the campaign in general. The only passion that sustained him, that gave him the motivation to rise in the morning was his hatred for Cardigan, the overwhelming desire to pester and belittle him. Lucan continued dispatching frantic orders to his brother-in-law at Yeni-Bazaar and demanding detailed reports, lest Cardigan's camping adventure should become too comfortable.

Part 4
Voyage to Calamity
September, 1854

Chapter 1
Lord Bingham Ponders the Benefits of Corporal Punishment

Wynfield's illness was accompanied by a string of most bizarre dreams. Luckily, they had nothing to do with the events that had happened. He dreamed of whales walking on the beach, arrayed in British uniforms. Their enormous tails split in the middle and turned into legs. Flying above them were winged lions with manes of fire. The tasseled tails snapped, sending forth colored sparks. This fantastical pageant was taking place to the sounds of a street organ.

He woke up to a strangest feeling of his blanket trying to escape from him, as if a dog was tugging at it. Right above his ear, he heard Lord Bingham's voice.

"Rise and shine, Jerry!"

Wynfield forced himself into an upright position. His head was still spinning a bit, but at least it did not hurt. The fever too appeared to have subsided.

"Good morning, Georgie," he greeted his future brother-in-law.

"Good morning, indeed! Jerry, haven't you heard? It's all over now!"

"What is over?" Wynfield asked, squeezing his temples.

The first thing that came to his mind was that the campaign had been recalled, and that they were returning to England.

"Our imprisonment—that's what is over!" Lord Bingham exclaimed jubilantly, his comely boyish face aglow. "We're moving, at last. We are sailing for Sebastopol without any further delay. I hear, it's beautiful there, a Crimean paradise. They call it the 'Isle of Wight of Russia'. Best of all, there is no cholera. The soldiers are positively ecstatic! They have been growing a bit restless here, to say the least. Come, Jerry! Let us see what Papa has in store for us."

Lord Bingham babbled so rapidly that Wynfield did not grasp half of the words. He only gathered that he needed to get dressed and report to Lord Lucan. There was just enough lukewarm water in the washbasin for him to rinse his eyes and his throat. Having completed this primitive grooming routine, Wynfield pulled his uniform over his wrinkled shirt, raked his hair with his fingers and followed Lord Bingham into the meeting room.

They found the earl brooding alone at the round table, with a half-empty rum bottle and a pile of cigar corpses. His face kept changing colors from burgundy to ash. Traces of blood were visible on his knuckles, as if he had punched a hard surface.

At the sight of two smiling young faces, he smashed his fist into the tabletop.

"What are you grinning about? Idiots! You think this is celebration?"

Wynfield and Lord Bingham did not know the cause of his rage, yet they hurried to retract the smiles. This was definitely not the manner in which they expected to be greeted. Lord Lucan should have been happier than anyone to hear the news of the embarkation.

The earl shoved a letter into his son's hands.

"There, see for yourself!"

As Lord Bingham began reading the document, his right eyebrow arched. It was an official order stating that the Heavy and the Light Brigades were to embark immediately, but that Lord Lucan, the divisional general, was not to take part in the preparations. More than that, he was to remain behind, as the men under his command were to sail to Sebastopol with none other but Lord Cardigan.

Lord Bingham cleared his throat, blinked, and read the letter over again, just to make sure that his eyes were not playing a trick on him.

"This must be a mistake," he concluded at last, folding the paper. "What other explanation can there be?"

Lucan yanked the document from his hands.

"You bet your sweet life, is a mistake! The entire bloody campaign is a mistake. Now it's official! Raglan has chosen Cardigan over me. Surely, they have grown chummy at Yeni-Bazaar, dining in the same tent, gossiping, laughing behind my back. My dear brother-in-law is heading to the quay as we speak, gloating and celebrating. Oh, I can see his loathsome, hideous face! He is riding towards his glory, while I am being shelved. There is nothing else for me to do. For two months those bastards have played me for a fool, kept me in this reeking, cholera-ridden town, only to discard me."

The sight of the earl's fit drove his son into a state of indignant panic. At that moment, Lord Bingham was willing to tear the throats of those who dared to insult his father. Instead, he found himself unable to move. Rage, the same fuel that Lord Lucan had grown to rely on, suddenly paralyzed his son. The young man had no idea how to shepherd himself out of that embarrassing state. All he could do was mutter:

"Oh, that is simply regrettable, Papa..."

That last word "Papa" was the final pin stuck into Lord Lucan's heart. Every day the earl was being reminded of his son's horse-riding accident. Georgie's memory and overall ability to reason appeared to have been restored, but not his aristocratic haughtiness. Something happened in those few minutes of his unconsciousness. Something was taken away from Georgie—and therefore, from the earl himself. What can be more devastating for an ambitious father than to see his once commendably sullen son turn into a drooling, yapping, tail-wagging, shoe-chewing, carpet-wetting pup? Lord Lucan felt that he had regained his son but not his heir.

The only instrument of punishment he could lay his hands on was a stiff belt with a giant brass buckle, an integral element of Lord Lucan's uniform, the same uniform he was not going to flaunt on the battlefield any time soon. Panting, the earl grabbed the belt and whipped his son across the face with it, the buckle hitting just below his right eye.

"If you insist on calling me Papa before the rest of your comrades, then by God, I shall treat you as a father would!"

Lord Bingham did not as much as touch his face or even wince.

At age twenty-four, he had grown accustomed to his father's outbursts, but this lash with a belt was something even he did not an-
ticipate.

"Out, both of you!" the earl shouted.

Wynfield, who did not have the same reasons for falling into
stupor, grabbed Lord Bingham's hand and pulled him out of the
meeting room.

As soon as they were outside, the young heir, who until then
had been conducting himself stoically, began producing strange
choking sounds, making it difficult to tell whether he was laughing
or sobbing.

"Please, Georgie, don't cry," Wynfield said. "Otherwise I shall
cry too."

"This is certainly not the way in which I would have preferred
to lose an eye," Lord Bingham replied between heaves. "If this
were meant to happen, if I were meant to become half-blind, I
would've chosen more heroic circumstances."

"Georgie, you won't go half-blind, I promise. Your eye is still
intact."

"Is it, Jerry? I can barely see. My face is all wet. Good God..."

"Those are tears, not blood, Georgie. Richard will testify to
that," Wynfield assured him and beckoned Dr. Ferrars, who tossed
aside his cigar and rushed to his young master's aid, having
guessed the origin of the crimson hematoma swelling under the
eye.

"Allow me to guess, Lord Bingham," he murmured, struggling
to preserve a semblance of diplomacy, "you walked into a lamppost?"

There was not a single lamppost in the vicinity.

"Let's say, I walked into the Lucan family crest," the heir replied, forcing a grin through tears. "For weeks Papa has had a
storm cloud hanging over his head. One should have expected for
thunder to strike. Poor Papa... The news devastated him. And I
made the most idiotic comment. No wonder he exploded."

The most sophisticated dressing material Dr. Ferrars happened to have at his disposal at the moment was his own handkerchief. He soaked it in lukewarm water from his own canteen and
applied it to Lord Bingham's face. The physician knew that this
sort of compress was completely useless. Still, he needed to create
an impression of providing medical assistance.

"I am truly sorry, Georgie," said Wynfield.

"Don't be. It is my own fault."

"I will take the next blow. Next time I will stand in front of you. Lord Lucan would have no choice but to go through me. I have acquired enough scars over the years, and another one would not make any difference."

"No, Jerry." Lord Bingham shook his head bitterly. "My father would never raise his hand on you. I am his son by chance, but you—by choice. Somehow I never measured up to his demands."

Since Wynfield did not wish to venture into the murky territory of brotherly rivalry, he hurried to change the subject.

"So, Georgie, you went to Rugby, right? How was it?"

"Ah, it's a miserable place." Lord Bingham flicked his hand. "I studied diligently, to a fault. True, I fell behind in theology, especially the Old Testament. But one cannot excel in all subjects, now can he? My professors did release me with a stellar review—if it means anything at all. What about you, Jerry? Where did you study?"

"I honestly can't tell you," Wynfield replied, looking before himself. "Even if I had a brief university career, it was knocked out of my memory."

Lord Bingham turned his unharmed eye to his future brother-in-law.

"Jerry," he began tentatively, "in all your ventures, have you ever seen the famous white light?"

"Have I seen what?" Wynfield asked, frowning.

"The white light... You know? It is related to the detachment of the soul. My theology professors discussed it in subdued voices, as it was not included in the official curriculum. There are accounts of persons who came close to dying. They report seeing the white light. So have you seen it, Jerry?"

"I would be lying if I said yes; but don't let my experience smash your metaphysical theory to bits. It could either mean that I have no soul—which strikes me as a perfectly viable explanation—or that I simply did not approach death close enough. Why, have you seen it?"

Lord Bingham nodded with an air of timid secrecy.

"It happened immediately after my accident, when I tumbled off my horse back home at Laleham Park. As consciousness abandoned me, the sun before my eyes faded, and then..." He let out a gasp of exultation. "Then the graying sky opened, and a white light descended upon me and pulled me out of my body as it lay there sprawled on the grass. I saw the blood trickling out of my ear and heard a male voice. At first, I thought it was God himself speaking to me. As I learned later, it was Dr. Ferrars."

"And that can only mean that I *am* God," Dr. Ferrars intervened with uncharacteristic humor. "After all, I did manage to relieve the pressure on your brain and repair the half-torn eardrum. You were in a pitiful state, my Lord Bingham. I intend to prove my divinity as the campaign advances."

"Don't let Reverend Bryce hear you talk like that," Wynfield curtailed him jokingly.

"Reverend Bryce will not dare to object once he sees the last of me," the physician bragged. "Gentlemen, I have been thinking and writing fanatically. I cannot divulge my findings to you just yet, but if you manage to stay alive, you will see the genius of Richard Ferrars before the year is over."

For the next two days, they had nothing better to do but philosophize about the afterlife, smoke, play cards, and polish their boots, just to kill time. The earl locked himself in his room and wrote feverishly. Nobody was allowed to even knock on his door. Every now and then a curse or the noise from an upturned chair would be heard in the halls of his quarters.

In the meantime, the chaotic preparations for the embarkation had begun. The anguished neighing of horses and the soldiers' moaning filled the late-summer air. Wynfield and Lord Bingham observed the commotion, unable to participate in it, as their hands were tied. At the same time, they felt obliged to stay out of their comrades' sight for fear that their idle wandering should ignite rumors about the awkward and humiliating position of Lord Lucan.

Wynfield could not help wondering if he would ever see Scarlett again. He had no idea when the Heavy Brigade was sailing. Given everything that had gone wrong and everything that was yet to go wrong, there was an excellent chance that he would never be reunited with his immediate commander. This realization filled Wynfield with a peculiar low-grade aching anger. Still, he did everything to harness his impatience before Lord Bingham, whose spirits were even lower. This hostile alienation from his father was eating a hole in the young man's stomach. He began spitting up blood-tainted acid, to the great alarm of Dr. Ferrars, whose initial suspicion was an onset of cholera. Luckily, the malady did not progress beyond nausea and stomach cramps. After a day of vigilant observation, the physician concluded that the culprit was not an infection but rather emotional suffering.

Chapter 2
A Tale of Two Biscuits

On September 1st, they received a completely baffling visit from Lord Raglan himself. Lord de Ros, who had settled previous conflicts involving Lucan, was indisposed that day, having come down with a fever as result of extensive sunbathing. Thus, the Commander-in-Chief had no choice but visit Lucan himself.

When Wynfield and Lord Bingham saw the one-armed silhouette, they fell silent and tensed up. Without acknowledging their presence, Raglan walked straight into Lucan's quarters.

"What do you suppose this means?" Wynfield asked.

"It means that the Commander-in-Chief received my father's letter," Lord Bingham said. "Papa spent two days writing it. He will either get everything that he demanded, or he will be discharged altogether. I have trouble envisioning any sort of compromise taking place."

The young heir began biting his cuticles.

"Stop it at once," Dr. Ferrars ordered unceremoniously, pulling Lord Bingham's hands away from his mouth. "Even the tiniest of scratches can lead to gangrene. Not to mention, those bits of dirty fingernails will aggravate your sensitive stomach."

Lord Bingham complied with the meekness of an ailing child.

After three hours, Lord Raglan emerged. The expression on his face made it impossible to determine the outcome of the conversation. He was wearing the same inconspicuous, serene smile that prompted Mrs. Duberly to compare him to a Renaissance theologian.

Wynfield and Lord Bingham saluted him as he passed. Dr. Ferrars cast his eyes down demurely. As soon as Raglan's figure disappeared from their sight, they glanced at each other, drew closer together, and held their breath simultaneously, waiting for the earl, who in turn was in no hurry to come out.

Dr. Ferrars was the first one to exhale, for he had the weakest lungs. He also had the sharpest ears of the three. He leaned his head against the door of Lucan's room, waiting, perhaps, for the familiar sound of breaking glass, paper being torn and chairs being toppled.

"I can't hear a thing," he muttered after a few seconds. "How odd... Not even the sound of breathing."

Lord Bingham covered his mouth with his hand, as if some horrifying thought occurred to him.

"God... What if Papa hung himself?"

"Don't be foolish, Georgie," Wynfield scolded him. "How on earth would he hang himself?"

"I don't know. He does have his belt."

"There is not a single hook on the ceiling. Believe me, this is not the easiest form of suicide. It requires practice. Many men have attempted and failed."

Suddenly, Dr. Ferrars raised his index finger.

"I hear something," he hissed. "His footsteps... He's coming."

The physician backed away from the door and assumed an exaggeratedly relaxed pose examining his knuckles.

The door flung open, and the earl appeared on the threshold. Tears were trickling down his face, settling into the creases of his trembling lips.

"Come in," he said half-audibly.

Wynfield and Lord Bingham followed him. Dr. Ferrars was about to enter as well, but the earl put his palm out.

"Stay out. This is a military affair." As soon as the door closed, the earl lifted his arms to the bare ceiling and twirled around his axis a few times.

"Ha-ha!" he exclaimed, stamping his feet. "I crushed them like a pair of stale biscuits."

He stamped his feet again and spun another few times.

Watching this odd ritualistic dance Lord Bingham concluded that his father's seclusion culminated in insanity.

"What biscuits, my Lord?" he inquired fearfully.

"Cardigan and Raglan, naturally! The Noble Yachtsman may have grown chummy with the One-Armed Hero, but I have the Duke of Wellington on my side! It was the Duke who appointed me the divisional general. I was chosen to command, and command I shall. Raglan cannot separate me from my cavalry. The crippled bastard attempted to barter with me. Imagine the nerve! He asked me if I would consider waiting and sailing with the Heavy Brigade later on. Hah! I could tell he was grasping at straws, trying to keep me away from Cardigan. Still, I did not budge. I know my rights all too well. With the Duke's blessing, I am sailing in three days, along with the Light Brigade. Have you seen *Simla*? It is an impressive steamer. My stateroom is being prepared as we speak. As for those two malicious gossips—let them find solace in one another. I spit on that friendship!"

Lord Lucan made a gargling sound, gathering the saliva to physically demonstrate his contempt for his enemies, but his throat, as if out of spite, happened to be dry. Instead of spitting, he stamped his foot one more time. Wynfield and Lord Bingham mimicked the stamp as proof of solidarity.

"Ah, my darling boys!" Lucan exclaimed, opening his arms. "I am so pleased that you are here to witness my glory. I would not wish to share it with anyone else."

Suddenly, the smile disappeared from his face when he saw the bruise under his son's eye.

"Georgie, what happened?" he asked with alarm. "In such an odd place, too... How on earth did you get it?"

"I walked into a lamppost," the young man blurted out without any hesitation.

Lucan pouted skeptically.

"That's bosh, Georgie. There's not a single lamppost within a fifty mile radius. Now tell Papa the truth: you got yourself into a squabble, didn't you?"

"My lord, there truly is no need to discuss this matter," Lord Bingham murmured, scratching the tip of his nose. "It's but a trifle."

"Not to me!" Lucan objected. "Some low-life assaulted my firstborn. How am I to look the other way? We are about to invade

Russia, and I want my precious boys to look their absolute best. Georgie, if you tell me his name, I will make sure that he pays for his audacity."

Clearly, Lord Lucan was determined to embarrass himself. He stepped towards his son, squeezed his face and turned it towards the light, peering into the purple mark across his cheekbone.

Eager to rescue his friend from this sudden onslaught of paternal love, Wynfield began fidgeting and coughing.

"What is it, Lord Hungerton?" Lucan asked with annoyance, still examining his son's bruise. "There's always something wrong with your health. You're either ranting, vomiting, or coughing. It wears on my nerves, you know."

"I am no longer ill, my lord. Dr. Ferrars has been tending to my health. I suppose, this is where our paths part, at least for the immediate future."

Lucan released his son's face and turned to Wynfield.

"Why are we suddenly talking about parting?"

"Well, your Lordship," Wynfield began, "since your audience with Lord Raglan had such a favorable resolution, and you will be sailing with the Light Brigade after all, I thought that, perhaps, I should make an effort to reunite with Sir James."

At the mention of the colonel's name, Lord Lucan made a grimace of disgust, as if he had tasted of rotten meat.

"Scarlett? Bah! And who on earth is this Scarlett, dare I ask?"

"I was under the impression that he was my direct commander," Wynfield replied in exaggeratedly casual tone, bobbing his head from side to side. "That is what I was told at Laleham Park. Forgive me if I was mistaken."

"No, you are not mistaken," Lucan replied with a spiteful shrug. "I suppose, that was the arrangement in the very beginning. True, Scarlett was there at Laleham, with his two boorish Indians. His name is not uttered frequently these days. Thus far, Scarlett's greatest achievement has been surviving cholera. For that alone he will be given a medal. At any rate, it is better not to bother him now. He is one frazzled, sickly old man. I assure you, he will not miss one lieutenant. I, on another hand, will miss you greatly, after all the effort I have invested into you. Or have you forgotten about the favors I have bestowed upon you?"

"How could I forget them, my Lord? I begin my morning prayers by offering thanks for all you have done for me."

"In that case, forget about Scarlett and the rest of the Heavies, as least for the foreseeable future. Your place is here with me, as another aide-de-camp. Now that I have been restored to my rightful position, I intend to take full advantage of it. I have a million tasks of utmost importance in store for you. It appears that my troops have forgotten who their real commander is. Surely, they will benefit from a gentle reminder."

"And what if gentleness fails, my lord?"

Lucan crossed his fists in the air, as if he had been waiting for this question.

"If gentleness fails, then we initiate a reign of terror! My first target is a certain brazen horsewoman that goes by the name of Mrs. Duberly. She has been irking me for quite some time, since the very start of the campaign. Flirting with the officers, distracting them from the drill, undermining my authority, compromising the solemnity of our endeavor... Recently it was brought to my attention that she has every intention of accompanying her husband to Russia, in spite of my direct prohibition. Wives or whores, there will be no women on the transports. I have always been against women on ships or in camps. The bitch must be stopped. Do you understand? Lord Hungerton, repeat what I just said."

"The bitch must be stopped," Wynfield spouted back energetically, looking straight ahead. "And stopped she will be. I will personally stop that bitch, with God's help. If necessary, I shall tear out her hair and tie her hands behind her back with it."

Lord Bingham threw a fearful side-glance at his friend. He had never imagined that Jerry, his sensitive, chivalrous Jerry, who mourned the death of his Balkan wench so deeply, could refer to a highborn Englishwoman as a bitch. No, Jerry could not be in earnest. Yet, there he was, standing before his commander, vowing to apply physical force against the beautiful and witty Mrs. Duberly.

"Bravo, Lord Hungerton," Lucan cheered him on with a round of slow, ceremonious applause. Then he turned towards his son. "Georgie, look at your future brother-in-law. You have a great deal to learn from him. This is precisely the sort of devotion and enthusiasm I expect from my aides. Now, starting tonight, both of you will patrol the quay around the clock. If you spot Duberly's wife attempting to embark—and I have no doubt that she will do so—catch her. If necessary, employ the natives to keep her sequestered on the shore until the last ship leaves. Her vile little notebook, where she scribbles the dirt about England's highest ranking generals, is to be confiscated from her and brought to me. Am I understood?"

"Perfectly, my lord!" Wynfield vowed and saluted him.

Lord Bingham, still refusing to believe the sincerity of his friend's vow, copied the gesture, avoiding eye contact with his father.

Chapter 3
Alliances Founded on a Shared Horse Fetish

Lord Lucan regretted not being there to see his brother-in-law receive the news of his demotion. Oh, he would pay a thousand pounds to see Cardigan's whiskers curl and his mushroom face redden in helpless rage, the same rage that he, Lucan, had experienced on so many occasions.

"I wonder what my darling James is doing at this moment," the earl would mumble, rubbing his thumbs against each other. "To have all his ambition dashed so unceremoniously and irrevocably... Oh, he must feel the pang! He rejoiced like an idiot, lost in the clouds, but I pulled him back onto the cholera-ridden land. Serves him right—after all the humiliation he had inflicted upon me! Ah, if only I could see his face... I would perish a satisfied man."

Having learned that he was no longer the sole commander of the Light Brigade, Cardigan secluded himself from his troops. He needed some time to absorb the shock of the news.

While wandering along the edge of the bay, he suddenly heard a familiar female sobbing behind his back. He turned around and beheld his beloved Amazon from Wiltshire, Mrs. Duberly. Over the course of their stay at Yeni-Bazaar they had become friendly. Having had the opportunity to observe his elegant manners, to hear his gallant compliments and to learn of his love of purebred horses, Fanny ceased mocking him in her journal. More than that,

173

she crossed out all the sections that depicted Cardigan in a grotesque light. She was not afraid to admit that she had been mistaken in regards to this gentleman, who proved to be much more than an extension of Lucan. All the glasses of excellent champagne they had drunk together! All the tales they had shared by the fire! Enchanted by Fanny, Cardigan became more lenient towards her husband and made it a point not to burden Captain Duberly with taxing chores.

Now they were standing face to face on a deserted shore.

"What's the matter, my darling Frances?" Cardigan asked. "Why are your beautiful eyes so red?"

"Oh, James, he betrayed me," she moaned.

"Who betrayed you, my dove?"

"My patron!" she wailed in disgust. "My saint, my Renaissance cardinal... Lord Raglan—that's who!"

Cardigan sighed and nodded silently, still looking Fanny in the eye.

"Oh yes, I too have been betrayed by him. He promised me exclusive command over the Light Brigade, and today I learned that the promise was broken. After all the effort I had invested into polishing my men, I must surrender my control of them. My loathsome brother-in-law is back in his saddle, and I am to obey his orders. On such terms we are sailing to Russia."

"Aw!"

They gasped simultaneously, as if pierced by the same bullet, and leaned towards each other, almost embracing, bound by mutual animosity towards the same man.

"Two months ago," Fanny continued, "Raglan granted me a private audience, over the course of which he was all benevolence, all tenderness. He presented me with a ruby ring from his amputated hand. He convinced me of his patronage. When I left his quarters in Skutari, it was with assurance that he would see that I would never be separated from my husband. Now I am told that I am not to sail with him. The order came from Lord Lucan. I pleaded with Lord Raglan, and he denied my request. He said he could not be bothered with such annoyances. It appears that in exercising his authority as commander, he has ceased to be my friend."

"You still have a friend in me, dear Fanny," Cardigan assured her, "whatever my friendship is worth. I am prepared to swallow my own defeat, but I cannot bear to see you crumbled by my brother-in-law. Should you think it proper to disregard the prohibition, I will not offer any opposition to your doing so."

Fanny glanced up at her new patron with disbelief and stopped breathing until Cardigan nodded, confirming her that she had heard him correctly. She exhaled noisily and pressed her face against the sash of his uniform.

"What shall we do, James?"

"I just might have a plan," Cardigan replied, stroking her hair. "And it just might work. Should it fail—I will take the weight of the consequences."

He bent over to Fanny and began whispering to her hastily. There was absolutely no need to whisper, since they were alone. Still, Lord Cardigan needed an excuse to brush his cheek against that of a beautiful lady who came to him seeking solace. It was his opportunity to tickle her earlobe with his mustache. He made sure to prolong his monologue.

"This is madness, James," Fanny said at last, drawing back and looking Cardigan in the eye. "This plot will never work."

"In all likelihood, it won't," Cardigan nodded, agreeing. "The alternative would be to comply, to accept our defeat."

"Anything but that," Fanny whispered through her teeth.

She removed the ruby ring from her thumb and turned towards the ocean, bouncing Raglan's gift on the palm of her hand.

"What are you doing?" Cardigan asked her nervously. "One does not discard such relics."

"It is no relic to me," Fanny replied. "It is a symbol of treachery. The very sight of it brings me grief."

"No, save it," Cardigan advised her, closing her hand. "Keep it until your next audience with Raglan. Then you can toss it in his face."

With an air of malicious determination, her nostrils trembling, Fanny forced the ring back on her thumb, making the ruby face inward.

Having forgotten that he was in the middle of a war, Cardigan contemplated his new protégée. Fanny had not asked her maid to curl her hair in weeks, and it had returned to its natural texture. The wind from the sea diffused her auburn stands, pulling them one by one from the bun.

"Fanny, we have a grueling journey ahead of us," he said somberly, thinking it his duty to give her one last warning. "More beautiful horses will perish before your own eyes. Are you certain you wish to subject your dear little heart to such pain?"

"My heart was broken with the loss of my beloved stallion," Fanny declared with the sort of pathos that Cardigan could appreciate. "There is nothing left to break, no more tears left to shed. If I witness another hundred horses perish, it will not make any difference."

Chapter 4
Lessons in Wartime Logic Continue

Patrolling the quay was not Wynfield's idea of heroism, but still, it was better than complete idleness. At least he had orders to fulfill, however ridiculous they struck him. Lord Lucan had sent him and Lord Bingham to supervise the embarkation of the transport ships. They were not to carry or even lift anything, even though every pair of capable hands was valued in gold. Their sole task was to prevent Mrs. Duberly, the vexatious bitch of the Light Brigade, as Lucan referred to her, from boarding.

With his future brother-in-law by his side, armed with field glasses, Wynfield witnessed one of the messiest, most disastrous embarkations of the century, a glorious celebration of incompetence.

The *Simoon* was the first vessel to be boarded. It was an old war ship from which the guns had been removed to make more room for the troops. Thirteen hundred of them were marched up the gangway and packed into the space below decks.

Lord Bingham nudged Wynfield gently.

"Jerry, don't usurp Papa's field-glasses now. Let me have a look too."

"Let me be, Georgie," Wynfield cut him off with annoyance. "I was the one entrusted with the task of watching the quay. Your duty is to watch my back."

"Then tell me what is happening, in God's name. I've waited my entire life to see such a sight. Jerry, please tell me."

He began stamping his feet impatiently, with the indignation of a five-year old.

"Georgie, if you do not stop pestering me, I will plant another bruise under your eye. Now, stand behind me, like your Papa told you."

Suddenly, Wynfield put down the field glasses and polished the lenses with his glove, as if disbelieving the image that they were relating to him.

"I'll be damned," he murmured, peering into the gangway.

"What are they doing?" Lord Bingham asked in an animated whisper, tugging at his sleeve.

"I don't know what the hell they are doing, Georgie. Whatever cargo they loaded on the ship, they are taking it all down."

"The ship simply cannot sail," they heard Dr. Ferrars' voice behind them.

Somehow, the young physician managed to find them in the crowd. He was carrying his medical case, which meant that he was not returning to Lucan's headquarters again. The arrangement was for him to board the *Simla*.

"Richard, I am glad you are here," Wynfield said, turning to him. "As someone who is versed in physics, can you explain to me what is happening?"

"The ship is overloaded," Dr. Ferrars replied casually, stretching both arms forward, as if holding an invisible vessel. "It will sink the way it is now. Or rather, it will never leave the bay. Therefore, the supplies must stay behind, so do the transport animals, since they will have nothing to carry."

"But the donkeys will starve to death!" Lord Bingham exclaimed mournfully. "It took so much time and effort to collect those beasts from the countryside; and now we must abandon them? It won't please Papa one bit."

"Lord Lucan better harden his skin," Dr. Ferrars replied through his teeth, struggling to harness his sarcasm, "for there will be a great many things that will not please him."

The physician glanced at the tents, medicine chests and stretchers being dumped on the shore, and wavered, as if overcome by sudden vertigo.

"I'll suppose, we'll be performing amputations with carving knives under the stars," he mumbled, rubbing the bridge of his nose. "That surely arouses the romantic in me. What an appetizing

178

sight that will be! Gentlemen, with your permission, I will retreat into my stateroom before I am trampled to death. Won't you be joining me?"

"Not just yet," Lord Bingham replied. "Jerry is on hound duty, sniffing out Mrs. Duberly. And I am hiding behind his back, where Papa's belt won't reach me."

"In that case, I wish you luck with your hunt, gentlemen."

Dr. Ferrars flexed his shoulders, tightened the scarf around his neck, and headed towards the *Simla*. Wynfield and Lord Bingham overhead his mumbling: "Breathe deeply, Richard... Breathe..."

The first flock of donkeys rattled down the gangway of the *Simoon*. The animals, not exactly known for their intelligence or grace, bumped over each other and brayed in panic, their hooves stubbing on the wooden planks and then sinking in the wet sand.

"I'm not sure which death would be preferable for these wretched beasts," Wynfield said pensively. "They can either starve on the shore of their native country or perish at sea and be dumped overboard. At least, now they have a slight chance of finding their way home. What do you think, Georgie?"

"Look at this, Jerry," Lord Bingham whispered suddenly, pointing towards the *Himalaya*, the steamer on which Lord Cardigan was supposed to sail. "Do you see what I see?"

Wynfield squinted and saw four men carrying a native Turkish transport cart up the gangway. One could tell that they were trying to take advantage of the commotion and keep the content of the cart hidden.

Having spotted two of Lucan's aides advancing towards the ship, the men speeded up their pace, nearly tipping the cart into the water.

"Halt!" Wynfield shouted, raising his arm.

The four men put the cart down and froze with their backs hunched, like a band of indentured servants caught stealing food from their masters' kitchen.

"Now, what do we have here?" Wynfield inquired with a smile. "You must be aware of the orders to strip the ship of all dispensable cargo. Remember—bare necessities only? This does not strike me as bare necessities."

"We are following Lord Cardigan's orders," one of the men stammered, blinking nervously.

"And we are merely following *Lord Lucan's* orders," Wynfield replied, intoxicated by the realization of being in command. He spoke slowly, dragging out every word, savoring every second of the anguish he was inflicting upon the four men. "Last time I verified, he was Lord Cardigan's direct commander. Now, let us take a look."

He pulled the curtain aside and saw a Turkish woman in native clothing. When Wynfield tore off the embroidered veil that was covering the woman's face, his smile instantly broadened. He recognized Mrs. Duberly. She was looking him in the eye defiantly, chin tilted, and eyebrow raised. There was no plea for mercy in her glance. Certainly, that was not a glance of a Muslim woman. It was not the pallor of her skin or the light texture of her auburn hair that betrayed Fanny's western origin—it was her posture and her facial expression.

Wynfield arched his back and laughed.

"Imagine that—Cardigan's new plaything!"

Lord Bingham, who had never seen Mrs. Duberly, did not know what was happening.

"Do you remember what Papa said?" he asked Wynfield in a tone of stern dutifulness. "No women of any kind—wives or whores."

"True enough; but this creature is not even human. She's a Turk, not much different from a transport animal, although she weighs less and isn't half as useful. If Lord Cardigan wishes to add another mule to his cargo—I say, let him! Come, Georgie. We must capture that Duberly bitch."

Wynfield snapped his fingers, letting the four men know that they were free to proceed, placed his hand on the back of Lord Bingham's neck and convoyed him down the gangway.

At the last moment, Wynfield turned around and caught a brief glimpse of Mrs. Duberly's face, just before the curtain of the cart was closed. She graced him with the same haughty, coquettish smile that had dazzled so many men of the Light Brigade. In return, she received a dismissive, condescending rolling of the eyes that erased her smile at once. This exchange of grimaces happened over the course of a few seconds.

"Papa will not let us board this ship empty-handed," Lord Bingham sighed. "He expected us to bring Mrs. Duberly's pretty head on a bayonet."

"Don't fret, Georgie," Wynfield consoled him. "I'm certain that your father will find new prey for us to hunt."

Contrary to their expectation, they found Lord Lucan in high spirits. Apparently, the loss of supplies and transport animals did not poison the sweetness of his victory over Cardigan. Equipped with a glass of rum and a cigar, he was parading around his stateroom that had already been made to look just like his headquarters in Varna. The furniture pieces had been arranged in the same order. The voyage was expected to take three days, and his Lordship needed to feel at home for that stretch of time.

"My dear boys!" he greeted them. "I cannot tell you how foolish I feel for having dispatched you on this scouting expedition. It was a clumsy mishap. Shortly after you left, a rumor reached me—from a very trustworthy source—that Captain Duberly and his shrew stayed behind in Yeni-Bazaar due to illness."

"All the better, my lord!" Wynfield replied flamboyantly, having assumed that the person who started the rumor was the same person who devised the plot to smuggle Mrs. Duberly aboard the *Himalaya*.

"Oh, I hope to God it is dysentery," Lucan continued, squinting with malice. He would have folded his hands for a prayer, but they were occupied with tobacco and alcohol respectively. "Please, let it be something agonizing and humiliating. Serves them right! This is their retribution for having flaunted their nauseating affection. Now look who's vomiting!"

Wynfield surveyed the stateroom and for the first time noticed Dr. Ferrars sitting in on the edge of the bunk with an open notebook. The physician was not feigning oblivion. He truly has become blind and deaf to his surrounding, if only for the sake of preserving his fragile sanity. Being trapped on the same ship with Lucan promised to be even more traumatic than sharing his headquarters in Varna. There was no possibility for physical escape, only for intellectual.

"Is this where we lodge?" Wynfield asked, unbuttoning his coat and searching for a place to hang it.

"Not so fast," Lucan warned him, wagging his index finger. "Initially, we were to board in this stateroom, all four of us, but then I remembered that I have a tendency to snore and talk in my sleep, and that would be undeserved cruelty towards all of you, for you need your rest. I don't want any rumors that I treat my men without consideration, torturing them with my abominable night-time habits. Thus, I decided to move you with the rest of my aides. True, their stateroom is about one-third of mine, and it doesn't have windows, and the ventilation is somewhat inferior, but otherwise, it is quite charming. Now, there are only three bunks, so the six of you will have to work out a sleeping timetable and take turns. Of course, you can always sleep two to a bunk, which should not be much trouble, since all of you are so slender. There are no slovenly men on my staff! Imagine all the merriment you, boys, can have without a grumpy old general like me. You can gossip, laugh, smoke, and play cards. And I shall be here all alone, with a map of southern Russia and a royal headache. Dr. Ferrars will escort you."

The physician did not as much as stir at the sound of his name. He continued scribbling with his notebook, until Lucan stood above him and barked.

"Dr. Ferrars!"

The physician's hand twitched and tip of the pencil broke off.

"Yes, Lord Lucan?" he asked, shutting down his notebook.

"Descend from your clouds for an instant," the earl said with an eerie softness. "Kindly show my two gallant and fearless aide-de-camps to their luxurious stateroom. They just wasted an entire afternoon hunting down someone who isn't even here. They must be exhausted. Help them get situated and stay with them until further notice. You and I will have a private discussion later."

Dr. Ferrars muttered in compliance and gestured for his two comrades to follow him. One could tell it did not break his heart to leave Lucan's stateroom.

Suddenly, a wave of stomach churning wailing, like that of the souls in Dante's Inferno, engulfed the quay.

"Gentlemen, you better close your ears," the earl said with a smirk, knowing the origin of the noise. "This Gregorian chant will render anyone deaf."

Wynfield and Lord Bingham rushed towards the window and saw a flock of women weeping by the shore. Those were the wives of the officers departing on the *Simoon*.

"What will become of them now?" Wynfield asked, his tone communicating superficial curiosity rather than profound concern.

"It's truly none of my business," the earl replied with a shrug. "I did not force them to come here. You know my view of women and war. I did not hold my revolver to their foreheads. They chose to accompany their husbands, assuming this campaign would be but an exotic picnic. Bah, they can use the donkeys we left on the shore to travel inland and explore the Balkan wilderness for all I care."

"Gentlemen, follow me," Dr. Ferrars said half-audibly, took both his comrades by the elbows and pulled them away from the window. When they were out of Lucan's hearing range, he added: "Believe me, this is not the last hideous scene you will witness."

He led them down the narrow stuffy corridors. Through the thin partitions, songs and laughter could be heard. The officers celebrated the long-overdue departure from Bulgaria, even though the action plan was sketchy at best, and the commanding generals were yet to agree on the exact disembarkation site. They were sailing, and that was all that mattered. As far as they knew, the first step was for the transports to rendezvous with the fleet at Balchik Bay and then head for the Crimea. In their minds, cholera, idleness, and futile drilling were staying behind. Unadulterated glory lay ahead. Their very voices appeared younger, livelier. Only yesterday, those soldiers sounded like apathetic old men. Neither the braying of the donkeys nor the wailing of their wives on the shore could ruin their euphoria.

"Oh, Jerry, are we the only idiots who are not rejoicing?" Lord Bingham asked.

"Believe me, Georgie, we are not the idiots on this ship," Wynfield replied.

"Do you truly believe that we will manage to cross the sea in three days?"

"Why wouldn't we? Everything else has been going according to the plan. It's been one stellar maneuver after another. What makes you so uncertain all of a sudden?"

Lord Bingham could not contain laughter.

"I simply adore you, Jerry," he sniffled hysterically. "Forgive me if I do not remind you of that often enough. Your sense of humor is delicious. I cannot wait to flaunt you to my friends from Rugby. They would sell their souls to have you for a brother-in-law. Three days, you say? You would bet on it?"

"This may not be my place to chime in," Dr. Ferrars said, "but whoever produced that ludicrous number clearly isn't very strong in geography or mathematics. Gentlemen, I saw the map. We are three hundred miles away from the prospective landing site."

"You don't trust the vessels, Dr. Ferrars?"

"I don't trust the commanders."

"So what is your verdict, Doubting Thomas?" Wynfield asked. "How much time do you think we will spend at sea?"

"Two weeks at least—if we are lucky. I am taking potential delays in the account."

"That's obscene!" Wynfield exclaimed dismissively. "Two weeks? We don't have enough provisions to last us that long."

"I know we don't!"

"Still, I refuse to believe that our commanders would be *that* careless," Wynfield continued, instinctively rushing to Lucan's defense. "My intuition persuades me that all the nonsense is behind."

"Lord Hungerton, your optimism terrifies me."

"Can a soldier hope?"

"My only is that you like your stateroom, as you will be spending quite some time there. Mark my word."

Dr. Ferrars pulled out a key from his pocket and unlocked the door.

"Gentlemen, welcome to your prison."

The smell of rotting wood and sweat greeted them. Lord Lucan certainly was not lying when he warned them about the poor ventilation in the stateroom.

The other three aide-de-camps were already fast asleep. Their boots and belts were piled up on the floor, as there was no furniture in the stateroom.

Dr. Ferrars covered the lower part of his face and rushed out into the corridor. He had not eaten anything all day, and long-repressed hunger sharpened his sensitivity to the smells.

Wynfield and Lord Bingham claimed the last empty bunk and lay on it back to back without removing their coats. They had a great deal to discuss, and plenty of time for it too, but not enough strength to verbalize their thoughts. Time wasting, beyond doubt, is among the most exhausting chores in the world. After watching the disastrous embarkation, the two young men were no less achy than those who took active participation in it.

"Oh, Jerry..." Lord Bingham moaned weakly. "If Papa knew we were sleeping in our coats, he would kill us."

The creaking of the boards signaled the unmooring of the *Simla*. The three sleeping aides began stirring on their bunks, sensing the rocking movement of the ship. Across the partition, howling and applause could be heard.

"Still, I think myself blessed," the sweet-tempered heir continued muttering. "On the same ship as my father, lying back to back with my brother... What of the men below the deck? There's no room for them to sit. Poor devils... Ah, yes... I am blessed."

Chapter 5
The Things Not Taught at Cambridge

When Dr. Ferrars returned to Lord Lucan's stateroom, his nausea did not subside. On the contrary, it worsened. Having compared his symptoms to those endured by Lord Bingham at Varna, the physician knew that the culprit of the tightness in his stomach was emotional turmoil. Truthfully, at that point he would have gladly surrendered to cholera, as it would have liberated him from the necessity to serve the tyrannical earl. Richard Ferrars was suffering from cholera of the spirit.

Lord Lucan was standing by the window, looking at the vanishing coast of Bulgaria. He sensed the presence of the physician behind his back but did not deign to turn around.

"It is no secret," he began, "that the numerous mishaps and misunderstandings of the past two months—mishaps to which I did *not* contribute—have compromised the morale of the troops. We are in no state to invade another country, certainly not one the size of Russia. Wouldn't you agree, Dr. Ferrars?"

"It is not my place to make such assessments, your Lordship," the physician replied. "Military maneuvers are not in my area of expertise."

"Bah! I am not consulting you as a military leader," Lucan huffed. "What is your opinion on their mental condition?"

"My lord, we all hold a similar opinion on that matter. Their despair is palpable."

"During the embarkation, I spotted you pouring out tea for those afflicted by cholera. You are not here to rinse their stomachs. You are here to rinse their brains. Are you not an expert on the human mind? Have you not been studying those men closely? Have you not been listening to their conversations as I had instructed you? Are they still eager to fight?"

Lucan slammed his hands into the glass and turned around to face Dr. Ferrars. This unexpected eye contact with Lucan paralyzed the physician's tongue for a few seconds. It was so much easier to talk to the back of the earl's head.

"My lord," he said at last, "those men have been eager to fight for months. Their melancholy is a consequence of idleness. However, things appear to have changed since the orders to embark were issued. As I was escorting Lord Bingham and Lord Hungerton down the vestibule to their stateroom minutes ago, I sensed a universal elation. The soldiers caught a new wave of hope."

While Dr. Ferrars was speaking, the earl kept nodding impatiently.

"And how exactly do you plan on sustaining that hope?" he asked. "Yes, I've heard them howl in delight. The partitions are made of cardboard. Every time one of them grunts or belches, I hear it. How will you personally ensure that their euphoria does not wane?"

"I cannot ensure such things, my lord."

Lucan gasped and placed his hand behind his ear.

"Excuse me? Did I just hear the word 'cannot'? What is a dirty word like that doing in your vocabulary, Dr. Ferrars?"

Saying "no" to Lucan was a costly but all the more irresistible pleasure.

"Your Lordship has heard me correctly," Dr. Ferrars confirmed. "I cannot forcefully arouse devotion in others, especially thousands of soldiers who had been ill used for months. I am a physician, not a magician."

"And you waited until now to inform me of that?"

"I have been attempting to inform you of that since the first day of our journey, my lord, but you have not been listening."

Over the course of his last three responses to Lucan, the physician's voice kept rising, assuming a more insolent tone. Unnoticeably to himself, Dr. Ferrars lifted his chin and assumed a more defiant, belligerent attitude. Perhaps, on a subconscious level he was hoping to provoke his commander into physical violence. Dr. Ferrars harbored no illusions about coming out victorious from a fight with Lucan. Even though he was almost thirty years younger than the earl, he did not possess the same strength or agility. Death from a blow to the head and an unceremonious burial in the waves seemed like an appealing alternative to being imprisoned on the same ship as Lucan. By then Dr. Ferrars had abandoned his fantasy about returning to England a hero and reuniting with his beloved benefactress.

Suddenly, Dr. Ferrars heard himself blurt out:

"I don't have any magical incantations to reverse the moral and physical harm done by certain incompetent commanders!"

There, he uttered those words that had been clogging his chest for so long. At least, his last few breaths would be deep and free. The fatal blow would come any second now. Lucan's hands rose above his head with the fingers fanned out and contracted into fists. With a beatific smile of a martyr, Dr. Ferrars turned his shoulders out, welcoming his demise.

To his surprise, the steel fists did not crash into his jaw or under his ribs. Instead, they landed on the top of the writing desk.

"You're absolutely right," the earl whispered, his body vibrating. "I know just of whom you speak. My life's work—our work—has been compromised by the likes of Raglan and Cardigan. They are the ones delaying the long-awaited bloodshed. Had I been the one making the decisions, we would be shooting our Orthodox brethren left and right. Our soldiers would be dying of wounds, as they should, instead of cholera."

The earl flew towards the astounded physician and seized him by the shoulders.

"Dr. Ferrars, thank you for reminding me who my enemies are. I needed that reminder sorely. Not for an instant may can I allow myself to forget about them. This is why it is more crucial than ever that you and I put our negligible differences aside. Together we must put this campaign back on its original path. Do you understand?"

Dr. Ferrars heard himself respond with surprising dignity and firmness.

"Yes, my lord."

"Grand. Thank you for reassuring me of your loyalty."

Lucan released his victim as suddenly as he seized it. The physician felt his calves liquefy and grabbed onto one of the chairs for support.

"I have been unreasonably harsh with you," the earl said, his sudden friendliness being directly proportionate to his fury a minute ago. "We both deserve a drink after such a hellish day. Would you believe it? I have not had any spirits since last night, and I cannot give out commands when my throat is dry."

He took out his famous rum bottle and two shot glasses but filled only one of them, having conveniently forgotten about the other one.

"I am anxious to hear about your findings, Dr. Ferrars," he began, blotting the rum from his mustache. "I understand that there are no quick miraculous solutions to ease the despair afflicting our men. However, I know that you have not been idling all this time. You have been writing ceaselessly in your notebook."

Without any hesitation, Dr. Ferrars picked up Lucan's bottle and poured some rum for himself.

"It is a protocol of selective sensory manipulations and chemical compositions," he responded in a most unaffected, businesslike manner, as if he expected his listener to understand every piece of the jargon. "The ultimate goal of the protocol is to enhance in soldiers a sense of loyalty to their commanders and to modulate their self-preservation instinct. However, in order to bring the desired effect, the protocol must be administered gradually and inconspicuously, over an extended period of time."

Watching the earl utterly confused and trying to mask that confusion with fervent nods gave Dr. Ferrars a delicious sense of superiority.

"So, what exactly will you need for your mind-rinsing experiments?" Lucan asked.

"As I mentioned earlier, I will need time and space. Without those two necessary components, my protocol will not work."

The request baffled Lucan.

"Time and space—is that all you need? By God, can you ask for something that would actually be in my power to provide for you?"

"My requests are not as extraordinary as they appear, my lord. I need one room without windows or any external light source where the men can congregate for spiritual fortification. I have written a few inspirational speeches and interspersed them with certain loyalty-enhancing slogans. Our own Reverend Bryce will deliver them. If repeated frequently enough, without any visual distractions, those speeches will put our soldiers in a particular state of mind. If they cannot see each other's faces, they will become temporarily oblivious to their physical differences and begin perceiving themselves as components of one whole. Their sense of individuality will fade. Stripped of their selfish interests, they will place a common goal above their own lives. They will be less likely to desert or to rebel."

Dr. Ferrars took a sip of rum, giving Lord Lucan a chance to appreciate his genius, but the earl did not seem particularly impressed.

"A prayer in the dark?" he asked, squinting spitefully. "Earth-shattering... Is that what you went to Cambridge for?"

Lucan's attempt at belittling him did not offend Dr. Ferrars but only confirmed that the earl was ashamed of his own ignorance.

"My lord," Dr. Ferrars continued in the same even tone, "they do not teach such things in Cambridge, at least not yet; and for fairness' sake, I never claimed to be a genius of any sort. Remember, it was not my personal desire to be here. I came along on your command."

"You are absolutely right," Lucan replied, raising the palms of his hands apologetically. "I had no business questioning your expertise. Please, continue."

Dr. Ferrars did not need an official permission to continue. He resumed babbling nonchalantly, as if discussing plans for a holiday dinner.

"It is imperative to change the collective dynamics at the root. Soldiers should seek their solace in their superiors, not their equals. No soldier should be allowed to spend too much time in the company of the same comrades. We must do everything to discourage the formation of preferential alliances. No frivolous personal friendship should compete with the soldier's loyalty towards his commander. All the while, the soldiers must have no suspicion that they are being in any way manipulated. This must be handled with utmost delicacy. If the troops suspect that some higher powers hamper their budding alliances, they will be all the more tempted to rebel. Then there are certain chemical formulas to help us reinforce the lessons we will attempt to impart on the troops. A colleague of a colleague of a colleague of mine, someone I had known in Cambridge, who claimed to have known the Sylvestre de

Sacy himself, had brought a recipe from his expedition to Persia. Allegedly, the Hashshashin sect used it during the Middle Ages before battles. Marco Polo himself had mentioned the tender relationship that the Muslims had with certain plants. With cannabis as the main ingredient, the potion is claimed to enhance one's courage. I admit I was somewhat skeptical at first about the validity of my friend's claims. He'd always been a bit of a braggart. However, we lose nothing by trying. I thought that this campaign would be a perfect opportunity to put the potency of the formula to a test. It may take some time for me to prepare the potion, as I am yet to gather the rest of the ingredients. Do you understand the task before us, my lord?"

Lord Lucan did not understand most of what was said a moment earlier. The physician spouted out too much too fast. The only thing that the earl took away from the conversation was that he needed to provide a dark room for Muslim prayers and ritualistic consumption of cannabis.

"It appears that you have already thought of everything, Dr. Ferrars," Lucan concluded. He bobbed his head from side to side, imitating deep thinking. "My involvement is not needed. Since we are to fight on the side of Turks, procuring the native herbs should not be difficult. They owe us that much, wouldn't you agree?"

"We have much to learn from our Oriental friends," Dr. Ferrars confirmed.

Chapter 6
What It Takes to Sink a Dead Body

Wynfield woke up to the sound of deep, resonant, rhythmical splashes. Since there were no windows, he could not tell what time of the day it was. The only source of light was a Turkish lantern dangling from the ceiling, but the oil in it had burned out almost entirely.

Dr. Ferrars was sitting on the edge of the bunk, trying to soften a biscuit in a pitcher filled with pale tea.

"What time is it?" Wynfield asked, rising on the elbow.

"About seven o'clock in the morning."

Suddenly, Wynfield noticed that the ship was not moving. The rocking sensation had diminished.

"Why have we stopped?" he continued interrogating, trying to remember how he ended up sleeping on the same bunk with his future brother-in-law. "Where are we now?"

"In Balchik Bay, waiting for the rest of the fleet—however long it will take. It all depends on what happens in Varna, how soon we can vacate the port. It would not surprise me if we sat here for two days."

Satisfied with the explanation, Wynfield crawled over Lord Bingham, nearly pushing him off the bunk, stood up and stretched, touching the ceiling with his fingertips.

"What was that?" he asked when he heard another splash.

"Why don't you see for yourself? My descriptive skills fail me once again."

Dr. Ferrars dropped the pitiful stump of his biscuit into the tea and pushed the pitcher away with disgust.

Without rousing the rest of the aides, Wynfield straightened out his wrinkled uniform and headed out on the deck.

In the rays of the rising sun, he saw the bloated faces of the dead soldiers floating by the sides of the ship. Contrary to everyone's hopes, cholera had followed them on the cramped ship. More deaths had taken place overnight.

Behind his back, Wynfield heard a familiar huff. A sound filled with so much contempt and fury could only belong to Lord Lucan.

"Do you recognize any of your friends, Lord Hungerton?"

"It is rather difficult to make out their features in this lighting," Wynfield replied. "I suppose, we shall learn their names from Reverend Bryce. He has been keeping the list of casualties diligently. Let us hope he does not become one any time soon. If you see a clerical collar floating in the waves, say a prayer."

The earl opened his cigar case and held it out before his new aide-de-camp. With a grateful sigh, Wynfield snatched the thickest and the sturdiest of them all. The gruesome sight of the mass sea burial killed his appetite entirely but at the same time increased his desire for tobacco.

"Incompetent idiots," Lucan continued. "They don't even know how to sink a body properly. The weights they are attaching to the feet are not heavy enough. By the end of the day, the ship will be surrounded by decomposing corpses."

"Remember: there is a beneficial side to every ordeal, including this one," Wynfield remarked, raising his cigar. "Now there is more room below deck."

The aide-de-camp's sangfroid perplexed the earl. Young Lord Hungerton had always been one to show distress over the sufferings and deaths of others, yet there he was, waving his cigar nonchalantly, talking about the collateral benefits of the epidemic. Could this be that the sentimental boy had finally started developing calluses on his heart?

In one sweeping, predatory motion, Lucan covered Wynfield's scarred cheek with his hand and peered into his eyes, trying to understand whether his subordinate was mocking or earnest. The gesture, that was supposed to communicate menace, did not perturb Wynfield. Without averting his eyes or as much as blinking, he released smoke through his nostrils, enveloping the earl's hand in a gray cloud.

"Lord Lucan, if you wish to inflict pain upon me, I recommend that you pinch the other cheek instead," Wynfield said. "This one is quite numb after being slashed with a knife. I don't want you to be cheated out of your due wrath. If you think that I merit pain, then I want to feel every bit of it."

The earl's hand trembled and slipped off Wynfield's face. For a few seconds the commander and the subordinate stood before each other, exhaling smoke. A seizure ran across Lucan's face, resulting in a strange, unnatural smile, as if some external force suddenly jerked the corners of his mouth upward. The earl dropped the cigar and burst into surprisingly cordial, generous laughter.

"God bless you, dear boy!" he exclaimed, engulfing his aide-de-camp in his arms.

"I am already blessed, my lord," Wynfield replied, returning the pat on the back, "being here with you, on the same ship. I would not wish to enjoy this gruesome spectacle with anyone else by my side."

Once again, Lucan did not know how to interpret his aide's words, for they were uttered without any definitive expression that would give the earl any clue regarding their sincerity. The boy was saying all the proper things. Nobody could reproach him for insubordination. After about a minute of deliberation, Lucan decided to err on the side of benevolence.

"Lord Hungerton, you should not be witnessing this," he said at last, releasing Wynfield from his embrace. "I hope you know that this was not my vision for the campaign. My heart bleeds at the sight of this horrendous mismanagement. Had I been in command from start, it all would have turned out quite differently. My one hope for you and my beloved son George is to see the glory of combat. I want you to exit this campaign knowing what war can and should be. What you see before your eyes right now is not war."

"Of course, it is not war, my lord," Wynfield continued agreeing in the same cool, velvety voice. "Just wait until we land and disembark. Then we'll show them!"

"Them—you mean the Russians?"

"Actually, I was referring to Cardigan and Raglan. They are our enemies too, are they not?"

Wynfield took one last puff from the cigar and tossed the stump overboard. It rotated in the air several times and landed straight into the gaping mouth of a dead soldier.

"Your aim is impeccable," Lucan commented. "I hope you shoot as well as you discard rubbish."

"I wasn't aiming, my lord," Wynfield corrected him calmly. "Our fallen comrade caught the cigar. Craving for tobacco does not end in the afterlife."

"This shall be our pastime for the next week or so," Lucan commented grimly and followed his subordinate's example. "The Black Sea shall be our rubbish yard."

Chapter 7
What's In a Name?

Contrary to Lord Lucan's fears, the stagnation in Balchik bay did not last very long. By September 7th all transports had arrived, their numbers totaling six hundred. They began forming rows half a mile apart and five miles long. Two sailing ships were attached to each steamer. They actual lining up of the vessels happened surprisingly smoothly. It was the first maneuver that went according to the plan. Around five o'clock in the morning, the fleet left the bay.

Having forgotten the floating corpses for a moment, Wynfield allowed himself to become entranced by the majesty of the nautical parade. It was the sort of spectacle that every English male must witness at least once in his lifetime. He stood on the deck with Lord Bingham and the rest of Lucan's aides, savoring the sensation of movement and the wind in his hair. They were moving at last, leaving stagnation, uncertainty and the smell of decay behind, anticipating the thrill of real warfare that lay ahead

.   Unfortunately, this bliss proved to be short-lived. The next day the English fleet met with the French near the mouth of the Danube, and the glorious procession of vessels came to a sudden halt. Wynfield hesitated to ask his commander what was the cause of this halt or how long it was expected to last. By then he and his comrades had grown accustomed to unexplained delays and complications. To escape from the disheartening sound of anchors dropping, they retreated back into their stateroom. There was nothing for them to do at any rate, so they killed time playing poker, which proved to be somewhat challenging since several cards were missing from the deck. The players had to invent their own rules.

Dr. Ferrars, who did not tolerate confinement in closed quarters very well, became the messenger to the aide-de-camps. For the next day and a half he scurried back and forth, between the deck and the stateroom, delivering news on the embarkation and political gossip.

Cardigan used this delay as an opportunity to aggravate Lucan with visits and letters. While their vessels remained anchored, the two in-laws went to and fro in boats. On September 8th the Noble Yachtsman issued an order demanding a court martial, but his demand was curtailed. Lucan took great pleasure in reminding his brother-in-law that only the Lieutenant General has the right to issue such an order.

Dr. Ferrars caught bits and pieces of the conversation on the deck and delivered them to the aide-de-camps. He enjoyed this spying game, as it offered a distraction from the job he was commissioned to perform. Once again, his sharp ears and his swift light feet were serving him.

On the night of September 9th he stormed into the stateroom panting and beaming, as if he had the best news in the world. The aide-de-camps stopped playing and looked at him all at once.

"Gentlemen," the physician began, "I have found out the real reason why we aren't moving. Are you ready to hear it?"

"Why, we've been ready to hear it for the past thirty-six hours!" Lord Bingham replied indignantly.

"Please, remain seated, gentlemen. We are anchored here because our valiant commanders still have not agreed upon the destination."

"Richard, this is absurd!" Wynfield exclaimed. "You're joking."

"I wish I were joking, Lord Hungerton. I can vouch for what I've heard. My ears don't lie. We still don't know where exactly we are sailing. And we shall not move until we know."

"What about the bay that Lord Brown had sighted?" Wynfield continued questioning him. "Didn't he make a reconnaissance?"

"It's much too small. The French will confirm that. Lord Brown—God bless him—is hopelessly shortsighted; and the other bay he had considered is too well fortified. If we land there, we'll experience immediate losses and won't be able to advance much further. There, you have it!"

Wynfield and Lord Bingham shook their heads with disgust. They could not believe that Richard Ferrars would interrupt their card game just to deliver more disheartening tidings.

"But wait, gentlemen," the physician continued, raising his index finger. "There's good news too. Lord Raglan and two French officers are sailing for Sebastopol as we speak! You know how seriously Lord Raglan takes reconnaissance. By the end of tomorrow, we should have a definite plan of action. We shall not stay here much longer. I thought this would lift your spirits."

Wynfield pointed towards the door.

"Richard, I do not cherish shooting messengers, but you have put yourself in this position voluntarily. You either leave the stateroom for good or stay put. This darting in and out is unnerving. I cannot promise you that I will not put a bullet through your head next time you slam the door."

Dr. Ferrars examined Lord Hungerton's face, considered his options for a few seconds, and then dashed out into the vestibule. Collecting military gossip was by far more entertaining than sulking in the stuffy stateroom.

He did not show his face before his comrades again until the morning of September 11th.

"Lord Hungerton, please do not shoot me," he pleaded with Wynfield. "This time I truly do have encouraging news. Lord Raglan and his two French companions had returned from their voyage to Sebastopol. They sailed so close to the shore that they spotted the Russian troops, who actually saluted them! I shiver just imagining that scene. There is a place near Eupatoria called Calamita Bay. It's wide enough and unfortified."

When Lord Bingham heard the name of the bay, he whistled loudly.

"Gentlemen, this is perfect! We are on a voyage to calamity, quite literally. What's in a name?"

"Our very fate," Wynfield replied with pathos. "I cannot speak for the rest of you, but I am growing quite excited."

"There's more grand news," Dr. Ferrars interrupted him. "Our beloved diplomat, our unsurpassed peacemaker Lord de Ros has fallen ill, leaving us commanders free to fight one another."

"I don't believe you," Wynfield challenged him. "Lord de Ros never falls ill. The man is made of steel."

"Well, this time steel melted. In earnest, Lord de Ros' fondness of sunbathing is legendary. He stayed behind in Varna with a fever and red blisters all over his body. Lord Raglan replaced him with General Airey, whose aide-de-camp is none other but our handsome, dashing, brilliant and, above all, universally loved Captain Nolan!"

All of Lucan's aides immediately began clearing their throats and rolling their eyes. Captain Nolan—bah! The amount of praise that show-off with his "equestrian Bible" had received was truly nauseating. All that talk about his enthusiasm, intelligence, worldliness, and courage could easily make him one of the most hated individuals in the cavalry. Too much praise does to a young officer's reputation what too much wood does to a fire.

"Gentlemen, we may as well drop on our knees at once," Lord Bingham said sarcastically. "Start rehearsing the phrase 'we are not worthy'. What are we doing here at any rate? The cavalry does not need second-class amateurs like us. It has Captain Nolan! He will win the war single-handedly."

Wynfield knew of one person who would be pleased by the news of Nolan's new position. That person was Mrs. Duberly. She and Nolan were on the same vessel, the *Himalaya*, and it was only a matter of time before they would collide. Wynfield knew of Mrs. Duberly's infatuation with the handsome captain. She had dreamed about meeting him in person since the beginning of the campaign, but for one reason or another their paths had not crossed yet. Knowing Mrs. Duberly's impetuous sentimentality, Wynfield could only imagine how the inevitable encounter would end.

By the end of the day the news of the upcoming landing had spread through the fleet, making spirits rise once again. The *Himalaya*, bearing Cardigan, darted ahead of the fleet. This maneuver could not go unnoticed or uncommented by Lucan and his aides.

"Behold, Uncle James is trying to lead," Lord Bingham sneered. "It is yet another expression of his silly vanity."

The young heir was standing on the deck next to his father and future brother-in-law. That night they did not retreat into their stateroom, as they wished to be among the first ones to see the land. They situated themselves on the deck for the rest of the night, having brought nothing but a few blankets for bedding, and slept in shifts, taking turns watching the horizon.

At dawn, Lord Bingham began shaking Wynfield.

"Jerry, wake up!" he called in a slightly hoarse voice.

Wynfield opened his eyes, tossed aside the blankets, and rushed towards the railing on the port side of the ship. Against the whitening background of the sky, he saw the dark line of the Crimean coast.

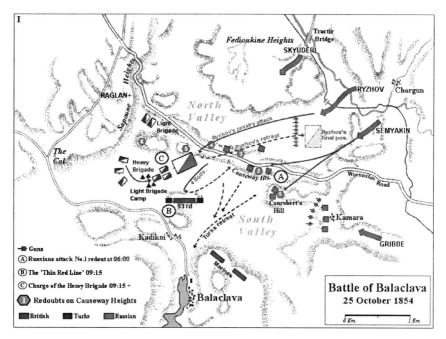

The Battle of Balaclava

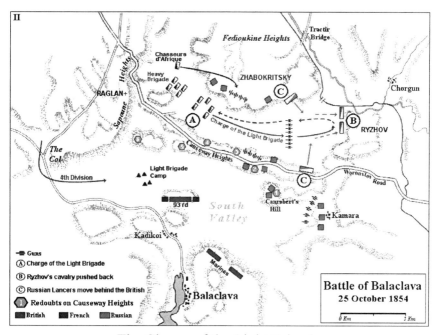

The Charge of the Light Brigade

Lord Lucan
George Charles Bingham,
3rd Earl of Lucan

Georgie
Charles George Bingham,
4th Earl of Lucan

Lord Cardigan
James Thomas Brudenell,
7th Earl of Cardigan

Lord Raglan
FitzRoy James Henry
Somerset,
1st Baron Raglan

Sir James Yorke Scarlett

Sir Colin Campbell, 1st Baron Clyde

Florence Nightingale

General Richard Airey,
1st Baron Airey

Captain Lewis Edward Nolan

Captain Nolan and the miscommunication of
the order for the Light Brigade to charge

William Russell,
Journalist

Fanny
Captain & Mrs. Henry Duberly

General Alexander
Menshikov
Russian Commander-in-
Chief in the Crimea.

General Pavel Liprandi
Commander of Russian
forces at Balaclava

Survivors of the Charge of the Light Brigade

Part 5
There Is Your Enemy!

Crimea
September~October, 1854

Chapter 1
Captain Nolan Employs
His Romantic Side

On September 13th, the governor of the charming town of Eupatoria received a visit from a handful of British officers. Neither the visit itself nor the demands presented by the officers were unexpected. The governor knew that the envelope extended to him in complete silence contained a summons to surrender. Russian generals were well aware that the British and the French fleets were approaching. Raglan's steamer was spotted just a few days earlier. It was only a question of when and where the ships would land.

Considering that his garrison consisted of two hundred men, many of whom were old or ill and totally unprepared to put up any kind of resistance, the governor of Eupatoria complied immediately, almost amicably. His only condition was to burn the summons for sanitary purposes, for he had heard about the legendary epidemics that had ravaged the British ships. The governor spoke enough English to communicate his demands, but his nonchalant guests were no longer listening. As soon as they obtained the official statement of surrender, they fluttered out of the city hall, enthusiastic and jubilant over such an effortless victory. They may have heard a word that sounded vaguely like "quarantine," but they did not give it much thought. They had a laborious enterprise ahead of them—disembarkation at Calamita Bay.

Having settled the political technicalities with the governor, they did not feel compelled to conceal their arrival. More than that, it appeared that they were making every effort to attract attention to themselves. The sounds of trumpets and bugles filled the air, making the atmosphere strangely reminiscent of the original embarkation in England back in May. Captain Nolan could not refrain from remarking that the lanterns hung from the masts at nightfall gave the bay a peculiar resemblance with a Venetian lagoon.

For Nolan, it was one of those moments when he needed to rouse and engage the romantic aesthete in him to keep the indignant realist under control. He kept making poetic comparisons, as it was the only way for him to keep from cursing at the sight of more dead horses being dumped overboard.

General Airey could not stop fuming at the members of the medical staff, who declared that the troops were too weak to carry their packs ashore. The men were ordered to leave all possessions behind except for what they could wrap in their blankets. They filled their canteens with presumably clean water and received three days' ration of cold pork and biscuits. They knew in advance that the food supplies would run out, just as they always have. With shapeless shacks over their shoulders, the exhausted troops looked like beggars. In order to appease his commander, Nolan attempted to persuade him that they looked like pilgrims rather than mere beggars. Yes, Pilgrims! Drained and foul smelling yet determined.

Airey proved to be unreceptive to Nolan's artificial euphemisms. He knew what exactly was on the captain's mind. Still, he applauded the young man's attempt at boosting the morale of the troops. The general and his aide were standing side by side, observing the distressing procession.

Suddenly, Airey adjusted his field glasses and twitched his shoulder.

"What on earth is he doing?" he mumbled.

Nolan glanced at his commander.

"My lord, to whom are you referring?"

"That officer..."

There were hundreds of officers on the beach. They were standing in full dress, with swords at their sides. Still, Nolan guessed very quickly at which man Airey was looking.

"Isn't that one of Lucan's aides?" he asked. "Lord Hunting... Lord Hungerton!"

"Yes, the one with a hacked up face. What is he doing?"

"Helping his men disembark?" Nolan suggested tentatively.

"Precisely! Why is he performing menial tasks? Do we not have sailors and servants for that?"

Indeed, the young officer was engaged in an activity below his rank. Standing with one foot on sand and another in the water, he was receiving boats and floats, helping the soldiers ashore. When another float with horses arrived, he took upon himself the task of reuniting the terrified beasts with their men.

"As much as I hate to admit, he has a way with animals," Nolan said. "Look how he pats the horses on the nose. He is a natural cavalryman!"

"He seems to have a way with everyone except for his equals," Airey replied sarcastically. "This crude display of camaraderie has one purpose: to make other officers feel morally inferior. 'Behold, I am a martyr! I am willing to pull the solders out of the water with my own hands. And the rest of you ought to feel shame!' His motives are thoroughly disgusting, wouldn't you agree?"

Nolan did not agree in his heart, but he could not express open disagreement either, so he flexed his shoulders and hummed.

"Just look at Lucan's son," Airey continued. "Lord Bingham is standing in the shade quietly, as a young officer should. He does not make it his goal to attract attention to himself. And this Lord Huntington—or whatever his name is—clearly expects a medal for his selfless acts."

Airey could have continued his rant about the inappropriate charitable excesses of Lord Hungerton, but Nolan suddenly snatched the field glasses from his hands.

"Why, my lord..." he muttered, peering into the cliffs no more than a thousand yards away from the beach. "It appears that our hosts are welcoming us."

With an indignant growl, Airey repossessed his field glasses and looked in the direction where his aide was pointing. He saw a Russian officer in a green uniform with a troop of Cossacks behind his back. Both the commander and his men communicated blood-chilling coolness. They did not appear poised for an attack.

The English silenced and halted their disembarkation for a few minutes, wondering if orders to fire would come, but the orders never came, even though the Russians were well within firing range.

"When do you suppose they will return?" Nolan asked his commander, when the Cossacks disappeared out of sight. "And what will their numbers be?"

General Airey hated admitting that he did not possess the answers. The gathering of the storm clouds on the horizon and his aide's relentless inquisitive stare had an unnerving affect on him. The general had nothing else to do but revert to change the topic of the conversation.

"That brazen Lord Hunting... Hungerton!" he growled, burrowing a pit in the wet sand with the heel of his boot. "Will someone teach him about military etiquette?"

Chapter 2
Brazen Lord Hungerton Searches for Fresh Water

By the late afternoon, the clouds over the bay thickened, the sea rose, and the first rattles of thunder were heard. The commanders agreed that it was no longer safe to continue the disembarkation. All procedures were halted for the rest of the day. Most of the cavalry remained on the ships.

Since the English troops had not been allowed to bring any tents from the ships, they had to find shelter elsewhere. Most of them simply collapsed on the beach, wrapped in their cloaks that provided absolutely no protection from the rain. They threw envious glances at their French allies, who were a little more fortunate, having individual *tentes d'abris* in their possession.

The officers had no better accommodations than their men. They claimed their spots under the artillery machines. Wynfield and Lord Bingham found shelter under a gun carriage. They both grinned and waved at Lord Brown and the Duke of Cambridge, who were hiding under a cart. Eventually Wynfield yielded his place to one infantry soldier who was beginning to show signs of respiratory illness. Through the thunder and the pattering of the rain, the two could hardly hear each other. The young soldier resisted the generous gesture, shaking his head obstinately, even though his teeth kept chattering. At last, Wynfield grabbed him by the neck and wrestled him under the gun carriage.

Airey and Nolan who witnessed the scene from the safety of

the tent that they had managed to smuggle aboard, rolled their eyes in disgust. Once again, the brazen Lord Hungerton was flaunting his selflessness. Perhaps, he expected the rest of the officers to crawl from their sanctuaries and yield them to their Indian servants? Perhaps, that was his primary goal for coming to the Crimea—to topple the military hierarchy.

Had Airey and Nolan been better acquainted with the Crimean climate, had they paid closer attention to the sky, they would have taken that opportunity to fill their canteens with water. The men aboard the ships were doing precisely that. Having all but run out of fresh water supplies, they stuck their tongues out, trying to catch every bit of moisture that was not tainted by cholera. Some of the cavalry officers went as far as taking their horses out of the holds, allowing the thirsty beasts to drink from the puddles forming on the deck. They had not thought that the storm would terrify the horses. Chaos arose aboard the transports, with hooves knocking against the masts and deafening neighing mixing with the thunder.

Dr. Ferrars, who had remained on the *Simla*, watched the storm from Lord Lucan's stateroom. There was no urgent need for him to disembark with the troops. He could wait for the madness to settle. Through the stateroom window he could see the beach covered with cholera patients who had been separated from their comrades and left to wait for the next sick transport, whenever it was due. Most of those men, he surmised, would not survive the night.

Himself being dry and warm, Dr. Ferrars felt something akin to remorse. It simply was not right that he should be apart from the troops. He should have been on that beach with them at least to support them with his words, since his hands were tied by the terms of the contract. Yes, he had been told a thousand times that the purpose of his trip to the Crimea was not to tend to the soldiers' bodies. His agreement bound him to Lord Lucan exclusively. Still, even if Dr. Ferrars could circumvent his Hippocratic Oath, his Christian—however loosely—moral code by which he did abide at least half of the time would not let him sleep that night. He suspected that there would be many more sleepless nights in store for him.

Deafened by a chorus of conflicting voices in his head, the hapless physician stood by the window until the storm abated.

*****

Having discovered in the morning that the fierce sun had evaporated every bit of moisture, General Airey fell into rage. Whose oversight was it? Who was to blame for having failed to notify him of the peculiarities of the Crimean climate? The only water available was what the more prudent troops had collected in their canteens.

Airey's first order was for the artillerymen to dig wells. Since the men had no shovels at their disposal, they had to make use of their bayonets. They began scraping the soil in blazing heat only to discover a few hours later that the water was brackish.

Suddenly, a brilliant idea occurred to Nolan.

"My lord," he whispered to his commander, "why don't you take advantage of Lord Hungerton's generosity. Make him dig too. You know his propensity to sacrifice personal comfort for a common good. He would not dare to refuse. The sight of an officer digging a well will provide much-needed entertainment for the troops."

Airey adored the idea and was slightly peeved that he had not thought of it himself. In all fairness, his head had been occupied with matters that were far more important. Yes, he would be happy to cajole the brazen Lord Hungerton into manual labor. Perhaps, that would teach the rest of the altruistically disposed officers a lesson. There was only one problem: Lord Hungerton was nowhere to be found. Several witnesses testified that he had vanished at dawn, having taken with him Lord Bingham and the young infantry soldier by the name Seamus Martin.

Now Airey and Nolan had a serious reason to huff and sulk. Their plan to make a spectacle out of Lord Hungerton was failing. To release their anger, they ordered to dig more wells, which proved to be a failure once again. None of them had drinkable water. All rivers and streams in the surrounding area were brackish.

"The land is cursed!" Airey exclaimed, surrendering. "Those Russians must have salted the water on purpose. They knew we were coming, so they dumped tons of salt into all their water sources. What other explanation could there be?"

Airey did not care that the troops were listening to him in bewilderment. When he saw their loose jaws and rounded eyes, he dug the heel of his boot into the sand after his custom and shouted:

"Back to work, you louts! Keep on digging! There must be fresh water somewhere. The natives couldn't have ruined all their water sources."

Reluctantly, the soldiers returned to their chores. It was not their place to question General Airey's sanity.

Salvation from their fruitless toils came from the blue. Suddenly, they heard a festive Irish song and saw three men approaching from over the cliffs. The soldiers recognized Lord Hungerton, Lord Bingham, and Private Martin. Each was carrying a small barrel on his shoulder.

"We've found fresh water!" Lord Hungerton exclaimed, tapping on the barrel.

Having heard that declaration, Airey turned green. Nolan rushed to his commander's aid, thinking that the general was about to faint.

"My lord, are you well?" the captain asked, offering his shoulder for support.

"Impossible," Airey hissed, his eyes burrowing the brazen Lord Hungerton. "Young man, this is no time for jokes of such nature."

"We are not joking," Lord Bingham replied triumphantly. "It's true. We found fresh water. This morning Lord Hungerton persuaded us to follow him on his expedition. There's a hidden spring about a mile away from here. It's not by any means enormous, but the water is unquestionably drinkable."

"You are welcome to sample the water yourself, my lord," Wynfield suggested, uncorking the barrel before the general. "Order a court martial for me if I am lying."

Airey gave Nolan a shove in the back.

"Captain—you first. After sampling brackish water from so many wells, I am afraid I cannot trust my own taste glands."

Nolan stepped forward with his hands cupped. Wynfield filled them with water from his barrel. With demonstrative squeamishness, the captain touched the surface with his lips. All eyes were fixed on him.

Finally, after a minute of suspicious lip smacking and sniffling, he straightened out and reported that the water indeed was fresh. He delivered the news with noticeable reluctance, because he knew what kind of reaction it would provoke in the troops. Having heard Nolan's verdict, they raised their bayonets in the air and began shouting praises in the address of the three men who saved them from the agonizing thirst.

The remaining two barrels were uncorked promptly, and the troops began lining up for their rations. Naturally, the officers jumped in first, leaving behind the men who had just spent hours digging the useless wells. At least, that was the officers' original impulse. When Lord Hungerton, their savior, cleared his throat and nodded in the direction of the exhausted troops, the officers, suddenly ashamed of their greedy haste, began stepping, aside and letting the wretched well diggers have the first serving of water.

"Gentlemen, wait," Wynfield said suddenly, plugging his barrel. "We must not forget our ailing comrades on the beach. I guarantee you that they have not had anything to drink since yesterday. I shall personally deliver the rest of my supply to them. You must go and refill your canteens. Private Martin will lead you to the spring."

The soldiers lined up to follow the comely young Irishman, who in turn was beaming with pride. Not every day does a native of Mayo chance to lead an English team. Above all, Private Martin was happy to be of service to a man like Lord Hungerton, who gave him his spot under the gun carriage. It was a shock to discover that the generous young officer was an aide to the fearsome Earl of Lucan. Being a village simpleton, Private Martin had not yet learned to conceal his emotions. Concepts of diplomacy or hypocrisy were still foreign to him. Having learned that Lord Hungerton was reporting directly to the Lieutenant General, the young Irishman let his jaw hang loose and his wide hazel eyes bulge. Another thing that shocked him that Lord Bingham was Lucan's son. How could a wolf have produced a lamb? The two young officers did not behave like lords at all, not towards each other and not towards their commoner companion. They called each other Jerry and Georgie, and they called him Seamus, although he would not dare to address them by their given names, at least not yet. In their company, Private Martin did not feel self-conscious about his Irish accent. A few times Lord Bingham asked him to repeat what he had just said, but it was done without any mockery. Bound by a sense of informal camaraderie, the three of them joked as if they had gone on a dozen fishing trips together. Private Martin wished that the expedition in search for water could last a bit longer. He knew that very soon he would have to separate from his new friends. Sooner or later, the laws of military hierarchy would take over.

They were not destined to fight side by side. Eventually, they would rejoin Lord Lucan, and he—the infantry.

"This day shall live in me heart f'ever," he declared with his characteristic bluntness. "If I don't do 'nother good deed fer the rest o'the campaign, I'll die a happy man."

Of course, the two officers began reassuring him in unison that he, Seamus Martin, had many heroic feats ahead of him, and that his brilliant military career was only beginning. The Irishman nodded, grinning, as at that moment he truly believed in those predictions. That grin remained on his face, as he was leading a team of troops to the spring. Every once in a while he would stop and look over his shoulder, surveying the line of gaunt sunburned faces, listening to the dull jingling of the half-empty canteens.

Wynfield followed through with his intention of visiting the sick on the beach. As he had anticipated, many of them were dead by the time he reached them. He could distinguish the living from the dead by the fact that the living were stirring and reaching out to him. When they saw him walking along the beach with a barrel of water, they began raising on their elbows and groaning. He held the opening of the barrel above their open mouths. From where he was standing, he could see down their parched inflamed throats.

The same night General Airey sent a note to Lord Lucan, who was still on the *Simla*, waiting for the sea to calm down sufficiently.

Your Lordship, I beg you to disembark promptly, as your valiant aide-de-camps are about to take over the command of the army. At this rate, we soon shall be a hair away from a mutiny.

When Lucan learned the details of the incident, he stretched like a lion and roared:

"Ah, my aquatic Prometheus!"

Finally, the situation was beginning to look up. His aides, his swift boys killed several birds with one stone. First, they became known as heroes, which was an instant reflection on their immediate superior, and second, they peeved General Airey. The fact that next to their names was the name of an Irish-born infantry soldier made the triumph all the sweeter. Airey had failed to procure water for the army. It took two young officers and a village idiot to save the day.

Chapter 3
March of the Sixty Thousand Ants

Lucan's pleasure doubled, when Cardigan botched yet another reconnaissance. Raglan sent him into the interior, having equipped him with two hundred and fifty cavalrymen and just as many infantry soldiers. When Cardigan returned, only half of his men were still with him. The rest of them had collapsed along the way of dysentery. The condition of the horses was ever more dismal than that of men. The expedition was an undeniable setback for the campaign but a personal triumph for Lucan. His precious boys maintained their status as unsurpassed heroes, to whom the troops owed their lives. The only water resource available to the army was the one that Lucan's aides had discovered.

Airey did not want his men to grow bored. Since there were no definite plans to march, and Cardigan's expedition did not lead to any valuable findings regarding the position of the enemy, there was nothing for the men to do other than carry the supplies to and fro between the transports and the beach. At least they were allowed to fetch and set up their tents. This permission received a mixed response. Being allowed to set up a semblance of a camp on the beach meant that the stay was going to last a while. Between the 16th and the 17th more than fifteen hundred men fell ill and had to be sent to sick transports. That probably was the record of cholera casualties in twenty-four hours.

Those who had miraculously managed to preserve their stomachs from the epidemic were busy putting up the tents and tearing them down. At last, Lord Raglan took pity on them and declared that they would march no matter what. There was no sense in waiting any further. Having a high concentration of corpses in one place was toxic to the morale of the survivors. It would be better to scatter them along the road. Thus the casualties will not look quite so devastating.

That was the rationale behind Ragland's orders to march. He did not know exactly in which direction the army would march, but he knew that they could not spend another night on that beach at Calamita Bay. The French were already skipping impatiently, blowing their trumpets, and pestering the English commanders with questions as to what was causing the delay.

On the morning of September 19th the Allies, their numbers totaling sixty thousand, finally left the bay, with colors flying and drums rolling. From a distance, the spectacle was surprisingly magnificent. Those who could not see a trail of bodies that the two armies were leaving behind could easily let out a gasp of reverence.

Once again, Wynfield was given a brief glimpse of glamour and glory that made him forget temporarily about the beach at Calamita Bay. He was riding on the left flank with the 17th Lancers under Lord Lucan. Lord Bingham and Dr. Ferrars were following with the 8th Hussars. The tacit agreement was not to make fuss over those comrades who were falling off their horses. The procession was to continue. The orphaned horses were to be seized by the reigns by the nearest rider and pulled along as if nothing had happened. As for the infantry, their deaths were not even to be acknowledged.

Wynfield was only hoping that his new friend Seamus Martin was not among the fallen ones, for he had grown attached to the Irish simpleton. This temporary separation from his friends gave Wynfield an opportunity to remember his fiancée at Laleham Park, the impetuous and childlike Lavinia, whose features, he was ashamed to admit, were growing blurrier in his head by the day. He should have at least brought a photo portrait of her. Of course, a piece of glossy paper would not survive in these conditions. Thus Wynfield had to rely exclusively on his memory, his treacherous memory that had a nasty tendency to embellish and distort the events. For instance, did that gruesome incident with the Balkan girl truly happen? What wouldn't he give to make it a bad dream, a fever-induced hallucination! No, it did happen. Elisaveta sneaked into his room with a basket of strawberries, and he bedded her repeatedly. The pleasure was immense. He would have continued bedding her, had her own compatriots not murdered her. Such stories were not for Lavinia's tender ears, and confessing right before the wedding would not ease his conscience. Perhaps, after thirty years of marriage, once their love had been tested in every way imaginable, he could finally relate the tale of the Balkan Slaughter to her. The time for confessions of this sort had not come yet. Was it too much to ask of an officer's wife to exercise tolerance and understanding?

Wynfield would like to imagine that his future heroic deeds on the battlefield would atone for his indiscretions between the sheets. He was also praying that in the future Lord Lucan would refrain from tempting him with such presents. Hopefully, with all the fighting that was coming, his Lordship would not have the time to coordinate such diversions for himself and his aides. At any rate, Wynfield's next birthday was not for another nine months, so he did not need to worry about extravagant gifts from his future father-in-law until the June of 1855. By then he would be home in England, preparing for his wedding or perhaps even married already. Where would they reside? Would Lavinia find his London property adequate, or would she long for the brooks of Laleham Park?

As Wynfield repeated his fiancée's name several times in his mind, the outline of her face became clearer. He felt her swift fingers on his forehead, heard her voice narrating the history of the Bingham estate.

When Wynfield descended back to earth, he noticed that the bands had stopped playing. Someone must have ordered the musicians to conserve their strength. Playing martial tunes seemed like mockery. Above him stretched the capricious Crimean sky—its color happened to be turquoise that particular day. To the right of him lay the sea, just as fickle and treacherous as the sky. The space between the two elements was filled with the singing of larks and the moaning of troops.

There was no sign of enemy thus far, no sign of any warm-blooded life for that matter, save for an occasional bird or hare.

"Water! Water!" begged the soldiers, leaning against the sides of artillery carts and eventually dropping to their knees.

To keep himself from fainting, Wynfield visualized the stream that he discovered a few days earlier. It was only that image that helped him stay in the saddle.

"I fear I shall never be able to enjoy the sound of a lark singing," Lord Bingham complained to Dr. Ferrars. "It is a dreadful sound. If I ever return to Laleham, I will have all the larks shot and their nests demolished. Oh, Richard... How will I get that hellish twittering from my head?"

Dr. Ferrars listened to the heir's whining with great interest. It was more than whining—it was valuable insight confirming his theory concerning sensory associations. He had heard from his Cambridge colleagues that smells and sounds had the power to invoke the memories connected with them. In extreme cases, when a memory was particularly unpleasant, the affected individual could easily succumb to panic and even belligerence. Dr. Ferrars had seen such behavior inside lunatic asylums, and he was hoping sincerely that this fate would not befall the impressionable, sensitive young heir. From now on, whenever Lord Bingham would hear a lark sing, he would also feel a wave of heat engulfing his body, regardless of what the temperature of the air happened to be. His throat would dry up, and perspiration would appear on his forehead, as he would imagine himself back on the blistering Crimean plain.

Chapter 4
Lord Lucan Acquires a Nickname of His Own

Seeing that the army would not progress much further, Raglan and Airey issued a halt, a decision they immediately regretted. Sitting on a scorching plain did not replenish the men's strength. On the contrary, it made them even drowsier. Convincing them to rise again was going to prove challenging. Having closed their eyes, the soldiers refused to open them again. They would rather be left for dead than progress another mile.

The intervals between halts were getting shorter and shorter. The columns bumped and bled into each other, with cavalry and infantry mixed together.

In the early afternoon, having climbed yet another ridge, the troops suddenly heard a chirping that did not resemble a bird's song. There could be no mistake: the sound was the babbling of a stream. Staring down into the hollow of the oasis, the soldiers hesitated to rejoice, as they did not know whether the water was drinkable. Even if it was brackish, at least they could rinse their sunburned faces. If anything, it was an excuse to make another halt. As they came closer to the stream, they spotted fresh water fish swimming by. That was the moment when all discipline and camaraderie was forgotten. A collective howl shook the army. Trampling over each other, the troops dashed towards the stream. Very quickly, the water became muddy from the sand being kicked up from the bottom by thousands of boots.

Watching the commotion below, Raglan shook his head bitterly and rubbed his inflamed eyes.

"Savages," Airey muttered spitefully. "How little it takes for men to lose their human dignity."

"And nobody is even thinking about the horses," Nolan chimed in indignantly. "Of course, we cannot expect the infantrymen to care about anything other than their own throats, but the cavalrymen? They have all but forgotten about their chargers!"

"Lord Raglan, I would not let the halt last too long," Airey advised to the Commander-in-Chief. "The troops will spend the rest of the day splashing in the stream if you allow them."

Raglan did not say a word in response to the advice. He merely raised his single hand, letting Airey know that he was still in command. He was suffering from an epic headache.

In the meantime, the men continued to crowd along the edge of the stream, hoping to fill their canteens before the water became too muddy. Gradually, as their bodies were cooling, the fierce shoves began turning to fraternal hugs. They began joking, prancing, and singing. Watching their frantic antics, listening to their hysterical laughter, one could imagine that there was alcohol in the stream.

A sudden volley interrupted the blissful water-worshipping ritual. The troops dropped their canteens and glanced up the ridge. At last—an engagement!

Having forgotten about his headache, Raglan rode to the top of the ridge above the stream and saw a handful of Cossacks, who withdrew instantly.

The Commander-in-Chief then dispatched Cardigan with several cavalry squadrons to scout out the position and the numbers of the enemy. The heat must have caused Raglan to forget that every other reconnaissance expedition led by Cardigan had failed. Fortunately, Lucan happened to be nearby, positioned with the 17th Lancers. He would not let his brother-in-law go unescorted this time. Glowing with malice, he rode towards Cardigan, instantly establishing his superiority, took command of the four squadrons dispatched by Raglan and began lining them up. Before themselves they saw about two thousand Russian cavalrymen.

"Is this all?" Lucan asked himself, smirking. "Is this what the noise is all about?"

Having forgotten their animosity for a second, the two in-laws exchanged fiery nods, anticipating an easy victory.

At the same time, on the opposite end of the ridge, Raglan and Airey were both turning pale; for they could see what no other British soldier could see.

On the plateau a colossal army was forming—countless regiments of infantry, several batteries of artillery and Cossack regiments.

Suddenly, Raglan's only goal was to return the four cavalry regiments unharmed. A major engagement needed to be avoided at all costs, as the British troops in their miserable state simply could not withstand one, not against seventy thousand Russians. As much as the thought of retreating infuriated Raglan, he had no choice but to send Airey to deliver the orders. Finding the word "retreat" distasteful, he substituted it for "extricate."

Having reached the four squadrons, Airey felt that he was intruding on a tender scene of family drama. Lucan was waving his arms and screaming at his brother-in-law, chastising him for the improper distribution of troops, while Cardigan was staring to the sky and whistling, demonstrative in his defiance. Each one was aiming to make the other look like a fool before the soldiers—Lucan with his insults and Cardigan with his lack of reaction to those insults.

To paraphrase Lord Paget, they had been like two blades of the scissors that snipped without harming one another but destroying everyone and everything that would get in between them. This time General Airey was to play the role of the unfortunate casualty of their war. When they heard the Commander-in-Chief's orders, they both darted forward, as if preparing to trample the messenger. Airey, recognizing his solemn role as Raglan's mouthpiece, did not flinch. Continuing to look past the two in-laws, he repeated the words of the orders.

Two minutes later the four British squadrons were riding back, followed by a volley of jeers from the Russians.

Lord Bingham, having made way through the lines of the 8th Hussars, found Wynfield.

"Jerry, what is all this?" he inquired in a fervent whisper. "I simply don't understand. What has just happened there?"

"What has *not* happened? That would be a more appropriate question, Georgie," Wynfield replied. "I suppose, we'll have to wait for Lord Lucan to deliver the explanation."

When the earl rejoined the 17th Lancers, his men recoiled silently, making way for him. It seemed that Lord Lucan's eyes would blind anyone who would dare to look into them. It was not until the nightfall that the troops learned about the reasons for recalling the engagement; but by then the earl had already been christened Lord Look-On. The nickname stuck with him, just like Noble Yachtsman stuck with Cardigan.

"What shall happen next?" Lord Bingham kept questioning Wynfield, as they were lying on the grass that night. "My poor Papa... Such undeserved humiliation! To be sent forth only to be called back a minute later?"

Lord Bingham appeared to have forgotten that his father had volunteered to lead the four squadrons. Cardigan was the one who had originally been entrusted with the task. Lucan left the 17th Lancers only to trample over his brother-in-law. Had he stayed with his regiment, the shame would have fallen on Cardigan.

The British were bivouacking along the edge of the Bulganek stream, sipping rum, tossing twigs, and dry grass into campfires, waiting for the Russians to strike. Six miles away, above the river Alma, the enemy was jeering.

"I know exactly what they are doing," Lord Bingham continued. "They have allowed us to enter the country. They wanted to lure us as far away from our fleet as possible. Then they will surely strike! Jerry, are you listening to me?"

"Of course, I'm listening, Georgie," Wynfield replied. "And I agree with every word. Perhaps, you should trade places with Lord Raglan."

"Well, perhaps I should!" the young heir shouted, raising his fist to the sky. "Oh, Jerry, my darling brother Jerry... In an ideal world, Papa would be in command, and we would be slaying Russians by now."

"Have patience, Georgie," Wynfield murmured, turning his back to Lord Bingham. "Fate is teasing us on purpose, to increase our eagerness to fight. Have you ever been teased by a woman? Fate is a woman, I'm convinced."

Chapter 5
A Feast of Burned Hare Meat and Toxic Fungus

Suddenly, in front of his nose he saw a pair of boots and heard a familiar voice:

"Good evenin', Lord Hung'ton."

Seamus Martin was standing over him, smiling his hearty juvenile smile, holding a freshly slaughtered hare by the ears.

Wynfield's drowsiness suddenly evaporated. He sat up on his blanket and touched the hare's belly. It was still warm.

"Seamus, what on earth..."

"I trapped 'im wi' me coat," the Irishman boasted. "And then I beat 'im on the head wi' a rock. Back home, I use to kill 'em by strikin' 'em wi' hammer right 'tween their eyes. There's a secret trick to it, yer see. I thought ye Lord Hung'ton grew weary of them salted pork 'n biscuits. So I brought 'im wee bunny-hare fer yer 'n Lord Bingham."

"Seamus, I'm positively speechless," the young heir muttered. "You didn't need to go through all this trouble."

The Irishman then reached into his pocket and pulled out a handful of wild mushrooms.

"Nay! I jus' thank to meself that any supper can be our last supper—no blasphemy intended—so I better share it wi' me mates. Fer we be mates, ain't we be?"

Wynfield and Lord Bingham nodded simultaneously, even

though they did not understand half of what the naïve infantry-man was saying.

"Come, I'll shows yer how I cooks 'im o'er the fire. I bet yer ne'er seen nothin' of this sort in yer lives."

Humming an Irish tune, Private Martin took a penknife from his pocket and began skinning the hare before his two bedazzled spectators. One could tell that he had performed that ritual count-less times. He could have done it in complete darkness. He knew just where to make the incisions, how to remove the pelt without harming it.

"Them hare pelts make fer a fine pillow," he remarked with a wink.

Having removed the meat from the bones, he chopped it into cubes and stuck them on skewers, alternating with mushrooms.

"Seamus, are you certain those mushrooms aren't poisonous?" Lord Bingham asked him timidly.

"Certain as me Ma's name be Cathleen Callahan. I knows how to tell 'em mushroom 'part. We had the same sort growin' in Cas-tlebar. They'd be the only thin' I'd eat when the soil stop givin' po-tatoes, when all 'em spuds rotted in one night. Them mushrooms kept me 'alive. I tell yer, a day come when there be nothin' you won't put in yer mouth."

Private Martin kept on ranting nonchalantly, sharing recipes for preparing wild mushrooms over the fire, periodically lapsing into his song, but Wynfield was not listening to the Irishman. His attention was focused on Lord Bingham, who suddenly started trembling and bit on the sleeve of his coat.

Wynfield gave his friend a little nudge.

"Georgie, what's wrong?" he asked when the infantryman turned to place the skewers over the coals.

"Nothing, Jerry."

"You don't expect me to believe it, do you? Something is trou-bling you, and I suspect it is not the smell of burned hare meat."

Lord Bingham blinked, as if trying to chase tears back under his eyelids.

"I'll tell you later Jerry."

"All right then, suit yourself," Wynfield replied with a shrug and began fixing his blanket, but Lord Bingham did not let him get too comfortable.

"No, Jerry, I'll tell you now," he whispered, squeezing his hand. "What the hell! This fellow, Seamus Martin... I never thought I'd come face to face with one of my father's tenants."

"What in the world are you talking about?" Wynfield asked, jerking his hand out of Lord Bingham's grip. "You are suffering from a mild heat stroke."

"What I'm suffering from is remorse," the heir continued whispering. "You know what happened in Castlebar six years ago, don't you?"

"Georgie, I don't even know where Castlebar is."

"That's where my father's Irish estate is, you fool! That's where we all were born, including my sister. Castlebar, County Mayo, on the West coast of Ireland? I don't have a map with me to show you. By God, Jerry, do you know anything about geography or history?"

"Why, thank you for bringing up my ignorance, Georgie. Given your vulnerable state, I shall not punch you for your insolence. Please, continue."

"I don't know the details," Lord Bingham continued, his hands moving frantically under the blanket. "Papa never initiated us into the matters of his estate. I only heard that when the crops failed in '48, Papa began issuing eviction notices to his tenants. They were unable to pay rent. One way or another, he acquired this monstrous reputation, even though is actions were not different from those of other landlords. He simply had no choice. The land could not support those people, so the people had to go. Knowing my father, his general compassion, however understated, towards his fellow men, I can vouch that he suffered greatly while issuing those eviction notices. He was not by any means taking his situation lightly. In a way, he was doing his tenants a favor. He was chasing them from a barren land. If not for him, they would have wasted more of their years there. He gave them an incentive to try their luck elsewhere. Some went to England, some—to the Americas. At any rate, he was not the heartless monster that everyone depicted. Certainly, it was a national tragedy, but my father did not cause it. If there's anything to blame, it would be Mr. O'Malley, his agent. He was the one responsible for overseeing the welfare of the tenants. My father could not possibly provide for forty thousand people on his own. I don't know if I can reiterate it enough."

"You don't need to keep persuading me of that, Georgie. You know well what opinion I hold of your father. What does this have to do with Seamus Martin?"

"Everything! It has everything to do with Seamus Martin. Don't you understand? He was one of the tenants that my father evicted. Now, looking back at my summers at Castlebar, I think I vaguely remember his family. His mother was a washerwoman. He had two brothers and three sisters, and all perished during the winter of '48. Only he and his mother had survived. Oh, God..."

Lord Bingham arched his neck, as if he were experiencing excruciating physical pain, blinked and began sobbing. Wynfield moved a few inches away from him.

"Georgie, do not fall victim to your own imagination," he said. "There are so many men bearing the same name, since it is so common. Seamus Martin! There must be at least ten of them in the infantry."

"No, Jerry, I remember his face. It's all coming back to me now, yes. I thought he looked familiar. He hates my father; he probably hates me too, and I cannot blame him for it. What if he kills me in my sleep?"

"Then don't sleep at all, Georgie," Wynfield curtailed him. "Stay awake all night, sobbing and shaking."

At that moment, the Irishman returned, carrying three steaming skewers.

"Here's our feast, gents," he said, fishing for praise.

He blew on the skewers and handed one to Wynfield. Then his gaze fell on Lord Bingham, who was still lying with his chin tilted up towards the night sky. "What's the matter? Why yer weepin'?"

"He feels sad over the death of the little hare," Wynfield explained. "Our darling Georgie is quite sentimental when it comes to small animals. Please, do not tell anyone. It's a secret."

"Ah, I sees!" the Irishman gasped and beamed again. "No worries, I won't tell a bloody soul. I s'pose, that leaves more food fer us, Lord Hung'ton."

The hare meat, though not particularly plentiful, turned out to be surprisingly tender. The wild mushrooms gave it a pleasant flavor. Wynfield ended up licking the skewers and his fingers—an act that was deliciously disgusting. Afterwards, he washed down the feast with what was left of his rum.

"Thank you, Seamus," he resumed, patting the chef on the shoulder. "After such a meal, I am ready to go to sleep."

"So am I, Lord Hung'ton," the Irishman replied cheerfully.

He had no intention of retreating back to the infantry unit that night. Having rolled the hare pelt into a tiny pillow, he wedged himself between his two new friends.

"Ah, that's the life..." he sighed sweetly. "What else can a soldier wish for?"

Chapter 6
Characteristic Insanity

On September 20th, a party of thirty young gentlewomen from Sebastopol descended upon the heights overlooking the Alma River. Arrayed in festive floral dresses, equipped with parasols, they resembled a flock of hummingbirds. The purpose of their expedition was to witness, over a leisurely lunch consisting of seasonal fruit and wine, a glorious spectacle akin to that of gladiator fights. Prince Menschikoff himself had invited them to watch the destruction of the Allies.

The sixty-seven year old nobleman with an impressive Russo-Finnish genealogy had been a friend of both Emperor Alexander I and later with his successor, Nicholas I, who in 1853 had appointed him commander-in-chief on sea and land. With his smooth skin, angular features, and a generous white mustache, Menschikoff looked like an older Slavic version of his English enemy the Earl of Lucan. The resemblance was only physical. Their tempers were complete opposites of each other. Menschikoff was methodical, diplomatic, and ceremonious. Those virtues endeared him to the Emperor in the first place. His skills as a military leader were questionable. Having proven himself as a fairly effectual officer in the army, from which he had retired thirty years prior to the Crimean conflict, he proved to be bad influence on the Russian navy, delaying its technological progress. Menschikoff's blunders did not diminish him in the eyes of the Emperor, who believed that good looks, eloquence, and stellar manners were the most valuable traits for a military commander.

Thus, in late September in 1854, the aging prince found himself on the heights, surrounded by thirty young beauties. That alone made it worth embarking on the campaign. Menschikoff took pleasure in communicating to his charming companions the technicalities of the upcoming engagement. He had to soften and simplify the dry military jargon for their delicate ears. He explained that the hills rising above the Alma made for a perfect fortress engineered by nature. On the lower slopes called the Kourgane Hill, there was a battery with twelve heavy guns called the "Great Redoubt." Above it towered another earthwork with lighter guns—the "Lesser Redoubt." Nature and advanced Russian technology had united to fortify the vicinity of Sebastopol. There was no chance of the Allies winning or even overcoming the obstacle course ahead of them. The British would have to descend the slopes towards the river, then cross it and continue advancing uphill, being under heavy fire all the while.

Suddenly, Menschikoff became aware that somewhere along his narration he had lost the attention of his listeners. Their sparking eyes of blue and gray were no longer fixed upon him. It came as somewhat of a shock to the prince.

When the enraptured girls began twittering about the handsome British infantrymen in their scarlet coats, Menschikoff began frowning and huffing, feeling pangs of geriatric jealousy, which made him even more determined to destroy the enemy.

This sort of angry determination only made him careless. He had been so preoccupied with eyeing out the British on top of the grassy slopes that he had completely neglected to fortify the area on his extreme left where the Alma ran into the sea. It was that blind spot that the French Light Infantry used to ascend a steep path.

Seized by panic and humiliation, Menschikoff galloped frantically on top of the cliffs. Luckily for him, the French infantry failed to advance since they did not receive support from the artillery.

In the early afternoon, an agitated French officer ran to Raglan, begging for support from the British. The crude intrusion irritated the Commander-in-Chief, who had been perfectly content ridging in front of his troops for the past hour and a half, teasing the enemy with the opulent white plumage on his hat.

Realizing that the French officer would not go away without having his plea answered in one form or another, Raglan gave the orders for the infantry to advance. The men jumped up with a collective howl of cheer and formed a line two miles wide and two men deep. As soon as they reached the edge of the river, a cloud of smoke enveloped them. Thinking that artillery fire was not enough to stop the British, the Russians piled up dry brushwood and set it on fire on the slopes before the Great Redoubt.

Losing formatting, tripping over the bodies of the comrades brought down by the rifle bullets, and swearing fiercely, the British continued to advance. Suddenly, to their astonishment they discovered that the Russians were retreating, pulling their guns away from the Great Redoubt. As it turned out later, the Emperor's troops were motivated by a bizarre principle that no piece of the artillery should fall into the enemy's hands. They would rather retreat than have one of their sacred guns captured. That was an explicit order from Nicholas I himself to Prince Menschikoff.

With yet another deafening howl, the mixed British battalions leaped into the earthwork of the Great Redoubt, but only to be forced out again a few minutes later, as the Russians kept bombarding them from above, and the reinforcements had not yet crossed the river. Very quickly, the Great Redoubt turned into a mass grave for the British.

Amazingly enough, the sight of the bloody soup did not shake the composure of the troops. Having crossed the river, the reinforcements consisting of the Scots Fusilier Guards, the Highlanders and the Coldstreamers marched on without altering their pace, as if they were taking part in a review.

Watching his men fall, Sir Colin Campbell declared:

"It is better that every man in Her Majesty's Guard should lie dead upon the field than they should turn their backs on the enemy."

In the meantime, on the extreme left, Lord Lucan was suffering excruciating tortures, once again waiting for the orders that would not come. The plan of engagement had been discussed animatedly, and the Light Brigade was poised against the four thousand Russian adversaries who were expected to attack any moment. However, Menschikoff pulled back his cavalry, leaving his men—and Lucan's—fuming. The cruelty of that order could be compared to pulling bread from a hungry man's mouth.

The British Cavalry had nothing left to do but observe the storm of the Great Redoubt. Perspiring profusely under his uniform, Lucan sat idly in his saddle, as messages laden with fury and desperation poured in from the officers. They were behaving like needy children, yanking their father by the trousers. His brother-in-law was making use of very strong expressions.

Even Lord Bingham, known for his sweet temper, was succumbing to the bout of universal fury.

"Is there no way to silence their whining?" he asked Wynfield in an agitated whisper when yet another note was delivered.

"I don't know Georgie. Perhaps, that is their way of releasing anguish."

"Jerry, I cannot bear to watch them pester my father like that," the heir continued lamenting to his friend. I've heard those bastards call him a coward. Imagine that? My father—a coward! While he's the one who's yearning to charge... The principal coward here is Raglan. Yes, I uttered those words. God forgive me. We are here because he has not given us any orders. Perhaps, he forgot that he has a cavalry. If the consequences of his command are disastrous, let it rest on his conscience and his reputation. Jerry, do you hear me? I cannot bear to watch my father being turned into a scapegoat."

"Hush, Georgie..."

Wynfield locked his fingers around Lord Bingham's forearm. The young heir felt the pain of the grip even through the fabric of his coat.

"You're sounding just like them," Wynfield said. "Your father will not be turned into a scapegoat. Not today. Look—"

Lord Bingham glanced in the direction in which Wynfield was pointing and saw his father riding towards the river. The horse artillery was following him.

"Dear God!" the heir gasped. "What in the world is he doing?"

"Taking matters into his own hands, I suppose," Wynfield replied.

No longer able to bear the torture of inactivity, the earl began ascending the slopes on the far left to protect the Highland Brigade. He acted on his own accord, since it became clear that orders from the Commander-in-Chief would not come any time soon. As for Raglan, he had left his troops and ascended to a spot from where he could have a better view of the battle, still tantalizing the enemy with his plumed hat. The Russians saw him in plain view bout could not believe that he was actually alone.

A sudden attack of filial adoration caused Lord Bingham to hyperventilate.

"This is my Papa," he whispered, beaming through tears. "I wouldn't expect any less of him. Come, Jerry! Let's follow him."

Wynfield attempted to reason with him.

"In all fairness, George, he did not order us to follow. This is our first battle. Don't you think it's a bit early for novices like us to break the rules?"

"To hell with the rules!" the heir exclaimed. "We are his aides, and we are his family!"

He spurred his horse and galloped towards the river, not caring whether his future brother-in-law was following him or not.

God, I hope Georgie and I do not turn into Lucan and Cardigan, Wynfield thought. *Who can promise us that history will not repeat itself?*

He did not give into Lord Bingham's provocation and chose to remain with the 17th Lancers. From their position, they could observe in amazement the progress of the battle across the river. Something unfathomable was happening. The meager string of Highlanders encircled the massive Russian infantry, firing inward at the tightly packed columns. The enemy began losing formation, scattering, and finally retreating across the hills. Once again, the British were inside the Great Redoubt, having recaptured it, this time permanently.

By the time Lord Lucan with the horse artillery appeared behind the Highland Brigade, Sir Colin Campbell proposed to chase the enemy. Having trouble accepting the thought that the victory had taken place without his active involvement, Lucan eagerly detached six artillery guns. Granted, that was not the sort of contribution to the battle he had dreamed about, but it was better than waiting on the opposite bank of the river. Just as Lucan was about to open fire on the retreating Russians, General Estcourt brought the instructions from Raglan not to attack on the grounds that the enemy might return and make a stand. The sole task of the cavalry was to escort the artillery guns, with Lucan on the left and Cardigan on the right.

It was not long before the two in-laws broke ahead from the artillery and began rounding up prisoners. Their liberal interpretation of the order compelled Raglan to repeat the instructions. Lucan let the demand slip past his ears: eagerness to fight made him deaf. He and Cardigan resembled two hounds that had been suddenly set loose after weeks of being chained. Aware and to an extent sympathetic of their state of mind, Raglan issued the third order for them to return to their guns, at which both earls began spitting and cursing right in front of their men.

The prisoners were sent loose, and the defeated Russian army was allowed to trickle back into Sebastopol. Raglan did not think it would be prudent or safe to pursue the enemy.

More "strong expressions" were heard in the ranks of the British cavalry that night. Lucan unleashed his fury on General Estcourt, and Nolan—on William Howard Russell, an Irish reporter for *The Times* who had been sent to cover the Crimean campaign. While Nolan was pacing around his tent and ranting, Mr. Russell was scribbling intently in a notepad lifted from a Russian corpse. The Battle of Alma, as the engagement was later recorded in history, was one of the strongest examples of "characteristic insanity" of the war.

Another famous term that Mr. Russell coined was "humane barbarity," referring to the lack of ambulance care for the wounded. Only one in six men had the privilege of being seen by a doctor. Those wounded who did not stir were left for dead. Dr. Ferrars' nightmare of performing amputations in the open air had materialized. Ignoring his commander's explicit prohibition to touch the patients, the physician rolled up his sleeves. Lucan was not in sight at any rate.

Once again, water was in short supply. Raglan had decided that bivouacking directly along the riverbank would be unsafe, lest the enemy should ambush them. The army moved up the waterless heights.

Somewhere amidst the bloody chaos, Dr. Ferrars reunited with Wynfield, who immediately asked him for instructions. He did not get the opportunity to fight that day or even ride his horse. He sensed that if he did not busy his hands with something immediately, his unused energy would come out in the form of curses of which there was no shortage in the air.

"Are you certain that we won this battle?" Dr. Ferrars asked, as they were propping the head of a wounded artilleryman against his comrade's corpse. "It simply doesn't feel like victory to me."

"And how in your opinion does victory feel?" Wynfield asked.

"I don't know," the physician mumbled hesitantly. "I imagined there would be a certain sense of elation."

"Next to a battle lost, there is nothing so dreadful as a battle won," Wynfield replied, quoting the Duke of Wellington. "Now you understand those words? Prepare yourself, my dear Richard. This is as victorious as one can feel. If you want sweet taste in your mouth, you may as well chew on some radishes."

They did not converse much after that philosophical exchange. Not that they could hear each other very clearly with all the moaning and cursing around them.

Suddenly, Wynfield heard a familiar voice behind his back.

"Lord Hung'ton!"

He glanced over his shoulder and saw a bloodied shattered hand protruding from under a mount of dead bodies.

"Seamus!" Wynfield exclaimed, forgetting about the wounded soldier he was helping at the moment.

He leaped to his feet and rushed to pull the Irishman out of the pile of corpses. A few second later, Private Martin's head was resting on his knee.

"Seamus," Wynfield repeated, wrapping the shattered hand of his friend in a dirty rag. In the dark, it was difficult to assess the extent of the injury. He could only see that the tip of the index finger had been blown off completely, and the wrist appeared to be fractured in multiple places. "Thank God you're alive, Seamus."

"They left me fer dead," the Irishman said resentfully.

"Tell me: does anything else hurt? Or is it just your hand?"

Private Martin lifted his head from Wynfield's knee and looked down to examine his body. "No, Lord Hung'ton, nothin' else hurts. Me hand don't hurt either, not any mo'. 'Tis like it's not there. I ain't sufferin' much, 'pon me word."

"You don't need to lie to me, Seamus," Wynfield said.

"I ain't lyin' to yer, Lord Hung'ton. Would I lie to an honest gent like yer? I don't need no pity. When I call yer name, I wasn't seekin' help. I didn't mean to distract yer from work. I'm as good as dead. I just wanted to say yer name one last time."

"Don't talk like that, Seamus. Of course, you'll say my name again, over and over, and I'll say yours. Let me call Dr. Ferrars right this moment. I'll make certain that he sees you next."

The Irishman shook his greasy head. "No, don't bother 'im good doctor. He's got plenty of men in far graver state than me. That lad over there got his ribs shattered."

"And that is precisely why the doctor cannot help him. The doctor's priority is to tend to those who are more likely to survive.

You were lucky this time, Seamus. With a tourniquet and a few stitches, your hand will be almost as good as new."

The Irishman did not sound convinced. He turned his head aside, breaking eye contact with his friend. He took a deep breath that sounded like a sob, and his youthful body turned limp with apathy. "I can't tell if I ev'n killed a single Russian," he whispered, "if I got any braggin' rights 'tall. I be rememb'd fer the water sprin' at Calamita and the roasted hare by Bulganek."

By then the rag around the soldier's injured hand was all saturated with blood. Wynfield remembered that in order to lessen the bleeding the patient had to be in an upright position with his hand elevated above the heart level. Without any offering any more verbal consolations to Private Martin, Wynfield began trying to lift him from the ground. The Irishman proved to be heavier than he looked. He refused to cooperate not so much because he lacked the physical strength but because he lacked the will. Still, Wynfield refused to give up. He became deaf to the moans of others wounded soldiers, who kept calling out his name and reaching out for him. At that moment, his sole purpose was to get Private Martin off the ground, slow down his bleeding and have someone else deliver him to the next sick transport.

Suddenly, Wynfield heard an exaggeratedly ceremonious cough. Lord Bingham was standing before him. "Lord Hungerton," the heir began with uncharacteristic formality, "the Lieutenant-General, the Earl of Lucan, requests your immediate arrival."

"Tell his Lordship that I shall be there shortly," Wynfield replied. "Give me another half hour. I need to deliver Mr. Martin into reliable hands."

Lord Bingham pushed his fists into his hips and let his jaw hang. "Well, my dear Lord Hungerton, forgive me for interrupting your philanthropic endeavor," he said. "When your commander said he wished to see you immediately, he did not mean in half hour. The rest of the aide-de-camps have already gathered. Everyone is waiting for you."

"Then it appears that his Lordship is already well-staffed. Don't let my absence interfere with the meeting."

Lord Bingham exhaled and dropped his arms, abandoning the artificial formality and lapsing into overt rage. "Ah, listen to yourself, Jerry! Now you take liberties with the orders! Unless my memory betrays me, earlier on today you refused to follow my father on the grounds that he had not received any explicit orders from Lord Raglan. Five hours ago you were a gem of subordination! You would not defy Raglan, yet you have no trouble defying your immediate commander. You would rather move mangled corpses than be by my father's side, especially now, when he needs you the most!"

At that moment, Private Martin squeezed Wynfield's shoulder with his unharmed hand. "Lord Hung'ton, you better go. I'll make me own way to them transports."

"Are you certain, Seamus?" Wynfield asked, helping him ease into a genuflecting position.

The Irishman nodded compliantly, having established balance on the ground. "Promise you, Lord Hung'ton. I won't be left fer dead. I'll go to the barracks and follow doctor's orders. And yer follow yer orders. Go."

This exchange doubled Lord Bingham's indignation.

"Ah!" he shrieked, squeezing his temples and distorting his features. "So you take orders from an Irishman? You brush off my father's demands. You need permission from some illiterate simpleton to obey your commander? Listen to yourself! Do you suspect of the magnitude of your audacity? You don't deserve to serve my father. And you don't deserve to marry my sister, you whoring, promiscuous bastard!"

Wynfield did not grace his future brother-in-law with a response. It was official. The fraternal idyll was souring. Their days of sleeping back to back were coming to and end. Wynfield had pondered that possibility, but he had not imagined this would happen so soon and so abruptly. Over the past few months he and Lord Bingham had grown suspiciously, unnaturally close. Impetuous friendship has a tendency to turn to impetuous animosity, especially for such openhearted individuals as Georgie was.

When Wynfield entered Lucan's tent a few minutes later, he could not help noticing that the other aide-de-camps regarded him with a sort of tentative sympathy. They were in no position to brand him a traitor or a coward, regardless of what Lord Bingham may have told them, since they had also remained on the spot with the 17th Lancers as the earl was crossing the river.

To his considerable relief, Wynfield discovered that his commander was not angry with him. Wynfield had fully prepared himself to be devoured and regurgitated in front of his comrades, but Lucan did nothing of the sort. The earl greeted his wanton aide with a casual nod. "Thank you for coming, Lord Hungerton. Please take a seat."

Wynfield grabbed a portable fabric chair and pulled up to the table. The earl's surprisingly calm demeanor proved that the perceived betrayal happened in Lord Bingham's mind only. The heir's indignation was of deeply subjective filial nature. He felt an instinctive need to protect his dear Papa. Since he could not sink his teeth into the rest of the aides—he did not share the same familiarity with them—he unleashed his anger on Wynfield. Perhaps, not all had been lost, and the two of them could still be friends after all.

That night not a word was uttered about the events of the past day. No more curses, no more insults were dropped. The earl took out a map of the Crimea and showed to his aides the loose itinerary. The plan was to march to Balaclava, a resort village frequented by the Sebastopol elite. It would serve as the military base for the British. It was a port, so the troops would not be cut off from the fleet, which was their only source of supplies and ammunition. The landlocked harbor was only half a mile long and too small to serve as a port for an army, but it was conveniently located. In addition, the troops would have access to the lush vineyards, vegetable gardens, and orchards. September was a perfect month for invading such a place. They would be able to feast on peaches, apricots, apples, and Muscatel grapes. Who knows? Perhaps, compulsive consumption of fruits and vegetables would help reverse the first signs of scurvy in the troops.

After the staff meeting was adjourned, Lord Bingham approached Wynfield outside Lucan's tent.

"Jerry," he began with tears in his eyes. "I'm positively mortified by the things I've said to you tonight. It wasn't me speaking."

"I honestly don't know what you are talking about," Wynfield replied. "I didn't hear a thing. All those soldiers moaning and carts rattling..."

Lord Bingham laughed nervously and then threw himself on Wynfield's neck. "Jerry, you're astounding," he muttered, choking. "I've never had a friend like you. If we were to have a falling out, I don't think I could bear it. To tell you the truth, I was growing a bit jealous of Private Martin. You seemed to understand his babbling, and I didn't. I couldn't help feeling left out. It must sound ridiculous to you..."

"You need not worry about Private Martin," Wynfield comforted him. "His fighting days are over. He's going home a cripple—with a modest compensation."

"But why, Jerry?" The heir looked perplexed. "I thought his hand was salvageable."

"That's what I told him to convince him to go on a sick ship. Georgie, I've seen his hand. It's shattered. There's not a whole bone in it. Still, I didn't want him to be left for dead. I wanted him to reach the hospital. The service there is slightly better—so I hear—and they have some anesthetics. I didn't want him to endure an amputation under the stars. Still, amputate they must, unless a miracle happens, and his bones magically reassemble themselves."

"Poor Seamus," Lord Bingham whispered, covering his mouth. "Now I feel guilty for not having bid him a proper goodbye. He did help us find the spring."

"Don't feel too sad for him, Georgie. Our Irish friend is not doomed, not completely. He can still perform basic work with his right hand. I've seen factory workers who lost their hands inside machines."

The last sentence made Lord Bingham frown. "Did you just say you've seen factory workers?"

"Yes, I have—with fingers and hands missing."

"Where would you have seen them?"

"In a previous life, I suppose." Wynfield sighed and sat down on the scorched grass. Lord Bingham joined him. "Every now and then an image arises in my head, an image so vivid, so detailed that it can only be an actual memory. Sometimes I see a giant bear charging at me, tearing up my face with its claws, and a little girl with the eyes of a wolf sharpening knives in the corner."

Lord Bingham glanced at his companion with a mixture of terror, amusement, and decadent curiosity. "Oh, Jerry, you mad jokester! Whatever drugs you take before bedtime I wish to sample them!"

Chapter 7
How Long Does It Take to Trample Down a Paradise?

On September 26th close to thirty thousand British soldiers marched into the village of Balaclava. Imagine an army of demons storming Eden. The troops spared nothing in their path. The vegetables in the gardens were trampled down and mixed with the soil. The fences and the barns were destroyed. The aroma of roses, honeysuckle, and plums was quickly overpowered by the stench of gunpowder and filthy ailing bodies.

The water in the crowded harbor became littered with refuse from the British ships.

Lord Raglan, who was observing the invasion from the shore, smiled approvingly when he saw his man-of-war the *Agamemnon* pull in. The Commander-in-Chief would have preferred for his men to behave in a less boorish manner. Much of the damage they had caused while making their way into the village was completely unnecessary. They did not need to smash the windows or drag down the grapevines. Those acts were not of mere carelessness but of deliberate vandalism. Now Russian civilians would remember the British as filthy, clumsy brutes. The same girls who were admiring the dashing infantrymen from a distance would now recoil from them in disgust. Still, Raglan had no intention of chastising his men for their lack of gallantry, as he had graver matters to attend.

In the interval between the Battle of Alma and the invasion of Balaclava, the conflict between Lucan and Cardigan had gotten worse, if such a thing was possible. Their beloved game of denouncing one another through letters to Raglan had resumed with a doubled passion. Cardigan had not given up his dream of separate command. He believed that if he pestered Raglan often enough, the Commander-in-Chief would eventually give in and release him from Lucan's yoke. Since his wishes were not being fulfilled, Cardigan continued to invent new ways to aggravate his enemy—and the rest of the cavalry. Everyone let out a sigh of relief when Cardigan was taken ill on board of the *Southern Star* in early October. Sadly, his illness did not last long enough. A week later, he returned back to the shore and began sticking his tongue out at Lucan.

Exhausted by the farcical spectacle, Raglan decided that the two spoiled children needed to be separated, if only to preserve the remains of dignity in the cavalry ranks. Cardigan was sent up the heights with the 11th Hussars and the 17th Lancers to form another camp. The thought of the cavalry being truncated left the men indignant—but then, it would not be the first time they were left indignant.

In mid-October, a gorgeous vessel entered the harbor. It was Cardigan's luxury yacht the Dryad, delivered from England by his dear friend Mr. Hubert de Burgh.

"My poor James!" de Burgh exclaimed, having pulled aside the curtain of Cardigan's tent. "How distressing it is to see a gentleman of your statue dining on some muddy soup in a jar and salt pork, rinsing it down with Varna brandy! This outrageous arrangement must be remedied at once."

That was the last night that Cardigan spent in his tent. From then on he would dine and sleep aboard his yacht, even though the distance from the harbor to the camp was several miles. Every morning he would travel to see the Light Brigade.

By then, the cavalry's ability to grow indignant with their commander's antics had been exhausted. The outrage was officially dead. Nothing that the Noble Yachtsman did could surprise them. The only thing that surprised them still was Raglan's tolerance of Cardigan's behavior. The Commander-in-Chief saw nothing criminal in Cardigan's desire to escape the discomforts and deprivations of the camp. If he had the means to enjoy meals prepared by his French cook, soak in a porcelain bath and sleep in a feather bed, who could forbid him? There was no official law obliging the commanders to share the sufferings of their men. After all, was that not the whole principle of hierarchy?

In the meantime, at the main camp, an unexpected friendship was kindling between Lord Lucan and Sir Colin Campbell, a hero of a dozen campaigns with over forty years of service. Even Lucan, with all his innate conceit, could not help removing his hat before this exceptional soldier, who had served in China, the West Indies and India but, because of his humble origin and lack of connections, had lingered in the ranks of a colonel, while his more privileged comrades kept getting promoted over his head. For an instant, Lucan abandoned his righteous self-pity and flung the gates to his dangerously underused heart wide open before his Scottish-born comrade. This friendship also had a collateral benefit—an injury to Cardigan's self-esteem. It pained the Noble Yachtsman to see his enemy on such good terms with a man like Sir Colin. Lucan showered Sir Colin with compliments in public, while Cardigan, in return made a spectacle of his friendship with Mr. de Burgh.

My best friend is better than yours, the two in-laws appeared to be saying to each other.

Chapter 8
There Is No God but You

One of Sir Colin Campbell's virtues was his intellectual humility and eagerness to acquire new knowledge. Experienced as he was in combat, he always grasped at opportunities to learn new tactics for training his soldiers. Being attentive and inquisitive, he could not help noticing certain peculiar rituals taking place at the cavalry camp. Every evening after dusk hundreds of troops would be led inside a dark barn where they would remain for periods of fifteen to twenty minutes. Then a trumpet would sound, the gate would open, and the soldiers would reemerge in complete silence, reeling slightly and grinning beatifically. Naturally, the ritual intrigued Sir Colin, who had never witnessed anything like this in his practice, so he asked Lucan to enlighten him.

"My lord," the Scotsman began coyly, "I pray you do not think my curiosity vulgar. It is of purely professional nature."

"From you, Sir Colin, I am willing to tolerate amazing amounts of vulgarity," the earl replied amicably. "Vulgarities from your mouth are far more pleasing to the ear than the gallantries of my other comrades. Ask away."

"What exactly is happening inside that barn?"

"A healing ceremony." Lucan's reply was just as direct as Sir Colin's question. "I'm so glad you asked. Nobody else in the camp seems to be paying attention to the meticulous preparations that are taking place under my supervision." Glowing with self-complacency, the earl began twisting the ends of his mustache,

245

curling them upward. "It is no secret that for the past few weeks our fearless cavalrymen have been suffering one blow to their dignity after another. So I needed to begin catering to their spiritual needs, since neither Cardigan nor Raglan seem to recognize them. Those two gentlemen are too engaged in their personal tribulations to care for those under their command. Fortunately, I have personally selected and engaged a few experts on the human soul—the soldier's soul, to be precise. They are working their magic on my men as we speak."

"Oh..." the Scotsman mumbled, overwhelmed by Lucan's speech. "Why... I don't suppose I could..." He suddenly stepped back and shook his graying head. "No, I would not dare."

"Bah, Sir Colin, such words do not belong in your vocabulary!" the earl scolded him in the same amicable manner. "Never use that expression in my presence. 'I would not dare'... Of course, you would dare! You have more rights to brag than Raglan, Airey and Cardigan put together. The two of us are probably the only competent, sensible generals in the entire British army. It is entirely possible that the fate of this campaign rests on our shoulders. Yes, you heard me correctly—mine and yours. What secrets can we keep from each other? Of course, you are more than welcome to attend one of the ceremonies. You have my blessing. This is what you were going to ask me, isn't it?"

"Yes, my Lord. I would be honored."

"The honor is mutual. Now, we must hurry. The next ceremony is at seven-thirty, and I do not like to dine later than quarter past eight."

The next batch of cavalrymen was gathering in front of the barn gates. The men were rising on their tiptoes, peeking over each other's shoulders, anxious to get inside. Clearly, whatever happened within those walls filled them with joy and reassurance. Most men came from the Light Brigade. There were some red-coated Heavies too—Sir James had finally brought them from Varna. The condition of Scarlett's men was noticeably better, considering they were spared the torments and humiliation of those comrades who were under Cardigan's command. Above all, they had been spared the ordeal of being caught in the crossfire between the two in-laws. Lucan held no grudges against Scarlett, so he let the lucky red coats dwell in their own oasis of neutrality. Overall, the Heavies appeared healthier, livelier, and more optimistic. They came to the barn in the company of their beloved commander, who maintained his benevolent silence.

The first trumpet call sounded, and the gates opened. The soldiers began to trickle in like ants inside their hill.

"My lord, time has come," Sir Colin said, tapping Lucan on the elbow.

"Wait until most of them are inside," the earl replied. "I would like for us to stand closer to the entrance. There are undeniable benefits to that. The later you enter, the sooner you'll leave."

Suddenly, to Sir Colin's astonishment, Lucan began stuffing rolls of wet gauze into his ears.

"What in the world are you doing, my Lord?" the Scotsman asked, while the earl could still hear him.

"Oh, this?" Lucan held one of the gauze balls to the light. "This is but a minor precaution. I've heard the same prayer countless times, and believe me I don't need to hear them again. I am only going in to accompany you. I wouldn't want for you to stumble in the dark and break an ankle. Raglan would never forgive me such an oversight, especially since the Russians can attack any day."

"Am I to plug my ears as well?"

"Then you will miss a meaty portion of the ceremony. I want you to experience it in full as I have."

Three minutes later, they were standing in complete darkness. Sir Colin knew that Lucan was nearby, because he could feel the plumes of his hat tickling his face and heard the earl's impatient growling.

The celestial drone of Reverend Bryce broke the lull. Without any preliminary speeches, he plunged straight into litany.

Praise and glory be to You, Oh God. Blessed be Your Name, exalted be Your Majesty and Glory. There is no God but You. Praise be to the Lord of the Universe, the Most Compassionate, the Most Merciful! Master of the Day for Judgment! You alone do we worship and You alone do we call on for help. Guide us along the Straight Path, the path of those whom You have favored, not the path of those who earned Your anger, nor of those who went astray. Amen.

The young reverend would pause after every phrase and give the men a chance to repeat after him. At first, the soldiers hummed indistinctly, dragging out the vowels and forgetting certain words, but after a few cycles of repetition, their voices became perfectly synchronized. They began sounding like a choir without music. Their drowsy mumbling eventually turned into an ecstatic chant.

An invisible trumpet sounded, and the gates of the barn opened. A gust of chilly evening wind drove the soldiers out of their collective trance. Reluctantly, they began leaving their place of worship, as another batch was waiting outside.

A young doctor was standing by the entrance, rationing out rum. Each soldier would present the cap of his canteen instead of a shot glass, and the doctor would reward him for his patience during the service with a splash of the blood-warming liquid. Following everyone's example, Sir Colin reached out for his serving, but Lucan caught his hand in mid-air and diverted it hastily.

"Don't bother with this murky rum," he said to the Scotsman, shaking his head discouragingly. "I have spirits of higher quality in my possession."

Lucan was not lying. He did have a bottle of excellent brandy inside his tent. He also had a set of elegant glasses that he would not share even with his aides. The sloppy boys had not earned the privilege of drinking out of such exquisite works of art. His own son, the giddy indiscriminating puppy, would still suck on whiskey bottles, smacking his lips and belching.

"My dearest Sir Colin," Lucan began when they were alone, "I have a strange feeling that you are dying to tell me something. Did you find the ceremony inspiring?"

"Exceptionally so, my lord," the Scotsman replied, sipping Lucan's brandy gingerly and reverently. "However, there is one part of the ceremony that left me perplexed."

"What part is that, Sir Colin?" the earl asked, resting his chin on his knuckles.

"My lord, I don't know how to break this to you, but the prayers recited inside that barn were not Christian."

"What do you mean? If those prayers were not Christian, what were they?"

"Islamic," Sir Colin replied firmly, planting the glass back on the table.

"Do elaborate!"

"Those are standard verses that Muslim soldiers recite before the battle. Of course, the text has been translated into English, and the name of Mohammed was removed. Apart from that, the British cavalry has just offered praise to Allah."

Lucan frowned with more confusion than anger.

"Are you certain of that?"

"If you don't believe me, ask any one of our Turkish troops, my lord."

"Don't be foolish, Sir Colin. Of course, I believe you. What I cannot believe is that Richard Ferrars would bother to dig up some Mohammedan scribble that isn't much different from what you would hear at Canterbury. Although, looking back at the conversation he and I had in my stateroom on the *Simla* a few weeks ago, I do recall him mentioning some Persian warriors, Muslim equivalents of Knights Templar."

"The Hashshashin sect?" Sir Colin asked enthusiastically, his eyes aglow.

"Something of the sort..." Lucan flexed his shoulders, embarrassed by his ignorance and poor memory.

"And the liquid served after the ceremony—was it truly pure rum?"

"Most of it was rum, yes. Dr. Ferrars may have added some herbs to calm the soldiers' nerves. Of course, I do not want to reveal this bit of truth to them. Otherwise they will be begging for the potion night and day."

The torch inside Sir Colin's head was growing brighter by the second. He finished the brandy in one gulp, slammed the costly glass into the tabletop, and seized Lucan's hand.

"My lord, would it be well by you if I brought my Highlanders to the barn? Their spirits are in dire need of lifting. My men have taken quite a beating at the Alma."

"Of course, Sir Colin," the earl replied, freeing his hand and rushing to examine the glass for cracks. "You can bring your men tomorrow—as long as I am credited for the method."

Chapter 9
Five Hundred False Alarms

On October 24th, Sir Colin and Lord Lucan received a visit from a Turkish spy who informed them of twenty thousand Russian infantry and five thousand Russian cavalry approaching Balaclava. The two generals received the news with a dab of skepticism—it was not the first time they were hearing rumors of an impending assault. There were several false alarms the previous week, and the troops were growing tired of being roused needlessly. Only three days prior a similar report was received, and the cavalry spent fourteen hours at their horses' heads, waiting all night in bitter cold that ended up killing Major Willet of 17th Lancers. Still, the army could not afford to brush off any rumors of hostilities. Every time a different boy was crying wolf, and every time the troops had to turn out.

"Five hundred false alarms are better than one surprise," wrote Lord George Paget.

However, having examined the swarthy messenger more carefully, Lucan and Sir Colin agreed that this time the threat was real. The great clash everyone had been waiting for was going to happen.

Without further deliberation, Sir Colin drafted an urgent note to Raglan and sent Lord Bingham and Wynfield to deliver it. When the two young men arrived, the Commander-in-Chief was consulting his French counterpart. The arrival of Lucan's aides irritated him so that he did not consider it necessary to comment on the

251

content of the message. With a dry "very well," he ordered the young men to leave his headquarters and return only if they had something new to report.

"We should've told Lord Raglan that the report came from an Englishman," Lord Bingham sighed. "His Lordship despises Turks. He says they are all bandits and not to be trusted."

"Nothing could be more logical," Wynfield replied. "We defend the interests of those whom we despise. Turks have gained our support but not our confidence. Here is another political paradox for you. But tell me, Georgie: what do *you* believe? What is your sparrow's heart telling you at this moment? Will the long-awaited bloodshed take place at last?"

"You have no right making such jokes, Jerry," Lord Bingham reproached him.

"I am not joking. I am asking you in earnest."

"By God, Jerry, after so many delays and false alarms, how can any soldier in the British army trust his intuition?"

Wynfield turned to face his friend, placed both hands on his shoulders, and declared with theatrical solemnity:

"It's coming, Georgie. I can sense it. I can smell the gray coats of the Russians. I can hear their barbaric prattle from miles away. The next twenty-four hours will change the fate of the world."

As much as the thought of returning to the cavalry camp empty-handed intimidated the two young men, they had no choice. They waited around for some sort of response from Lord Raglan, but it never came.

Lord Lucan took out his anger with the Commander-in-Chief on his entire division. One of his beloved practices was rousing his men a good hour before daybreak. At five o'clock in the morning on October 25th he was already galloping in front of his troops, who were already poised at their horses. Lucan noticed that his brother-in-law was not present that morning—he was sleeping late on his yacht, with Lord George, the commanding officer of 4th Light Dragoons, serving as his unofficial substitute. Lord William Paulet, Assistant Adjutant-General of the Cavalry, and Major Thomas McMahon were riding on each side of him.

As they were passing Redoubt No. 1 on Carnrobert's Hill, Paulet could not refrain from drawing his comrades' attention to the fact that two flags were flying. It could only mean that the enemy was approaching.

"Are you quite sure?" McMahon asked dubiously. He was not entirely awake yet.

A second later a cannon inside the redoubt fired. Lord Lucan and his staff lifted their heads to see the cloud of smoke rising, blending with the clouds in the dawning sky.

"Mark the hour," Sir Colin whispered solemnly, as if he had never heard a canon blast. "The battle has begun."

"Imagine how foolish Raglan will feel for having dismissed our message of yesterday," Lucan said. "That drowsy, arrogant old sot! How are we to make a stand now without assistance?"

He spurred his horse up and galloped about a hundred yards forward. The sky was brightening by the minute. Having looked through his field glasses, the eagle-eyed earl let out a string of profanities that contained a certain element of reverence. Approaching the heights were two enormous columns of Russian infantry with artillery, there number exceeding ten thousand.

Having found himself once again without orders to charge, Lucan decided to put on a show for the advancing Russians.

"I shall make threatening demonstrations and cannonade as long as my ammunition lasts," he declared before dispatching the same two aides to Raglan's headquarters.

Before departing to carry out his father's orders, Lord Bingham glanced at Redoubt No. 1, as if bidding it farewell.

"I do not envy the poor Turks sitting inside of it," the heir confessed to his companion. "Without any support from the rest of us, they will be smashed to bits in a matter of minutes. It will not take long for the Russians guns to silence them."

"At least we won't be here to witness it," Wynfield replied. "If this provides any consolation, your father has shown extraordinary mercy by sending us away."

The assault on the redoubts proved to be a disheartening sight indeed for reasons other than the abundance of Turkish blood spilled by the Russian guns. Having watched half of their comrades in Redoubt No. 1 slaughtered, the defenders of Redoubts 2, 3 and 4 fled without putting up any resistance, leaving the twelve-pounder guns in the hands of the enemy. "Ship, ship, ship!" they squealed, scurrying towards Balaclava. This spectacle of panic and cowardice merely confirmed Lord Raglan's statement about Turks being unreliable.

As for the Commander-in-Chief himself, he had situated himself and his staff on the Sapouné Heights from which he could see the unfolding battle. At his side stood Captain Duberly with his wife, who had sacrificed breakfast on the *Southern Star* to witness this glorious moment in history. The tireless journalist William Russell who kept ravaging his notebook, burrowing holes in the paper with the tip of his pen was also there. Since the Turks had failed shamelessly, Raglan was hoping that the Scots would prove to be worthier allies. With God's help, the 93rd Highlanders would duplicate the heroism first seen at the battle of Alma a month ago.

The Highlanders, aided by a small force of Royal Marines, were situated in the North Valley, poised to deflect the Russian cavalry three thousand men strong under the command of Ryzhov. Sir Colin had formed his troops into a row two men deep, even though the convention dictated that the rows should be at least twice as thick. The grizzly Scotsman had a low opinion of the Russian cavalry and did not think it necessary to form four lines.

"We have only Balaclava and the Black Sea to our backs," Sir Colin spoke to his men. "Remember there is no retreat from here. You must die where you stand."

"Aye, Sir Colin," his aide John Scott replied. "If needs be, we'll do that."

All his men were clear on the suicidal nature of their mission. Emerging alive and victorious was not a possibility they considered. The best they could hope for was to slow down the progress of the enemy. The previous evening they attended their last prayer ceremony inside the dark barn and drank their last serving of rum. Additional words of inspiration from Sir Colin were welcome but not necessary. The troops could not be any more at peace with their fate than they already were.

Watching the enemy dash towards them, the 93rd Highlanders, discharged three volleys, the last one being a three hundred and fifty yards. In spite of the immediate casualties, the Russian Hussars and Cossacks could have easily overrun the British, if only for the sheer inequality of forces—three thousand against five hundred.

Suddenly, Ryzhov ordered his men to retreat, for he had trouble believing that the Highlanders were standing alone. Surely, the thin red line was a mere diversion, and there were heavy reinforcements behind it.

At the sight of the enemy retreating, the 93rd Highlanders, who had already made peace with their impending death, leaped forward for a counter-charge, when their commander barked:

"93rd, damn all that eagerness!"

Not all of Sir Colin's men stopped at once. Some continued dashing for another fifty yards or so. They had trouble believing that the same man, who only five minutes ago cheered them to meet death with pride and defiance would attempt now to hold them back. The mass death, with which they had already reconciled, bypassed them this time.

A cry of jubilation volleyed through the North Valley and reached the ears of Dr. Ferrars, who was watching the battle from the same spot as Lord Raglan and his staff. Unaware of the tears streaming down his sunken cheeks, the physician squeezed the flask in his pocket. Could it be that he, Richard Ferrars, had something to do with the victory? The Turks may have proven to be incompetent spies and cowardly soldiers, but at least they had helped him procure the herbs needed for the potion.

William Russell assaulted his notebook with a doubled vigor, immortalizing the feat of the 93rd Highlanders as "the thin red line."

Lord Lucan was waiting for orders by Redoubt 6 with the Light Brigade, jogging his horse to and fro, aggravating his men whose nerves were already stretched quite thin. During one of his crossings, Lucan glanced over his shoulder and saw his son, who had returned from the Sapouné Heights.

"Where in Devil's name is your future brother-in-law?" the earl exploded, seeing that his heir was standing alone. "Where is Lord Hungerton?"

Chapter 10
Red Specs in the Sea of Gray

At quarter past nine, Sir James Scarlett was moving the eight squadrons of the Heavy Brigade southeast in the South Valley, as per Raglan's instructions.

Suddenly, he noticed a young officer in 5th Dragoons uniform galloping next to him. Having examined the fanciful pattern of scars on the young man's face, Sir James remembered meeting him briefly at Lucan's estate. The earl had pompously introduced Lord Hungerton as his protégé and made him Second Lieutenant on the spot. Sir James never bothered to gather the details of the story, for, God knows, he had plenty to occupy his mind. However, his two advisors, Elliot and Beatson, seemed genuinely happy to see Lord Hungerton. They both smiled and saluted him with an air of amicable informality.

"What are you doing here, Lieutenant Hungerton?" Scarlett asked sternly.

Truthfully, after the initial introduction at Laleham he did not expect to see the young man ever again—at least not on the battle-field. Scarlett had interpreted that spontaneous elevation of the injured foundling to the ranks of a junior officer as one of Lucan's whims.

"I am here to perform my duty, Sir," Wynfield replied.

"Where have you been for the past six months?"

"I can explain my absence, Sir. If you could only give me a chance..."

"I have no time for your explanations, young man. We are about to charge uphill an army outnumbering ours three to one."

"Lord Lucan has kept me on his staff!" Wynfield needed to scream in order to be heard through the howling of the wind and the clicking of the horses' hooves. "I could not disobey him. All this time I've been yearning to be by your side, Sir! Please, believe me."

Scarlett's advisors began doubling with laughter in their saddles, in spite of the gravity of the situation. They had heard about Lord Hungerton being forced to teach the soldiers the old drill in Varna. Poor lad!

"Does Lord Lucan know where you are?" Scarlett asked.

"I'm afraid he does not," Wynfield answered. "I implore you, Sir: please let me ride with you! I've dreamed of this moment for the past six months. If I am to die in this campaign, I would rather die today, by your side."

Scarlett could hear only half of what was being said to him, but the gist of the young officer's plea was expressed in the words "ride with you" and "dreamed." Damn Lucan and his foundlings! Was he, General James Yorke Scarlett, expected to indulge the heroic dream of every whimpering little boy?

Intuition told Sir James that getting rid of Lord Hungerton may prove to be more time-consuming than simply allowing him to join the Heavy Brigade, however belatedly. The general was no longer looking at the young officer. His eyes were fixed on the mass of Ryzhov's cavalry advancing towards them. He had very little time to align his troops.

"Left wheel into line!" Scarlett shouted, turning the two advanced regiments into line to face the enemy.

Wynfield hurried to join the 5th Dragoons, ignoring the quizzical stares from his comrades who had never seen him before. For an instant, he thought he heard Lord Lucan's voice. Indeed, the earl had left the Light Brigade and galloped towards the Heavies to order Scarlett what he had already started doing—charging the enemy. Fortunately, Wynfield's position in the second line hid him from Lucan's view. Still, he lowered his face as a precaution.

Riding around the commander of the Heavies in frantic circles, the earl reveled in the illusion that he was the one initiating the charge. Scarlett took the liberty of ignoring his vexatious commander. At a moment like this, he could not be bothered by a nuisance, no matter what rank. Because of the dismal location and the unevenness of the ground, the lines were broken and had to be restored quickly. As soon as his men were in perfect alignment, he ordered his trumpeter Trumpet Major Monks to sound the charge. Russian trumpets responded from the top of the hill. The Heavies began advancing at a trot. The pace of their horses never progressed to a gallop, because the distance between the two cavalries was so short.

Peeking over the shoulder of a Scots Grey officer riding in the first line ahead of him, Wynfield saw an enormous, seemingly impenetrable square of Russian cavalry five hundred yards away. The giant gray wave was rising to swallow the tiny Heavy Brigade. The monstrous inequality of forces gave the picture a surreal quality.

Wynfield's hearing began playing tricks on him. Some sounds became muffled and others grew louder. He could not hear the clacking of the hooves, yet he could hear a Royals soldier behind him muttering a prayer. Gradually, other voices joined in: chants, chuckles, whispers, moans. Wynfield could swear he was struck suddenly with the gift of reading other people's thoughts.

I am to die today, certainly, he said to himself. *God must be giving me the first taste of the afterlife. My body hasn't been destroyed yet, but the soul is already striving out of it.*

The conviction of being already dead scattered what was left of Wynfield's apprehension. In perfect serenity, he watched Scarlett and his staff advance fifty yards before the first line, crash into the square of gray coats, and disappear. The first line of the Heavy Brigade mimicked its commander.

At that moment, six hundred feet above the valley, Lord Raglan leaped out of his chair for the second time that day—the first time happened when Sir Colin's Highlanders chased away Ryzhov's cavalry. For the Commander-in-Chief this movement was purely instinctual. By jumping to his feet, he was not gaining better view of the valley. The soldier in him was honoring the soldiers on the battlefield. The men of the Heavy Brigade did not vanish out of sight. Their red coats loomed in the somber gray mass. Through his field glass, Raglan could recognize individual soldiers. It brought him unspeakable delight to see Scarlett alive and fighting ferociously, slashing the enemy with his sword. A handful of Heavies were causing the massive Russian square to sway and quake. Neither pistols nor carbines were used in this pure hand-to-hand engagement. The main weapons in this battle were swords and curse words. At some point, the mass became so tight that the fighters had trouble moving from the bodies of their fallen enemies blocking their way.

Next, the second squadron of the Inniskillings and the 5th Dragoons dove into the Russian mass to reinforce their comrades. To his surprise, Lord Raglan spotted Lord Hungerton, whom he had seen earlier that morning in the company of Lord Bingham. What was Lord Hungerton doing fighting with Scarlett? Was he not supposed to stay with his immediate commander and the Light Brigade? On another hand, the young officer's participation in the charge proved to be most beneficial. His ferocity and agility made him stand up from the mass. It was not long before Raglan realized that Mrs. Duberly was staring at the same man, her youthful chiseled face beaming with admiration and reverence.

Suddenly, she turned pale and touched her lips.

"What's the matter, my dear?" her husband asked her.

Captain Duberly was on staff duty that day and therefore not taking part in any engagements.

"Nothing," Fanny whispered through her fingers.

"If the sight is too overwhelming for your pretty eyes," the captain continued, "feel free to turn away. I shall let you know when it is safe to look."

Her eyes still on the battlefield, Fanny sought her husband's hand.

"Pray for him, Henry," she said.

"Pray for whom, my dear?"

"Lord Hungerton. He appears wounded. See how he droops over his horse's neck?"

"I may as well pray for the entire Heavy Brigade," the captain responded. "What makes Lord Hungerton so privileged?"

"By God, Henry, do you not remember?" Fanny could not have been more indignant had the captain forgotten her birthday or their wedding anniversary. "Back at Varna, as we were embarking, he had an opportunity to denounce me, yet he did not. It was Lucan's will to separate me from you. Thanks to Lord Cardigan's generosity and Lord Hungerton's discretion, we are here together, watching history unfold before our eyes. Pray that he remains on his horse."

"As you wish, dear..."

As much as his wife's sentimental whim perplexed him, Captain Duberly felt obliged to indulge it. He could not think of a single battlefield prayer, so he lifted his hand to begin crossing himself.

Completing the pious ritual proved unnecessary for Captain Duberly, as sounds of British cheers emerged from the wavering mass. Dispatched by Lord Lucan, the 4th Dragoons crashed into the Russian force, causing it to break and flee uphill.

The men of Light Brigade joined their comrades in cheer. Plumed hats and helmets were tossed to the sky. Raglan sent one of his aides down to the valley with a terse appreciative message: "Well done, Scarlett!" The Russians were chased out of the South Valley. There was no chance of them penetrating Balaclava now.

Having witnessed such a tense situation resolve itself so favorably, Raglan collapsed back into his chair and demanded that Airey open a bottle of scotch. The show was not over as far as they were concerned. They fully expected Cardigan to pursue the retreating Russians to finish them off, yet the Noble Yachtsman remained in the same spot, even though Lucan had explicitly permitted him to take advantage of an obvious opportunity, should it arise. Captain Morris of the 17th Lancers, nicknamed "pocket Hercules" for his short, stocky, and incredibly powerful body, pleaded with his commander to charge to no avail.

"My God, what a chance we are losing!" Morris lamented to his comrades.

Lucan had nothing left to do but chastise his delinquent brother-in-law in a letter delivered by his son. Once again, Lord Bingham had the pleasure of communicating his father's disappointment to his uncle. Ah, there is nothing that delighted the young man more than being tangled in a family farce.

The fatalities on the side of the Heavy Brigade were surprisingly low—ten against Ryzhov's fifty. Most of the wounded, their numbers approaching one hundred, were able to stay in the saddle. One by one they returned to Redoubt 6.

Having forgotten his obligations as aide-de-camp, Lord Bingham would run up to every officer in the 5th Dragoons and examine his mud-stained face, hoping to see the familiar features of his future brother-in-law. With every disappointment the tremor in his hands intensified.

"Jerry, Jerry..." he kept whispering to himself. "Please, be alive. Come back, in God's name."

Another minute of fruitless waiting, and he would go to the scene of the battle to look for his friend among those who remained on the ground. Suddenly, he heard a weak, triumphant laughter above his head.

"Georgie, what a show you've missed!" a familiar voice exclaimed.

Supported on each side by Beatson and Elliot, Wynfield stood wavering. Blood was gushing from a slip on his neck, trickling down his spine, having soaked his shirt and his uniform. Having disengaged himself from Scarlett's advisors, Wynfield stepped towards Lord Bingham.

"Jerry!" the heir let out an indescribable cry, catching his friend in his arms. "I wish to know everything. Tell me how it felt, being in the heart of the battle."

"First you must tell me how it looked from the outside."

"Red specs in a sea of gray," Lord Bingham replied without a moment's hesitation. "I cannot wait to marry and have children of my own, if only to tell them their Uncle Jerry's bravery. I know what I saw."

Their fraternal idyll was interrupted by the sudden arrival of Lord Lucan. Without a word, the earl began circling his two aide-de-camps.

"If you wish to strike me, my Lord," Wynfield mumbled, trying to keep his eyes on his commander, "you know which side of my face is the more sensitive one."

Still, the earl remained silent. Watching Lucan ride in circles exacerbated Wynfield's vertigo. A thin stream of blood gushed from both corners of his mouth.

"Papa, Jerry needs a doctor!" Lord Bingham gasped, ignoring the titular formalities, for at that moment he was not a soldier but a frightened child begging his father to save his brother.

The earl vanished as unexpectedly and silently as he had appeared, leaving his son glancing around helplessly and murmuring: "Jerry, stay awake, I beg you..."

Wynfield had every intention of staying awake, because he longed to tell Lord Bingham about the marvelous thickness of the Russians' coats that actually dulled the blades of the British swords. Still, he was losing blood too quickly from the severed arteries on the back of his neck. There could have been other minor wounds not yet accounted for.

It was not the first time that Wynfield's body was suffering from moderate exsanguination. The sensations of fogginess and extreme weakness were already familiar to him. He imagined himself chained to a giant pendulum that flung him in and out of consciousness. He could vaguely hear Lord Bingham's frenzied appeal for help followed by a grateful exclamation when the help finally arrived. Several pairs of warm callused hands lifted him from the ground and carried him away.

When the fog enveloping his head thinned out for a moment, he found himself lying on his stomach inside a tent. Someone had placed a pillow under his ribs and another one under his chin. His uniform coat and his blood-soaked shirt had been removed. Dr. Ferrars was giving instructions to someone on how to stitch up and dress wounds.

"The Russian soldier had clearly aimed to decapitate our Lord Hungerton," he said, his statement immediately met with a benevolent chuckle. "I cannot blame the enemy, though. Who would not want to bag such a hot head for a trophy?"

"Gentlemen, who wishes to make a bet?" another voice asked. "I say, Lord Hungerton will receive a promotion."

"If he does not, I shall take personal offense to it and desert."

"We all deserve medals after what we have done today."

"I don't want any shiny trinkets! One edible dinner is all I ask. Even rats appear more appetizing than another serving of uncooked salt pork."

"Who will be brave enough to suggest this splendid idea to Lord Raglan?"

"What makes you think that Lord Raglan is the one composing our menu? I would settle for one night aboard the *Dryad*. I would like to trade places with the Noble Yachtsman for one night."

"Not in a million years would I sleep in Cardigan's bed. Bathing in his bathtub would make me feel filthier than I am now. The entire yacht is tainted."

How Wynfield longed to join in that conversation! He could have contributed a dozen clever remarks that would make the men in the tent double with laughter, but every time he opened his mouth, bloodied saliva would foam forth. The jokes would have to wait.

Anesthetized by pride from his accomplishments for the day, veiled in the euphoric laughter of his comrades, Wynfield drifted off into sleep.

Chapter 11
"Advance On Both Fronts"

His awakening was accompanied by gnawing alarm. He had no idea how much time had passed, but he sensed that while he was sleeping, something dreadful had taken place. The dressing on his wounded neck made it impossible for him to turn his head. He took a deep breath and pushed himself up from the pillows on which he had been resting.

Sitting across from him were two men from the Light Brigade.

One of them was Captain William Morris of the 17th Lancers, and the other one was Henry Wilkin of 11th Hussars who also served as a field surgeon. Their dark-blue uniforms looked black from the dirt, and their heads were uncovered.

"What's happened?" Wynfield asked, having guessed that another engagement had taken place.

"That is an excellent question, Lord Hungerton!" Morris replied sarcastically. "What has happened, indeed? There are at least five versions of the story. My friend Henry and I seem to agree on the account that our brilliant generals know neither how to read nor how to tell right from left. Isn't that so, Henry?"

Wilkin twirled his hussar's hat as if it were a useless toy.

"Down with it, William," he curtailed his friend. "Don't take your anger out on Lord Hungerton. Your riddles will perplex him even more. Don't you see the man is wounded and delirious?"

"I am not delirious!" Wynfield objected indignantly and rose to his feet, holding onto a pole of the tent for support. "Can someone tell me where my commander is? Where is Lord Lucan? I'd like to speak with him."

"I wish I could say he was burning in hell," Morris continued through his teeth, "along with Cardigan and Raglan, but alas, it is not so. All three bastards are alive and well, which cannot be said for the men of the Light Brigade, who were practically fed to the Russians. Almost three hundred casualties in less than twenty minutes! Now that is what I call military brilliance. It takes talent to destroy that many lives at once."

"William!" the hussar tried to curtail him again. "If you do not stop ranting, I will be obliged to sedate you with morphine, even though it would be a waste of precious substance, considering how many amputations I am to perform before the end of the day. I have been listening to you for six hours now. A shell must have landed on your head. You simply cannot spread rumors and incite insubordination. Nothing is certain as of now. All the facts are yet to be collected."

"Henry, my friend, do you honestly believe those bastards will tell us the truth? They are in conference right this moment, con-spiring, inventing a believable story that will remove the blame from them. Captain Nolan is conveniently dead—lucky for him! He twisted Raglan's orders and then took a gallant tumble off his horse before everyone. Once again, he turned everything into a spectacle, even his own death. Recall his last words?" Morris in-flated his cheeks and imitated Nolan pompously: "*Advance on two fronts! Attack immediately! There, my Lord, is your enemy! There are your guns!*' Bah! Hell isn't hot enough for him."

"William, it is not becoming of a Christian man to slander those who are not present to defend themselves. Let Captain No-lan rest in peace."

Watching the two survivors of the charge bicker, Wynfield re-alized that he would not get any reliable information from them. He squeezed his head, let out a moan and stumbled out of the tent.

The picture revealed before his eyes made him waver and draw back a few steps. As distraught and as absorbed by their conflict Wilkin and Morris were, they could not stifle a bitter laugh at the sight of his reaction.

"I told you, William," the surgeon commented. "Lord Hunger-ton's brain is not primed for the truth."

Wynfield rubbed his eyes to make sure that he was not dreaming. The cavalry camp, illuminated by several orphaned bonfires, served as both as hospital and a graveyard. The survivors clustered in small groups, bickering, cursing, and weeping. In their current state, they resembled Napoleon's soldiers caught in the middle of a Russian blizzard.

Like a father searching for his child in a crowd, Wynfield began pacing from one cluster of soldiers to another, seizing them by the sleeves of their uniforms, shaking them and receiving nothing but bewildered stares in return. Some sort of stupefying spell had been cast upon the entire cavalry.

"Has anyone seen my commander?" he kept asking. "Has anyone seen Lord Lucan?"

Suddenly, he felt a pair of sturdy heavy hands on his shoulders. The man standing behind Wynfield's back did not see the bandages under the collar of the uniform and therefore did not realize the agony his touch was causing. Struggling not to howl, Wynfield turned his whole body around and saw Sir James Scarlett. The general's white mustache and eyebrows now looked gray from the dust and the smoke. The top of his brass helmet had been indented by the enemy's sword. His face, now black and blue, glistened, its expression remaining that of understated benevolence and determination.

"Thank heavens, it's you!" Wynfield exclaimed. "I feel like I'm strolling through a lunatic asylum. Perhaps, you can explain to me what has happened."

Having noticed the bandages on the young officer's neck, Scarlett hurried to remove his hands from Wynfield's shoulders.

"Lord Hungerton, I owe you an apology for having treated you with needless harshness on the battlefield earlier," the general said. "No doubt, you had legitimate reasons for absence, reasons beyond your control."

"Oh, it was my fault, sir," Wynfield replied. The pain prevented him from shaking his head, so he laid his hand on his heart instead to enhance the sincerity of his words. "I should have known not to pester you with my excuses at a moment of such tension."

"Still, I had no right to scold you before your comrades and undermine your reputation. Will you forgive me, Lord Hungerton?"

"Sir, I still cannot see any transgression towards me on your part, but if it would make you sleep better, then yes, I do forgive you. But for the love of God, tell me what happened."

"I can only tell you what I know. There are enough rumors circulating already. I will not contribute to them." Scarlett gestured towards his tent. "Would you like to sit down?"

"No, sir," Wynfield replied stoically. "If I sit down, I may have trouble standing up again. Did you see the charge happen?"

"I certainly did, though not as much as Lord Raglan saw from his altitude. It now appears there was a misinterpretation of the orders, absurdities, ambiguities that were not clarified in a timely manner."

"Oh, I have time, sir. I would very much like to hear your telling of the story. I suspect there will be many versions of it circulating."

Scarlett sighed and beckoned Wynfield into his tent, where he lit a lamp and unfolded a map. "I beg you not to be overly critical of my narrative skills, Lord Hungerton."

Chapter 12
The Valley of Death
(As told by Sir James Scarlett)

Around 10:45, the Commander-in-Chief had requested Brigadier Airey to draft an order to Lord Lucan stating something along these lines: "Lord Raglan wishes the Cavalry to advance rapidly to the front, follow the enemy, and try to prevent the enemy carrying away the guns. Troop Horse Artillery may accompany. French Cavalry is on your left. Immediate." It would pain Lord Raglan to lose the naval guns from the redoubts on the reverse side of the Causeway Heights; but what seemed clear to him from his vantage-point on the west of the valley was not clear to the men below.

Captain Nolan was the one delivering the note from Raglan. Having reached the cavalry, he began gesturing frantically and shouting that the cavalry was to attack immediately. When Lord Lucan asked the messenger to clarify to which guns he was referring, Nolan made another wide sweeping gesture. "There, my lord, is your enemy. There are your guns." The commanders were perplexed, as Nolan was pointing not towards the Causeway redoubts but a cluster of Russian guns in at the end of the valley.

Nolan never made a secret of his contempt for Lord Lucan, but today he took an opportunity to flaunt it before the entire cavalry. His demeanor was most arrogant and insolent. Lord Lucan appeared put off by it and refused to engage in any further discussion. Still, he was, determined to follow the order, however absurd it appeared to him, so he dispatched his brother-in-law and his six-hundred-some calvalrymen straight into the valley between the Fedyukhin and the Causeway Heights.

Upon hearing the order, Lord Cardigan questioned its sanity and pointed out that there was a battery in front, battery on each flank, and the ground is covered with Russian riflemen. Lucan agreed but then remarked that they were bound to obey Lord Raglan's orders. So, Cardigan formed his men in two lines—the 13th Light Dragoons, the 17th Lancers and the 11th Hussars in the first and the 4th Light Dragoons and the 8th Hussars in the second.

Shortly after 11 o'clock, the Light Brigade began advancing towards the Obolensky's battery at the end of the valley, where Liprandi was waiting with twenty battalions of infantry and fifty artillery pieces. Russian forces were framing the valley. As for Lord Lucan, he was to follow with us, the Heavies.

As soon as Cardigan set off down the valley, we saw Nolan rushing across the front, cutting his lordship off, screaming indistinctly, as if he had seen the devil himself. I thought I could make out the words: "Turn, turn!" We never learned what it was that he had tried to communicate to the cavalry. An artillery shell exploded near him, mortally wounding him. For a few seconds he tried to stay in the saddle, with blood gushing out of his mouth. Then he tumbled to the ground. As for the cavalry, it continued on its course—and was torn to shreds by fire from three sides.

To be sure, Cardigan's men did reach the Russians at the end of the valley, and they did force them out of the redoubt, but at an incredible cost. They could not keep up the fight for long and retired. The Russian artillerymen resumed fire with grape and canister. They did not care about hitting their own men.

We—the Heavies and I—were fully prepared to follow Cardigan's men with reinforcement. We entered the mouth of the valley but did not move much further. When Lord Lucan realized that the Light Brigade was doomed, he recalled us. His argument was that he did not wish to lose the Heavies too. So, we stood and watched the mêlée at Obolensky's battery.

It was the French who helped rescue what was left of the Light Brigade. The Chasseurs d'Afrique broke the Russian line on the Fedyukhin Heights and covered Cardigan's men. As for Cardigan himself, he did not seem terribly concerned by the fate of the men behind him. He led them to the Russian guns and decided that his leadership ended there. We spotted him galloping alone, and that was the last we've seen of him. Later we were told that he retired to his yacht.

By noon, the survivors had returned. The whole engagement took less than twenty minutes.

Chapter 13
French and Russian
Commentaries on English Tactics

Having finished his terse narrative, Scarlett drummed his blackened fingers against the map. "So that is the Charge of the Light Brigade as I saw it. Forgive me if my telling of the story was dry and prosaic. I tend to favor verbs over adjectives. No doubt, there will be many a poem written about this. You know what Marshal Bosquet said: 'C'est magnifique, mais ce n'est pas la guerre'. It is splendid sight, but this is not how one fights a war. I must agree with him. The Russians must have thought we were drunk."

Wynfield peered into the map, as if he could actually see tiny dots moving down the valley. That was the picture that Raglan must have seen from his plateau. "I dread asking you this question, sir, but I shall ask nevertheless. What is left of the Light Brigade?"

"After regrouping, less than two hundred men were with their horses."

Wynfield took a few seconds to register the number in his head. "Less than two hundred out of... more than six hundred?"

"There would have been more casualties, had it not been for Lord Lucan's caution," Scarlett continued. "He withdrew my brigade at the last minute. He himself was wounded lightly in the leg. His horse was hit twice. One of his aides was killed."

"Dear God..." Wynfield whispered. "Please tell me it was not his son."

"No!" the General interjected hastily. "Do not be alarmed. Lord Bingham is alive. I have not seen him since the battle, but I am certain that he escaped unharmed. He must be by his father's side at this very moment."

Scarlett spoke without any pathos, sentimentality, or judgment, as a man who had nothing to hide or to justify.

"I should be by his side as well," Wynfield said lowly. "He is my patron, my commander, my future father-in-law. Sir James, you are an honest man. Tell me: is there any truth to the accusations? I don't want any merciful lies. I will stand by my commander regardless of his responsibility. Did Lord Lucan lose the Light Brigade?"

A ghost of a smile appeared beneath Scarlett's dusty mustache.

"Young man, leaning on my theoretical military knowledge, I do not believe that one man could be responsible for a tragedy of this magnitude. Can I say in good conscience that Lord Lucan played absolutely no part in it? No. He probably should have been more thorough in receiving and interpreting Captain Nolan's message. At the same time, it would pain me to see Lord Lucan shoulder all the blame. If I understand anything about military politics, the Commander-in-Chief will look for a single scapegoat. I am sorry to say it, but right now all the fingers are pointing at Lord Lucan."

Wynfield lowered his eyes and suddenly seized the general's hand.

"Sir James, can I count on you to advocate for my commander?" he asked in a trembling voice, pulling on General's fingers. "After all, he spared your men, didn't he? You said so yourself. He withdrew the Heavies, and now he is branded an incompetent coward for it. Promise me you will put on a word of defense for him."

"Young man," the general responded without a hint of apology in his voice, "I cannot promise such things, simply because I hold very little authority. Nobody cares for my opinion. I am nobody here."

"That isn't true!" Wynfield objected. "You are a hero."

"Same can be said for you, Lord Hungerton. Let God be the judge of that. At any rate, we were not promised peace or justice in this life. Perhaps, in the next one... One can always hope."

Wynfield released the general's hand and drew back with an air of resignation if not defeat.

"So what is our next maneuver, Sir James?"

"The state of the cavalry will not permit any engagement in the near future. Lord Raglan understands that. We have not even assessed our losses properly. Tomorrow's daylight shall bring more answers."

"So what are we to do now—pray and wait?"

"I wouldn't expect that of you, Lord Hungerton. A man like you does not tolerate idleness or uncertainty well. Perhaps, something can be done about it."

Wynfield's eyes blazed up with timid curiosity.

"Do you have an assignment for me?"

"As a matter of fact, I do. After today's mixed fortunes, we have a considerable number of wounded. They need to be escorted to the hospital and situated."

Wynfield could not believe his ears. "You are sending me to rot in Scutari?" he asked, squinting indignantly.

"Do not interpret my proposal as an insult, Lord Hungerton," Scarlett continued in his habitual steady voice. "Take a minute to consider your alternatives. You will be in greater danger of rotting if you stay here indefinitely. You can either collect military gossip in the cavalry camp, or you can provide sorely needed physical and spiritual support to your injured comrades. The hospital, one would imagine, is already overcrowded, and the atmosphere is chaotic. In all likelihood, the wounded are not separated from the cholera patients. I cannot speak for Lord Lucan, but I personally would feel comforted knowing that my men have an advocate."

"What makes you so convinced that I am fit for such a task?" Wynfield asked dubiously, even though he suspected he should have been flattered. "Would your men find my company comforting? They hardly know me."

"My men have seen enough of you and tasted of your character. It is my conviction that you possess the necessary traits to kindle the morale of your comrades. My other task for you is to oversee the rehabilitation of the recovering troops. Once their wounds heal, the men will need to regain their combat skills. It will amaze you how quickly those skills are lost. It would pain me to see such fine soldiers discarded prematurely. They will need to practice target shooting and mounting their horses. I have already drafted a letter for Miss Florence Nightingale, asking her permission to establish some sort of rehabilitative facility on the hospital grounds. With your assistance, they will be able to rejoin their profession. I hope you do not consider this assignment beneath you, Lord Hungerton."

Wynfield stepped forward and saluted the general.

"Yes, Sir James. Thank you for your confidence in me. Please, forgive my initial reaction to your proposal. It was not my intention to communicate ingratitude or insubordination. It would be an honor to accompany my comrades to Scutari."

"Very well," Scarlett concluded tersely. "The transporting procedures will begin tomorrow at dawn. Reverend Bryce will be joining you. In the meantime, do try to get some sleep."

Chapter 14
Shadows on the Cloth

Wynfield returned to the tent that he had been sharing for all those weeks with Lucan's aide-de-camps and Dr. Ferrars. There was nobody there, as Wynfield had expected, which brought him strange relief. At least he would not have to explain his departure. Not to mention, he was in no condition to face Lord Bingham and endure another "everyone hates Papa" lament.

The meager possessions of the occupants of the tent had been mixed up and piled up in the middle: belts, shirts, boots, blankets and crumbled journal pages. It was not safe to leave so many flammable objects next to a burning Turkish lantern.

Wynfield found a blank scrap of paper for his farewell note to Lord Lucan. The best writing tool he could locate was a stump of a pencil covered in bite marks. With any luck, Wynfield would be able to squeeze about fifty words.

By then he had learned to move without aggravating his wounded neck. Using the sole of Lord Bingham's boot as a hard surface, he began to scribble.

My Lord, I depart for Scutari in accordance with the orders from Brigadier-General Sir James Scarlett to escort the wounded to the hospital. May God...

The tip of the pencil broke, and Wynfield did not have a pen-knife on hand to sharpen it. Clearly, the same God did not want him to finish the sentence. Perhaps, the Almighty thought it blasphemous to have His name used in a letter addressed to Lord Lucan.

Wynfield folded the unfinished note, slipped it inside his pocket, and stepped outside the tent to smoke a cigar. By then, the rustles in the camp had abated and almost all bonfires had withered. Every now and then, a wounded horse's neighing would break the lull.

Wynfield remembered Sir James's advice to get some sleep but sensed it was not likely to happen that night. In spite of the fatigue from the blood loss, he felt strangely alert, as if every nerve in his body was communicating with the universe. All the elements around him—the sky foggy October sky, the chilly air, the muddy soil beneath his feet, even the waves of the Black Sea splashing behind his back at Balaclava Bay were whispering secrets to him, the chosen one. He was the only Englishman in the Crimea who was truly awake.

Inhaling the life-giving smoke, he heard his name being called.

"Lord Hungerton..."

The universe was speaking to him in a woman's voice. Stranger things have been known to happen. Wynfield responded with an attentive hum, letting the invisible speaker know that he was eager to listen.

The initial call was followed by a stretch of silence. Wynfield started wondering that, perhaps, the universe changed its mind about initiating him into its mysteries. He drew another puff, flexed his wrists, cracked his knuckles, and prepared to go back inside. Then he heard shallow, agitated breathing and saw a slender shadow moved across the fabric of the tent.

The spirit of the universe appeared to him in the shape of Mrs. Duberly. She was wearing her wrinkled riding dress, the same one in which she first disembarked on the Turkish shore five months prior. Her hair, usually arranged in a low loose bun and covered by a net, was streaming down her back.

Wynfield laughed, dropping the cigar from his mouth.

"Good evening, Mrs. Duberly," he greeted her with affected gallantry. "I hope the events of the past day provided plenty of material for your journal."

"I prayed for you," she said in a trembling voice. "I was told you survived the charge. I came to see you with my own eyes."

"What a waste of time, Mrs. Duberly," Wynfield replied, feeling a sudden need to light another cigar. "I am not worth one of your hairpins. A bone from Lord Cardigan's mutton chop has more dignity than me."

Silently, Fanny subsided to her knees before him. The hem of her riding dress bunched up, revealing the muddy edge of her petticoats. Wynfield had forgotten how much fabric women of the upper class wore. Mrs. Duberly's wardrobe must have weighed more than his uniform, the sword and the brass helmet included.

Wynfield angled his both thumbs and index fingers to form a square and glanced through it.

"You look particularly ravishing from this angle, Mrs. Duberly," he said. "The army photographers are capturing all the wrong moments. Please, do not rise to your feet. There is something infinitely endearing about a kneeling woman."

Trembling with reverence, Fanny looked into the young hero's eyes, the wide steel-colored eyes of her dead stallion.

Suddenly, Wynfield understood the universe's will for him. He was to lay with Mrs. Duberly, the thorn in Lord Lucan's side, the defiant arrogant bitch who viewed the massacre from her throne. He, Lieutenant Hungerton, was going to do the honors on behalf of the entire Light Brigade. One could not fathom a better closure to a catastrophic day! He could hear the voices of the fallen cavalrymen, cheering him on.

Fury can trigger the same physical responses as tenderness—Wynfield was discovering this peculiar anatomic phenomenon. Blood rushed to his fingertips, making his hands tremble, while his knees became weak. The wound on his neck started bleeding again, and his parched mouth started salivating. He had to struggle not to seize Mrs. Duberly by the throat.

Having misinterpreted the cause of Lord Hungerton's agitation, Fanny stretched her arms towards him, beckoning and imploring. A second later they were both lying on the muddy grass before the entrance to the tent. Fanny heard the clanging of the buckle on his belt and the sound of her skirts tearing.

Her body was not prepared for such an abrupt and vigorous assault. Fanny had been with the same man for too long and had grown too accustomed to his predictable lukewarm caresses. At the same time, she was enlightened enough to know that what she had brought upon herself qualified as violence, not exactly undeserved and not exactly unexpected. The burden of ambiguous, unidentifiable guilt that had been afflicting her for the past six months was suddenly lifted. Without fully understanding the nature of her crime, Fanny had already sentenced herself to punishment and chosen her executioner. Staring up into the bleak sky, struggling not to vocalize her pain, Fanny concluded that justice smelled like blood, tobacco and withered grass. It was one observation she could not publicize in her journal.

Part 6
A Nightingale Among Vultures
Scutari
November, 1854

Chapter 1
On Various Forms
of Phantom Pains

General Scarlett's proposal for rehabilitative arrangements for his wounded men had left Florence Nightingale fuming. Her hostility could be explained by the fact that she had never met the man in person, and his letter reached her at an exceptionally trying hour. How dared he even think about returning his men to the battlefield, when she barely had enough gauze to dress their wounds? How typical of an ignorant, detached general! He must have thought they were bathing in luxury in Scutari, serving gruel out of gold bowls, and playing cricket between amputations. Now his newly acquired status of a hero gave him even more reasons to present his demands. Perhaps, he expected her to abandon the rest of her patients and devote all her efforts to returning the Heavies to their fighting shape? Naturally, those suffering from cholera did not count as legitimate patients. No, they did not have any bleeding wounds and therefore did not merit her time.

The letter was dated October 26th. Nearly a month later, Florence was still fuming over it. At this stage of fatigue and frustration, her imagination was beginning to triumph over common sense. She nurtured this absurd hatred for Scarlett, her invisible, unreachable enemy. Had they met in reality, they would have gotten along splendidly, given their similarities in temper.

The only man she loathed more than Scarlett was his ambassador—Lord Hungerton. Just like his commander, Hungerton was considered a hero and therefore above all regulations. The official purpose of his arrival in Scutari was to accompany the wounded of the cavalry unit after the Balaclava travesty, yet after the first day it became clear that his personal goal was to turn the hospital into a circus or a tavern. He brought madness and blasphemous merriment wherever he went. For instance, he kindled an entirely outrageous tradition of sing-along. Whenever Florence heard his husky tenor starting a battle tune, it was safe to bet that another fifty voices would join in a minute. Before long, the entire hospital would be buzzing and pulsating. Not all men had beautiful voices, by the way. Most of them howled like hungry dogs. No dutiful member of the medical staff could function in such a savage environment.

At night Lord Hungerton would strut through the halls with his hands in his pockets, shirt unbuttoned, a cigar in his teeth and a brazen fiendish grin on his disfigured face. Nobody dared to inquire when he acquired those scars and under which circumstances. One thing was clear: the scarring did not detract from his masculine vanity. He winked and whistled at the nurses, even those who were Roman Catholic sisters. His hands did not always stay in his pockets. Often they would end up where a gentleman's hands had no business being, and a gentleman he was—allegedly a baron!

Florence tried to seek solace in the possibility that Lord Hungerton's outrageous behavior was an unfortunate side effect of a profound mental trauma. Perhaps, the atrocities that he had witnessed made him embrace vulgarity and debauchery. If Florence permitted herself to believe that he was acting in clear conscience, she would certainly strangle him. She did not have much tolerance for a man aiming to lay down his law in her domain, to mock and dismiss her rules regarding cleanliness, holiness and quiet, to sabotage all her efforts to create a medical establishment that would produce more survivors than corpses. It was all a prank to him—the entire war, the entire life!

The only benefit of having him there was that he kept the Heavies under control. They worshipped him for their own peculiar reasons. True, he could turn them into a jackal chorus in a matter of minutes, but he could silence them just as easily. In addition, he appeared to be immune to all infections diseases. The man had a million chances to contract dysentery and cholera, yet he managed to bypass them—and she had never seen him wash his hands! Lice did not cling to his thick black curls, and his gums did not bleed. In that respect, Lord Hungerton was something of a medical enigma, and Florence did not like enigmas, especially when they defied her theories.

Luckily, Lord Hungerton had been gone from the hospital for the past few days. He took a transport back to Balaclava to meet with one of his superiors, either Scarlett or Lucan. Florence prayed that his absence would last a while, preferably until the end of the war. What a relief it would be never to see him again!

To her credit, Florence was aware of her growing propensity for internal tirades, and she hated this new mental habit. If only she knew how to break it!

Passing through the hall with her lamp, she saw Private Seamus Martin, a former infantryman, clutching the stump of his recently amputated hand, rocking back and forth, and moaning, his eyes wild. The Irishman must have gotten out of the room again. That particular patient was not particularly compliant and difficult to keep in one place.

"It burns... Me hand burns!" he ranted. "From the elbow to... where the fingertips once were. The hand's gone, but the pain stays."

Instead of scolding him for leaving his bed once again, Florence sat behind him on the bench and held him by the shoulders, trying to console him. His case of phantom pains was one of the most severe ones she had ever seen in her practice. Even those soldiers who lost their legs at the hip did not suffer as much as he did after losing his hand.

"Hapless boy..."

"I asked 'im fer drugs, I begged 'im," the Irishman continued groaning. "But he'd give me none!"

Florence detached from Martin slightly and tried to look him in the eye.

"Who is it of whom you speak?"

"The bloody surgeon... I hate 'im! I could kill 'im, I swear. The bastard, he passes by, grinnin', mockin' me..."

Florence drew a small flask from her bag and held it to Private Martin's lips.

"Here's some valerian root. It can't hurt. Drink up."

He took a few sips and collapsed back on the bench, panting. Florence cradled him as she would a child. After a few seconds, he appeared a little calmer.

"Talk to me," he implored. "'Bout anythin'. I only need to hear yer voice."

"Just think: you'll be sent home soon," she began with forced enthusiasm. "But first you'll receive your pay. Spend your money wisely. Consult your mother."

Florence knew she had touched a sore subject when she saw her patient wince after her last word. By then she could distinguish physical pain from emotional. She knew that the culprit of Martin's grimace was not his lost hand.

"Ma died whilst I was in pris'n fer stealin'," he muttered. "I never seen 'er face after I got meself arrested. She came to visit me, but I ne'er came out. Don't think I could bear it, not after what she done fer me, takin' me from Castlebar to Liv'pool. Yer know? Ma knew there was no chance of us survivin' 'nother winter home in Ireland. So she brought me to a real workin' English city; but I was no good at any trade save stealin'. That's how I got meself in prison."

"Ah, the whole world is a prison," Florence said, stroking his hair. "Just because you aren't chained, it doesn't mean that you are free."

"I hope Ma ain't too cross wi' me. Wher'er she gone, I hope she seen me when I found water at Calamita Bay. 'Twas a good day fer all of us, the best day in me life, that's fer sure. Lord Hung'ton, Lord Bingham and I found water. I could see me Ma smilin' at me."

Suddenly, Martin lifted his head from Florence's lap and glanced at the envelope peeing from underneath the collar of her blouse.

"A letter, eh?"

"From a dear old friend."

"What's his name?"

"Sidney," she replied faintly, staring into space.

"Well, does Sidney have any good news?"

"It's an old letter, filled with promises yet to be fulfilled. When I have a dismal day, I reread it."

The Irishman sank back into Florence's lap, but her fingers did not resume stroking his hair, as her thoughts shifted onto another subject.

"'Tis pity I'm unlettered, Miss Nighin'ale," Martin spoke, attempting to draw her attention to himself once again.

"I'll teach you how to scribble your name. Your writing hand is unharmed." She took his right hand and shook it in the air. "There's no excuse for continuing to communicate in muffled grunts, young man. I hope that your writing will be more articulate than your speech."

Florence's tone was changing rapidly. She was sounding less like a mother and more like an impatient schoolmistress. Tenderness must be rationed in moderation, or else it will have poisonous effects.

"Where's Dr. Grant?" the Irishman asked suddenly.

At the sound of her colleague's name, Florence twitched and nearly dropped Martin's head from her knees. That random question posed in a most innocent tone sent a chilly seizure through her body. Yet, there was decidedly nothing criminal about Private Martin's curiosity. Dr. Grant had been a prominent fixture at the hospital, an icon of stability and competence. It was only natural that the patients would wonder about his whereabouts.

"He was sent back to England," Florence replied after a few seconds of silence, struggling not to reveal her agitation. "I was informed earlier in the morning."

"Why?" Martin continued inquiring with the persistence of a curious child, unaware of her unease. "Why was Dr. Grant sent away?"

"I can only guess. Another friend leaving my side..." Florence was no longer speaking to her patient but to herself. "Oh, I should've expected something of the sort. It's happened to me before. The moment I find a worthy conversation partner, someone who can construct elaborate phrases and use Latin terms, he is snatched from me. Fate continues to tantalize me, feeding me morsels of hope."

"And that's why yer day's dismal?"

Those were the last distinct words that emerged from Martin's mouth. His body grew limp as he began dozing off.

A flock of vultures circling above the hospital drew Florence's glance towards the open window. They were no farther than a hundred yards. She could almost feel the fanning of their wings on her face. Before the war broke out, those birds were rare guests in Turkey or the Crimea. However, after the arrival of the Allie forces, those scavengers began migrating from as far away as North Africa, following the trail of corpses.

Being a woman of science, Florence harbored no sentiments akin to squeamishness or superstitious fear towards those birds. They were Nature's sanitarians. She knew that their stomach acid was particularly corrosive, making them able to devour carcasses that would be lethal to other scavengers. The hospital became a coveted attraction for them. Frequently the vultures would beat the gravediggers to the corpses. If one of the gravediggers attempted to frighten them away, the birds would use their reeking vomit as defense. *The Lord God made them all.* Florence remembered well that line from a popular religious hymn. The vultures would initiate the process of breaking down dead flesh, and the worms would finish it. Whoever found these simple scientific facts distasteful had no business working at a hospital. Dr. Thomas Grant would certainly support that statement.

"He better make himself known when this travesty is over," Florence continued her monologue, still staring at the night sky through the window. "He better find me home in England, or I'll find him. He promised to give me his book. If I discover that he allowed another woman to read it first..." A hint of female jealousy loomed in her voice. "So help him God! Oh, the sparkling dialogues we could've had. I can almost hear his cough behind my back. It's not unlike that lingering pain from a hand that's been severed."

Chapter 2
Those Big and Mighty Men

A rustle followed by a squeak interrupted Florence from her lovesick musing.

What sort of creature would roam the halls at such an hour? It was not a mouse—it was Rebecca Prior, the dimwitted blonde nurse prone to swooning and vomiting spells. She looked like she needed an audience.

Florence removed Private Martin's head from her knees and laid it cautiously on the bench. Then she grabbed Rebecca by the arm and pulled her aside, lest their presumably meaningless conversation should rouse the patient.

"Miss Prior," Florence began, folding her arms, "you have exactly two minutes to spill your tribulations. I hope to God they are grave enough."

"It's Mr. Bennett..." the nurse whined, twisting her plump pink hands nervously.

"Does he still scold you for that incident in the tent?"

The yellow locks around Rebecca's face bounced as she shook her head.

"No, he hasn't spoken of that night. It's not his words. It's his glances. They leave me unsettled."

Florence looked down and covered her mouth, formulating an appropriate answer, then nodded and glanced up at Rebecca.

"Miss Prior, I can't fathom what I could have done to encourage this sort of familiarity between us, to position myself as your confidant. When you barged in I thought for an instant that there was an attack or a fire. You distract me from my patients only to inform me that Mr. Bennett's glances leave you unsettled? Why, do you think, he chose you of all women as his target?"

Rebecca shrugged in contempt. The answer was obvious. How could Miss Nightingale not understand such simple things?

"Why, the rest of the nurses are nuns! Molly Fields and I are the only laywomen. Most of them are too bloody old, some well over thirty, and some—over forty!"

"God forbid!" Florence gasped in horror. "What business they have being alive! The audacity, to last that long! You and Molly are like yellow-beaked fledglings among old hens. What a lonely life it must be for the two of you."

Rebecca did not grasp the sarcasm in Florence's response and interpreted the head nurse's horror as genuine. She did not have a slightest idea how old Miss Nightingale was. Being eighteen and endowed with the intelligence of someone younger, Rebecca had trouble identifying other women's age. Completely ignorant of anatomy, biology and the natural signs of aging that one could expect at any given decade, she would not be able to tell the difference between a thirty and a fifty-year old. Had Miss Nightingale told her that she was twenty-five, Rebecca would have believed her.

"When Mr. Bennett stares at me," she continued agitatedly, drawing closer to her sympathetic confidante, "I simply can't work. My knees tremble, and my hands freeze."

"I think I know why your knees tremble, Miss Prior," Florence declared. "There's a scientific explanation for it." She leaned closer to Rebecca and sniffed the air. "Have you been drinking sterilizing solution?

The young nurse raised her hands and widened her cornflower eyes. She resembled a rabbit cornered by a hound.

"I swear it's not my fault! It's Molly... She carries a whiskey flask."

Florence smiled, as her intuition proved correct once again. One should not have expected a different answer from Miss Prior. Pointing her plump little finger at another girl was her instinctive defense. Florence could picture Rebecca as a child accusing one of her siblings of spilling the milk or eating the last butter biscuit.

Naturally, it was all Molly's fault. Molly must have pried Becky's jaws open and poured the content of the flask down her throat. Then Molly must have curled Becky's hair forcefully, stuffed rolled-up gauze down her blouse, and smudged old rouge over her cheeks.

"My, what wayward, scandalous girl, that Molly is!" Florence concluded, shaking her head. "Perhaps, I should have a private talk with her."

"Please, don't be cross with Molly!" Rebecca entreated, changing her attitude in a matter of a second. "She mustn't worry in her condition."

"What condition?" Florence asked mechanically. "Oh, sweet mother of God..." she whispered in disgust, having realized what the silly drunken girl was trying to tell her. "Not wasting any time is she! Who's the lucky partner in crime?"

"She's not quite sure," Rebecca replied nonchalantly, without a hint of embarrassment.

"Not quite sure? What a surprise! A fortunate baby, indeed! Some are born fatherless, but this one will have the entire British cavalry for a father."

One of the possibilities that crossed Florence's mind was the prime suspect was Lord Hungerton. Perhaps, that was one of the reasons why he left the hospital. He impregnated one of the nurses and vanished to avoid the consequences. How convenient indeed! Fortunately, for the young officer in question, Miss Prior scattered Florence's suspicion.

"Molly was already in that way when she came here," Rebecca giggled awkwardly. "For three days she vomited. We feared it was cholera; but it wasn't! Imagine our relief. So Molly came to Dr. Grant in hopes that he would help her put this mishap behind her." She kicked her foot up furtively and bit her lower lip. "But he refused! How shocked we were."

Florence's breathing quickened, her disgust escalating. Her hospital being used as an abortion den!

"What possessed Molly to approach Dr. Grant with such a request?"

Once again, Rebecca shrugged, mystified by Miss Nightingale's failure to grasp the obvious. Had she not been following the rumors? Truly, it is unhealthy to be so preoccupied with one's work and pay so little attention to what is happening around.

"We've all heard about his past, his days in Southwark," the young nurse continued in a matter-of-factly tone, as if stating that the moon was yellow and the grass was green. "There are all sorts of tales going around; but Dr. Grant swore that he had never rendered such services to women. He persuaded Molly to keep the baby and stop drinking. So she gave me her whiskey flask, and I gave her my shawl to hide her belly as it grows."

"Why, this is female solidarity at its finest!" Florence exclaimed, throwing her head back. "And then you wonder why Mr. Bennett stares at you. Look at yourself! You're a walking circus, drunk and painted while on duty! Then you run to me for protection! How do you expect me to protect you? I would have to dunk your head into a bucket with cold water first."

"Miss Nightingale," Rebecca whimpered on the brink of tears, "I thought that you'd understand, being a woman and all..."

"I am not a woman!"

This outrageous declaration prompted the girl to burst into hearty, sonorous laughter, the kind that would rouse a whole wing of the hospital. Now Rebecca knew that Miss Nightingale was joking. She was capable of making jokes after all.

"I am not a woman," Florence repeated through her teeth, seeing that once again her words were taken at face value. "Not in the sense that you and Molly are." She straightened before the mortified girl and clicked the heels of her shoes. "Allow me to make myself clear. I am a sergeant in petticoats. Truth be told, I feel very little affection for women, weak and foolish ones in particular. Their lot does not concern me. If my work reflects well on them, if it raises their standing, it will merely be a fortunate coincidence. My mission is not to advocate for the females of the species. I've reaped no benefit from associating with them. I prefer the company of powerful men."

Florence had hoped it would never come to her delivering that speech. She had hoped that subtle hints would suffice to make Rebecca understand the intellectual and spiritual gap between the two of them. They were made from the same clay and therefore could not be confidantes. That was the gist of what Florence attempted to communicate to her subordinate. Not surprisingly, Rebecca interpreted the head nurse's words in a way that made sense to her. She nodded feverishly, her attitude changing from imploring to aggressive.

"I see now!" she shouted, sticking her pink finger out again.

"You're envious of me, old maid that you are. Those big and mighty men of whom you speak—they won't bed you in a thousand years!" Having dropped all inhibition, Rebecca chattered like a squirrel, bobbing her curly head from side to side and making grimaces short of sticking her tongue out, her face brightest pink. She did not care that the patients in the next room began stirring and whispering. "That's right. They have no use for you. Wouldn't you love to trade places with me! Scrawny spinster... With a gray face and gray hairs..."

Having spouted out her last batch of insults, Rebecca suddenly fell silent and retreated, panting, terrified by her outburst.

"Dear girl," Florence said with astonishing composure, "if you carry on in this manner, you won't live to be an old maid. You will die a young hussy—if that is a more appealing fate."

Rebecca slouched and scurried off, as she did on the night of Private Martin's amputation. As for the Irishman, he moved on the bench, coming out of his slumber, and raised himself on the elbow.

"Was Rebecca here?" he asked in a drowsy voice.

"Yes, she just left," Florence replied curtly.

"I knew I heard 'er voice, so near..." Martin continued droning with moronic tenderness. "Seen 'er shadow. Couldn't get me eyes to open."

"You were sleeping."

"P'haps," he whispered, resigning. "Ah, wouldn't it be heavenly? Havin' her fer a mistress and you fer a mother... Why, I'd be the jolliest one-handed thief in the whole of England."

His elbow gave in, and he collapsed back on the bench.

Standing over the crippled simpleton, Florence threw her arms in despair. Why was it that every pickpocket under the sun considered her his mother?

"Dear boy," she said, "if you were my son, you would've turned out quite differently, I assure you. For one, you would've developed a more discriminating taste in women."

"I don't und'stand," the Irishman murmured, taken aback by her hostility.

Not that Florence expected him to understand. Perhaps, he and Rebecca would make a fine pair after all. They both had limited vocabularies and limited control over their impulses. Alas, she could not cure them of their origin. It was not in her power—or in her contract. She could only bandage Martin's stump and pour some sedatives under his tongue.

"Let us not pamper our illusions," she concluded out loud. "I am nobody's mother. I am but a frigid spinster. And you are an orphan, and a thief, and an invalid. And Rebecca is a hussy. What's even more tragic? We're all English citizens. We have allied with a Muslim nation against our fellow Christians. That alone can unsettle your stomach worse than cholera."

Chapter 3
Dialogue with an Iron Scarecrow

Wrapping gauze around her index finger had become nerve-calming technique for Florence. She feared that if she would let her hands rest for a second, she would lose control over her mind. She used that wretched piece of fabric to keep her thoughts tied together.

Suddenly, she felt on her cheek a chaste, filial kiss, mocking in its reverence. She shuddered, turned around, and saw the insolent scarred face of Lord Hungerton.

"Your prodigal son has returned, Miss Nightingale," he said. "Are you pleased to see me?"

"To be perfectly honest..." she blurted out and stammered.

The rogue nodded lightly, encouraging her to finish the sentence.

"You can be as honest with me as your conscience dictates, Miss Nightingale. I am sure you are forced to tell hundreds of noble fibs every day."

"I had hoped you would not return, Lord Hungerton."

"You are breaking my heart! How could I abandon my beloved Heavies? What would they do without me? You are merciless."

"I thought you wanted the truth. Every night I prayed that your engagements at Balaclava would keep you there. God appears to have ceased answering my prayers."

"Now, don't blaspheme, Miss Nightingale. Every prayer is answered, but not always to our satisfaction."

Florence kicked herself for having allowed the clown to pull her into an idle exchange of venomous phrases. He managed to engage her in his game, and now she did not know how to exit it.

"What do you want?" she asked abruptly.

Wynfield had no intention of abandoning his game so easily.

"You know exactly what I want, Miss Nightingale," he replied in the same smug, flirtatious tone. "It's the same thing I wanted three weeks ago. I am a man of simple desires."

"Not another word about your rehabilitative endeavors."

"Please, understand, it is not my whim. It is the demand of Sir James Scarlett. All that he requests of you is to designate an open space two hundred yards long to practice target shooting. I have kept a close eye on the Heavies. At least twenty of them are in the final stages of recovery. It should please you to hear that. Soon they will be ready to resume active duty."

"I cannot have the noise from the rifles and revolvers disturb my patients. I am a woman of medicine. Do not expect me to sympathize with incompetent military leaders and go out of my way to accommodate their requests. My duty is to see that my patients leave the hospital alive. What they do after their release is none of my concern."

"Bah, classical female logic!" Wynfield smacked his lips spitefully. "You reason like a quintessential woman."

"I beg to differ, Lord Hungerton," Florence retaliated, wagging her index finger that was still wrapped in gauze. "I am anything but a quintessential woman. If Sir James wishes to lay demands on me, he will have to see me in person. I will not conduct discourse with him through his flunkies."

Wynfield hummed in perplexity and rubbed his upper lip.

"If I suffered from insecurity," he said, taking Florence's arm and leaning to her ear, "I would conclude that you were not terribly fond of me, Mrs. Nightingale. That is how an outsider would interpret your behavior towards me. Of course, I know that to be untrue. The only reason why you wish me gone is because I am too much of a distraction. When I am here, all you desire to do is converse with me; and who could blame you? I am an obscenely engaging person. You shall be seeing more of me. If you are to have a tryst with Thomas Grant, you must realize its stipulations. You will be gaining more than an aging, sickly lover. You will also be gaining a son, a hideously disfigured, lecherous, irreverent, fearless, witty son, who will kiss you on the cheek every night, just like he did a few minutes ago."

Florence freed her arm from his grip and shoved him in the chest, but Wynfield did not even waver, slight as he was.

"You look perplexed, Miss Nightingale," he remarked. "Your dear friend never mentioned having a son, did he?"

"Dr. Grant may have mentioned an adopted son in passing," she replied, glancing up at him. "The young man had died."

"What a curious bit of news. Why wasn't I informed of my own death? How convenient for Dr. Grant! Is that what he told you?"

"Yes, and I believe him. I have trouble imagining a man like Dr. Grant putting forth into the world a creature like you."

Disagreeable as this admission was to Florence, in her heart she could conceive of Lord Hungerton being Dr. Grant's son. Intuition told her that stranger things have happened.

Having sensed falsity in her voice, Wynfield sighed sorrowfully and shook his head.

"Poor, poor Florence... You do not mind my familiarity, do you? I cannot help feeling a kindred sort of affection for you. How fiercely you cling to your illusions. How desperately you wish to believe in Thomas Grant's decency. You are too arrogant to admit that your taste in men is abysmal. After Sidney Herbert, you have truly stepped down. Imagine your mother's outrage if she saw you in the arms of an opium-trading vivisectionist!"

Having said that, Wynfield burst into convulsive laughter, and he continued laughing even after Florence had struck him across the face. It was not a female slap delivered with the palm and the fingertips. It was a hard blow of a fist. Sadly for Florence, it proved to be just as ineffective as the shove in the chest a minute earlier. The scarecrow was made of iron!

"Miss Nightingale, do you treat all your children with such tenderness?" he asked. "You are in the wrong profession. You should have led the army at Balaclava, dear lady. Or should I say 'dear sir'? The Light Brigade would've been left intact."

Florence had to give justice to the hacked-up rogue: he did understand her better than others did. As much as she desired to continue loathing him, she could not. Perhaps, this ill-mannered and horrendously misguided young man was the last thing she would have left of her beloved Tom.

She did not stop Lord Hungerton when he went over to pinch the sleeping Irish cripple.

"Awake, Seamus," Wynfield chanted, kneeling by the bench. "Jerry is here."

Private Martin stretched convulsively, lifted his head, and a second later his dirty face beamed.

"Lord Hung'ton... Yer came back? Am I dreamin' still?"

"Of course, I came back. You're been sorely missed, Seamus."

"Now there's less o'me to miss," the Irishman snarled, nodding at his stump. "'Tis all o'er now. I'm but an orphaned cripple. Miss Nighin'ale said so h'self."

While it was not Martin's goal to denounce his nurse, Wynfield cast an interrogative over-the-shoulder glance at Florence, who exhaled nervously and fanned herself, even though it was chilly in the hall.

"Well, Seamus, I have news for you," Wynfield continued, having turned back to face the Irishman. "You are not a cripple. You are my friend. When this ordeal is over, I shall take you to London with me. I want you as a guest of honor at my wedding. You shall dance a jig before everyone. Your feet are intact, aren't they?"

The Irishman responded with a series of shallow nods. From a distance it looked as if he were simply shivering from the cold.

"Aye, lord Hung'ton, wouldn't that be grand?"

"I only wish for you to know that you are not alone," Wynfield continued, rubbing the elbow of Martin's mangled arm. "You shall not find yourself on the streets, or in a poorhouse, or back in prison. I forbid you to entertain such thoughts. Hundreds of soldiers owe their lives to you. If not for the water you helped us find, they would not have made their way out of the Calamita Bay. I shall never let anyone forget."

Suddenly, Martin's face changed. His forehead creased, and he pulled the stump of his hand away from Wynfield.

"Say no mo', Lord Hung'ton..."

"What's the matter, Seamus," Wynfield asked. "What did I say?"

"Yer sayin' all good thin's—too good to be true. I've trouble believin' yer. Recall the time we spoke on the banks o'the Alma, right aft' the battle? Didn't yer say me hand could be saved? Yer said the wound wasn't grave. Yer lied to me then, didn't yer? Whilst yer intent was noble..."

Still kneeling, Wynfield recoiled from the bench, looking downward. Suddenly, Florence stepped in.

"He did not lie to you, James."

Wynfield and Martin both looked up at her.

"What yer sayin', Miss Miss Nighin'ale?" the Irishman asked.

"I am saying," Florence began, struggling to sound convincing, "that the loss of your hand was an unfortunate consequence of the dire conditions in the hospital, conditions that I have fought to improve. Your hand could have been saved, had we possessed a larger medical staff and more abundant supplies. The people who work here are very skillful and dedicated, but there simply aren't enough of them. Do not blame Lord Hungerton for misleading you. He was not mocking you or feeding you false hope. He simply was unaware of our limitations here. I can see plainly that he cares for you deeply. Perhaps, he is not a doctor, but he is certainly your friend. And if he promised to take you to London with him, you have every reason to believe him."

The answer seemed to satisfy Martin. He sighed and reclined back on the bench. The fingers of his good hand found Wynfield's hand.

"F'give me, Lord Hung'ton," he mumbled. "I had no business lashin' out at yer."

"Don't give it another thought, Seamus. I was perfectly earnest and sincere when I invited you to my wedding. I truly want you there, as a witness to my happiness."

Florence turned away to hide the blush and the sweat on her face. It was one of those rare instances when she chose sentimentality over practicality. She would rather endanger the reputation of the hospital than the friendship between the two young men.

Chapter 4
Polite Ways of Asking for Promotion

Corrupt minds think alike. Approximately at the same time, Lucan and Cardigan became overwhelmed by the same desire: to flee. Having to look at the fading remnants of the Light Brigade was becoming more and more burdensome with each day. The only place to which they could flee without being branded cowards was Scutari. To visit the wounded and the ailing subordinates was a noble excuse, one to which Raglan could not object. A few weeks after the Battle of Balaclava, the warring in-laws, independently of each other, rushed across the Black Sea to the same destination that they perceived as their sanctuary.

Cardigan sailed on his yacht *the Dryad*. He would not give up his customary luxuries even after the travesty with the Light Brigade, or rather, *especially* after the travesty. After all the hardships he had endured on the battlefield, he felt entitled to his comforts more than ever.

Cardigan's cavalier demeanor could not leave the onlookers unimpressed. He behaved like an innocent man, who had made no mistakes and had no reasons to feel ashamed. There have been rumors of his alleged desertion. One of Raglan's staff officers, Colonel Calthorpe, claimed that he saw Raglan gallop away from the front lines on his charger Ronald, bred on the Deene Park estate. Lord Paget had also noticed Cardigan's absence. However, none of the officers dared to make any overt accusations.

Having reunited with his troops after the Charge, he declared:

"Men, it is a mad-brained trick, but it is no fault of mine."

Later on, when Raglan attempted to confront him, the earl retaliated smoothly and nonchalantly.

"My lord, I hope you will not blame me, for I received the order to attack from my superior officer in front of the troops."

He was referring to the Lieutenant General, his brother-in-law.

Lucan's worst nightmare was materializing. Just as he had feared, Raglan, Cardigan and Airey allied against him to make him the scapegoat. Since Nolan, the man truly responsible for the disaster, was dead, the treacherous trio needed to find someone with a heartbeat. It was convenient to blame Lucan for having been too obedient and not having questioned the orders.

"You have lost the Light Brigade," Raglan declared on the night after the charge.

He would not let Lucan say a word in self-defense—not that the Lieutenant General had much to say that evening. Of all the generals involved, he grieved the calamity most acutely and most sincerely, even though he suspected that his men would not believe it.

The fact that Lucan embraced the Spartan conditions endured by the rest of his men made him look like repentant sinner. His behavior suggested that was punishing himself for something, therefore he must have been guilty. For weeks, he slept on the ground, shivered in the late autumn wind, rolled in dirt and lice, his fury rapidly turning to apathy. Occasionally, he would reach out and rest his weather-beaten hand on the disheveled head of his son. To Lord Bingham's astonishment, his father did not take his fury out on his staff. Now that one of the aide-de-camps was dead and another one away at Scutari, Lucan made an effort to draw the rest of them closer one another.

"I wonder how Lord Hungerton is faring," he would mutter.

In late November, the earl sailed to Scutari incognito on a transport ship, accompanied by Dr. Ferrars. Having disembarked at the crowded dock, they made their way to the hospital by foot, in spite of Lucan's leg wound. Suddenly, it occurred to the earl that he should have made arrangements to deliver supplies to the hospital.

You're growing senile, George, he scolded himself silently. *Thank God, your children cannot see you.*

That phrase became his litany over the next few days, a form of verbal self-flagellation. He resumed his Spartan lifestyle at the hospital, having lodged in the same room as the Heavies. Very soon, he discovered that his presence had an oppressive effect on his men. His awkward attempts at jovial familiarity sowed suspicion and unease. The soldiers would grow silent and cluster together, secretly hoping he would leave. One evening Lord Hungerton managed to cajole the Heavies to play a round of cards with their commander. The men agreed reluctantly, but only as a favor for their beloved patron.

"They despise me," Lucan confided to Wynfield later that night. "I dare not imagine what rumors are circulating about me. No doubt, my dear brother-in-law has contributed his part to my defamation."

"Be patient, my lord," Wynfield attempted to comfort him. "The truth will emerge—it always does. Perhaps, I could use my influence over the Heavies to help redeem your reputation."

"No!" Lucan raised his hand proudly. "Leave this battle to me. Besides, you were not even there when the charge of the Light Brigade took place. Your testimony will not sound authentic at any rate."

Fortunately for Lucan, over the course of his stay at Scutari he did not run into Cardigan once. The two in-laws managed to avoid one another. The Noble Yachtsman was much too squeamish to enter the halls of the hospital. He spent most of his time aboard *the Dryad*.

Their exile could not last forever. Raglan, who was aware of their whereabouts, sent a letter to Scutari demanding their immediate return to the camp.

"The means of my execution must have been decided," Lucan joked to Wynfield. "Raglan wishes for everyone to be present at my court-martial."

One morning, as the earl was smoking his cigar outside the hospital, a scrawny freckled surgeon by the name Timothy Bennett approached him. With his head bowed and his hands clasped on his chest, he looked the epitome of servility.

"Thank you, my lord, for granting me this audience," he began.

"Your crude interruption of my morning walk hardly constitutes an audience," Lucan replied, looking ahead and blowing smoke through his nostrils. "Consider yourself lucky. Ordinarily I would have you removed from my path by the scruff of your neck, but today I'll make an exception. You see, in the near future I too have an audience, one that promises to be tiresome. Perhaps, if I indulge a creature like you, even for an instant, God will credit me this good deed and shorten the impending ordeal. You chose a good day to ambush me. Speak, young butcher."

"My lord, you are in grave danger," Timothy blurted out.

"What shocking news." The earl yawned. "Who is after me this time?"

"Your own brother-in-law, my lord."

"Dear old Jimmy?" Lucan inquired, feigning shock. "Who would've imagined? I thought we were getting along so splendidly. Tell me, young butcher, whence do you derive such wild ideas?"

"My lord, it's true!" Timothy shouted, sensing he was being ridiculed. Agitation made him salivate profusely. He swallowed, filled his narrow chest with air and continued with doubled speed. "Lord Cardigan plotting your overthrow as we speak. He had recruited that diabolic doctor, Thomas Grant, who has been on his yacht since yesterday. I do not know what your brother-in-law had promised Grant, but that man has no principles, no honor. He won't think twice before breaking the Oath for his personal benefit. Take my word for it. I've worked under his watch. Sadly, my colleagues do not seem to grasp the full extent of Grant's moral depravity. He had fooled everyone, from the chaplain to Miss Nightingale. She is smitten by him! And the soldiers worship him. It's quite gut-wrenching."

"Are you finished, young butcher?" the earl asked, still looking ahead.

"Almost, my lord." Timothy rubbed his gloved hands together. Hungry sparks began jigging in his beady eyes. "In light of the situation, I assume that Thomas Grant will not be returning to the hospital corps. Now that he has a new personal benefactor in the face of Lord Cardigan, he will surely abandon his medical responsibilities. The unit will need a new physician. I hope it is not overly presumptuous on my behalf to recommend myself for the vacant position. True, I do not have a diploma from Cambridge, but I am familiar with the patients, their wounds, and their conditions. They trust me. And I in turn am bound to them by duty and compassion."

Timothy delivered the last three sentences with a hand on his heart, practically chanting, projecting theatrical self-deprecation.

"In other words, you came to ask for a promotion?" the earl asked. The hand holding the withering cigar froze. "Then you should've started with that. You should've said: 'Lord Lucan, Thomas Grant is in my way. Please remove him from his post, so I can to slice and dice my patients freely.' That would've saved us both a few minutes."

Timothy gasped and recoiled, insulted to the bottom of his heart.

"My lord, you are mistaken in regards to my motives. I swear on my life that my primary concern is for your wellbeing—and that of England."

Lucan tossed aside his cigar turned towards Bennett abruptly. The expression on the earl's face made the puny surgeon jump up like a startled squirrel.

"Am I expected to believe such declarations? You pitiable gossip boy!" Lucan roared. "If anyone deserves to be removed from his post, it is you!" He pulled out his model Adams and poked the barrel it into the surgeon's chest. Paralyzed from his toes to his eyelids, Bennett could not even blink. "First you interrupt my morning walk, which alone merits court-martial," Lucan continued, accompanying almost every word with a shove of the revolver. "Then you insult me by suggesting that I have something to fear from my imbecile brother-in-law and that hairy abortionist from Southwark. You truly fathom yourself so significant to imply that I cannot solve a family trifle without your assistance? Back to your victims, butcher!"

As soon as the revolver stopped pointing at his chest, Bennett regained his bravado.

"My lord, you will regret not heeding me."

"Out of my sight!" snarled the earl.

Chapter 5
Variations on James Braid's Method

Dr. Ferrars awakened on the floor of the provisions cellar. At his head, he found a petticoat and a shawl, the former belonging to Rebecca Prior, and the latter to Molly Fields. The two lay nurses were sleeping a few feet away from him with their heads on a flour sack. The physician was proud to have remembered their names and which article of clothing belonged to which girl, even though he had only spoken to them once. He took even more pride in the act he committed with them in the cellar. It was so deliciously gauche, so piquantly against the code of professional conduct! His former colleagues from Cambridge would be outraged and envious. God, did he need that release, after months of deprivations, suffering and ceaseless intellectual work. He had not bedded a woman since he left Laleham in late spring. It was late autumn now. He had been so preoccupied with studying and manipulating other people's minds that he had been unforgivably neglectful towards his own physical needs. When the two giggling girls grabbed him by the hands and dragged him into the cellar, how could he resist? No, he did not feel any remorse, not towards Molly Fields at any rate. She was already pregnant by someone else, so she could not claim that he ruined her reputation.

Suddenly, he noticed the two nurses.

"What are they doing here, Richard?" he asked Dr. Ferrars, gesturing in their direction.

"They are sleeping," he physician replied smugly. "Can't you see? Or rather, they *were* sleeping until you barged in and awakened them."

Rebecca and Molly both opened their eyes, propped themselves up on the sack and assumed inviting poses, preparing for a second tour of duty.

"Richard, you cannot subject yourself to such danger," Wynfield reproached him, having forgotten the reason why he came into the cellar. "These two fine ladies will make you ill, and I'm not referring to cholera here. Even I do not bed them. And neither would you after seeing what sort of company they keep."

Dr. Ferrars picked up Molly's shawl and twirled it in the air.

"Lord Hungerton, did you come here to compare our respective activities below the waist? I am touched by your concern for my wellbeing. I assure you, it is unnecessary. I know better than you how to avoid communicable diseases. Unfortunately, Lord Lucan does not like me well enough to present me with Balkan or Crimean virgins on my birthday. My humble position confines me to the company of my fellow countrywomen, and I do not consider myself deprived."

"Look, Richard, you must send these lovelies away," Wynfield demanded. "Get rid of them."

"In the middle of the night?" Dr. Ferrars asked indignantly.

"Believe me, there are other beds for them to warm," Wynfield assured him. "I need to speak with you right this instant. I demand your undivided attention. No external audience."

Rebecca and Molly did not need to wait for Dr. Ferrars to dismiss them officially. They collected their garments and scurried up the staircase, whispering and giggling. They had already made up their minds to come back. Befriending the personal physician of the Lieutenant General was too profitable an opportunity to pass by. This friendship promised to bring both of them fantastical prosperity.

As soon as their footsteps abated, Wynfield plopped himself down on the vacated flour sack and dropped his head on his knees.

"Your story better shake me to my core," Dr. Ferrars began menacingly. "Do you know what one man can do to another man for interrupting his orgy?"

"Richard, I think I'm losing my mind," Wynfield said without lifting his head.

The declaration was music to Dr. Ferrars' ears. Individual cases of insanity ranked among his favorite professional challenges, right below massive brainwashing.

"Do you have reasons to fortify your theory?" he asked, remains of sleepiness melting away.

Wynfield lifted his face but avoided looking Dr. Ferrars in the eye, apparently embarrassed by his forthcoming confession.

"I was in the room with the Heavies, as usual," he began. "We had just finished the last round of poker and put the cards away. Suddenly, when I glanced around, I discovered myself was in an entirely different place. The room changed its shape and turned into the dining hall of a tavern. The Heavies turned into sailors and factory workers. There was the dark-haired girl with knives sitting in the corner, and an old bear was pouring drinks for the customers. Remember that bastard who slashed me up for some stupid transgression? I saw him from the back."

"Perhaps, you were having a nightmare," Dr. Ferrars suggested innocently.

"No, I was completely awake and not even terribly exhausted. All of a sudden, my face began to burn. I could feel the skin tearing, the scars opening. I stormed out of the room, howling like a madman."

"That is perfectly in line with Carpenter's ideo-motor reflex theory," Dr. Ferrars concluded triumphantly.

"Could you repeat it in English now?"

"Certain ideas and images can trigger physical sensations. All this is very good, Lord Hungerton, however inconvenient and ill timed it may appear to you. Perhaps, you are not losing your mind but rather recovering it."

"For the love of God, stop speaking in riddles. They confuse me even more."

The physician squinted pensively, flipping through the archives of his theoretical knowledge that he had not used in a while.

"You think you can stay awake a bit longer?" he asked suddenly.

"I can't imagine falling asleep after this experience," Wynfield replied, throwing his arms up. "I would be afraid to close my eyes."

"Perhaps, I can help you," Dr. Ferrars murmured, looking around and patting the pockets of his trousers. "Remain where you are."

He removed the lantern from the ceiling and placed it on the floor between himself and his patient. They both could see each other's faces, evenly illuminated.

Next, the physician took out his pocket watch and held it about ten inches away from the patient's eyes.

"What are you doing?" Wynfield asked, frowning.

"I am attempting to initiate James Braid's hypnotic induction method," Dr. Ferrars replied softly and steadily.

"Didn't I ask you to speak English?"

"Just keep your stare fixated on the watch. Let me know if I need to bring it closer or remove it farther away. I do not wish to strain your eyelids too much."

"I told you, Richard, I do not wish to fall asleep."

"You will not fall asleep, I assure you. On the contrary, you will be in a state of heightened awareness."

Wynfield exhaled, abdicating, and fixed at the brass case of the watch.

"Why, this must be the pinnacle of idiocy," he declared after a few seconds. "I have no time for this."

"Of course, you have time for this," Dr. Ferrars replied soothingly, having taken no offense to such a blunt criticism of his technique. "You have all the time in the world. All the time in the world... All the time... in the world..."

As he spoke, Wynfield's pupils began dilating, and the crease between his eyebrows began smoothing out. The neck and face muscles became more relaxed.

"It is the year of our Lord 1852," Dr. Ferrars continued, having assessed that the patient's state allowed for the treatment to continue. "We are in England, enjoying another muddy, foggy spring. It rains almost every day. You cannot distinguish morning from evening."

"God damn the government," Wynfield mumbled. "Those whoresons raised the taxes again. Half of the shops on our street are closing. There are piles of broken furniture in the middle of the road."

"And that concerns you because—"

"My landlord may be next in line to the debtors' prison. He keeps his books hidden from the Irish cow. She wipes the tables at his tavern and likes to poke her freckled nose everywhere, particularly where she shouldn't. My landlord had once kept the books under the counter but then hid them under a lock inside his cabinet."

"What is the cow's name?"

"Brigit... And there's another cow by the name Ingrid. That one is from Sweden, speaks her own version of English. And there's a tiny she-wolf by the name Diana, hiding in the dark corner with her knives... And a famished bear by the name..."

Suddenly, the patient blinked, and the crease reappeared between his eyebrows. Dr. Ferrars did not let him slip out of the trance.

"Tell me more about your neighbors," he requested, shifting the position of the watch slightly. "Life cannot be horrible for all of them. Is anyone prospering?"

"Mr. Langsdale certainly is," Wynfield responded at once. "He never splurges on soap, and he does not hire help. He performs all tasks with his own filthy hands. As for my landlord, he fancies himself a gentleman. He would sooner forgo bread than soap."

"And how did you come to board with such a man?" the physician asked. "Can you describe your first encounter?"

For the first time, the patient hesitated to respond.

"I cannot remember," he admitted at last.

"In that case, what is your earliest memory involving that man?"

"The reflection of my bandaged face in the mirror that he handed to me... Layer by layer, he unwrapped the gauze. He told me not to be disheartened and that many women were drawn to interesting disfigurements."

Wynfield raised his hands to his face and began rubbing his scars as if trying to erase them. His jagged nails left red traces on his cheeks. His eyes were no longer focused on the shiny object.

"Enough for tonight," Dr. Ferrars ruled, putting the watch away. "We shall resume our dialogue tomorrow."

The patient's hands stopped ravaging his face and dropped. With his eyes still open, he slipped from the flour sack down to the floor. He resembled a puppet abandoned by the puppeteer.

Chapter 6
The Lamp and the Canteen

The lack of intellectual equals in her immediate vicinity kept Florence engaged in silent dialogues with her former lovers. Sometimes both Richard Milnes and Sir Sidney Herbert would appear in her thoughts and begin arguing amongst each other, forcing her to intervene.

"Down with it, gentlemen!" she would scold them, not realizing that sometimes she would say those words out loud. "You are both wrong on all accounts."

Ironically, the activity geared towards preserving her sanity was in fact destroying it. Her patients and subordinates could not help noticing the new peculiarities in her behavior, and having noticed them, they could not refrain from discussing them.

"Poor Miss Nightingale," the nurses would whisper. "Her condition is worrisome."

"Have you seen the shadows around her eyes?"

"She is growing negligent."

Indeed, Florence was paying less attention to the tidiness of her wardrobe. Instead of changing the white cuffs on her dress, she removed them altogether along with the buttons and simply kept the sleeves rolled up. She no longer invested much effort into braiding her hair neatly and could go for a week without undoing her bun. Every day more loose tresses were framing her pale, angular face. Her movements, formerly so graceful and authoritative, became abrupt and uncertain. She would waver, bump into objects, stumble, and mutter words for which she would have chastised her subordinates only a month ago. Her demeanor bordered on hostile. Her voice would fluctuate in volume, fading and breaking. Over the course of delivering one sentence, she could go from shouting to whispering.

"God save Miss Nightingale," her patients would pray.

"Something is gnawing her from within."

"She is going mad!"

Oblivious to her surrounding, Florence did not suspect that she had acquired a most sincere albeit passive sympathizer—the Earl of Lucan. The sight of an exquisite stoic woman drained by her thankless mission aroused long-forgotten chivalrous sentiments. He could not promise providing more staff and supplies for her hospital, but he could offer his broad shoulder as a prop for her disheveled pretty head. He knew when Florence made her rounds and timed his promenades through the halls of the hospital accordingly. Did she not notice how dashing he looked in his uniform? Did she not see his sincere concern for his wounded men? Did she not hear him inquire about their condition? He would lavish his compassion on them in her presence, and she would not as much as glance in his direction. Foolish woman! She was always drowning in her ludicrous internal conflicts, always inventing new tortures for herself instead of extracting pleasures out of life! No wonder she never married. What sort of feat did he, the Earl of Lucan, Lieutenant-General need to accomplish in order to attract her attention? Did his nobility title and military rank count for anything? In the past, he had been able to tempt women far wealthier and more notorious than her. Perhaps, Florence was only feigning disinterest in order to fuel his passion. Yes, that must have been the reason for her chilly demeanor! No other explanation fit. On the other hand, perhaps, she was deterred by the fact that he was still officially married to Anne Brudenell? No, that did not seem like a valid reason. Sidney Herbert's family status did not stop her from becoming intimate with him. Perhaps, she was intimidated by the age difference?

Lucan thought about the two decades separating them, her thirty-four against his fifty-four. He had always preferred younger women. The Balkan girl he had bedded in Varna was fourteen, young enough to be his granddaughter. His ability to impress younger women with his trim torso had always been a source of pride for him. His beauty was ageless and effortless. What woman would not want a kiss from a man with such firm lips and sparkling teeth? Contrary to popular assumptions, he was not a selfish, demanding lover. He made sure that his mistresses experienced at least some pleasure. He was no expert on female physiology, but at least he knew how to avoid causing pain. When he had finished with the Balkan virgin, she looked pleasantly surprised. She must have expected carnal tyranny, and instead she received a rather gallant initiation into womanhood. There was hardly any blood on the sheets. Had he no right to take pride in the diplomatic manner in which he had handled such a delicate case?

A swarm of questions buzzed inside Lord Lucan's head. One evening, having grown tired of fruitless gentlemanlike pursuit, he ambushed Florence inside the nurses' tower, right by the door of her bedroom.

"Miss Nightingale," he whispered fervently, pressing her against the wall with his uniform-clad chest, "when shall you stop ignoring my tokens of devotion?"

His coarse, tobacco-saturated mustache brushed against her neck. The handle of his sword cut into her hip.

Sensing that she would need both hands to defend herself from the onslaught of unsolicited affection, Florence dropped the lamp. The heated glass broke, the oil spilled on her dress, and a second later the hem of her skirt caught fire.

Not a single gasp escaped from Florence's chest. Her lips squeezed tightly, she snatched the canteen from the belt of the astonished earl. Fortunately, there was enough water to put out the flames. Five seconds later the empty canteen was lying on the floor next to the broken lamp. Florence and Lucan were standing three feet away from each other, both staring downward and panting.

"Miss Nightingale," the earl began in a tone of repentance and humility. "Undoubtedly, you have heard some rather unflattering descriptions of my person."

"I do not pay attention to military gossip," Florence replied coldly, brushing out the folds of her skirt.

Her imperturbability stunned the earl, who had expected a hurricane of reproaches and threats. No, she did not even cry for help. Perhaps, she thought there was no use in trying to appeal to his conscience. She behaved around him as she would around an unruly patient or a rabid animal, a creature to be dreaded but not judged. As far as she was concerned, he did not possess a moral dimension, only a baggage of crude instincts.

"I know how horrifying this scene would have appeared to an innocent onlooker," Lucan continued, "but I swear on the lives of my children..." He took a moment to rethink such an extravagant pledge. "Miss Nightingale, I do not wish for you to consider me the sort of man who would ambush a woman in a moment of weakness."

"Do not flatter yourself, my lord," she replied, buttoning her collar. "You did not catch me in a moment of weakness. I have not experienced such a moment in a very long time. And for the future, please be advised that I am more skilled with surgical scissors than you are with your sword. Good night, my lord."

There was a hint of squeamish pity in her voice.

Lucan heard the creaking of the key and the slamming of the door. He was standing in a puddle of oil mixed with water. Bits of broken glass glistened at his feet. Somewhere in his turbulent romantic tenure, he forgot how to express his sentiments with dignity. What sort of creature was he becoming? Considering his monstrous reputation, no woman would ever believe in the sincerity of his affection from now on. Any gesture of gallantry would be interpreted as attempted rape. Having lost his credibility as a general, he was beginning to lose his credibility as a gentleman. The Crimean campaign was turning out to be a disaster on more than one front for his lordship.

Chapter 7
The Yellow Notebook
Finds a New Owner

It would be an exaggeration to say that the incident in the dark hall scarred Florence deeply. The earl was not the first man who had attempted to reinforce his verbal compliments with hand action. It took her less than an hour to repair the burned hem of her dress. The loss of the lamp distressed Florence considerably more. Growing attached to other human beings was an impermissible luxury, so she grew attached to inanimate objects. She would have been more willing to forgive Lord Lucan the violation of her chastity than the breaking of her beloved lamp. At almost thirty-five, she would not allow a minor sexual mishap devastate her. If anything, she became a little more vigilant while ascending the staircase of the tower at night and made sure that at least one other nurse was accompanying her.

In the meanwhile, her exhaustion kept accumulating. She was entering the same sleepwalking state as the chaplain. One evening, while making the rounds for the last time, she bumped into a leg of a bench, and the ring with keys slipped off her wrist. Florence bent over to pick them up and suddenly discovered that she was unable to stand up. She let out an exhausted laugh, laid her head on the bench, and closed her eyes. Apparently, that was where God wanted her to spend the night. An invisible wing wrapped around her shoulders, persuading her to surrender to sleep.

As soon as Florence complied, the same wing ushered her inside an edifice resembling giant surgical tent made of dark-blue silk and studded with diamonds. Florence reached out with her hand towards the heaving dome, and suddenly, it lowered upon her. The universe itself was meeting Florence halfway. Entranced by the ringing of hundreds of tiny brass bells, she began snatching stars from the sky as she would currants from a bush. Separated from their element, the stars would extinguish and turn to dust in her fingers. Suddenly, the dome wavered, and a vulture's claw tore through it. On one of the talons shone Lord Raglan's famous ring from the Waterloo era.

Florence froze with her head up, expecting to see the rest of the vulture's body through the ripped fabric of the universe, but the vision began fading, as a sensation from the physical world began pulling her from the dream—a man's fingers brushed against her bare forearm.

Her first thought was that Lord Lucan had returned to resume his courtship. Would she have the bodily strength to resist another amorous onslaught? Perhaps, if she remained perfectly listless, he would eventually lose heart and go away on his own accord. Florence remarked that the strokes were uncharacteristically reverent and did not move past her arm. Apparently, his lordship was attempting to prove that he was not a lascivious monster and that he was capable of chaste caresses.

Suddenly, above her head Florence heard a hoarse cough, a familiar sound that could not be mistaken with any other. Still unable to move a limb or even lift her head, she forced her eyelids open and perceived the slouching figure of Dr. Grant, shrouded in pale light breaking through the window.

Now Florence knew for certain that she was still dreaming; or perhaps, her heart had stopped suddenly and she died in her sleep. Yes, she had heard of such occurrences. No doubt, Tom's spirit must have come to fetch her.

"What time is it?" she heard herself ask.

Of all the questions she had for him regarding the nature of the afterlife, she chose the most mundane one. She could not even recognize her own voice, so detached and foreign it sounded.

"It appears that I lost my pocket watch," Tom replied, lowering himself on the ground next to her. "Are you surprised to see me?"

Florence leaned forward and found herself in the embrace of his emaciated, weak, burning arms. Feeling the pulsation of his neck vein against her cheek, she concluded that she was dealing with a living man rather than a ghost. They both were still alive.

"I don't understand," she whispered at last, pushing her hands into his bony chest and struggling to look him in the eye. "I was told that you were sent back to England."

"Not until all my evil deeds in the Crimea are completed," Tom replied with his usual weary self-deprecation. "Tell me now: do you like boring tales of political conspiracy?"

"If they are told by you—surely!"

"In that case, you're in for such a treat."

There were sitting at a slight distance from each other, leaning against the bench. Florence continued stroking the fringe of Tom's scarf, as if to verify that he was real. This swing from despair to euphoria, from drowsiness to extreme alertness, proved to be a shock for her weakened body and mind. Her blood vessels began expanding rapidly under the intensifying blood flow. The tingling pain coursing through her limbs was akin to that of lightly frostbitten flesh dipped into hot water.

"What if I told you," Tom began, leaning closer to her, "that Cardigan offered me ten thousand pounds to drug Lucan?"

Florence released the edge of his scarf, shook her head, and laughed.

"I know, I couldn't believe it either," Tom commented in solidarity.

"No!" Florence objected, her tone suddenly changing to that of hostility. "I cannot believe that you did not grasp at this opportunity."

"To stuff my pockets?" Tom asked, still believing her hostility to be feigned.

"No—to free England from a mid-caliber tyrant!"

By God, she was not joking. Once again, she began wrapping the edge of his scarf around her wrist, this time more frantically. Hastily, Tom pulled the woolen rag off his neck and handed it over to Florence, lest she should strangle him by accident.

"But the Oath..." he muttered.

"The Oath!" she gasped, tugging at the ends of the hapless scarf ferociously. "The Oath applies to people, those illiterate no-names who groan on the surgical table, die of infections and are thrown into a mass grave. Cardigan and Lucan do not belong to that category. Don't you know, by now?"

Florence rose to her feet and began pacing in front of the bench, babbling like a madwoman.

"Some epidemics come in the form of other two-legged creatures that look distressingly human." She stopped and raised her index finger. "But we, as medics, must make such distinctions and take necessary actions. Amputate Lucan, as you would a gangrenous limb. By God, there are no victims on that yacht, only predators of various sizes, all equally despicable."

Tom caught her by the wrist and rubbed in the area of the pulse.

"And this is precisely why I cannot bring myself to destroy Lucan," he said, looking up into her blazing eyes. "Raglan will replace him with someone even worse. Lord knows, the British army does not lack for incompetent leaders. I simply don't have enough chemicals to drug them all."

For a few seconds Florence stared down at Tom in silence, panting, fighting to slow down the racing of her heart and her thoughts. Then, having replayed the words of her previous tirade, she shook her head so fervently that several pins came out of her bun, and more tresses escaped.

"Forgive me," she whispered. "Mr. Bennett was right—I have let the chloroform go to my brain."

"We all have—the entire Western civilization. You are not alone in your delirium."

"God, Tom, you look abysmal," Florence said, remembering her duties and hurrying to change the subject. "I suppose, there's no use asking you how you feel."

"I do not feel much pain, only fatigue," he confessed. He was not lying. Pain had been the least bothersome symptom of his illness.

Florence resumed her place next to him, this time much closer, practically on his knee, unbuttoned his shirt, and pressed her ear to his chest. The last pin fell out of her bun. They both found themselves covered in the crinkled black silk of her hair. Was this truly happening? The most beautiful, most brilliant female member of the medical profession had her arms and her tresses wrapped around his neck. How would his Cambridge colleagues comment on this mockery of fate?

"What do you hear?" Tom asked jocosely. "A requiem for the Famished Bear?"

"What I hear," she replied, straightening up, "is fluid in your lungs. By God, Tom! How could you have been so negligent? Did you take the medicine I gave you? Naturally, you didn't!"

"I did..." he muttered, but Florence could not hear his last statement.

"Arrogant fool!" she exclaimed indignantly. "You fancy yourself omniscient, immortal... And why should my patients take me seriously, if my own colleague, who sings my praises, dismisses my advice? Well, congratulations, Tom. You have earned yourself a splendid case of pneumonia. What am I to do with you now?"

"Please, calm down," he implored her. "I have something to give to you."

She detached herself from him and fell her back against the bench, arms crossed and still fuming.

"What is it?" she asked, struggling hard to appear disinterested.

Tom reached into the inside pocket of his jacket and pulled out a yellow journal tied with a rope.

"This is my intellectual dowry," he said, holding the journal before Florence.

"I am not ready to read it," she replied, moving his hand aside. "You said it wasn't finished yet."

"You see, I may not have the time to finish it."

"Of course, you'll finish it—upon your return to England! Once this military circus is over, you'll have all the time in the world."

Tom laid the journal on Florence's lap and squeezed her flushed face between his hands. The gravity of his condition granted certain privileges. Such exhilarating abandon only the proximity of death could afford.

"I won't be returning to England," he said, stroking her temples and burying his fingers in her hair. "We both know it. In a week or two the chaplain will be wrapping me in sailcloth."

She did not react in any way to his caresses that were growing bolder more insistent by the second. Her arms remained crossed on her chest.

"I shall not allow you disparage my abilities, Dr. Grant," she said sternly through her teeth. "Forgive me for not concurring with your grim prognosis for yourself. I have had patients in my care recover from pneumonia."

"How old were those patients?" Tom asked with a sigh. His fingers slipped down her face and lingered on her shoulders where the collar of her dress opened. "I am no longer twenty... or thirty... or even forty... I have close to five decades of relentless self-abuse. Dear Florence, my body is a museum of horrid habits. It should be donated to Cambridge University."

"Very well," she insisted, ignoring his arguments. "Your illness can be still be reversed, if you surrender yourself to my care."

"I've outlived many patients, including my own children," he said, running his thumbs over her collarbones. "This time I shall join them. I have made my peace. Forty-nine is not such a terrible age to die. My life has not always been fruitful or virtuous. In fact, my best decades were wasted on brooding and stagnation. Perhaps the last few months have offset my transgressions. I thank God for the chance to be at least somewhat useful in my last days."

As Tom was uttering those words, Florence kept shaking her head and humming faintly, like a stubborn child dismissing news that were not to her liking. Tempted as she was to cover her ears, she realized that the gesture would be unpardonably juvenile.

"But Tom," she said at last, "you've had so many opportunities to die, and you've bypassed them all. Why now? What shall I do?"

The last question was posed in a tone of selfish female panic that Tom had never heard in her voice before, not even on the night she told him about Milnes and Herbert.

"You shall read over these lines and hear the Famished Bear, growling from the slums of Southwark."

This sudden lapse into lyricism was more than Florence could bear. She covered his mouth with her hand.

"Do not ruin a perfectly scientific moment with poetic drivel," she said, applying pressure to his lips.

Almost immediately, she slid her fingers aside and gave Tom a sorrowful kiss the purpose of which was similar to that of a slap. How else could she sober up this romantic, self-deprecating idiot? He had his mind set on dying! And the most infuriating part was that he actually believed that she would allow him to do something so foolish.

"I would not mind prolonging my life just a bit," Tom mumbled, his eyes still closed, "not for any worthy cause but for my own selfish pleasure."

"Everything we do is for our own selfish pleasure," Florence said, her forehead still touching his, "even the acts that are deemed as noble by onlookers. There is no altruism. There's only vanity that can take so many forms. Behind every lofty cause, there is a low motive. I am no better. My mother has been right all along. From the very beginning, I've been indulging my own whims, even while wrapping gauze around bleeding stumps."

Tom responded with weak laughter.

"What is it now?" she inquired defensively. "You find it hard to believe?"

"No, I do believe it. That is precisely why I laugh. It is altogether amusing. First Cardigan offers me ten thousand pounds, and then the unconquerable Florence Nightingale graces me with a kiss. These adventures are worthy of Dickens or Hugo. If you despise lyrical poetry, you must appreciate political satire." He looked up and folded his hands jokingly. "Oh please, God, give me another few months. I'm curious to find out how all this ends."

For once, Florence had nothing to say in response, at least not immediately. Encouraged by her silence, Tom initiated a second kiss, one he had pondered and rehearsed in his mind for weeks. Leaning on his limited, sporadic experience, he endeavored to overshadow Florence's previous lovers. He remembered that she assigned great significance to the ritual of lip locking, for he had heard her mock Richard Milnes for his timid prudishness. The last time Tom kissed a discriminating, experienced woman, whose rejection could inflict considerable pain, was twenty-five years ago at Lord Middleton's estate. Blasphemous as it sounded, but the Irish maid from the Golden Anchor who perished in the fire did not count. While Tom appreciated Brigit's devotion to him at a calamitous time, he never aimed to impress her or compete with the men she had bedded before him. Quite honestly, her evaluation of his amorous skill never concerned him. With Florence, he would rather perish, than disappoint her. Even a hint of her contempt would be enough to finish him off. Rejection from her would merely accelerate his demise. If she laughed at him, he would die right there under the bench.

Fortunately, his anxieties did not come to fruition. After the first few seconds, it became clear that at least the first rival, the one by the name Robert Milnes, was eliminated. The enthusiasm with which Florence responded to Tom's initiative effaced half of his fears. Suddenly, this muse of cleanliness seemed to have forgotten that kissing was an excellent way of communicating infectious illnesses. Having abandoned her very self-preservation instinct, Florence surrendered to his monstrously anti-sanitary method of showing affection. Their kiss could have lasted an eternity, had it not been interrupted by a fit of Tom's cough. Having tasted his salty blood on her tongue, Florence broke the embrace reluctantly.

"Does that mean you will at least try to delay your departure?" she asked, her tone being more declarative than interrogative.

"I promise to obey you if you in turn promise not to marry Sidney Herbert, even if he does become widowed," Tom replied, remembering that he still had a second rival to eliminate.

Florence drew back in bewilderment.

"How in the world did Sidney's name surface?"

"His name always hangs in the air, spoken or not," Tom blurted out with annoyance. "Every tourniquet you apply is dedicated to him. I know it, and it irks me to no end. Be honest: am I hopelessly inferior to Sidney?"

"Only socially," Florence replied without a second's hesitation. "Not intellectually or even physically. Although, he is younger and better preserved..." She examined Tom's features. "Your jaw is every bit as defined as his, and your brow every bit as high. If a man possesses those features, he is handsome already. As a matter of fact, you and Sidney would get along quite well."

"You can't expect me to harbor amicable sentiments towards him."

The fit of masculine jealousy struck Florence as endearing and entertaining. If it fueled Tom's determination to recover, she was more than willing to feed it.

"In Sidney's defense," she said, "he is my patron, the one who sent me here. We owe our meeting to him."

He forced himself up into a kneeling position.

"Then marry me," he spouted out without a blink. "Together we'll quake the academia, with or without Cardigan's bribe."

For once, Florence's instinct and upbringing were in agreement. A lady must not receive a marriage proposal sitting down, especially if her intention is to accept it.

"I suppose, we should go and awaken the chaplain," she said, springing to her feet. "Reverend Bryce must be bored of funerals, poor soul. Surely, he'll welcome a chance to perform a different ceremony."

"We'll celebrate with moldy bread and contaminated water. A splendid feast!"

"But there will be no guests," Florence cautioned him hastily. "We must maintain discretion. It shall remain our secret."

Chapter 8
What Happens When a Young Man Feels Excluded From a Party

The euphoria from her reunion with Tom had caused Florence to forget that a military hospital was not the safest place for a secret. Absorbed in their own bliss, the lovers did not suspect that they had a witness, and a rather malevolent one. While they were exchanging caresses and making plans to revolutionize the English medicine, Timothy Bennett was grinding his teeth behind the corner. From his hiding place, the young surgeon could not make out every word they had exchanged, but their pantomime sufficed to make his blood boil. Nothing is more infuriating than the sight of another man's happiness, especially if that man was as despicable and immoral as Dr. Grant. Not only did the filthy vivisectionist return to the hospital, which immediately ruined Timothy's meager chances for a promotion, but he also appeared imbued with some mysterious enthusiasm. That barking black-haired witch was pouring ideas of grandeur into his disheveled graying head! They were groping each other, oblivious to their age, with the shamelessness of adolescents.

Damnation! How fickle and murky are women's hearts! He, Timothy Bennett, so young, virile, and ambitious, had been forced to pay to have his carnal hunger satiated. The favors he extracted from women never included any elements of prelude. Although far from hideous, he had never been kissed on the lips. It was one favor for which he would not pay. The sight of his two enemies embracing, cooing and stroking had infused burning venom into his veins. How could God allow such deviants to find such pleasure?

Feeling that hot blood was about to squirt from his ears, he ran outside into the chilly night. Walking through the yard, he noticed light and movement in the surgical tent. He heard laughter, shushing, belching, and glasses clanging. Two of the voices he recognized immediately. They belonged to that pregnant whore Molly Fields and the libertine doctor Richard Ferrars. There was a third man with them, most likely a certain Heavies' officer by the name Lord Hungerton, who took more pride in his hideous face than he did in his beautiful body. Another handful of perverts! They had all conspired to drive him to insanity. Wherever he turned, he encountered consensual fornication, cheerful intertwining of tongues. The hospital was engaged in a constant clandestine orgy, to which he was not invited.

The only thing that kept Timothy from exploding was the thought of his beloved work. He was looking at a very busy, very promising week. Six amputations were scheduled for the next day, four of them above the knee. Certainly, it was not going to be easy to perform such complex surgeries without any competent assistants, but Timothy always welcomed a professional challenge. More hardship also meant more glory for him. Working alone, he would be spared the nauseating chore of saying "please" and "thank you." At a closer examination, the Universe had not been horribly unjust to him after all. He occupied his own place in it, and that place was not on the lowest tier of the pyramid either. For starters, he needed to sharpen his saw, his trusty saw to which he had developed a tender lover-like attachment. Weeks of endless work had made the blade dull.

Having regained his equanimity in part, Timothy exhaled, brushed his sweaty forelock away from his eyes, and headed towards the shed to fetch a sharpening file. The wooden box that was used for storing surgical supplies was inhabited. Male snoring and grunting could be heard, mixing with female whimpering. Right by the entrance, Timothy saw a familiar pair of woman's shoes. They glistened in the moonlight like a pair of tiny leather boats. Dusty pompoms adorned the tips of the shoelaces. Timothy had seen those shoes drag across the hospital halls, heard them squeak. They belonged to a certain golden-haired Cinderella who had a habit of vomiting and swooning for no reason. She was there in the surgical tool shed, in the holiest of holies where neither patients nor nurses were allowed! She was using it as her personal brothel!

Feeling his equanimity evaporating again, Timothy pulled the handle. The hinges were well greased, and the door opened noiselessly. The workbench where he usually sharpened his saw was lined with withering candles, shapeless and pathetic, like the stumps of amputated limbs. Their fading light illuminated a classical military idyll: a nurse between two soldiers. Shrouded in her shapeless cream nightgown, with her pink fists clutched under her dimpled chin, Rebecca resembled a sleeping angel. On her left lay a lancer with a head wound. On her right lay a one-armed dragoon—Timothy had sawed off the other arm himself only three weeks ago. Both heroes had their trousers unbuckled—undoubtedly for comfort alone.

A gust of wind extinguished all the candles but one. Disturbed by the sudden sensation of cold, Rebecca raised on her elbow, feeling for her shawl. Suddenly, the gaze of her swollen eyes froze on the menacing silhouette in the doorway. She saw a panting man with a saw in his hand. That figure had appeared to Rebecca before in her nightmares—a common punishment for eating supper too late. She rubbed her eyes and pinched herself on the cheek, but the image did not disappear. Having realized that she was not dreaming, Rebecca parted her puffy lips, but the only sound she could produce was a sorrowful, helpless meow.

There was no possibility of escaping from the shed. Nevertheless, Rebecca glanced behind in a desperate hope that, perhaps, the walls would miraculously part for her. A second later a hand seized her by the hair and dragged her across the dusty floor of the shed.

The snoring soldiers did not as much as stir. Those men could sleep through a cannonade. Intuition told Rebecca that they would not rise to her defense at any rate. Only an hour ago they were bickering with each other as to who would have her first. The one-armed dragoon insisted that his injury was graver and therefore he deserved to be serviced first. The lancer with a brain concussion demanded preferential treatment based on the fact that he was older and better paid. Unwittingly to themselves, they taught Rebecca a brief lesson in military hierarchy. Fearing that their shouting would awake the medical staff, Rebecca stepped in between them and proposed a maneuver that would eliminate the need for one of the soldiers to wait. She managed to put an end to their quarrel and satisfy them both at once. Before turning their backs to her, they growled appreciatively and patted her on the rump. That was as far as their appreciation of her generosity and ingenuity ended. Now, having had their tension relieved, they would not mind to pass their plaything to another man. After all, peace in a military hospital depended on everyone's patience and willingness to share. That principle concerned all commodities, from clean water to women.

Knowing that no champion would come to her rescue, Rebecca made a weak attempt to use her nails, but they were too short and soft from the abrasive soap. Her teeth could not be of service to her either, as her hair was wrapped around the attacker's hand. Although she still had not seen his face, she knew almost certainly that it was Mr. Bennett, in which case any resistance on her part would bring even more pain. He took particular pleasure in suppressing his victims.

"What's the matter, Miss Prior?" Timothy asked, jerking her to his feet and pulling her head close to his. "You've turned the hospital corps into a whorehouse, and when I hold you up to your duties, you back down. You are a useless nurse, but apparently, you have other gifts. It would grieve me to see them go to waste. "

"Please, don't," she whimpered half-audibly.

"Why not? What can I do to you that other men haven't done already?"

That was an excellent question, one that Rebecca could not answer immediately. For the sake of fairness, there was very little that she had not already endured from the opposite sex. She had tasted of just about everything, from basic battery to forced intercourse; but all her previous abusers were ordinary men who still possessed traces of compassion. This creature by the name Mr. Bennett was not human. There was something diabolic about him, in spite of his outward boyish beauty. Rebecca had the intuition to sense it, but not the vocabulary to articulate it. The thought of being violated by him terrified her more than the thought of being violated by the entire patient population of the hospital.

Unable to answer Timothy's question directly, Rebecca attempted to divert his attention to higher matters.

"The God sees," she droned mysteriously.

She paid with a tuft of hair for this sudden plunge into theology.

"He sees!" Timothy shouted, not caring if someone could hear him. "Why does He see only *my* transgressions? You still play a virgin with me, even after I catch you half-naked between two drunken soldiers." He pulled her head even closer to his, so that their cheeks were touching. "What? What was that, Miss Prior?" he asked in response to her whimpering. "Were you about to tell me that the sin of flesh is lesser than that of pride? Perhaps, we should consult the chaplain. What do you think?"

Rebecca tried shaking her head, but Timothy sunk his nails into her scalp. He trapped and immobilized her face between his elbow and his shoulder.

"Give us a kiss," he snarled and bit into her bleeding lower lip.

At last, his mouth came in contact with a woman's mouth. That was the moment when the Universe was supposed to freeze, at least for him. Rebecca stopped fluttering and relaxed her jaw like a fish dying on the sand. After a few clumsy wags of the tongue, Timothy realized that the Universe was not going to freeze after all. There, he had his first kiss! So this was the subject of so much noise?

Disappointment and relief are frequent companions. He was ready to release the stupid nurse. Miss Prior could give him nothing that he could not find in a traditional English brothel. He could send her back into the world in peace.

He felt sharp pain slashing across his back. Thousands of damaged nerve endings screamed at once. His mouth immediately filled with a mixture of blood and vomit.

Timothy released Rebecca and collapsed, his feet twitching. Above his head he saw the twisted face of Private Martin. The crippled Irishman was holding the dripping surgical saw in his good hand. Even on the verge of a pain shock, Timothy took a few seconds to appreciate the irony of the situation. His own patient had slashed him with his own tool. The stupid piglet of a nurse had an avenger after all.

"Not shabby," Timothy groaned, mocking Martin through his teeth. "You handle a saw well. Had I known, I would've trained you as my assistant. I was telling Miss Prior moments ago how I hate to see talent wasted." He lifted his head off the ground and nodded towards Rebecca. "It wouldn't mind sharing her with you. It would be an honor. She can amuse two men at once. It is a proven fact."

The Irishman jumped on top of Timothy and plunged the tip of the saw into his throat. The surgeon's body twitched and froze.

"He can't hurt yer now!" Martin howled, dropping the saw and darting towards Rebecca.

The nurse would not look him in the eye. When he squeezed her shoulder, she winced and pulled away.

"Look at me!" the Irishman implored, pointing at the corpse. "He's dead. The bloody bast'rd... He won't cripple 'nother man, nor will 'e touch 'nother woman. 'Tis all o'er."

Rebecca continued backing away, shaking her head in disgust.

"I can't..."

Martin dropped on his knees and stretched his intact hand towards her.

"Don't pull 'way from me," he continued begging. "Yer have nothin' to fear. I'm not like 'im. I done many a rotten thin', but I never harmed a woman. I swore to yer I'd be yer vassal 'til the end of me days. Recall that?"

He remained standing on his knees, hand outstretched, until Rebecca's form dissolved in the shadows.

Chapter 9
On the Futility of Allies

Lucan and Cardigan could not avoid each other indefinitely. Scutari was not big enough for both of them. Inevitably, their paths crossed, in front of the hospital, of all places, over the dead body of Timothy Bennett. It pleased the two generals to oversee a scandal in which they, for a change, played no key roles.

The scene of the crime resembled one of Shakespeare's finales. The victim in a pool of his own blood, the kneeling criminal with his arms pulled behind his back and the astonished onlookers were arranged with theatrical precision. Still, Lucan had trouble focusing on the victim and the criminal. His gaze would periodically shift to Florence Nightingale and the haggard physician who was leaning on her shoulder for support. It was not difficult to guess that their intimacy transcended professional solidarity. So that was the creature who had stolen Florence's affections! How humiliating it was to have an old bear for a rival! It only strengthened Lord Lucan's conviction that female logic was beyond his grasp. What woman would choose some sickly, mucus-spouting physician over a healthy, dashing general?

Lord Lucan tried to find solace in the presence of his two trusty allies, Lord Hungerton and Dr. Ferrars. Cardigan had come unaccompanied—Hubert de Burgh had stayed behind on the yacht. On the surface, Lord Lucan appeared better fortified. Nevertheless, for some strange reason he could not help feeling alone. The two men who were supposed to be his allies were not entirely with him in spirit that morning. Clearly, they had more important things than supporting their commander. Dr. Ferrars was enjoying his new friendship with the pregnant nurse a little too much. One could not judge the young physician too harshly for that. A starving man will feast on scraps gratefully. As for Lord Hungerton, the cause of his dissipation was unknown. He looked as if his cranium had been partially evacuated. A portion of his brain must have been sucked out with a syringe. That blank stare that shifted from Private Martin to Dr. Grant, that drooping lower lip and those dangling hands indicated trouble. Perhaps, Dr. Ferrars was testing cannabis-based potions on him?

One way or another, Lord Lucan found himself without allies that morning. He had to rely on his own authority and eloquence to exercise justice.

"The one-handed thief killed the butcher surgeon," he summed up the travesty with the solemnity of a one-man Greek chorus. "I should've expected something of this sort to happen. It was getting suspiciously quiet at the hospital corps. We were due for a little bloodshed." Suddenly, he turned on his heels to face his brother-in-law. "Lord Cardigan, what exactly do you intend to do with Private Martin?"

Such an unexpected direct address surprised the Noble Yachtsman, who had been buffing his fingernails with the cuff of his coat.

"Private Martin shall receive the same treatment as any other murderer," Cardigan responded at last.

Tom detached himself from Florence's shoulder and stepped forward, suffocating.

"In God's name, this man can't be held responsible for his deed," he said, addressing the two in-laws. "Clearly, he is out of his mind."

"How peculiar," Cardigan remarked spitefully, curling his mustache. "As far as I recall, it was Private Martin's hand that was injured in the battle, not his head."

"His head suffered too! Loss of a limb can bring on insanity. Gentlemen, listen to me. This is my medical testimony. You cannot try Private Martin as you would a healthy man."

Having finished grooming his mustache, Cardigan stepped forward with the majesty of a peacock.

"Dr. Grant, as you recall, you have been removed you from your post as a doctor," he said. "Your opinion is of no relevance. If

I make an exception for Private Martin, what message will it communicate to the entire army? Then every soldier will claim insanity as an excuse for insubordination and violent outbursts. He will be executed tonight, as an example to his comrades."

The Irishman burst into hoarse laughter, breaking his silence for the first time. "Bah! I killed the wrong bast'rd... So many pigs to slaughter, and only one hand..."

Disregarding Martin's outburst, Tom continued pleading with the two generals.

"How are we expected to win this war, if we have Englishmen killing one another?" he asked, pointing at Timothy's corpse. "Family members plotting each other's overthrow..."

Cardigan interrupted him nervously. "Dr. Grant, your supervision of the medical unit has proven to be most inefficient. All these atrocities happened on your watch."

That was the moment when Florence, lost her temper. "Oh, for heaven's sake!" she shouted, darting forth. "Look who's talking about inefficiency!"

"Easy, Miss Nightingale," Cardigan curtailed her, embarrassed by the fact that her leap made him draw back instinctively. "You can dig your dainty little fingers into surgeons and physicians, but please harness your temper with commanders of my rank. Everyone is aware of Sidney Herbert's patronage over you, but even that has its limits. Another outburst on your part and you shall be on the ship back to England. Personally, I always thought it imprudent to allow women into a war camp. You may have wrestled your way into medicine, but do not dab into politics. You have already witnessed many things that aren't intended for a lady's eyes."

"Easy, Jim!" Lucan intervened with crude familiarity. Another pang of chivalry prompted him to come to Florence's aid as well as gave him a chance to throw Tom back into the arena filled with lions. "Let the mad scientist speak. He started mumbling something about family conspiracy—I'd like to hear the rest. Let him elaborate on that topic before he kicks the bucket." He turned back to Tom. "Speak as long as you like, Dr. Grant. You have my explicit permission. Nothing you say will be held against you. By the time I come up with an adequate punishment for your audacity, you shall be dead already."

"I have run out of tirades," Tom muttered, lowering his head.

"In that case, does Private Martin have any final wishes?" Lucan asked, slightly disappointed.

The question made the Irishman's ears perk up instantly. Not often did men of Lord Lucan's status inquire about his desires.

"Yes, yes 'e does!" he exclaimed, referring to himself in the third person to capture the solemnity of the moment. "As matt'r of fact, 'e does. A few days 'go, I had my last pinch of t'bacco stolen. Nothin' would please me bett'r than one last cigar, rolled by Miss Prior's lovely hands."

Lucan liked simple men with simple wishes.

"Miss Prior," he addressed Rebecca with exaggerated courtesy, "you heard your patient's request. His chivalrous attempt to defend your honor has cost him his life. He will be executed because of you. Remember that as you roll his cigar. Be sure to tuck the paper in around the corners. It is an art."

"I can't," Rebecca responded with her most versatile phrase. "My hands are trembling."

"Your hands are always trembling," the earl scolded her dismissively. "Now is not the time to be skittish. Imagine that you are working with someone else's hands. When I am overcome by anxiety on the battlefield, I imagine that I am leading someone else's army, not my own."

"But I don't have any tobacco," she said, gradually regaining composure.

Lucan looked around, clapped his hands, and whistled like a hunter summoning his hounds.

"Does anyone here have a pinch of tobacco to spare?" Then he turned to Cardigan. "Jim, will you do anything today to justify your existence, or will you be your usual self? I thought so." The next victim of his sarcasm was Tom. "Good doctor, in your fantastic assortment of chemicals, do you have anything as simple as tobacco? Do you have anything besides rat poison and hallucinogenic substances?"

After a few seconds of silence, Lucan threw his arms up in despair.

"As usual, I must take leadership into my own hands and sacrifice my own goods! I did not come here to be star of the spectacle, but you leave me no other choice."

He rummaged in his pockets, pulled out a fabric pouch of tobacco and a sheet of paper. Having placed the treasure into Rebecca's trembling hands, he instructed her:

"Miss Prior, do the honors. Be sure to tuck the edges."

Rebecca grunted and began fumbling with the paper. She had never rolled a cigar in her life.

"Young man," Lucan continued, addressing the soldier, "this is top quality tobacco, the likes of which you've never smoked. Be sure to savor every puff. Every criminal should be so lucky to sample such a treat before his execution."

Having finally captured enough tobacco inside the paper tube, Rebecca approached Martin and placed the cigar between his teeth. Her hands were perfectly steady by then.

Cardigan gestured for Martin to stand up. "Walk!" he barked, not realizing that his finger was pointing at the hospital wall.

His eyes still fixed on the nurse, the Irishman struggled to his feet. Before receiving the inevitable shove in the back, he glanced over his shoulder one last time. Miss Prior was standing with her back straight, her hands locked over her apron, proud of a task she did not botch. Lord Hungerton, his new dearest friend, his adopted brother, at whose wedding they were supposed to make merry, stood agape. No, there was no chance of advocacy of any sort coming from Lord Hungerton. An unlettered peasant from Mayo should know better than take promises from a young nobleman.

Martin inhaled, preparing to speak, but Rebecca lifted her pink finger.

"Do not open your mouth," she instructed him calmly. "You'll drop your cigar. And I worked hard to roll it for you."

Cardigan convoyed the condemned cripple behind the barracks. Having been relieved of both her tormentor and her vassal, Rebecca scurried off. Tom lost his balance and fell to his knees on the ground. Florence subsided behind him, supporting his back.

Now Lucan could exact his revenge on his rival in full. Nothing could stop him from tearing the decrepit physician apart with mockery. He only wished he had a larger, more appreciative audience. Dr. Ferrars continued yawning and shivering sweetly, still thinking of his pregnant whore. Lord Hungerton's jaw continued dropping lower, and his eyes kept widening, as if he were choking or struggling to say something. Clearly, the boy had not recovered fully from his wound. Could it be that his poor head had sustained one too many blows?

I will have plenty of time to box those rogues' ears, the earl promised himself.

For the time being, his new archrival, the man who claimed Florence, was on his knees, and that was all that mattered to Lord Lucan.

"I hope you last another hour or two, good doctor," the earl began, hovering over the two lovers. "We have too many deaths, and only one chaplain. Now that Mr. Martin has had his final whim satisfied, it is your turn. Ask away. I've already started on a frivolous note, and now I can't stop. What do you wish?"

"Restore me to my position," Tom implored, looking the earl in the eye. "I still have enough air in my lungs for a few rounds."

Lucan clicked his tongue and shook his head.

"My poor Tom, you have not mastered the art of elegant leisure. This is precisely why you are dying. You have exhausted your nervous system."

"What an astute observation..." Florence injected bitterly.

Lucan did not glance in her direction, for he wanted to poke his enemy a bit more.

"When was the last time you ate a three-course meal?"

"Twenty-five years ago, at Lord Middleton's house," Tom responded after a few seconds of recollection.

"And when was the last time you slept for eight hours without interruption?" The earl patted himself on the chest contentedly. "Look at *me*! Would I be as effective a leader if I did not cater to my physical needs? Human body is fickle and frail. Ah, I forgot! You are not human. That's right, you are a bear." The earl curled his hands into claws and let out a jocose roar. "Well, do you truly consider yourself a bear, Tom? Bears sleep a fair amount, don't they?"

"For God's sake, stop interrogating Dr. Grant!" Florence exclaimed, losing the remains of her composure. "You've sacrificed a whole pinch of your precious tobacco for Martin and you didn't ask him so many questions. Lord Lucan..."

"Please, call me George," the earl responded with a gallant bow, satisfied that his mockery of Tom produced the desired effect on Florence. "Unlike my brother-in-law, I do not mind familiarities from a pretty woman, even if she is past her prime." Before Florence had a chance to recoil, he seized her elbow and evaluated her with a critical glance. "If it will please you, dear Florence, I will honor your lover's request. If he wants to bark bloody mucus all over his patients, who am I to stop him?"

He stretched his hand over Tom's head.

"Thomas Henry Grant, doctor of medicine and philosophy, I hereby give you my blessing to resume your dirty and thankless work of which there will be no shortage."

Seemingly oblivious to the mockery, Tom grasped Lucan's hand and pulled himself to his feet.

"Aren't you forgetting something?" the earl asked. "Here's where you say—"

"God save the Queen!" Tom chanted, looking straight ahead.

"I would have preferred to hear 'God save Lord Lucan'," the earl commented with a whimsical shrug, "but I suppose, one is never wrong to mention Her Majesty. After all, it was her idea to send us all here. We must thank her for presenting us with this opportunity to show our heroism in such hellish conditions. And if my brother-in-law summons you again, tell him..." He glanced at Florence once again and changed his mind. "No, I mustn't say such things before a lady. She hears her fill of profanities from others during the day. By the way, Florence, Sidney Herbert will be thrilled to hear that you have found a new lover. What a relief it will be for him... and Elizabeth... and their six children."

"I have found more than a lover," she replied, looking at Tom. "I have found a husband."

"Even better!" the earl exclaimed, applauding. "Why wasn't I invited to the wedding? No matter, I'll be sure to attend Dr. Grant's funeral. I shall ask the chaplain to wrap him into something more regal than sailcloth. The British flag, perhaps? That will be my personal gift."

Lucan tossed his head back and broke into languishing, malicious laughter, making the plumes on his hat dance. Having run out of breath, he paused, refilled his lungs and went for another round.

His gloating fest was interrupted by a sudden exclamation from Lord Hungerton.

"Papa Bear!"

The earl stopped laughing and stared at his aide indignantly. The foggy-brained young man, who had been standing agape all this time, suddenly trembled all over, as if someone had dumped a bucket of icy water on him. His eyes, completely vacant only a minute ago, blazed up with a mixture of tenderness, terror, and remorse.

"Papa Bear," he repeated and lunged towards Dr. Grant with the impetuousness of a little boy rushing towards his father.

Lucan appeared noticeably embarrassed. His insane aide had just ruined his moment of gloating.

"Now, Lord Hungerton, your behavior borders on indecent," the earl reproached him quite earnestly. "Only one man is allowed to mock Dr. Grant at any given time. If we both attack him at once, it will make us look like cowards. Is that how you wish to be remembered among your comrades?"

The young man did not hear him. He knelt next to the dying old bear and took his limp claw in his hands, mumbling something that sounded like a string of hasty, fervent apologies. Florence did not try to stop or question him.

Lucan's first reaction was to attack Dr. Ferrars.

"What is the meaning of this? What have you done to my aide?"

"I haven't done anything," the physician replied without any hostility or defensiveness. "I did not put anything foreign into Lord Hungerton's head. I merely stirred what had settled on the bottom. Take a look, my lord. The two gentlemen recognize each other."

Lucan turned around sharply and saw a stomach-turning family idyll. Dr. Grant was wedged between Lord Hungerton and his new wife, who were supporting him from both sides.

"Florence, my love," Tom spoke, beaming with pride, "I don't believe I have formally acquainted you with my son. This is Grinnin' Wyn, the most wicked jester in Southwark and a champion dart player. Did you know? He can juggle six whiskey bottles blindfolded."

"Grinnin' Wyn?" the earl mumbled, completely confused. "I'll be damned if I understand a bloody thing."

"You do not need to understand, my lord," Dr. Ferrars said. "Just observe the scene from a safe distance and try to be happy for them."

"Happy!" the earl roared. "After everything I've done for that ungrateful brat, he calls another man his father!" Lucan removed his hat and began tearing at the plumes. "Well, what does all this mean for me? Does this Grinnin' Wyn still regard me as his commander? Does he even remember my name? And do you truly expect me to rejoice for Tom Grant? First, he stole my woman, who was rightly mine, which is deplorable enough. Now he steals my son too! All he needs to do is fake illness, and everyone rushes to his side, showering him with pity. Perhaps, I too should employ that trick. All the affection it shall win me! Next time I see Raglan, I shall feign an attack of gout. A sure method of gaining a promotion! Decidedly, all principles of human loyalty and gratitude are dead."

The earl continued raging, even though nobody was listening to him, not even Dr. Ferrars. The young physiologist clasped his hands together and brought them to his mouth. From a distance, it was difficult to tell whether he was praying or just trying to keep warm. At a closer look, one could see tears streaming down his fingers.

Dear God, if this is my only deed of merit, I shall die a happy man.

Chapter 10
First Snow

Lord Lucan's grudge proved to be short-lived. By the end of November, his new rival Dr. Thomas Henry Grant was laid down to rest in a grave outside the hospital. Reverend Edwin Bryce came out of his walking slumber and actually recited an original eulogy. Those patients who had the strength to get out of their beds congregated around his grave. To his credit, Lord Lucan had kept his word and arranged for Tom's body to be wrapped into a British flag. He did not utter another malicious word in reference to his deceased rival, nor did he publicize the secret of Florence's marriage. The abruptness of Tom's departure tempered Lucan's heart. In all honesty, the earl had expected the Famished Bear to linger a bit longer. In spite of all his condescending remarks, Lucan had viewed the deceased doctor as a physical and intellectual equal. It was not his custom to bully those he considered inferior to himself. If he had mocked Tom, it was only because he had viewed him as a tangible threat. The departure of this unrecognized medical titan made his lordship think of his own demise.

In early December, Lucan returned to the camp in Balaclava, taking his physician and his aide-de-camp with him. Contrary to the earl's fears, Lord Hungerton did not lose any of his reverence for his commander. If anything, the young man became more even more attached to his only remaining father figure—after a brief period of withdrawal. Fortunately, Lucan possessed enough prudence and tact not to not to provoke fate and question his aide about the scene he witnessed outside the hospital. He never asked how the young man acquired his scars or his bizarre nickname Grinnin' Wyn. Those stories were left behind in the Famished Bear's grave in Scutari.

Before departing, Lord Lucan did make a promise to Tom's widow to expedite her requests for medical supplies. Knowing that Florence would in all likelihood not speak to him in person, he wrote her a terse, unembellished letter stating that he was aware of her unfavorable working conditions and that he would make every effort to improve them. Perhaps, in his heart he aspired to become her new Sidney Herbert. It would have delighted Lord Lucan to learn that Florence had kept the letter on her bosom, but it would have distressed him to learn that she had never opened it or even read the addresser's name. She had simply stuffed the envelope under the collar of her dress right next to the latest correspondence from the Secretary of War. Seeing her in such a state would have left Lord Lucan heartbroken and enraged.

In the week following her husband's death Florence fell into the same walking slumber as many other members of the medical staff. The rest of the nurses interpreted her stupor as extreme fatigue. No doubt, her melancholy was of impersonal, universal kind, triggered by the daily death toll. They had agreed not to aggravate Miss Nightingale needlessly—and she remained Miss Nightingale to them. They continued addressing her by the only name known to them. They had no suspicion that the woman presiding over them was a bereaved Mrs. Grant. They continued persuading themselves that her frequent trips to the dead doctor's grave were dictated by the grief for an admired colleague, an emotion perfectly natural and understandable but hardly devastating, until one night in before Christmas they found her lying by his gravestone unconscious, covered by a thin layer of snow.

When they carried her into the tower and removed her cloak, they saw a well-worn notebook tucked into the inside pocket. "England on Her Deathbed" read the title. Nothing could stop them from opening the notebook. They did not expect to find anything terribly secretive or criminal.

Having heard the voices of her sisters, Florence stirred, her hand feeling for the notebook. They slipped it under her arm hastily and left the room.

When Rebecca Prior tiptoed in later that night, she found her superior sitting on her bed, clutching Dr. Grant's notebook to her chest, a new lamp at her feet. Florence's superhuman ability to recuperate after a brief physical collapse inspired awe in those around her. Just a few hours of sleep enabled her to maintain upright position and speak in complete sentences without lapsing into sighs or sobs.

"Miss Nightingale," Rebecca began cautiously, placing a cup of hot tea before Florence, "there's much work to be done. The gents are gone."

"The gents are gone..." Florence echoed expressionlessly and wrapped her discovered fingers around the cup.

"Ah, yes, Dr. Grant..." the girl sighed nostalgically and suddenly cringed, as her thoughts shifted onto a more sinister figure. "Mr. Bennett... Uh! Reverend Bryce says it will be weeks before the new doctor arrives. Dr. Hall will not be bothered. It's you and me for now. Surely, we'll have our hands full."

"The gents are gone," Florence repeated in a slightly elevated voice and laughed like a madwoman, spilling the tea over her dress and the notebook. "They are gone!"

Rebecca drew back tentatively. "Why are you repeating yourself, Miss Nightingale?"

"Indeed, why am I repeating myself?" Florence asked, turning to face Rebecca. "I honestly don't know, Miss Prior. Nobody is listening, whether I mumble or shout. Young lady, I owe you an apology. I had no business lecturing you on the dangers of premature death." She pointed her fragile finger at Rebecca. "You shall outlive all of us. Yes! You'll stand over our mass grave and say: 'Fiddle-dee-dee!'"

The girl, with her gift for grimaces, pouted and rounded her eyes in horror. "Don't jest like that, Miss Nightingale."

"No, I'm perfectly serious." She brought the cup to her lips for the first time, smelled the content, and decided not to drink it. The tea was only good for warming her fingertips. "Girls like you have a guardian angel. There's infinite wisdom in your stupidity; and I have much to learn from you. And you were absolutely right: I was indeed envious of you, for all the reasons mentioned above."

The grimace of horror on Rebecca's face gave way to that of giddy vanity. Did she hear Miss Nightingale correctly? "Envious, of me?"

"I do not grudge you your yellow locks," Florence explained hastily, lest the girl's limited fancy should carry her off in the predictable direction. "They are the least of your advantages. It's the hollowness under the locks that I covet. The benefit of being meager and useless is that nobody profits from your death. The chances of someone removing you from the face of the earth are minimal. You may as well be left where you are."

The brutal frankness of that admission appealed even to someone of Rebecca's intellect.

"But I don't want to be meager and useless anymore," the girl confessed, sitting down next to Florence. Since Miss Nightingale was brave enough to share her innermost thoughts, perhaps she, Rebecca Prior, could reciprocate. "I want to be grand and famous. No more being cornered by drunken soldiers. Those days are over. I want to receive letters from scientists and generals, have audiences with the queen."

Rebecca purposely stretched the vowels in her last word to give Miss Nightingale a chance to appreciate the magnitude of her dreams.

"Is that all you want, dear girl?" Florence asked, tilting her head. "Please, don't stifle your ambitions."

"There's more," Rebecca continued, rubbing her hands greedily and growing more agitated by the second. "I want to have other nurses in my command." She jumped up from the bed and twirled ecstatically, trying on her new persona with the same frivolity as she would try on a new petticoat. "I shall march ahead of them, carrying my own lamp, lighting the way. And everyone around shall bow and say: 'Behold: a saint!'"

"Your modesty is astounding," Florence commented, placing the half-empty cup on the floor.

"I know! I've promised myself to be humble and modest from now on. No more rouge. No more stuffing gauze into my blouse. Miss Nightingale, you'll be proud to hear that I have ended my friendship with Molly Fields."

From the tone in which Rebecca delivered the last statement one could have guessed that she expected a medal for such a heroic sacrifice.

"Why on earth?" Florence asked. "I thought your shared adventures bonded you for eternity."

"That friendship was not wholesome for my soul. I need a worthier friend, someone like you."

"Someone like me," Florence muttered, not quite sure whether such a comment merited offense or amusement on her part.

"I need someone to teach me how to tie my hair in a bun and

scold surgeons when they don't do their job properly. Will you do the honors, Miss Nightingale?"

Surprisingly, that was the very question Florence had dreaded. The prospect of becoming Miss Prior's personal mentor struck her as a rather questionable honor.

"I could begin by teaching you how to apply tourniquet."

"Oh, must I?" Rebecca whined reluctantly, for that was the very response that Rebecca had dreaded. "Is it truly necessary?"

"Dear girl," Florence continued, her voice regaining its usual sternness, "before you start barking orders at others, you will need to learn to carry them out first. This transformation will take time and, as my heart tells me, many more swooning spells."

Rebecca bowed her head compliantly. Florence noticed that for the first time her hair was not curled.

"I am willing to do whatever is necessary, Miss Nightingale. Anything to be the next Lady with the Lamp!" Having made her pledge, Rebecca suddenly remembered something far more important. "But wait, I have more news to share. I have a new gentleman friend."

"Who is the lucky victim?"

"The chaplain! Our very own Edwin Bryce. A future saint needs a godly suitor. Wouldn't you agree? See, Miss Nightingale, I have thought of everything. You can no longer fault me for negligence. He's been giving me lessons in theology. He's also privy to the latest military scandal."

Florence nodded with a tired, benevolent smile. Once again, Miss Prior resumed flirting and gossiping, her favorite activities. The incident with Mr. Bennett had not taught her a thing. No, she had not been struck by a lightening after all. For a second Florence had grown slightly alarmed, wondering if some fairy spirit had kidnapped the empty-headed girl and replaced her with an actual purposeful woman.

"There's talk of Lord Lucan being sent home to England," Rebecca continued in a mysterious whisper, resuming her place next to her headmistress. "During his latest audience with Lord Raglan, he had a fit. He started ranting, and cursing, and rolling on the floor. The chaplain was invited to exorcise him. How does the story strike you, Miss Nightingale?"

"I am a woman of science," Florence responded. "What would I know about demonic possessions or military scandals?"

"But wait!" The girl hissed, fanning her pink fingers. "That's not all. There's a rumor that Lucan's madness was induced, that someone had drugged him."

Florence tightened her cloak around her shoulders and glanced at the door, hoping that Rebecca would understand the hint and leave.

"Miss Prior, if you are committed to becoming a respectable, graceful, enlightened woman, you must give up the pleasure of spreading rumors. Now go back to your patients. I shall join you shortly."

Self-complacent and eager to leave, Rebecca fluttered away, leaving her headmistress to her reverie.

Alone once again, Florence Nightingale Grant began unbraiding her hair that was still wet from the melted snow. She needed to restore her habitual businesslike appearance. Prolonged grief was a luxury reserved for widows who were not forced to keep their marriages secret. Thousands of patients have gone through my hands—and thousands more were destined to. She had already started composing the content for her handbook under the most mundane, unimaginative title "Notes on Nursing." Pity, she had to leave out some astute observations and theories. Her audience, she suspected, would not reconcile them with the image of the Lady with the Lamp. The events of the past two months only confirmed her belief that some epidemics came in the form of fellow humans. That was why she did what her husband did not have the heart to do.

I stand at the Altar of the murdered men, and while I live, I fight their cause.

Part 7
A Lull More Deafening
Than A Cannonade

Crimea—England, 1855

Chapter 1
"I Cannot Remain Silent..."

"I will not bear one particle of the blame," Lord Lucan kept repeating to himself, sometimes out loud, sometimes in his thoughts.

Raglan's words "You have lost the Light Brigade" continued ringing in his head. With each day, it became more apparent that all fingers were pointing at him.

He could not remain silent. He could not allow himself to open his mouth either, for it had a will of its own. His Lordship found it more and more difficult to control his diction and not lapse into profanities. The men in his immediate surrounding had conspired to provoke him, to purposely cajole him into a temper fit and then declare him incompetent. Even the sedative potion given to him by Dr. Grant's widow did not help.

Lord Lucan regarded his last days at Scutari with bittersweet fondness. Shortly after the old bear's funeral, he and Florence reconciled, if only out of respect for her deceased husband. Both agreed that there should be no bickering over a fresh grave. The earl apologized from the bottom of his heart for the nasty things he had said, and Florence assured him that those things were forgotten. As a sign of her forgiveness, she gave him a flask containing an herbal concoction, something to help him keep his nerves sedated, as he was about to reenter an extremely hostile environment. Before sending him off on his transport ship, she pressed his hand and even laid her head on his chest briefly, partially fulfilling Lucan's fantasy. Naturally, he would have preferred for that moment to last longer and lead to even greater intimacy, but for the time being he had to content with the memory of her concave cheek pressed against his uniform.

"Now, George, return to your soldiers and set the example they sorely need."

Those were her last words to him. Florence had taken his frivolous request to heart and addressed him by his given name. Perhaps, not all was lost. She was beginning to see the heart behind the caricature painted by the entire cavalry collectively. After the war they could resume their friendship under more agreeable circumstances. Lord Lucan had heard of great romances starting with playful hostility. He had never read Jane Austen's "Pride and Prejudice," but his estranged wife had fed him bits of the plot. After a few episodes of venomous verbal exchange, the young heroine and her suitor eventually fell into each other's arms. Now, he and Florence were not as young as the lovers from Austen's novel, and he was not entirely free from the shackles of his failed marriage, but he was willing to expedite his divorce from Anne, now that he had a perfect reason for it.

In the meantime, he needed to clear his name. He could not publicize his budding relationship with Florence if the rest of the world thought him an idiot and a coward.

In his quest to reform himself and become a graceful, reasonable, diplomatic man, Lord Lucan decided to compose a letter to the Secretary for War, the Duke of Newcastle, detailing his own account of the events at Balaclava. Yes, he could still articulate his thoughts in a written form. In his letter, he simply reiterated the tragic ambiguity of Raglan's last two orders and his own inability to disobey them.

I cannot remain silent, he concluded. *It is, I feel, incumbent on me to state those facts which I cannot doubt, must clear me from what, I respectfully submit, is altogether unmerited.*

There, he had said it all. There was nothing left to add. Overall, Lord Lucan was extremely pleased with his letter, for good reasons too, and harbored high hopes for it. His optimism only proved how little he knew about military politics.

The effect of the letter was totally opposite to the one he had expected. In early February Lord Raglan received Newcastle's order to inform Lucan of his dismissal.

"It is Her Majesty's pleasure that you should resign the command of the Cavalry Division and return forthwith to England," he said to the earl.

Contrary to what everyone had surmised, Raglan took no pleasure in breaking the news to Lucan. In spite of their continuous friction, the Commander-in-Chief did not relish seeing the earl turned into a laughing stock. He delivered the blow with great reluctance.

Words could not describe the extent of Lord Lucan's astonishment. What went wrong this time? Was the tone of his letter misinterpreted?

Without a word, he retreated into his tent. The campaign was over for him. There was nobody else to whom he could appeal, nobody in a higher position except for God, and God did not make military decisions.

Lucan's only consolation prize was that the command of the cavalry transferred over to General Scarlett. There was nobody else the earl would rather see replace him. Had the vacated position been given to his brother-in-law, Lord Lucan's fury could have proven fatal. Luckily, the medical board proclaimed Cardigan unfit for duty and dismissed him home to England. Given the fragile state of his health, he was permitted to travel on his yacht in the company of his friend Mr. de Burgh. Cheers and laurel garlands were waiting Cardigan in Europe. Wherever he went, he was paving the road of shame for his brother-in-law.

"I pity that wretched old fellow," one of the young cavalry officers admitted in regards to Lord Lucan's dismissal. "But I'm not sorry to see him go! Such an irate, obstinate old man he was!"

By then confessions of this sort were uttered in the open without. The morale of the survivors had sunk to the level where there was no more fear, as there is no plant life on the bottom of the ocean. Many soldiers would have preferred to be shot for insubordination rather than try to survive a Crimean winter.

After the disaster of Balaclava, the remnants of the Light Brigade were posted inland. Since the early November, the horses have been receiving no more than a handful of barley for the day. To trick the hunger, they gnawed at their straps and saddle flaps. The soldiers were forbidden from putting the animals out of their misery. No horse was to be shot save for a broken leg. They shivered in the sleet without shelter, while their men had to content with wind-beaten tents. Before departing for Europe, Lord Cardigan had not bothered to make any arrangements to have forage delivered. Feeding his men and their horses was no longer his responsibility.

On Valentine's Day in 1855, Lord Bingham went for his final stroll through the frozen cavalry camp. The young man was experiencing an inexplicable desire to subject himself to suffering. Having grown weary of the insects biting his scalp, he picked up a dull blade and shaved his hair off entirely, leaving countless cuts on his temples and crown. His head looked as if it had been thrashed with a horsewhip. He smiled wickedly at his own wretched reflection and poured whiskey over the raw skin. When the stinging pain settled, Lord Bingham regretted his decision to shave his head. Perhaps, it would have been more stoical to leave the hair and the lice inhabiting it.

Suddenly, he felt a familiar hand cupping his shoulder. Those thin but unusually strong fingers belonged to his future brother-in-law, Lord Hungerton. Lately, their rapport had been far from fraternal. The resentment that kindled first after the Battle of Alma began stirring again.

"Georgie, look up at me," Wynfield said.

"Go away, Jerry!" the heir growled like an irate child, shaking the hand off.

"I intend on going away. That is why I came to say goodbye to you. General Scarlett is waiting."

"Oh yes, Scarlett! How could we forget him? I hope you blossom under your new patron. What a cozy spot you've occupied, Jerry! Whoever happens to be the hero of the day, you latch onto him."

Lord Bingham had no objective reason to hate Scarlett or resent his promotion. At that moment, he would to hate any other man appointed to his father's position.

"George, you know it was not my whim," Wynfield justified himself, disregarding the venomous remarks flying at him. "Lord Raglan appointed me as Scarlett's new aide-de-camp. Please, understand."

Of course, Lord Bingham understood. That did not mean he was going to behave reasonably, at least not at that stage of grieving, when the wound was still so raw.

"And you jumped at it, clapping and smacking your lips. Didn't you, Jerry? Now you wish nothing to do with my father, who is the laughing stock of the British Empire."

Lord Bingham sat down on an empty wooden box and covered his eyes with his fists, mixing tears and the melted snow.

"Georgie, please don't cry," Wynfield begged him.

"Or what—you shall cry with me? Is this what you meant to say?"

"No, if you cry, your Papa will cry too. He mustn't see you sad. That would finish him off. You must remain brave, calm and staunch for him."

"Easy for you to say!"

"Easy indeed," Wynfield smirked sorrowfully. "I buried my own father not too long ago. He died in my arms. I heard his last growl. There was a segment of time when I blamed him for all the misfortunes in my previous life. Imagine that? I had blasted him with fantastical accusations, that man who had nurtured me for fifteen years. Ah, the wicked tricks of one's memory... You weren't there to witness it, but Dr. Ferrars will confirm that I'm telling you the truth. I was so busy apologizing to my father for the horrid things I had spouted in my delirium that I simply forgot to tell him that I loved him. He expired to the sound of my frantic babbling. What would I know about bereavement?"

"That is entirely different!" Lord Bingham objected fervently. "Your predicament cannot compare to mine. International humiliation is far worse than death. Dr. Grant became a martyr of the English medicine. His departure was mourned. As for my father, the whole of England is praying for some terrible accident to happen to him! They call him an old dolt and a coward in the open."

"But Georgie, you and I know it isn't so, don't we? Right now your uncle Jim is harvesting his laurels back in Europe, bathing in everyone's adoration, slandering your father. Sooner or later Lord Cardigan will make a bombastic ass of himself. The mass hysteria will settle, and the truth will emerge, inevitably. Crowds cannot remain loyal to the same idol for too long."

"All right, then," Lord Bingham said, straightening out and wiping his tears off. "If you believe my father to be a worthy commander, then prove it. Go back to London with him and support him in the House of Lords. You are a medium-size hero now, so your word shall count for something. Perhaps, it will not restore my father to his position, but it will reverse some of the slander.

Leave Scarlett and stand by my father. Then I shall truly believe that you are my friend."

Wynfield let out a sigh and sat down next to Lord Bingham.

"Georgie, there is no easy way of saying this."

"Then don't say another word. Your answer is quite clear."

"Please, let me finish. I have grown tremendously fond of you, and I am completely devoted to your father. If circumstances prohibit me from accompanying him to London, I shall still be there in spirit."

Lord Bingham raised his reddened eyes to the sky, shook his head, and cursed under his breath.

"Be there in spirit... Why, this is the most insulting, condescending, blatantly unimaginative excuse I've ever heard. Damn you, Jerry! Have you no cheek to admit that you simply no longer wish to be associated with my buffoon of a father?"

Lord Bingham's weepy pathos was beginning to wear on Wynfield's patience.

"You want honesty from me, Georgie?" he asked with sudden abruptness. "One day, with proper training, which you have been denied thus far, you could probably make a mediocre military career. There are many soldiers of such caliber in the British army already. One more or one less would not make a world of difference. England would not lose or gain much. Why waste yourself on mediocrity, when you already are a remarkable brother and son? Your place is with your family, which is something I, regretfully, cannot say for myself. The Devil knows better where my place is. I do know that came here to serve my country, not to win affections. If you make me choose between my duty and your friendship, I cannot promise that I will choose in your favor. Now you understand why it isn't easy for me?"

The heir sniffled and nodded.

"I understand. I wouldn't expect any less of you, Jerry. You consider me a worthless soldier, and you were bold enough to say it to my face. I thank you for that. I pray that your own military career proves to be more successful than mine."

The two former friends exhaled in tandem and marked their upcoming parting with a moment of silence, their elbows touching. The sound of snow crunching beneath the boots made them both turn around. They saw Lord Lucan in the company by Sir Colin Campbell and William Howard Russell, his only two friends who had volunteered to see him off.

"Stop burdening Lord Hungerton with your whining, George," the earl chided his son. "He must preserve his strength. He has formidable challenges ahead of him."

"Lord Bingham was not burdening me at all," Wynfield defended his former friend. "We were only bidding each other goodbye. I was the one who sought him out. I did not want him to depart without..."

The earl did not look in his direction.

"Are you ready, George?"

"Yes, Papa," Lord Bingham replied. "Homeward we go."

What a relief it was to be able to address his father in this manner without the fear of being whipped on the face with a belt. No more formalities. No more intrigue. No more fear of getting killed.

Walking up the gangway of the transport, Lord Bingham felt his despair letting up. He was beginning to feel sorry for those remaining behind. From a distance the sleet-covered cavalry camp looked even more pitiful.

"Are you still going to let *him* marry Lavinia," Lord Bingham suddenly asked his father, investing particular contempt into the word "him" while referring to Wynfield.

"If he survives the next few months—surely," the earl replied indifferently. "I don't know what plans the Commander-in-Chief has for his men. It is no longer my dilemma. The provisions are running out. Very soon the men will be chewing saddle straps and chewing their own fingernails. If Lord Hungerton comes back alive, I will be more than willing to give Lavinia to him."

By then Lord Bingham should have grown accustomed to hearing blasphemous absurdities, but his father's last declaration left him hyperventilating.

"Why... Why, I cannot believe my ears, Papa!"

"I see no reason to oppose their marriage."

"You will have *him* for a son-in-law even after the cold, treacherous way he turned his back to you?"

"Well, *somebody* has to marry your sister," the earl said, raising his palms to the sky, like a man in a desert praying for rain. "Why can't that somebody be Lord Hungerton? Dear boy, this is not the time for me to pamper my pride. I must remain practical and businesslike. During this phase of my life, I cannot afford to be trapped with a spinster daughter on my hands. Then your mother shall never set me free."

Lord Bingham gasped apologetically, remembering the core of the tension between his parents.

"Of course, Papa! How could I have forgotten? Parental politics, the murky labyrinth..."

"Uh-huh!" Lucan affirmed with a belligerent nod. "One day you will find out the painful way."

"I don't think I shall ever marry, Papa," Lord Bingham declared. "I shall devote my life to being your son, serving you, always being by your side."

The earl huffed, sending a cloud of white steam into the frigid air.

"That would be a foolish sacrifice, one I would not appreciate! Unmarried children are always a burden, regardless of their sex. Earnestly, George, I want you to marry, and marry well. I too have plans for the future, grandiose plans—a lecherous old man that I am. My military career is done for, it appears. I shall use my newly acquired freedom to pursue a personal happiness that I have been denied for decades. Now I am convinced that God led me to the Crimea for a particular reason, and that reason was not to conquer the enemy, but to find love. I have met the woman of my dreams, and I intend to woo her. You are the first one to know this."

"When did all this transpire, Papa?" Lord Bingham asked with astonishment although without judgment. "When and where?"

"A few weeks ago, in Scutari," Lucan replied, smiling. He looked like a cat that had just lapped an entire bowl of fresh cream. "Before the year is over, I hope to introduce you to your new stepmother—Florence Nightingale Grant Bingham!"

Lord Bingham thought it would be better not to ask any more question. Clearly, his father had lapsed into temporary insanity from all that grief and indignation. Those outrageous declarations were his way of dealing with the profound moral blow he had been dealt recently.

Before the transport moored off, Lord Lucan shook his fist at the heights where the main headquarters stood. He knew that Raglan could not see his gesture, but he hoped that the Commander-in-Chief would feel the punch from a distance.

358

Chapter 2
Good Intentions Come Full Circle

Captain Scarlett did not enjoy his new position nearly as much as everyone had expected him to. Taking charge of the British cavalry in such a deplorable state could only compare to assuming responsibility over a bedridden invalid. It did not appear like Scarlett's dream for a rehabilitative facility for the recovering soldiers was going to materialize. Dr. Hall would hear nothing about it. The hospital was a place where men went to have their limbs amputated or die, not a luxury sanatorium for those who could stand on their own two feet. Thus, Scarlett's initiative was shut down. Most of his men were sent home to England as soon as their wounds closed. It was not his fate to command them or even see them ever again.

New cavalry reinforcements began tricking into the Crimea. Most of them were very young lads, frightfully inexperienced, looking up at their new commander with their yellow beaks open. The chore of training them fell on Lord Hungerton's scrawny shoulders, who had been elevated to the rank of Major for his courage during the Charge of the Heavy Brigade. His former commander, Lord Lucan, was not made aware of the promotion. Everyone agreed that there was no need to infuriate the disgraced earl any further. Lord Hungerton spent his afternoons drilling the newcomers.

"God bless them," Scarlett muttered, his voice muffled by his mustache. "I wouldn't put them through another Balaclava."

Scarlett's only consolation was the presence of Dr. Richard Ferrars, who once had served as Lord Lucan's personal physician and who had chosen to stay behind after the earl's recall from the Crimea. Scarlett's initial impression of Dr. Ferrars was that of a sheltered theorist who would swoon at the first sight of blood. Now the general could not be more pleased to admit that he was wrong. The young physiologist proved to be a composed, decisive expert, completely devoid of squeamishness or arrogance. He could appease even the most bitter and aggressive of patients.

One day, as General Scarlett and Dr. Ferrars were enjoying a meager supper in their tent, Lord Hungerton came in from the cold.

"I hate disturbing you, Richard," he said, rubbing his hands, "but I need your advice."

"You are not disturbing me at all," Dr. Ferrars replied, pulling up a third chair. "How can I help you?"

"Perhaps, could you recommend some exercise for my right arm? It is still a bit weak from the wound."

"What are your symptoms? Are you still in pain?"

"No, pain is the least of my worries. I can handle impressive amounts of it. No, it is mostly numbness and weakness that bother me. Today, as I was training my men, the sword slipped out of my hand. I didn't even feel my fingers unlock. I just heard the jingle it made as it hit the frozen ground. It was the strangest thing. Imagine that? The soldiers thought it was some new maneuver, so they repeated after me. It was almost amusing. At any rate, I'm sure it's nothing serious. It must have been the cold."

As Wynfield was ranting about the incident, a barely noticeable crease formed between Scarlett's eyes.

The physician blotted his mouth with a shapeless rag that had in lieu of a napkin and beckoned his patient.

"Take off your coat and come to the light. Let us take a look."

Wynfield complied promptly and stripped himself to the waist, unconscious of the terribly draft seeping in through the gaps in the tent.

"Now, keep your arms straight and raise them above," Dr. Ferrars instructed him. "Both arms, all the way... Lord Hungerton? Did you hear me?"

"I heard you, Richard," Wynfield replied. "I heard you the first time. What must I do next—stand on my ears?"

The physician glanced back at Scarlett, who was watching the scene without blinking, his red face growing stiffer by the second.

"Lord Hungerton," the general said at last, "it appears that you have trouble elevating your right arm beyond a certain point."

The arm in question remained frozen at a ninety-degree angle.

"No, I'm not having any trouble," Wynfield denied in a shaky voice. "I'm cold and exhausted, that's all."

His right arm began vibrating, bent in the elbow, and finally hung. The patient remained standing with his hunched over back turned towards his companions.

"Take a look, Sir James," the physiologist said, palpating the muscle that ran from Wynfield's neck to his right arm. "This is where the muscle was damaged. This tight lump in the upper shoulder is all fresh scar tissue. It appears that the nerve endings have been severed irreparably. Furthermore, the muscle in his forearm is slowly becoming atrophied. It is an unfortunate chain effect."

The unceremonious manner in which he was being treated left Wynfield speechless. Dr. Ferrars and Sir James were giving him the same courtesy they would an inanimate object or a corpse in the lecture hall of some medical college.

"Gentlemen, I am still here!" he reminded them. "I can hear you, and I can feel your fingers on my neck. Is it safe for me to turn around?"

"Of course, Lord Hungerton," the doctor replied calmly. "You may turn around and put your clothes back on. God, it's freezing in here... I saw what I needed to see."

Wynfield grabbed his shirt and his coat from the chair. Suddenly, he discovered that he had trouble buttoning up. The fingers on his right hand would not obey.

"All right," he whispered, having given up on his collar. "Would someone care to explain to me what the hell is happening on the right side of my body?"

"I just explained it to Sir James, but I'll be more than happy to repeat myself: you have muscle and nerve damage."

"I heard that! What does this mean for my military career?"

"It means you'll be going home and planning your wedding," Dr. Ferrars replied, returning to his supper. "How can you continue serving in the cavalry if you cannot handle a sword? The new troops need to learn the proper technique, and you are not in the condition to demonstrate it, not if the sword continues slipping out of your fingers. Your career ended when that nameless Russian sot hacked you across the neck."

Wynfield turned pale and grabbed onto the table for support.

"What... What the hell..." he muttered. "I thought you said it was but a scratch!"

Dr. Ferrars took a few seconds to finish chewing.

"It was a scratch," he affirmed, lifting his finger, "a very deep one—in a bad place. The *worst* possible place, I should say."

"And you knew that while you were sewing up the wound?"

"Such assertions cannot be made at the time of surgery. With any injury, there is a possibility of permanent loss of nervous responsiveness. I did not wish to leap to any premature conclusions. That would have hindered your recovery."

"Hindered my recovery? In other words, you lied to me!"

Suddenly, Wynfield realized that he was in no position to judge Dr. Ferrars, as he had done the same to Private Martin, knowing that the Irishman's hand was not salvageable. Wynfield considered of the string of tragedies that his own white lie had triggered. Perhaps, it would have been better for Martin to die on the banks of Alma. He would have been spared the gangrene, the amputation, the delirium, the grapple with the surgeon and the execution. The hapless Irish lad could have died a natural death as a pseudo-hero, but instead he was shot as a murderer. He had endured all that needless suffering because of the good intentions of a certain friend.

One of Wynfield's tragic flaws was his tendency to ascribe too much fatalistic significance to his actions. He continued blaming himself for Elisaveta's violent death and for Martin's disgrace. In his self-flagellating fantasies, he elevated himself to the ranks of a minor deity who had the power to ruin the fates of fellow creatures. Had Wynfield's rational streak been more developed, he would have viewed his actions in a warmer, brighter light. Thanks to him, Elisaveta had tasted of tenderness and Martin—of friendship. Deplorably, he only perceived the destructive results of his intervention into the lives of others. The injury was his punishment for all the harm he had caused.

"So, I'm officially a cripple now," he muttered, running his fingers through his hair. "I might as well consign myself to a rubbish yard."

"You are not a cripple by any means," the physician objected. "You can still use your right arm for daily tasks. Your life is not over only because will never hold a sword. Considering that the Russian you were fighting aimed to decapitate you, I would say you were quite fortunate. Honestly, I do not understand what makes you so distraught. You are behaving as if your very livelihood depended on your military service. You are a baron, for Heaven's sake! If you find your leisure burdensome, there are hundred of other occupations you can pursue. Go back to London, get married and start a theater company."

"A theater company..." Wynfield echoed weakly.

Dr. Ferrars had already lost interest in his patient's case of post-traumatic atrophy. He suddenly frowned, brought the rag to his mouth, and spat out a chewed-up morsel of salted pork.

"I don't think this is fresh," he muttered through the fabric. "Sir James, I wouldn't eat that meat if I were you."

"Don't worry about me, Dr. Ferrars," the general replied. "My stomach is lined with iron. Having survived a bout of cholera in Varna, I can now digest anything, even the soles of your shoes."

"Not the soles of my shoes!" the physician joked, waving his arms in protest. "I need them. They are my last possessions that haven't fallen apart yet."

They chuckled over the leftovers and began wiping the biscuit crumbs off their wobbly little table. Neither one of them was paying any attention to Lord Hungerton, who in turn had no intention of leaving.

"This isn't over!" he declared. "I won't allow you to write me off so easily. I demand a second opinion."

"You wish to go before a medical board?" Dr. Ferrars asked without even turning around. "That will be a perfect waste of everyone's time. Those doctors won't tell you anything different. You may as well spare yourself the hassle and start making your boarding arrangements now. The wind is expected to die down in the next few days. It will be good sailing weather. Take advantage of it. February is a treacherous month."

Wynfield drew his sword and smashed it into the tabletop in front of Dr. Ferrars. He then rolled up his right sleeve all the way up to his shoulder.

"What are you doing?" the physician asked in a spiteful, fatigued voice.

"Chop off my bloody arm!" Wynfield shouted. "It's of no good to me now. Then I shall truly be a cripple! I shall look and feel like one!"

Sir James, who had hoped until the very last moment that the tiff would resolve without his intervention, felt obliged to remind his aide-de-camp that his demeanor was becoming unworthy of a soldier.

"Lord Hungerton, it grieves me to see you treat your weapon so disrespectfully," he said. "A sword is not a toy."

"I don't care!" Wynfield cried out. "I shall never use it again."

"You are behaving like a spoiled child!" the general cut him off, in a sterner voice. "What if your comrades saw you in such a state? What sort of example would it set for them? I would expect you of all men to receive unpleasant news with more dignity."

Sir James found himself somewhat at loss. Unaccustomed to witnessing such theatrical performances from his aides, he did not know quite know how to approach this situation. Beatson and Elliott had always been marvels of composure and stoicism.

While Scarlett realized that Lord Hungerton's outrageous behavior merited disciplinary actions, he hesitated to carry them out, held back by a sense of Christian compassion. The young man must have adopted some rotten habits from his former commander, Lord Lucan. Six months in the company of the snarling earl would turn anyone into a lunatic.

No, Scarlett did not wish to chastise his aide, whose days in the army were counted at any rate. At the same time, the young man could interpret leniency as encouragement.

While the general was searching for a humane yet effective way of putting an end to the performance, the physician did something unexpected—he slapped Lord Hungerton across the face, knocking him to the frozen ground.

"Jeremy, stop it at once!" Ferrars ordered.

Scarlett's bewilderment intensified. Vulgarity and insubordination ravaged the camp like an infectious illness. For a physician, even as accomplished as Dr. Ferrars, to address an aristocratic-born officer by his given name constituted an unthinkable liberty. Amazingly, it was the physician's blow that ended Lord Hungerton's juvenile tantrum.

"Thank you, Richard," Wynfield murmured, his sincerity unquestionable. "This is precisely what I needed."

"You are very welcome, my lord," Dr. Ferrars replied. "I am merely returning the favor. Remember our score?"

"I certainly do, Richard."

Wynfield rose to his feet, dusted his breeches, and rolled down the right sleeve of his shirt. Then he took the sword, ran his fingers over the blade apologetically, and placed it back into the sheath.

Sir James sighed with relief: the dramatic amputation was not going to take place after all.

"Gentlemen, I think we better forget this incident," he concluded in the tone of a peacemaker. "Hopefully, it passed without any witnesses. Dr. Ferrars, I applaud you for settling the matter single-handedly. Lord Hungerton, I better begin signing your discharge documents. You can expect a glowing character reference from me. Whatever you choose to do for the rest of your life, you shall always have an advocate in me."

Wynfield attempted to salute his commander, but his right arm did not cooperate, so he bowed instead. He could not allow himself to depart without a physical display of courtesy.

"Thank you, Sir James," he said. "God bless you and your men. How I shall miss the sound of cannonade."

Chapter 3
Peaches and Cabernet
(London, March 1855)

There is something infinitely decadent, daring and exquisite about hosting a picnic in early March, with blankets spread out on the last snow. Anne Brudenell Bingham, Countess Lucan, decided to celebrate the first day of spring. The location was Kensington Gardens, immediately to the west of Hyde Park, and her companion was none other but Adeline Louisa Maria de Horsey, the mistress of her older brother James the Earl of Cardigan, who had just arrived from the continent covered in laurel leaves and rose petals.

Cardigan's first estranged wife Elizabeth Tollemache Johnstone was on her death bed, and it was only a matter of time before the fresh-faced Adeline would take her place. It was a bit of a gloating party for the two women, since Anne had never been terribly fond of her brother's first wife. Everyone knew that Queen Victoria would never allow Adeline in her court, given the scandalous nature of her relationship with Cardigan. That was why Anne felt obliged to assure the young girl that she was always welcome at Laleham. In addition to Elizabeth's illness, they had other reasons to fill their glasses with excellent cabernet.

They had situated themselves by the Long Water. The stream was still frozen over, but the ice was beginning to crack, creating fanciful lacy pattern.

"To me nothing is more beautiful than the skin of a peach,

frostbitten ever so slightly," Ann declared, holding a fragrant fuzzy fruit to the sun. "Do you see how the light plays up with the texture?"

In response Adeline scattered a handful of pomegranate seeds over the snow.

"See how they glisten? Rubies against white silk! How I wish I could be a painter, or a jeweler. On days such as this, I pity the blind."

"Believe me, dearest, sometimes I wish I were blind," Anne muttered suddenly.

Her hand holding the stem of glass shuddered, and the cabernet spilled on the snow.

"Is anything the matter?" Adeline asked.

"I had hoped that our delightful outing would not be spoiled," Lady Lucan replied through her teeth.

They saw a sinister silhouette of a tall man crossing over the Serpentine Bridge, approaching them. Young Adeline recognized Anne's loathsome husband George. As for the Countess, she pretended to be ignorant of his presence as long as possible. She began filling her mouth with grapes and pomegranate seeds, as they would prevent her from speaking with him.

"My poor Anne," Adeline whispered, pressing the fingers of her future sister-in-law. "To have lived with this dreadful man for so many years... I know how you prayed he would never return from the Crimea."

Anne wiped the peach juice from the tip of her nose and helped herself to another serving of wine. When her husband approached, she greeted him with a full mouth and a full glass.

"Will you not join us, my lord?" Adeline piped giddily, exploiting the opportunity to aggravate her beloved James' enemy. "Did they serve peaches and cabernet in the Crimea?"

Lord Lucan did not even acknowledge the presence of Cardigan's mistress, whom he considered a base whore. Without a greeting, he placed his foot into the fruit basket. Pink and golden juice streamed from under the sole of his boot.

"My lady, I'd like a word with you in private," he demanded, his nostrils flaring.

Anne began extracting pomegranate seeds from her mouth one by one, ceremoniously and defiantly.

The next casualty of Lord Lucan's wrath became the bottle of merlot. The loaf of French bread and paper-thin slices of Swiss cheese followed. A minute later, what had started as a light and elegant English picnic resembled the aftermath of a Roman feast. When there was no food left to destroy, the earl cast his glance on Adeline's lap dog. The tiny Papillion, having sensed danger, whimpered and hid in the folds of its mistress' tartan skirt. As fond as Adeline was of her future sister-in-law, she did not wish for her dog to become a victim of the Lucan marital feud.

"Perhaps how would be a good time for me to go for a stroll," she said in a trembling voice, clutching the dog to her chest and rising to her feet.

Before Adeline had the chance to turn her back to the spouses, the earl reached down and squeezed his wife's jaw, forcing her to spit out the chewed-up grapes.

"There, give them up, my lady," he said. "Too much sour fruit is unwholesome for your stomach."

Even after the last of green pulp had emerged from Anne's mouth, Lucan continued squeezing her jaw to assure that she could not turn away from him.

"How dare you distract me from my picnic?" Anne asked, looking him in the eye, aiming to communicate to her husband that she was not afraid of him. "I never disrupt your political meetings, do I? Or, perhaps, you deem my engagements less important."

The earl released her jaw with disgust.

"My lady, I have news for you. I have met the woman with whom I intend to spend the rest of my life."

The Countess yawned demonstratively.

"Does this woman even exist?"

"She certainly does! More than that, she is gaining international notoriety. She is beautiful, compassionate, and fearless. Those are just a few of her virtues. Of course, it is impossible for you to conceive that some women can accomplish something. God forbid! You spend your afternoons gossiping and rolling fruit in the snow."

"Why, I do believe that such a woman exists," Anne replied, fanning her frozen fingers. "But is she aware of your existence? I only ask because I know your propensity to brag about imaginary trysts. Assuming this nameless heroine is real, why in the world would she give herself to an incompetent soldier who is rapidly becoming the subject of military jokes? If the lady is as extraordinary as you describe her, should she not be a little more discriminating in her choice of a husband? My dear, I cannot help sensing that your story is embellished. Clearly, you are exaggerating something—either her virtues or the extent of her devotion to you."

Anne could have continued mocking her husband in her lazy, frivolous voice, but he stamped his foot into the ravaged basket.

"I want to end this marriage!"

Anne rolled her eyes; she had been hearing this phrase for the past ten years.

"I did not come here to boast about another mistress," Lucan continued. "The woman I love will not settle for a mistress' position. I came to inform you about my intentions to start the divorce procedures in earnest. I do not expect you to behave with dignity and make this ordeal painless for us both. No, you shall attempt to place every obstacle in my path, for you cannot bear to see me happy."

The countess yawned again, putting her jaw at risk for being dislocated. This time her boredom was not feigned. Her husband's grumbling, combined with the alcohol, made her drowsy.

"Are you finished already?" she asked, rubbing her eyes. "For an instant I thought that you for once had something truly significant to report, something other than your latest imaginary affair. If you are finished delivering your news, I would like to share something with you as well. You see, I too have news. Congratulations, my lord! You have a grandson."

Lord Lucan extracted his foot from the crashed picnic basket and wiped the sole against the snow.

"I don't expect the news to thrill you," Anne continued. "No doubt, you've heard it many times before, since your bastards have already procreated. Still, this little bastard is precious, for he is the first one that you and I share in common."

The earl began shaking his head violently.

"Don't you dare!" he shouted. "Do not even endeavor something so base! There is a limit to how low a bitter wife can stoop. Fabricating some fable about Georgie! To injure me, you would slander your own son? Is nothing sacred to you, woman?"

"But darling," Anne cooed, taking her husband's arm softly, "what leads you to believe that I was referring to Georgie? The mother of the little bastard is none other but our dear daughter Lavinia."

The conversation was growing progressively more distasteful, even though Lord Lucan did not think it was possible.

"Remember your house guest last summer?" Anne asked, burrowing her chin into her husband's shoulder. "Remember the charming gun-thief with a shattered jaw? You mandated Lavinia to exercise hospitality, and she interpreted your words as a carte blanche for fornication."

Anne became silent, giving her husband a chance to digest her narration. Judging from the way his body suddenly tensed up she concluded that he no longer was thinking her a liar. At last, they could converse like two reasonable adults, bound by parental solidarity. Still clutching the earl's arm, Anne made a step forward, inviting him for a little stroll.

"Lavinia had been withdrawn and teary-eyed all summer," the countess continued, "but I blamed her melancholy on the usual source—her father's abominable behavior. Then one evening, as we were preparing for a ball, I noticed that corset would not come together. After a brief and gentle interrogation on my part, the girl crumbled and confessed. Oh, George, you should have seen her!"

Anne glanced up to see her husband's face. It looked a little paler and stiffer than it did five minutes earlier, though its expression did not change much. The countess filled her lungs with chilly March air, preparing to relate the best part of the story.

"This one-time frivolity nearly cost Lavinia her life. If you were to open a medical textbook and read about all the possible complications of childbirth, she endured all of them, including severe blood loss and fever that lasted for ten days. That ordeal ought to kill her appetite for fornication for the next fifty years. She did not show particular distress when I told her that the child had died. She blotted her eyes, nodded, and agreed that it was God's will. Then she embraced my knees and begged for my forgiveness. I tried not to be excessively stern with her. After all, the girl had already received her lesson. Do you hear me? I forbid you to scold her. Next time you see her, be gentle and cheerful. Bring her some pretty trinket to lift her spirits. You know how to choose useless gifts. Act as if nothing had happened. Not a word about her ordeal. Do you understand?"

Lucan stopped and turned his wife around to face him.

"Where is the child?" he asked, seizing her elbows and pressing them to her sides. He knew that she could not feel pain through her fur-trimmed coat.

Anne threw her head back and laughed, sending a cloud of cabernet-scented steam in her husband's face.

"God bless you, darling! You truly expect me to reveal all my cards? This much I'll tell you: the little bastard is safe; and I will see to his continued safety as long as you promise to play your part. Knowing your intellectual and moral limitations, I shall not ask you anything unreasonable. Keep that raven-haired clown and other vermin that you bring from the street away from this family."

Lucan blinked tightly and then opened his eyes wide, as if chasing away an apparition. He always knew of his wife's passion for gossip and scheming, but he never thought that she would indulge that passion at her own children's expense.

"I don't believe it," he muttered. "You actually would—"

"Yes, my darling, I would sink this low to protect my own daughter's reputation. I shall see that she makes a suitable match, in spite of her errors. There is enough Brudenell blood in her to make her a worthwhile human specimen. Her father's negligence nearly killed her, but her mother's love shall restore her to life. Yes, mother's love can work even greater miracles."

The earl released her from his grip and shoved her into the snow. She fell on her back with her arms spread.

"My lady, you know about mother's love?" Lucan asked, hovering over her. "An unsuspecting listener would find your words almost moving. It is astonishing how you manage to veil your lowest revenge campaigns against me into maternal sacrifice."

Anne responded with a peeling, provocative laughter and flapped her arms, stirring a cloud of flurries. From a distance, the scene looked like a jovial rendezvous, just an affluent middle-aged couple enjoying the last snow.

"All your actions are dictated by female envy," the earl continued. "You cannot bear the thought of your daughter feeling carnal pleasure, the kind of pleasure that no man has given you in a long time. You are suffocating in your loneliness, in your incurable uselessness, so you want Lavinia to suffocate with you. I do not believe for a second that you wish her to marry well. Nothing would please you better than to keep her a spinster, to share your misery. You would turn her against her own father and all other men in the world, including those who could make her happy. By the way, that scarred clown whom you despise so is a national hero. You may wish to consider that."

"Lavinia does not need a hero," the countess said, having stopped fidgeting in the snow. "She needs a gentleman. Unfortunately, her father is neither. It is a tragic fact of which the world is becoming aware. Lavinia's only chance at a redeeming life is to marry a man superior to her father." Suddenly, Anne's demeanor became businesslike. "Perhaps, I should inform you of my recent conversations with Viscount Henry Hardinge. Yes, you heard me correctly. I am referring to the Commander-in-Chief, whom you have failed to impress. That worthy gentleman has a son Charles, who one day shall inherit the family estate in Lahore. They are a demanding, fastidious bunch. Interaction with them requires impeccable diplomacy. I must choreograph my every move. One careless twitch of the pinky finger, one awkward flip of the eyelashes—and all my prospects shall collapse. This process is more intricate and perilous than commanding a cavalry unit."

"Why are you telling me this?" Lucan asked, pretending that he did not understand his wife's hint. The child-stealer was now playing a matchmaker?

"I know how anxious you are to embrace your new life, darling," Anne concluded, "even if it is confined to your imagination. You have convinced yourself that there is a woman in this world who wishes to marry you. I cannot forbid you to fantasize. I can, however, stop you from bring more shame upon this family. This talk about divorce must stop, at least until my transaction with the Hardinges is complete."

Chapter 4
Lord Lucan Rouses the Actor in Him

Lucan's first civilian task for his son was to meet with Lord Hardinge and demand a court martial. The request was denied, as one may have expected. Less than twenty-four hours later, the earl was standing in the Parliament, addressing the House of Lords on the regarding the circumstances of his recall. He was not ready to put the issue to rest. No, he was willing to resurrect it as many times as would be necessary, reiterating the points covered in his letter to Newcastle, the same letter that cost him his command of the Cavalry Division. The angry energy bubbling in his breast needed release. At that stage of humiliation, Lucan believed he had little to lose. He could not possibly make himself any more unpopular than he already was. He had grown immune to the whispering and the eye rolls from the peers in response to his attempts to clear his name. That was the mission to which he dedicated the first two weeks of March. A day would not pass by without him trying to expose Raglan's incompetence before the peers. Lord Bingham kept running tirelessly back and forth between his father and Lord Hardinge, dispatching demands for a court martial and letters of refusal. The young heir covered more distance in the first two weeks in London than he had in the six months at the Crimea. He certainly felt more useful.

Panmure, Newcastle's successor as Commander-in-Chief, confessed to Raglan that he did not want to scandalize the army any further by allowing Cardigan and Lucan to clash in the open. A court martial would bring the fragile morale even lower.

On March 19th Lucan finally received his long-awaited and well-earned avalanche of rotten tomatoes, when he rose with his speech once again. He spoke with the same imperturbability and solemnity, without a hint of frustration and exhaustion, just as if he were presenting the facts for the first time.

I rise, my Lords, in pursuance of notice, to move for a copy of Lord Raglan's report of the Battle of Balaclava. I consider it due to your Lordships and to myself not to forego this, the first opportunity which has occurred to me, to make a statement of what was my conduct on the day of that battle, and at the same time to show what has happened since in reference to it. It will be necessary, I fear, to trouble your Lordships at some length, and in the statement I am about to make, it shall be my endeavor, as it is my wish, whilst exculpating myself, not to inculpate others. It is my wish to make my statement as clear as possible, and to do so I shall have to take your Lordships to the Battle of Balaclava.

The speech was over three and a half thousand words in length. Lord Cranworth, the Chancellor, saw no way out of this closed circle of Lucan's grievances but let him finish his speech and then allow an open debate. The peers took turns stabbing the hapless earl and pouring acid over his wounds. In their eyes, his gravest offense was his lack of discretion. According to Duke of Richmond, it was distasteful to hear accusations and private conversations brought forward. Lord Lucan had no business attacking Raglan, his direct superior, out in the open. No, there would be no court martial.

There was little less Lucan could do. He tried earnestly and he failed. The realization of the failure no longer brought him the same searing pain. By then his indignation over the matter had dulled. He could not rage over the same travesty indefinitely. This juvenile bickering with Cardigan, this fruitless discourse with the Parliament had grown stale. He needed to find himself a fresh new conflict; but first he decided to visit his Irish estate and vent his brain. With his eyes set on Castlebar, Lord Lucan walked out of the House of Lords.

Having approached the stairwell, he suddenly spotted former aide-de-camp and protégé Lord Hungerton on the lower level. Had it not been for the familiar scars on the young man's face, the earl would not have recognized him. Hungerton was sporting an elegant charcoal waistcoat, the newest style, and a burgundy tie. His unruly dark curls had been cropped shorter and combed aside, leaving the forehead exposed. A third party must have helped him choose the suit. There was no way this Bohemian urchin could have dressed in that fashion on his own. Overall, his apparel and his demeanor indicated a firm determination to be the most dashing lord in the Parliament.

The little cur is learning quickly, Lucan thought to himself. *A hero's status is making him bold.*

Their glances intersected. The young man flashed his beautiful teeth and waved. There was no chance of avoiding a conversation now. Lucan would not meet his former aide halfway. The earl crossed his arms and leaned his hip against the banister.

"What are you doing here?" he asked coldly, when his former protégé ascended the stairwell.

"Same thing you are, my lord," Wynfield replied. "I arrived as fast as I could. Believe me, I wish I could have come sooner."

"I meant: what are you doing in England?" Lucan asked, detaching from the banister and shifting the weight of his body. "Whatever became of your friendship with Scarlett? Weren't you appointed to train the new cavalry? Did you disappoint our red-faced hero so quickly?"

"Not at all! Sir James and I parted on excellent terms and rather reluctantly. It appears that the injury I sustained at Balaclava was graver than we had originally thought. My right arm has been behaving unpredictably. Dr. Ferrars did not sound very optimistic."

"How is he?" Lucan asked with subtle curiosity. "I am referring to our cunning genius. Did he mention coming back to work for me?"

"To be honest, I have no idea," Wynfield replied. "My thoughts have not been with them as of recent. I have mostly been thinking of the life waiting for me in England. My lord, I am here now."

Wynfield opened his arms before the earl, not as an invitation for an embrace but as an expression of amicable surrender.

Through the musk notes of the cologne in which his neck and hands were dabbed so generously, one could still smell gunpowder. Several weeks would pass before that smell would rinse out of his skin and hair completely.

"Very well," the earl replied, arching his eyebrow. "Welcome back to the Parliament, Lord Hungerton. What else is there left to say?"

Lucan's exaggerated coldness did not surprise Wynfield. One would have expected the earl to withhold his affection after everything that had happened.

"My lord," Wynfield continued, "I wish to reassure you of my devotion. It is enraging how the House has been treating you, and I have no intention of condoning this injustice. Perhaps, we can demand another court martial?"

The earl let out a short, malevolent laugh.

"Hah! I wish you the best of luck!"

"Not all is lost," Wynfield whispered insistently. "Ideally, I should have been here by your side on March 2, but I just arrived this morning, quite literally. Perhaps, I could offer my testimony, to reinforce yours."

"Your testimony? Don't be foolish, Lord Hungerton! Allow me to remind you that you were unconscious in the surgical tent when the Charge of the Light Brigade happened. Who will take your testimony seriously? If you wish to receive a round of ridicule, by all means, proceed!"

The scene between Lucan and Hungerton could not pass unnoticed. Young lords, whose sharp ears were always ready to perk up at the sound of a quarrel, began clustering at the top of the stairwell. Wilton and Granard, who still remembered Hungerton's performance in the Parliament almost a year ago, were tickled by his arrival.

"Behold, gentlemen, our favorite clown has returned!" Wilton squealed, rubbing his hands. "I wonder what prank he has in store for us this time."

"What a scrumptious treat," Granard murmured, his eyes igniting. "Lucan and Hungerton tearing into one another, with button flying! Someone must fetch Ellenborough. Quickly! He mustn't miss such a spectacle."

Lord Lucan and Wynfield would not give the spectators such satisfaction and secluded themselves inside one of the libraries.

"My lord," Wynfield began when they were alone, "if I have in any way offended you, I would like an opportunity to redeem myself. Please, understand, I had direct orders from Raglan himself. I was to remain at the cavalry camp as Scarlett's aide. It was not my choice. Do you begrudge me my subordination? You should understand better than anyone the ordeal of receiving questionable orders."

"Stop apologizing," Lucan said, stretching his arm out. "It is all water under the bridge. You have seen me angry before. Do I look angry to you right this moment?"

"Believe me, my lord, I would rather have you scold and curse me. Why are you treating me like a stranger? Are we not family? Am I not to marry your daughter?"

"No," Lucan replied with a slight shrug.

Wynfield tilted his head and smirked, still thinking that the earl was trying to punish him for not taking a firmer stand in his defense.

"I see, my lord," he said with theatrical humility. "I suppose, Lavinia has found a more enviable suitor." "As a matter of fact, she did," Lucan confirmed imperturbably.

"Ah, I see," Wynfield replied, squinting. "Very amusing, indeed."

"Then laugh to your heart's content. Now, if you do not mind, I must hurry off. My business here is finished for the foreseeable future. I'm off to Castlebar tonight. Good day to you, Lord Hungerton."

Lucan glanced at his reflection in the glass of the bookcase, fixed his tie and smoothed his mustache.

"No," Wynfield said lowly, shaking his head. "This cannot be."

"Oh yes, it certainly can. Now, with your permission..."

Wynfield leaped in front of the earl, blocking the door handle with his back.

"Impossible! I must see her."

"She won't see you, Lord Hungerton. She has nothing to say to you, nor does she owe you any explanations. Your engagement was never official at any rate. I cannot be held accountable for the fantasies arising from your shaken mind. Lord Hungerton, with all due respect, I have graver matters to settle. I have no time for your puppyish infatuation. You consider your alleged love so unique and your feelings so precious that you expect the world to stop spinning and tend to them?"

Of all the disagreeable surprises that fate could have hurled at him, it was one Wynfield had imagined the least. In his mind, parting with Lavinia had been even less likely than getting shot on the battlefield or contracting an illness. The bitterness from the discovery of his shoulder being permanently damaged and his career in the cavalry being over had already begun fading. The possibility of Lavinia shifting her affections onto someone else in his absence was not something he had considered.

"No, I demand an opportunity to meet with her!" he exclaimed. "If she had stopped loving me, she must inform me of that in person."

Lucan repeated his malevolent chuckle from the hall.

"In time you shall learn to curb your demands and reconcile with your disappointments, young man. I too came to London full of demands. If I can accept the refusal of a court martial, you can accept rejection from a woman."

"I don't believe you."

"Then you are calling me a liar?"

"I wouldn't dare, my lord. Nevertheless, I cannot help feeling that a rather significant portion of the truth is being withheld from me. Lavinia would not cast me off without a reason. I suspect that you are privy to something but aren't at liberty to share it with me."

Wynfield's perceptiveness was making Lucan nervous. Love sharpened the young man's intuition. The earl knew that a minor twitch of a facial muscle would shatter his façade. Truth be told, Lucan was not a skillful liar, especially when it came to keeping someone else's secret. He needed to awaken and call the inner actor to his aid.

"You are an imaginative, highly emotional young man," the earl said, clapping Wynfield on the shoulder patronizingly. "You perceive conspiracy behind most trivial occurrences. The reality is much plainer than your fantasy. Your pride will not allow you to believe that a woman could prefer another man to you? Let us cast juvenile sentiments aside and look at the numbers. Shall we? You are a mere baron, and her future husband is a viscount. He has a larger fortune, and his lineage goes further into the past. As you can see, it is nothing personal, pure mathematics."

Wynfield pushed away the earl's hand.

"I refuse to believe that Lavinia would be guided by mere mathematics."

"You mean to tell me that you know my daughter better than

her own father does? Of course, you spent whole two weeks in her company! That is enough time to examine one's soul back and forth. My dear boy, I've known that girl for nineteen years. Yes, she may have pampered your vanity while you were recovering. I am not saying that she is entirely devoid of compassion. Still, compassion is hardly the best reason to marry someone. Otherwise, Florence Nightingale would marry the entire Light Brigade. In all honesty, I a bit surprised that you were naïve enough to interpret Lavinia's hospitality as something greater. I would have expected a man like you to possess a healthy dose of cynicism. Let that be a lesson for the future. Next time a woman makes an extravagant promise in the throes of Christian charity, you may think twice before taking it as face value."

Watching the changes occurring in Wynfield's face, Lord Lucan felt his own apprehension lifting. His first attempt at composing fiction ended in success. He managed to convince the enamored boy that Lavinia had left him for a more impressive candidate.

Still leaning against the door, Wynfield covered his eyes with his hands.

"Allow me a minute, my lord," he murmured, pressing his thumbs into his eyeballs. "Ah, I should have anticipated it. I am paying for my transgressions. This is only the beginning."

Watching his protégé in pain, Lucan felt his own throat tightening. Suddenly, he became overwhelmed by pity for both Lord Hungerton and himself. Circumstances, which in his mind were beyond his control, forced him to exercise unspeakable cruelty towards a loyal, pure-hearted, well-intentioned boy who loved his daughter sincerely, albeit carelessly and boorishly. What a messy, unenviable predicament they got themselves into!

"Leave your eyes alone," the earl said. "You shall blind yourself."

Obeying some impetuous urge, he stepped towards the young man and took him in his arms.

"Do not lose heart," he whispered, clapping Wynfield on the back. "We do not need to part as enemies. You are still my son, perhaps even more so than ever. Forgive me my aloof demeanor earlier. I simply did not know how to break the unpleasant news to you. It is not an activity I relish. Believe me when I say this. It pains me to see you suffer. You've had a streak of ill fortune, haven't you? First Dr. Grant, then your arm, now Lavinia... Alas, there is nothing I can do about Lavinia. I have very little say in matters of her heart. She and her mother have their own designs. If it is of any consolation, my year has started rather badly. I shall not burden you with any details. Please know that you are not alone. Both you and I need time to replenish our spirits. As a matter of fact, why don't you come to Castlebar with me?"

Wynfield lifted his head and looked his fickle benefactor in the eye. The man who was mocking him five minutes ago was now consoling him.

"I am being perfectly earnest," the earl continued with paternal enthusiasm. "You've never been to Ireland, have you? It is a beautiful country."

"So I hear," Wynfield mumbled, staring at the pattern on the rug under his feet.

"The landscape shall leave you breathless. Imagine eating freshly caught salmon for supper every evening, washing it down with ale from a local brewery. And the women! You shall never revert to English girls, I promise."

"I doubt I shall be looking at any women in the near future," Wynfield replied skeptically, "regardless of their nationality."

"Ah, this is what you claim now." Lucan winked mischievously. "Wait until you walk through the streets of Castlebar and see those flocks of copper-haired beauties. Wait until you hear them sing Gaelic ballads. Please, say that you shall join me on my trip. It would mean a great deal to me."

Wynfield scratched his temple, and then threw his arms up apathetically.

"Surely! Why not? If it will please you, my lord..."

At that point, he was too exhausted to think of a reason not to go.

"Excellent!" the earl exclaimed, rubbing his hands. "And for heaven's sake, stop calling me 'my lord'. There is no reason for us to continue with formalities after everything we have endured together. You are no longer my aide-de-camp or even a future son-in-law. From now on, I insist that you address me as George. And I in turn can call you..." Lucan paused for a second and tapped his lower lip. "What was that clownish nickname you sported—Grinnin' Wyn?"

"No!" Wynfield cried out in terror, stretching his hands before him. "Please do not call me that, my lord. I mean, George... That name is from another world, another era. I am not certain it fits me any longer."

"I understand completely. That was Dr. Grant's endearment for you. Of course, his memory is sacred. I would not endeavor to replace him. May he rest in peace! I suppose, I can call you Jeremy. Or do you prefer Jerry? That is what my son calls you, isn't it?"

"It is entirely up to you, my lord... George! But please, let us leave this place at once. I cannot breathe here."

When they emerged from library, they saw Wilton, Granard and Ellenborough in the hallway. The three scandal-savvy lords seemed disappointed that their two feuding peers were not sporting bruises or any other signs of physical altercation.

Chapter 5
Flavored Tobacco
and Chocolate Truffles

One of the most famous attractions at Castlebar was the plaque on the city hall commemorating the violent clash in late August 1798 when a Franco-Irish force of two thousand routed a British force three times its size through the town streets. The battle became known as the Castlebar Races and was recorded as a triumph of the United Irishmen under the leadership of Theobald Wolfe Tone. The Castlebar Castle, the original residence of the Lucan dynasty, was burned down the same year. Decades later a modest square villa was built in its vicinity, becoming Lucan's summer residence.

The brass plaque was one of the first that Wynfield asked about when he arrived at Castlebar in the company of the earl. They had traveled by coach from Dublin, traversing the entire country. Lord Lucan made a reluctant tour guide. He just poked a limp finger at the plaque and murmured something about "freckled apes rebelling every decade or so." His attitude towards the Irish nationalism was that of superficial, nonchalant contempt. He did not view the movement as a serious threat, more of a nuisance.

"My love for Mayo was slow-growing," he confessed over tea, when the two of them finally settled at Castlebar House. "In my father's time, it was backward and inhospitable. There were no farms or industries, only rocks, heaths, and mud huts. It took us decades to make this green desert suitable for living. And the agent we've had until my father's death—ah! Those O'Malley thieves! I better not even touch that topic."

The topic was indeed unpleasant for Lucan. He blamed the financial problems at Castlebar on the O'Malleys, who had agented the estate for thirty-five years. In the absence of the Lucan's father, St. Claire O'Malley behaved almost like the owner, taking all sorts of liberties that ordinarily would be off limits for an agent. He lived in the family mansion, slept in the master's bed, hunted on the master's grounds, and never enforced the payment of rent. Half of the tenants at Castlebar were his relatives, so he treated them with unforgivable leniency, all at the expense of the landlord.

"When I glanced at the books back in '39, I almost had a fit!" Lucan continued ranting between sips of tea. "That Irish thief had gutted my accounts! For years he had practically been feeding his gluttonous relations out of my pocket."

"You do not say..."

"My dear Jerry, some Irishmen are worse than Jews! The travesty had to be remedied somehow. I discharged O'Malley at once and started processing the evictions. Of course, the tenants did not like my action one bit. You see, they had grown spoiled by O'Malley. God forbid, someone should demand that they pay rent. They thought they could continue living on my land free of charge. They can neither farm nor manufacture. The Irish are good for nothing except for begging, rebelling, destroying, burning someone else's property. Would you believe it? They christened me the 'exterminator', as if I were the only landlord to evict his tenants. I did nothing immoral or illegal. I was merely exercising my rights. Jerry, I have great ambitions for this property. It will be turned into a prosperous farm, with or without the Irish tenants. I have been researching new agricultural techniques. I shall make good use of my land, even if I must purge the parasites that drain it. But first, I want to show you my cricket grounds. You know how to play cricket, don't you?"

Wynfield was not listening to the earl, even though his facial expression suggested moderate interest. Examining the wallpaper in the dining room, he kept thinking: *This is the house where Lavinia was born.*

Surprisingly, for how unpopular Lord Lucan among his tenants, they organized quite a lavish reception in his honor, illuminating Castlebar, and launching fireworks. In the evening, a group of Irish children appeared in front of his mansion with a welcome address, delivered in the most servile tone. The earl responded with a sour condescending smile. He could not wait for the well-wishers to leave. The smell of rotting potatoes and curdled goat milk perpetually hovering over them nauseated him. He had been forced to bear all sorts of disagreeable odors at the cavalry camp, so he would not suffer the same inconvenience in his own estate.

No later than the next morning, he summoned his tenants to announce great news: he was going to begin agricultural endeavors, which meant creating paying jobs for the locals. He had his mind set on growing wheat in Mayo, against all odds, against all laws of nature and agriculture. His ambition was his generous gift to his tenants. Golden rain was going to spill over the heaths of Castlebar. Yes, they heard him correctly: wheat was going to replace potatoes, and he, the 3rd Earl of Lucan was going to pioneer the conversion. It was going to be the most daring experiment of the century.

The tenants stared at the landlord in bewilderment, some in outright terror. His ambition was akin to that of growing figs in the North Pole. However, he did promise to pay them. He mentioned nothing about their wages being contingent on the outcome of the experiment. Everyone could profit from Lord Lucan's stupidity. Having concluded that they had more to gain than lose, the tenants began applauding.

By the end of his first week at Castlebar, the earl issued first instructions to start clearing the land. The plots reserved for planting potatoes would be used for planting wheat instead. His lordship soon discovered that he liked being in command of peasants very much. For a change, he had full control of his endeavor. He did not need to put up with superior commanders and their aide-de-camps. Words of orders left a delicious aftertaste in his mouth.

As one should have predicted, Lucan's enthusiasm did not last very long. Unconditional subordination becomes tiresome after a while. Once the novelty of pushing around flocks of peasants wore off, he set off for London, leaving his trustworthy friend Lord Hungerton in charge.

While Wynfield did not mind shouldering the responsibility—he had no other matters to occupy him—he had great difficulty understanding what the tenants were saying. His ears were yet to grow accustomed to the sound of western Irish accent. Half the time he could not tell whether they were speaking broken English or Gaelic. It caused him great embarrassment to ask the men in his command to repeat what they were saying, but he had no other choice. Whenever one of them would approach him, muttering rapidly, and waving his arms, Wynfield felt like he was back at Varna, bartering with local vendors. Even his short-lived friendship with Seamus Martin could not have prepared him for communicating with the natives of Castlebar. About once a week, a note from Lucan would arrive. The content was almost always the same.

Dear Jerry, do not indulge those Irish thieves in my absence. Keep the cellar locked at all times. Do not disclose the location of the wine. Do not let the women and their children beyond the gate of the house. Once you let them through, you shall never be rid of them. Is there anything I can bring you from London? Would you like some flavored tobacco or chocolate truffles?

Contrary to his promise to put the collective blunder at Balaclava to rest, Lucan resumed his war with the Parliament. He and his old enemy Anthony Bacon engaged in a game of trading insults, writing expository pamphlets and sending angry letters to *The Times*, which the editor always published eagerly.

Then in late June, England received the news that Lord Raglan had died in Balaclava. Crimean fever was cited as the official cause of his death. However, those who were with him in his last hour claimed that the Commander-in-Chief had suffered a complete nervous and physical breakdown. The failed assault on Sebastopol on June 18th was the final straw. "I could never return to England now," he whispered on his sickbed. "They would stone me to death."

In other words, Raglan was indirectly admitting his responsibility for the disaster. At least, that was how Lucan interpreted his former commander's last phrase. The earl viewed Raglan's sickbed admission as an excuse to buy a new Parliament suit and apply for another court martial. Perhaps, he did have a chance at vindicating himself after all. Inspired by this sudden spark of hope, Lucan scribbled a brief letter to Wynfield.

Dear Jerry, I hope those Irish thieves are not causing you too much trouble. When I come back from London, I shall bring a few heads on a stick. My guardian angels are whispering to me that there is justice after all, even on this earth. Expect me some time in August. You still have no answered my question regarding your choice of a souvenir. Do you want flavored tobacco or chocolate truffles?

Lucan never made it back to Castlebar that summer, as he was called to Laleham for the funeral of his youngest daughter Sarah Anne. The girl was fifteen years old at the time of her death. The bereavement made Lucan forget his political tiffs or even his hatred for his wife. Ordinarily, whenever one of the children fell ill, the earl would inevitably accuse their mother of negligence, but in the case with Sarah Anne, it was the first time that an illness had actually resulted in death. The estranged spouses embraced over the narrow coffin of their daughter. Even Lord Cardigan came to his niece's funeral. It was a brief moment of truce between the Binghams and the Brudenells.

In early September Wynfield received an uncharacteristically emotional letter from Lucan.

Dear Jerry, my trustworthy boy, it comforts me to know that you look after my estate and my tenants, as I take this time to grieve the untimely departure of my beloved daughter. I am not so delusional as to question what I am being punished for. The answer is quite plain. The young ones who perished of hunger on my property also had parents. You must understand why I cannot show my face to those people. Boorish, lazy, and wayward as they are, they need an enlightened patron. I cannot think for anyone more suitable for the role than you. I leave you to instruct, to protect, and to discipline them. In the meantime, pray for me as I pray for you. May the Almighty keep you!

Wynfield had never met Sarah Anne or even seen her portrait. Still, the girl was Georgie and Lavinia's sister, and that sufficed for Wynfield to feel a twitch of physical pain. Some mysterious invisible thread tied him to the collective flesh of the Binghams. Whenever something would happen to one of them, a portion of the pain would radiate onto Wynfield as well. The symptom could be as seemingly minor as a cramp between the ribs. The principle was not even spiritual but chemical. He had made love to Lavinia and he had slept back to back with her brother.

As much as Wynfield longed to respond to the letter and express his condolences, he remembered Lord Lucan's insistent request not to publicize their friendship. The letter could end up in the hands of the children or the Countess, which would be even worse. Thus, Wynfield limited his sympathy to prayers.

The tone of the letter was illustrative of Lucan's state of mind at that particular moment, certainly not of any permanent moral transformation. That onslaught of humility triggered by grief lasted but a moment. Alas, no great epiphany was in the stars for his lordship. It would take more than one of his children's deaths to make him see the light. He was destined to live through the same tragedy again two years later with another daughter, one by the name Elizabeth.

By early November 1855, the earl was back on his horse, having received a Knights of Bath batch of honor and command of the 8th Hussars. The appointments sparked more controversy, which the earl relished.

Wynfield was not there to see Lucan prance amidst his adversaries in the Parliament. All he had was the letter drenched in tears of paternal grief and remorse. He continued to have faith in human virtue and the possibility of redemption, even after all the deceit he had witnessed. Reading over Lucan's last letter, Wynfield knew he could not abandon his new flock.

Chapter 6
Black Thumb of Death

In spite of his new tasks at Castlebar that obliged him to interact with dozens of workers, Wynfield was growing increasingly lonely. As he was growing adjusted to their heavily accented babble, he understood more and more that had nothing in common with those people. All attempts on his part to initiate a lighthearted chat drove the workers into a state of hostile bewilderment. The harder Wynfield tried to win their trust, the more suspicious they grew. Those men responded well to direct orders but not to questions of personal nature. There was something unnatural about an Englishman, especially a lord, inquiring about their families. His very presence in their midst must have been an act of some whimsical perversion. That Englishman was there to watch them labor in vain.

This passive animosity could not compare to anything Wynfield had received before from anyone else. Even in the Crimea, he felt less of a foreigner. The glances of the Irish workers caused his skin to itch. His whole body began rebelling against the new environment. Wynfield had grown so accustomed to inhaling soot, sawdust and gunpowder smoke that fresh country air had the effects of poison on his respiratory system. He craved factory pollution as if it were ambrosia. In his dreams, he wandered through foggy workshops, bumping into pieces of machinery, listening to the melody of gears shifting and clashing into each other.

Unfortunately, even sleep was becoming a scant luxury for

him. Until he came to Ireland, his understanding of the word "insomnia" was rather sketchy. To him it was an imaginary disease that afflicted idle middle-aged women. It posed no threat to a vigorous twenty-five year old man who spent his days outside. He simply could not understand how one could lie in bed perfectly still with one's eyes closed and not fall asleep. After two nights spent in that state he was ready to howl and beat his head against the wall. After a week, he was ready to jump off the cliffs, just to silence that low buzzing in his head. The most curious part was that he did not even have any great moral dilemma at that time. He was not battling remorse or alarm for the wellbeing of a loved one.

For the first time his head, heart and hands were completely vacant. He had no war, no love, or even manual work to occupy him. Strolling through the streets of Castlebar at night did not exhaust him sufficiently.

His most disturbing discovery was that he appeared to have stopped noticing female beauty. The women of Mayo did not treat Wynfield with the same hostility as he received from their brothers and husbands. Irish girls were notorious for their chastity, but they would consider selling it to a benevolent Englishman who could promise them a more comfortable life. Wynfield encountered many comely young creatures in town and on the country roads, but neither the sound of their breathy laughter, nor the swaying of their hips could drive him out of his carnal hibernation.

On the edge of town, there lived a buxom, cheerful washerwoman, allegedly a widow. She could not have been older than thirty. To his amusement, Wynfield learned that the infant she carried in her laundry basket was not her son but her grandson born to her fifteen-year old daughter.

One time, the washerwoman came to Castlebar House without the baby. Having covered Wynfield's bed with fresh linens, she lay down on it, her blouse unbuttoned.

"Lord Hung'ton," she called, arching her back and smiling. "Mast'r look so lonesome... Come tae Marg'ret."

Some time passed before Wynfield realized that he was looking at a fairly young, still attractive and above all readily available woman. He had completely forgotten what a man was expected to do in such situation. Having rummaged in his pocket, he took out a shilling and threw it at her. The coin landed between her naked breasts.

The washerwoman laughed, thinking that the young lord preferred to pay in advance. Once she realized that he had no intention of getting his money's worth, she leaped to her feet in terror, buttoned her blouse hastily and rushed outside, leaving her empty basket on the table.

"Splendid," Wynfield muttered, staring at the door through which the washerwoman fled a few seconds earlier. "Now she'll tell her sister-hens in town that Lord Hungerton is a pervert who pays his whores without bedding them."

As Dr. Ferrars had predicted, Wynfield's right arm began atrophying and growing thinner. The loss of muscle was becoming more and more noticeable with each month. Without any pronounced emotion, Wynfield watched his body lose its symmetry gradually. The sight of a withering limb did not stir any grief or anger. It was just another injury his body sustained. Looking back at his temper fit inside Scarlett's tent and his demand for Dr. Ferrars to chop off the useless arm at the shoulder, Wynfield could not believe it was he saying those things.

On a detached intellectual level, he understood such apathy to be unhealthy. If he noticed Georgie slip into this state, he would make every effort to save his friend. Wynfield would probably slap him, get him drunk or take him to a brothel—anything to drive him out of his stupor, to reawaken his raw instinctive masculinity. Alas, he could not do such things for himself. Perhaps, he did not consider himself worth saving.

"Ireland shall be my burial ground," he said, strolling through the Castlebar cemetery, mesmerized by the intricate pattern on the tombstones.

Examining Celtic crosses became his new interest. Whoever came up with the idea of an endless knot was a genius. Mr. Walsh, the butler at Castlebar House, the only man with whom Wynfield could have conversations, explained the technique of etching Celtic designs.

By mid-October, it became obvious that Lord Lucan's ambitious experiment had failed miserably. To be exact, it had been obvious since the summer, but the tenants chose to remain in denial. Up until the bitter end, they clung to the hope that the crops would rise. Had they toiled in vain? There was no mention of Lord Lucan paying them for their fruitless work. The earl had vanished into thin air along with his promises. The tenants were looking at a winter without grains or potatoes.

When Wynfield called for a meeting in front of Castlebar House, an impressive number of tenants turned up. The men were gnashing their teeth and flexing their fists. Some carried with axes and shovels. The sight of those stiff jaws and flaring nostrils would make anyone in Wynfield's position at least a little nervous, but by then, he was almost entirely indifferent towards his fate. The prospect of dying in the hands of a furious Irish mob did not frighten him. He did have to admit, however, as much as it shamed him, that the men crowding around him did bear considerable resemblance to apes. So, that was where the illustrators of the *Punch* magazine drew their inspiration. Granted, it was a horribly blasphemous and unchristian thought, and Wynfield forbade himself to cultivate it.

"Dear friends," he began, "as you can see I am no farmer, but I am a baron. True, I have a black thumb of death, but I also have an inheritance that I have not tapped into yet. Now would be a perfect time to break the seal on my father's fortune. Rest assured, this winter you shall not go hungry. There will be meat and bread. I shall see to it myself. I made a promise to Lord Lucan that I would look after you. In the meantime, I want you to halt all fieldwork and return to your homes."

The first week in November, supplies of flour, grain, and canned beef began arriving. They were being delivered to the front yard of Castlebar House and then rationed out to the families on the tenant list. Wynfield realized that buying provisions out of his pocket was not the best maneuver from a pedagogic point if view. It went against all principles of the rewards system. He could not possibly feed them all indefinitely. At the same time, he could not let them starve either.

Chapter 7
As Final As Waterloo

December brought a string of moist squalls, covering the barren fields with a thin layer of sleet. Thus, the tenants no longer had to look at the proof of their fruitless toil. Right before Christmas, an outbreak of infectious cough spread through the town. Wynfield spent his days ordering provisions and medicine from Dublin. He even arranged for a physician to arrive, paying him twice the regular fee. He needed someone to help him administer the medicine. Wynfield was afraid of killing his tenants by advising them to take wrong doses of the potion. In the meantime, no new letters from Lord Lucan were arriving.

One evening Mr. Walsh informed his master that he had visitors—a woman with a small child. Initially Wynfield assumed that it was one of the tenants who came to ask for an extension on rent or a sack of flour. It was not uncommon for the people of Castlebar to wrap themselves in rags and imitate limps or coughs only to trigger pity. Sometimes they would bring their scrawniest, sickliest children as theatrical props. Having tasted of Lord Hungerton's soft-heartedness, the tenants took every opportunity to turn it to their advantage. They had suffered long enough under Lord Lucan, so they felt no guilt exploiting the idiotic generosity of his unofficial agent.

Having expected to see an emaciated peasant, Wynfield instead saw a gentlewoman dressed in a road dress of Glasgow tartan and a green velvet jacket. A veil attached to the brim of a bowler hat hid her face. Wynfield had never seen a woman sport anything of this sort on her head, not even someone as outrageous and daring Mrs. Duberly. Who would think of attaching three layers of black gauze to a man's hat? Perhaps, that was the new fashion in the cities. What did he know about such things?

The woman was holding an infant boy just under a year. The tiny creature was going out of its way to make her life miserable, fidgeting, whimpering, pulling on her veil, and sucking on the buttons of her jacket.

"Ah, Wynfield!" the woman greeted him genially and casually, as if they had been apart for mere hours. "I am relieved to see that you don't have a succession of butlers and house servants. What a chore it would be to go through a dozen of people! You practically answer your own door. Impressive! Then again, I wouldn't expect any less of Grinnin' Wyn."

Wynfield had not heard anyone address him by that name and so casually in ages. He thought he was beginning to recognize the woman's voice, that sharp, authoritative alto that appeared somewhat out of harmony with her slight frame. Whatever the lady lacked in height, her voice compensated for it.

"Come, lift my veil," she requested impatiently, seeing that her host still had trouble recognizing her. "My hands are occupied. Can't you see?"

Instead of merely lifting the veil, Wynfield removed the whole hat, revealing a mop of ruffled light-brown curls. Before him was Miss Jocelyn Stuart, the unofficial duchess of Clarence and the muse to all orphan boys. Looking into her amber eyes framed by copper eyelashes, he remembered the spring of 1854. He saw the outlines of St. Gabriel's school and of Horsemonger Lane Gaol from which his elusive patroness had rescued him.

Having shifted the restless infant in her arms, Jocelyn crossed the threshold. When Wynfield's hand accidentally came in contact with the velvet of her jacket that was damp from the rain, he succumbed to the familiar vertigo of vanity. This woman had actually taken the time to investigate his whereabouts and traveled to see him, especially after the hostile manner in which they parted. He sensed that she did not come to make war. He had seen her militant expression, and she was not wearing it at that moment.

"I heard you were feeding the poor, so I came to provide you with some practical guidance," she explained before Wynfield had a chance to enquire about the purpose of her visit. Her tone was most businesslike. "If you are serious about philanthropic endeavor, there is an intelligent way of going about it. Hunger relief is a science, just like any other."

"I wouldn't say I was relieving hunger," Wynfield said, fidgeting bashfully. "That is an overstatement."   "On the contrary, that is a gross understatement," Jocelyn objected. "What you are doing here is preventing an outbreak of cannibalism. You heard what happened seven years ago."

"Perhaps, some obscure rumors..."

"Those are not some obscure rumors! That is history—unpalatable and unpublicized but very real. Nobody wants to hear of such atrocities, least of all those who own this land."

"I shall simply have to take your word for it, Miss Stuart," Wynfield abdicated. "Thank you for coming here. Your abnegation is deeply moving, especially given your new family obligations. Which reminds me: I still have not congratulated you on your marriage."

Jocelyn clutched her heart in horror.

"Me, married? Heavens, no! I'm a proud spinster."

"And the child?"

"Oh, he's not my son. He's your son," Jocelyn blurted out nonchalantly. "He is one of the reasons why I am here."

Wynfield hunched over and began laughing. Miss Stuart's talent for delivering the most outrageous jokes with a straight face deserved applause.

"Surely, laugh your fill," Jocelyn scolded him. "His mother was no so amused, I assure you. She nearly died giving birth to him, and I nearly died delivering him to you across the stormy sea. Do you know what effort I exerted to find and extract him from his hiding place? The little devil bit me on the neck and yanked out a tuft of my hair! He is impetuous and ungrateful, just like his father."

Wynfield stopped laughing, although his shoulders continued twitching. For the first time he looked at the baby, whom until then he had perceived as a lump of squirming pink flesh.

Jocelyn separated the boy from her chest and held him to the light, so that Wynfield could examine his features properly.

"Take a look at this gem of Anglo-Celtic breeding," she proclaimed solemnly. "In the veins of this innocent creature runs the blood of Binghams, Brudenells and Hungertons. Do you realize

397

what a perilous concoction this is? Two pompous bullies and a mad republican! Many men would sell their souls for such a pedigree. Just imagine the extraordinary things this child can accomplish. Sadly, his own mother shall never know. Poor Lavinia...”

"Lavinia!" Wynfield called out, as if his exclamation could magically make Lucan's daughter appear before him. "How in the world..."

"You of all men should be able to answer that question. A physician raised you, after all. You must know how children are conceived. Sometimes little brats come into this world uninvited. Blessedly, I was not there to witness the love scene between you and Lavinia, though I doubt it was a pretty sight, given her lack of experience and your utter lack of patience. Whatever you did to avoid consequences, you did not do it soon enough. Whichever questionable precautions you took, they clearly failed. Somehow your respective pedigrees intertwined in her womb."

Wynfield sat down on his filthy unmade bed and shook his head.

"I always sensed that something between us was not finished," he murmured.

"Oh, it's finished, my dear friend," Jocelyn assured him categorically. "It is as final and irreversible as Waterloo. How hastily Lavinia washed her dainty hands of her romantic blunder! How eager she allowed others to bury her secret. The little girl was startled. Surely, she had imagined that her initiation into womanhood would be more ceremonious. You do not want a trembling coward for a wife, whose actions are guided by her tyrannical mother."

"How do you know all this?" he asked, jerking his head up.

"You mean how I learned about the existence of your son before *you* did? There is nothing unusual about this phenomenon. The man, the hero of the tryst, is often the last one to find out. Some fathers of bastards remain in the dark for decades, and some—for their entire lives. You, my dear, have only been in the dark for less than a year, so consider yourself fortunate."

"You still have not answered my question, Miss Stuart. How did you become privy to this?"

"I must be a magnet for intrigues. My veins are like telegraph wires. I breathe Morse code. I know people who know things. While looking for a discrete family for her bastard grandson, Lady Lucan turned to a soft-spoken minster from a small, poor, inconspicuous parish in Bermondsey. The countess assumed her scandal would be safer with him since he appeared so remote from the society. Can you guess the minister's name?"

"Reverend Barclay," Wynfield whispered.

"Excellent!" Jocelyn exclaimed and kissed the baby on the head. "I am pleased to see you regain your memory. As you know from personal experience, Reverend Barclay is very good at keeping secrets—but not from me. Our friendship overrides all pledges of confidentiality. He was the one who recommended the adoptive family and moderated the handing over of the child. Lady Lucan could not have done it without professional assistance. She surely would have blundered and exposed herself, given her flammable emotional state. Reverend Barclay, on another hand, is an expert in such matters. He makes arrangements of this nature quite frequently. Over the past few years there seems to be a surge in bastards. Young people are growing careless. At any rate, Lady Lucan paid the new parents good money to keep the child, but I paid them even better money to give him up. Now they can leave their pitiful little cottage in Middlesex and start a new life in another country under new names. This child is much too good for a peaceful, dull life in the countryside. His temper is too erratic, and his pedigree is too exquisite. In time, he would destroy his adoptive family. They simply would not know what to do with him. He belongs with you."

Wynfield did not say anything in response to Jocelyn's last declaration. The idea of any child belonging with him struck him as absurd. What accolades did he have as a father, as a human being? What could he possibly teach a child?

"You still do not believe me?" Jocelyn asked. "You think I have fabricated this fable for the sake of making a hostage of you? How can I convince you that I want nothing from you? I have plenty of enthusiastic allies who will join me on my next crusade without any cajoling on my part."

Wynfield arched his eyebrow, recalling his last meeting with Jocelyn a year and a half ago. At that time, she was trying to persuade him to assassinate Lord Cardigan. Looking back at the events at Balaclava, Wynfield began wondering if, maybe, he had made a mistake by refusing to assist Jocelyn. Perhaps, her schemes were not so outrageous after all. Of course, she would never ask him to help her again, not after his refusal the first time.

"There, hold him!" she said at last, placing the squirming infant onto Wynfield's chest. "My arms are quite numb from rocking him. See if your flesh recognizes him. No lie from me or anyone else is stronger than your instinct. Animals recognize their young by the scent, and we are not that far removed from our four-legged friends."

When the baby's hot forehead bumped into his mouth, Wynfield felt a spell of dizziness. His damaged arm began to tremble from the weight of the little bundle.

"And for God's sake, do not drop him on his head," Jocelyn warned him. "I fear that his foster mother had already dropped him several times. That woman did not strike me as very dexterous. Look, he has your eyebrows and your pupils. What other proof do you need? Well, do you believe now?"

"I don't know what to believe," Wynfield confessed. "It does not matter where this child came from. What matters is that he is tired."

He was looking for an excuse to break the physical contact with the child. After months of emotional drought, he experienced a chemical surge. He was about to lay the baby down on his bed, but then he noticed how filthy the sheets were. The washerwoman had not come by in months, and Wynfield did not have the motivation to change the bedding himself. On some nights, he would lie down without even undressing or taking his boots off, knowing that he would not be able to fall asleep at any rate. The only clean piece of fabric in the whole house was an embroidered tablecloth that had never been used. Wynfield wrapped the baby in that tablecloth and placed him on the bed.

"What's his name?" he asked, reluctant to look at the boy's face.

"I forgot what it was," Jocelyn admitted negligently. "His foster mother may have told me in passing. I prefer not to clog my memory with unnecessary facts. Right now he is Edmund. I took the liberty of renaming him after my late fiancé, the only man I have ever truly loved."

"Edmund is a fine name." Wynfield nodded reverently, remembering his departed half-brother. "If the child grows up to demonstrate one tenth of Mr. Barrymore's generosity and wisdom, I shall ask for nothing more."

Suddenly, the child squirmed his way out of the tablecloth and began crying. Wynfield jumped to his feet, ready to pick him up.

"Don't move," Jocelyn ordered calmly. "Do not tell me that Grinnin' Wyn cannot bear the sound of an infant whimpering.

He's probably hungry. Neither he nor I have eaten anything since this morning."

"I have some canned beef in the pantry," Wynfield proposed timidly. "I can ask Mr. Walsh to heat some on the stove."

"I don't think that Edmund is ready for such delicacies yet. By the way, if you think that there's honest-to-God beef sealed in those tins, one can only envy your optimism. For all we know, it can be cat's liver."

"There might be some goat milk and bread at the house next door. I shall send Mr. Walsh."

"No, don't send him in this weather," Jocelyn discouraged him calmly. "He'll slip and break a leg. Food can wait until tomorrow."

"No, it cannot wait!" Wynfield objected. "I'll go myself. The child is hungry. You said so yourself."

"He won't die of starvation overnight. Have you never gone hungry? By now, you should know that those pangs rise and subside. Edmund needs to learn to control urges of the stomach early on. The sooner he masters the art of silencing his body, the better off he will be. Children who are picked up and fed at the first call grow up spoiled weaklings."

The child fell silent as unexpectedly as he started crying. Having found comfort in his thumb, he fell asleep.

"Still, I find it deplorable that the boy should be separated from his mother," Wynfield said.

"Believe me, you have nothing to deplore. This separation is no great loss for the child—or even Lavinia for that matter. Like most women of her station, she is devoid of maternal instinct. As soon as their babies emerge from their bodies, they are snatched by the nurses—if they are alive, or by gravediggers—if they are dead. If this is of any consolation to you, Lavinia never laid her hand or her eyes on the child. She does not even know that he is alive. I saw her at Hyde Park with her fiancé, Charles Hardinge. Lavinia did not look like a bereaved mother, rather like a blissfully ignorant bride. Everyone is better for it. Although, the viscount may be surprised on his wedding night when discovers that his peach blossom of a wife is not a virgin. I wonder what sort of explanation Lavinia will offer him. I am certain that her mother will instruct her. The Countess has an invisible fox's tail that she uses to wipe over her tracks. She should have been an international spy. It is a shame that her gifts are wasted on family scandals."

"Miss Stuart," Wynfield suddenly interrupted her, raising his hand like a schoolboy before a stern schoolmistress, "I have not slept in three months. This is no exaggeration. Mr. Walsh shall see you into the guest room. You deserve to rest comfortably after your recent troubles. I swear on my life, I am not trying to get rid of you. If I do not lie down, I shall fall down, and the floorboards shall crack. Believe me..."

"Why, I do believe you," Jocelyn reassured him hastily. "You look like hell, Wynfield. I have seen insomniacs, and you display all the signs. Go to bed at once."

"God bless you, Miss Stuart," he sighed gratefully. "Tomorrow morning you will find me an entirely different man. Then we shall continue this conversation."

His eyes already half-closed, he stretched his hand forward, and Jocelyn pressed his fingers.

Left alone, Wynfield cautiously moved the sleeping baby closer to the wall and stretched out on the edge of the bed with his back turned to Edmund. A second later, Nature took mercy on him. After months of flattening his pillow with his fists, he was finally granted the long-denied forgetfulness.

Conclusion
Thirteen Miles to Clare Island
County Mayo, Ireland—December, 1855

Chapter 1
The Divine Healing Powers of Burned Porridge

In the heart of every father obliged by whatever circumstances to share his bed with his offspring lives the fear of inadvertently crushing the child. Fortunately for Wynfield, his sleep was so deep that he did not even move an inch through the night. He woke up in the same position in which he had dosed off. As for the child, he had freed himself completely from the confines of the tablecloth and began kicking his father in the back as if to make more room for himself. Nature had blessed him with long, lean, impressively strong legs. Physically precocious infants do not cry as much, as they are accustomed to getting their way through sheer force. Little Edmund was determined to drive the stranger off his territory. Without a squeak or a grunt, he pushed his pink sweaty heels into the stranger's spine. Another shove would send the unsuspecting father tumbling to the floor.

Suddenly, through his sleep Wynfield heard Jocelyn's whisper.

"Easy now, Edmund—this gentleman is not our enemy."

The kicking of the tiny heels stopped. A second later Wynfield heard the sound of curtains being drawn aside and felt the late morning light spilling over his face like cold water. It was an amicable slap reminding him that it was time to open his eyes. Decent people do not stay in bed past ten.

His eyelids unsealed without particular exertion on his part. Twelve hours of uninterrupted sleep sufficed to restore his vigor.

He saw Jocelyn standing in front of the window holding the child. She was still wearing the same road dress, only without the jacket. In the daylight, the tartan colors appeared unusually rich. Her hair had been brushed out and rearranged in a less fastidious fashion.

"You are still here," he whispered in awe. "You truly are here—both of you."

"If we are a nuisance, we can leave at once," Jocelyn replied. "I shall take Edmund to America or, perhaps, to Australia."

"Then I shall follow you."

"Wynfield, you are not fully awake yet. By the way, do you know that you shout in your sleep? It sounded like cavalry drill from thirty years ago."

Wynfield laughed and dropped his head back on the pillow.

"Now you are privy to all the military gossip. Oh, I hope that Mrs. Duberly mentions me in her memoirs. One day I can tell my son how I copulated with a married woman under the smoke-veiled sky."

Jocelyn graced him with a sympathetic but at the same time commanding look.

"For God's sake, Wynfield, eat something before you utter another stupid thing."

He nodded compliantly and rubbed the bridge of his nose.

"How right you are, Miss Stuart. I have not been in the presence of a lady for a long time. It only takes a few months of seclusion to turn a man into a savage. I promise to watch the drivel pouring out of my mouth."

Wynfield glanced towards the table and saw a bowl of buttered oat porridge and a steaming teapot.

"Forgive me the Spartan nature of the breakfast," Jocelyn apologized. "It was the best Mr. Walsh could procure in the morning. Do not be alarmed by the smell of smoke. There's no fire. We burned the first pot of porridge. Mr. Walsh was amusing me with his anecdotes in the kitchen. We laughed so heartily that we forgot all about the bubbling pot. Now the entire stove is covered in brown starchy substance."

Wynfield sat up on the bed and stretched his bruised back.

"Why is it that Mr. Walsh never jokes with me?" he asked. "Many months passed before he deigned to explain to me the rudiments of Celtic stonework. Miss Stuart, I'd like to give you a tour of the cemetery after breakfast. I think I've found a perfect spot for my grave."

After a few spoonfuls of burned and greasy porridge, Wynfield felt his sanity returning to him. Jocelyn knew just what to serve him. It was almost as terrible as army food. He almost wished there were more burned lumps in the porridge. When Lucan stayed at Castlebar House, he demanded smoked salmon on pumpernickel bread with dill and egg whites on the side. Wynfield found that his stomach rejected such delicacies so early in the morning. His body demanded crude, boorish nourishment. The smell of overcooked oats brought back the cheerful memories of London workhouses. The only thing missing was the subtle taste of industrial soap.

In the meanwhile, Jocelyn was trying to explain Edmund the peculiarities of the western Irish climate.

"This is not the best place for you to live if you do not like surprises," she spoke, tapping the window with her finger. "In the summer it can rain as often as seven times a day. The sun hides in the clouds and then emerges. Those flashes of light can make you go blind or at least give you a dreadful headache. The crops come up when they please and if they please."

Wynfield continued to avoid looking at the child's face in daylight, perhaps, for fear of identifying Lavinia's features and losing equanimity. His had not yet reached that stage of acceptance where he could ponder Lucan's daughter without exposing himself to pangs of bitterness. Any reminder of his crumbled infatuation still roused nostalgia, if not spiritual then certainly physical. Of the few women he had bedded, Lavinia may not have been the most skillful one, but she was most certainly the most eager one to learn. That awkward abandon with which she climbed the Olympus of sensuality could not leave a man unimpressed. Wynfield would be lying if he declared that the thought of not bedding her ever again did not grieve him at all. While in the Crimea, he had devised a string of most outrageous amorous fantasies. Now he would simply have to realize those fantasies with some other woman.

What kind of lover will that Viscount Hardinge prove to be? Wynfield asked himself, thinking of Lavinia's new fiancé. *How many children will they have? Not that it matters at this point. It is to me that she gave her virginity. I was the one who fathered her firstborn. No, I have not been defeated completely. Hardinge and I shall have to split our victory between the two of us—and I shall get the better half of it. Lavinia will miss me, for certain. Hardinge shall be a frequent guest in her bed, but I shall frequent her thoughts.*

Suddenly, Wynfield shoved the empty teacup aside, leaped to his feet, and immobilized the child's head between his hands.

"All right now, let us take a look," he said with the determination of a physician preparing to examine his patient.

To his great relief Wynfield discovered that Edmund's eyes were not gray like his or Lavinia's but hazel. This must have been the legacy of the boy's maternal grandmother, Ann Griffin, an exquisite Welshwoman who in her time had dazzled the men of Oxford, students and professors alike. Neither the Binghams, nor the Brudenells, nor Helmsleys had such eye color in their bloodlines for several generations. Edmund's eyebrows were well defined and mobile, like his father's.

"A handsome devil," Jocelyn remarked impartially, as she had seen many children in her life and could predict which ones would grow up to be beautiful. "By the way, it is the voice of esthetic sensibility, not of blind maternal instinct or Christian piety. No, I do not subscribe to the idea that all God's creatures were equally pleasing to the eye. I have seen homely children, and Edmund is not one of them, for better or for worse. Wait and see how much trouble he causes."

Chapter 2
White Blood and Celtic Solidarity

Wynfield stayed true to his promise of showing Jocelyn the cemetery, one of Castlebar's most famous attractions. By early afternoon, the snow had stopped, and the temperature rose. What can be more delightful than strolling through cold mud amidst gravestones?

Wynfield insisted on carrying the child himself, even though he knew in advance that the task would prove challenging. Since he had only one arm he could rely on, he pressed the child tightly against his chest, which was not the most comfortable position for either one of them. The grip and the smell of the stranger terrified the little boy, who kicked, fidgeted, and scratched his father's face. In spite of all the hardships, the little creature was causing him, Wynfield attempted to maintain a conversation with Jocelyn.

Just for Jocelyn's amusement, Wynfield showed her the fields where Lucan had ordered to sow wheat.

"Take a good look at my humiliation," he said, gesturing at the patches of barren land. "Have a hearty laugh."

"Then I would have to laugh at the entire British Ministry of Agriculture," Jocelyn consoled him. "Something similar is happening in England. Crops are failing everywhere. The prices on grains are expected to double. The next few years will be rotten for the whole of Europe. So may stop flagellating yourself for Lord Lucan's idiotic whims."

"I am pleased to hear that, Miss Stuart."

"That Europe is going to starve?"

"No—that you do not condemn me. And I'm not referring to the harvest."

Jocelyn sighed and wrapped her hands around his atrophying arm. They slowed down their pace.

"If you expect stones to be cast your way, they will certainly not come from me. It grieves me to disappoint you. I myself am a fruit of unsanctioned love, and so was my late fiancé Edmund Barrymore. We were both bastards, however privileged, and that fortified our solidarity."

Wynfield paused to glance at his reflection in the puddle. He had a baby on his left arm and a woman clutching his right arm. Was that possible? Only twenty-four hours ago he passed by the same puddle, and the picture looked quite different.

"Were you sincere when you said that you loved my brother?" he asked suddenly.

"What makes you doubt my sincerity?"

"The length of your engagement," Wynfield replied blatantly. "Seven years... I confess I do not know much about matrimonial formalities, but seven years strikes me as a bit long. Most people would either marry or part ways."

Jocelyn pointed at a stone bench by the entrance.

"This looks like an excellent place to take a rest," she said, taking the baby from Wynfield. Apparently, his sudden question knocked the breath out of her. She inhaled a few times, bracing herself for what promised to be an unpleasant but necessary conversation.

Wynfield sat down at a slight distance from her, beginning to regret his crude intrusion into the matters of her heart. He honestly did not expect that his question would make it necessary for her to sit down.

"To indulge your obscene curiosity, yes, I did love Edmund," Jocelyn continued. "And I was eager to bear his children, even before the formal ceremony. Plainly put, two bastards do not mind producing more bastards. Unfortunately, our children kept dying inside me early on. I lost three of them in the first year of our intimacy. No doctor could give me a satisfactory explanation. My womb was a ready-made grave for the unborn. I never initiated Edmund into my ordeal lest he should become distressed. By God, the man had already lived through so many losses. His first wife died of consumption."

"I am aware of that," Wynfield intervened, feeling a sudden urge to advocate for his late brother. "Edmund—or Capt'n Kip as I knew him—told me the story the very first night I came aboard his schooner. If I can trust my judgment of character, he was not the kind of man who would abandon a woman due to her illness or inability bear children."

"Precisely," Jocelyn confirmed, leaning her chin on her frost-bitten hands and looking straight ahead. "He would stay with his woman and uphold her, even at the expense of his own desires. For that very reason I wanted him to remain free. Every year I invented a new reason for delaying our wedding. Perhaps, one day he would find a healthy woman who could fulfill his dream of fatherhood. I could not bring myself to break the engagement. What convincing excuse could I invent? If I told him that my heart had grown cold, he would not have believed me. He knew I loved him. It was plain to see. My mother, an actress, told me that for a woman feigning love is easier than feigning indifference. I could not tell Edmund a lie, but I could not tell him the truth either, so I kept buying time. No, it was not the most admirable manner of handling the matter, but at the time I could think of nothing better. God in His mercy put an end to my seven-year performance. Edmund died of white blood. What a shock it must have been for him to meet his brood in Heaven—assuming Heaven is the place where unborn children and men of his moral caliber go. At least, that is what Reverend Barclay tells me. Reverend would not lie to me, even out of mercy. Now Edmund and our children are with God. And I am here, seeking solace in various crusades."

Wynfield chose to abstain from making any remarks. Tempted as he was to express condolences, he did not wish to insult Jocelyn inadvertently. His knowledge of this woman was too superficial, and his indebtedness to her too profound. One thing he could not deny: Jocelyn was not without her contradictions. With all her vehemently liberal views and an army of enlightened allies, she ascribed an awful deal of importance to a woman's ability to provide a man with natural heirs. Her vision of the afterlife was also surprisingly traditional, not a hint of Eastern mysticism, not a word of reincarnation. She believed in a Biblical Heaven. The same woman tried to cajole him into killing an English general less than two years ago.

"So, what is your next crusade, Miss Stuart?" Wynfield asked, presuming the question to be safe.

"Are you genuinely interested," she asked, folding her hands on her knee and turning to face him, "or are you merely asking out of politeness?"

"And now you are the one doubting my sincerity, Miss Stuart," he reproached her jokingly.

"I do not know what to think of you, Wynfield," she admitted. "You appear so content rationing canned cat liver to people who clearly loathe you."

"Come now, Miss Stuart, it isn't so terrible here—once you grow accustomed to a few things."

By then little Edmund had calmed down a bit. No, he had not grown tired of fidgeting and kicking. He could have continued tormenting the stranger by bouncing on his knee, pulling his hair and banging his forehead into the man's teeth for another few hours. Luckily for Wynfield, the boy discovered the enormous shiny buttons on his overcoat. Those shiny metallic disks looked so appetizing, that the child began salivating and twisting them. The buttons were sewn on firmly, and Edmund would have to exert considerable effort in order to detach one of them.

"Do you see yourself living here for the rest of your life?" Jocelyn asked. "Tell me in all honesty."

"I can certainly see myself dying here," Wynfield replied, honoring her request for unadulterated honesty.

"Why, that *is* the meaning of 'the rest of one's life'," she reminded him diplomatically. "Allow me to rephrase my question: do you hope that your life here will be a long or a short one? If someone told you that Castlebar was the last home you would ever know, that you would never venture farther than five miles from the town, what would your response be?"

"I would not be thrilled, but I would not be devastated either."

"And what if someone propositioned you to leave? What if someone approached you with a tempting offer that would require you to abandon Castlebar immediately?"

Wynfield was not prepared to respond to all those questions at once, as he had not even thought about leaving Castlebar

"I made a promise to Lord Lucan," he replied at last. "I cannot betray him."

Jocelyn reclined against the back of the stone bench and closed her eyes.

"Lord Lucan was the one who betrayed you," she reminded him. "He knew you had a son, and he allowed for your separation from him. He did it out of cowardice, not malice. He may not be a conscious enemy of yours, but he is certainly a traitor. I know their lot all too well. Power but no strength, big opinions but no principles..."

Wynfield found that he could not argue with Jocelyn on any of the accounts she brought forth against the earl. He knew that any attempts on his part to vindicate his former benefactor would come across as insincere. There was truly nothing left to say in Lord Lucan's defense.

"Miss Stuart, regardless of my sentiments towards the earl himself, I have grown attached to his people. I have an obligation towards them."

"Those people do not need charity. They need freedom."

Her last word, uttered in a faint whisper, soared to the sky. The same instant, the flock of crows sitting on the bare branches above the graveyard, scattered, as if Jocelyn's last word startled them. Wynfield was startled too.

"What did you say, Miss Stuart?" he asked, blinking with both eyes. By God, was she referring to Irish separatism?

"Freedom!" she repeated, having sensed that he did not understand her the first time. "Yes, to be the masters of their land, to make their own laws. What a wild concept! Wynfield, you have Celtic roots, don't you?"

"I suppose so," he replied, shrugging. "My mother was Welsh."

"And my mother was Scottish."

"Is that supposed to mean something?" Wynfield asked, maintaining his innocent tone. "I am not provoking you, Miss Stuart. I honestly do not understand."

"Can you look me in the eye and swear that you do not feel an ounce of Celtic indignation? Do you not hear the voices of your material ancestors?"

Blessedly, Wynfield had not been hearing any voices as of late. Of course, that was about to change. When he found himself in Jocelyn's presence, he would start hearing and seeing things. Her aggressively theatrical manner of delivering ideas, undoubtedly inherited from her mother, had had intoxicating effect on Wynfield. Jocelyn did not even need to raise her voice. Perhaps, that is what they mean by "charismatic orator." For Jocelyn's sake, he was willing to hear anything, even the inner cry of the Celts, or whatever she called it.

"In God's name, Wyn, have you truly become so slow-witted?" she asked, squinting. "A few minutes ago you asked me what my next crusade was. Well, this *is* my next crusade!"

"And who are your new comrades-at-arms?"

"If I shared their names with you, they would not mean much to you at any rate."

"Go on, test my ignorance."

"Does the term *Young Ireland* mean anything to you?"

As a matter of fact, the term was not entirely foreign to Wynfield. Lord Lucan had mentioned a movement in the late 1840s involving a handful of young reporters from *The Nation* newspaper, who aimed to repeal the Act of Union of 1800 and sever Ireland from Great Britain. The potato blight and the string of evictions that followed had galvanized the young journalists to violence. Their rebellion was quickly suppressed, as one should have expected. Through they were originally sentenced to death, but then their penalties were reduced to exile in Van Diemen's Land in Australia, a popular destination for criminals. The Young Irelanders were kept separate, lest they should conspire again. There was nothing unique about their uprising. It was like any other European uprising that took place in the 1840s.

"I have been corresponding with two of them, who found refuge in Paris. One of them fled to America a few years ago. The other one still lives in Paris, the capitol of secret societies. Monsieur Hugo acquainted us. He must have grown tired of our correspondence, so he handed me over to another idealist, and I am grateful to him for that. The French are the most profound masters of revolutionary science. My new Irish friend has been educating himself. His quest is to master the technique of conspiracy, which he shall use to overthrow the British rule."

The little boy let out a triumphant cry, as if to confirm the last statement of his patroness.

"Hear that, Miss Stuart?" Wynfield asked, bouncing the child on his knee. "You have an enthusiastic young sympathizer. I must admit, your confidence is infectious."

"I would not commit myself to a cause unless I considered it was worthy and viable. I am convinced that we can establish an independent Irish republic. The vision is spelled out right here."

She reached into the breast pocket of her jacket, pulled out a letter, and brandished it as if she would a flag.

"Please, Miss Stuart, do not wave his piece of paper over my head," Wynfield said, sliding closer to her. "Slap me across the face with it instead. That would help me gain a deeper understanding of your passion. You know how well I respond to physical violence. Anymore, slaps and punches are the only way to communicate any ideas to me. Do not think for a second that I ridicule your dreams? If it appears that way, it is only because I no longer have any of own."

"Your stupor is temporary," she said with sudden tenderness, brushing the envelope against his cheek. "Your thirst for blood shall awaken."

"I have been called a hero, but I certainly do not feel like one."

"Perhaps, it is because you have been fighting on the wrong side." She spoke calmly, without a shadow of pathos, as if reiterating a universally accepted fact. "The cause of your unrest and dissatisfaction is quite apparent. All this time you have been defending the interests of a thoroughly evil entity. The British army is next to Satan's."

"Is it really? In that case, I should be relieved that you've never seen me in my cavalry uniform. You would probably see horns growing through the helmet. You certainly would not allow me to hold the child. Although, Mrs. Duberly thought that the Heavies looked quite dashing."

"Ah, what is a uniform?" Jocelyn asked sorrowfully and tucked a graying strand behind his ear. "It's but a few square yards of red wool and a handful of shining buttons. You were deceived, my poor friend. Deceived..."

Her weather-beaten fingers with cracked nails lingered on his face, smoothing out the creases. The sudden lapse from austerity to tenderness threw Wynfield into utter perplexity. Of course, that could have been her very intention. Still not certain whether she was mocking or encouraging him, Wynfield could not bring himself to respond to her caresses, so he accepted them passively. He appeared to have forgotten about the child on his knee.

"It just occurred to me that we have not kissed yet," Jocelyn whispered, brushing his mouth with her knuckles. "How could we have allowed for such an oversight? All this talk about white blood and Celtic solidarity distracted us."

The creases on Wynfield's forehead deepened.

"You are mocking me," he said, separating his lips from her hand.

"Not in the least. This is a perfect place for our third kiss. The first one happened on Camberwell Green seventeen years ago, and the second one—inside the library of Hungerton Lodge right before the war broke out. Do not think me sentimental. I have an excellent memory, that's all."

They simply had not reached that stage of familiarity where two people lose count of their kisses, where caresses seize being revelations and turn into mere affirmations. Wynfield and Jocelyn were shivering on a stone bench in the middle of a cemetery, ankle-deep in mud, with ravens circling above their heads. In another life, in the realm of their chaotically intertwined dreams, they had already become lovers. Had their hour finally arrived? Was their dormant affair that had begun on the fairground in the spring of 1838 destined to consummate at last?

Wynfield could not embrace Jocelyn with his right arm. The cold air exacerbated the weakness and the stiffness of the muscles. The most he could do was cup her knee with his trembling hand.

The disapproving growl of the infant reminded them that they were no longer mere lovers. Overnight they had become something of a family, a clique of conspirators. Wynfield still felt that the blood tie between him and the child amounted to little more than a formality. Edmund was Jocelyn's son to a greater degree. She had known of his existence longer. She risked and endured more for his sake. She had occupied the place vacated by Lavinia. If there were any woman who could claim the title of Edmund's mother, it would be Jocelyn. It was her approval that Wynfield needed if he wished any rights to that child. At the same time, if Fate deemed it necessary to make him indebted to a woman, he would not have chosen any other.

They had not discussed their immediate future explicitly, but Jocelyn's demeanor indicated that she had no intention of simply leaving the child in the hands of his natural father. It was possible that a journey was in store for the three of them, perhaps as far as another continent. If they were destined to sail to Australia after all, so be it! At least they would be sailing there free people. If Jocelyn wanted to build barricades, he would supply the broken furniture gladly. What the devil! He had not maimed and killed Russians in the Crimea? Indulging the whims of an idealistic woman cannot be more degrading than taking orders from cynical men. In the meantime, Wynfield made every effort to prolong the kiss, partly because he had not indulged in this ritual in well over a year and partly to delay the conversation regarding what was to happen next.

Chapter 3
The Fox Swifter
Than Ten Hounds

Suddenly, Jocelyn tensed up and looked over Wynfield's shoulder towards the cemetery gate. The butler from the Castlebar House, the man who never hurried anywhere, was running towards them, looking unusually disquieted.

"Is anything the matter, Mr. Walsh?" Jocelyn asked.

The butler stopped and bent over to catch his breath, with his hands pushing into his knees. Apparently, he had been running for some time.

"There are English gentlemen looking for Lord Hungerton," he replied.

"And what did you tell them?"

"I told them that Lord Hungerton went out for a walk—alone. And that he was not expected back until the evening."

"Well done, Mr. Walsh," Jocelyn praised the butler, helping him straighten out and pressing his hands.

They exchanged mysterious cavalier smiles like two partners in crime whose camaraderie had been tested by time. The smile vanished from the butler's face a second later.

"The gentlemen did not leave," he proceeded in a trembling voice, "nor do they intend to. Four of them remained outside the house, and the other six dispersed in various directions. They were armed."

Wynfield stood up from the stone bench and threw the baby over his left shoulder.

"Miss Stuart, would you care to explain to me what is happening? I was not expecting visitors, especially ten of them, bearing arms."

"I was not expecting them so soon either," Jocelyn muttered aside, releasing the butler's hands. "Oh, I knew they would come. I thought I was several steps ahead and making excellent time. Unfortunately, it appears that they are not far behind me, not as far as I had hoped they would be."

"For God's sake, of whom are you speaking?"

"You know perfectly well of whom! Do you think that Lady Lucan would allow her bastard grandson out of England so easily? The child is her only leverage over her husband. She will do anything to keep him here. Ah, damnation... I prayed for another day of peace. No such luck! The vicious hag sniffed me out and sent her hounds. She must have asked her buffoon brother, Lord Cardigan, to help her. They know that the child can only be in one place."

Watching Jocelyn pacing back and forth in the mud, Wynfield felt his ribcage expanding. The volume of blood in his veins must have doubled miraculously. At last, he could breathe! He had been denied the thrill of adversity for ages, it seemed. Once again he had enemies, people who wanted his head on a stick! Above all, he no longer had to agonize over his promises to Lucan. The decision had been made for him. He could not stay on the island.

Having regained composure, Jocelyn looked at the butler again, now with a businesslike air.

"Mr. Walsh, where is the nearest port?"

"Newport Town, Miss Stuart, no more than fifteen miles from here."

"I need two horses, sturdy horses that can travel in such weather."

"You can have my brother's," the butler replied without blinking. "His house is half a mile away down in the valley. In winter you see the rooftop from here."

"God bless you, Mr. Walsh."

Wynfield could not help but marvel at Jocelyn's ability to win the loyalty of complete strangers. Driven by some vague instinct of chivalry, Mr. Walsh was willing to put himself at risk for her sake.

He certainly was not doing it for Lord Hungerton. The butler hardly glanced in his new master's direction. Mr. Walsh's main goal was to protect the beautiful woman and the child that he perceived as a part of her. Without being privy to all the details, he realized that the ten English gentlemen were after the boy, aiming to take him away from the charming and generous lady. With God as his witness, Thomas Walsh would not allow it.

The butler's brother, Robert Walsh, was the most accomplished and prosperous mason in Castlebar whose work had become famous even in the neighboring counties. His chisel carved half of the headstones at the cemetery. His house was an enormous workshop. When the frazzled strangers arrived, they paused at the threshold for a few seconds to marvel at the multitude of half-finished sculptures.

"I need two of your best horses, Robert," the butler declared. "And your ugliest, dirties work clothes for our guests to change into. They cannot travel in their present apparel. Do not ask any questions."

The mason was not even going to ask any questions. He saw the beautiful lady untying the strings of her purse.

"This is for your troubles, Mr. Walsh," she said, leaving a handful of coins on his workbench. "The Almighty shall cover the rest."

Without touching the coins, the mason counted them with his eyes.

"Why can't we have such intruders every day?" he asked his brother, when the guests disappeared in the cellar with a heap of rags.

Robert Walsh lived alone and therefore did not have any women's clothes in his house. Jocelyn took great pleasure transforming herself into an adolescent masonry apprentice. The transformation played in her favor, as it would confuse the Englishmen, who would be looking for a lady.

"What is the itinerary, General Stuart?" Wynfield asked.

"We ride from here to Newport and then take a boat to Clare," Jocelyn explained, wrapping her hair in a bun and hiding it under a boy's cap. "It's a picturesque island no more than seven square miles right at the mouth of Clew Bay. The quartzite hills on the north-west peaked at fifteen hundred feet, while the east and the south are quite flat. If you like Celtic stonework, I must show you the remains of the late 15th century Cistercian friary. Galway monks founded it. Perhaps, one day we can return there. For now, pray that we do not run into a storm. From there we shall take a bigger boat and sail around the west coast of Ireland to Guernsey to visit Monsieur Hugo, who, I am certain, will be delighted to see you. From Guernsey we proceed to Calais, and from Calais—straight to Paris, to reunite with my Young Ireland friend."

Jocelyn blurted out her plan on one breath, as if traveling by sea in late December with an infant was a usual activity for her.

On the way out of the mason's house, they stuffed their mouths with dusty bread and gulped down warm ale. Robert wrapped a few boiled potatoes in a towel for the child. It was the only food in the house suitable for the toothless gums of an infant.

"God bless you both!" Jocelyn exclaimed and kissed the two brothers on the foreheads fervently. "We shall never meet again. I shall pray for you."

She ran into the yard, where Wynfield was waiting with the two horses. Suddenly, she heard the butler's voice behind her back.

"Wait now, Miss Stuart. I shall ride with you. You do not know the way. Robert, give us a third horse!"

Just like before, the mason obliged without asking any questions. He had been carving stones for so many years that his own face had stiffened, resembling one of his own sculptures.

Before mounting her horse, Jocelyn took the baby from Wynfield.

"You shall need at least one hand on the reigns," she explained. "Besides, the arms of a woman are more enduring than those of a man."

There was one main road leading from Castlebar to Newport, but Mr. Walsh took them down the less traveled paths. Luckily, the horses were sturdy and accustomed to traveling on soft wet soil, but the ride itself took much longer than anticipated. The fugitives did not hear the sound of the sea until after dark.

The coastline of Clew Bay was lined with fishing huts and boats. Very few of the huts were illuminated from within. There was virtually no sign of life or movement ashore.

"When they hear the jingle of coins, they shall wake up at once," Jocelyn remarked smugly.

She dismounted from the horse, handed the child over to Wynfield, and began descending the slope towards the fishing village. Mr. Walsh followed her.

Jocelyn pointed to the biggest boat, a Norwegian-Scottish hybrid known as the Skaffie, with rounded stems, raked sterns, two masts with a tall dipping lugsail and a mizzen sail.

"Do not be deceived by the size of the boat," Mr. Walsh warned her. "You can maneuver it easily when the water is still, but in bad weather they become quite unstable. Not to mention, it takes at least five people to crew it."

"Then which boat do you recommend?"

"This one!" The butler pointed at the least impressive vessel that looked like an upturned shell of a walnut. "Now pray that the owner is willing to lend it to you."

Wynfield, who remained on the top of the cliff with the horses and the child, could not hear what they were saying or see their gestures very well in the dark.

"Some adventure we've gotten ourselves into, little one," he whispered to Edmund.

Edmund fanned out his fingers and reached out towards the sea, as if to grasp the glistening black abyss. He did not appear frightened in the least. To Wynfield's relief, the child remained calm throughout the journey from Castlebar to Newport. He did not cry or protest once, even though he had not anything to eat since morning. The boiled potatoes given by the mason remained untouched in the saddle sack. The giant rocks, the starless sky and the roaring waters fascinated him. He received signals from the universe that the adults around him could not capture.

At the foot of the cliff, Wynfield saw a string of moving golden dots, like fireflies in a row. Those were the lights of sea lanterns used by fishermen. Jocelyn was returning with Mr. Walsh and two villagers.

Wynfield pressed the child to his chest and began descending the cliff, careful not to lose footing in the dark.

"The gentlemen were kind enough to barter with us," Jocelyn explained to him once he was close enough to hear. "For thirty shillings they will take us to Clare. I told them they could keep two of the horses."

Does this woman eliminate all her troubles with money? Wynfield asked himself when Jocelyn returned with a fisherman tagging behind her. He appeared to have forgotten that he did precisely the same when he ordered food for Lucan's tenants.

When Jocelyn turned around to say goodbye to Mr. Walsh for the second time, he had already dissolved in the storm. The massive rocks devoured him. Their enigmatic guide abandoned them as suddenly as he had come to their aid. His task was finished.

The two young fishermen began untying the boat, exchanging bewildered growls among themselves. They did not receive such proposals every day. An Englishwoman dressed like an Irish apprentice had just paid them thirty pounds to take her and her companions to Clare Island. When presented with such a sum of money, one does not ask questions.

Jocelyn lifted the lantern over her head and beckoned Wynfield. The orange yellow illuminated her flushed face haloed in wet curls escaping from underneath the cap.

The wind muffled her voice, but Wynfield guessed her words by the movement of her lips.

"One day you shall thank me."

Epilogue
In the Spirit of
Fenian Brotherhood

A letter from James Stephens to John O'Mahoney
February, 1856

Greetings, John! I am pleased to inform you that my French exile is coming to an end. I intend on making my way back to Ireland. God willing, before the year's end, I shall be in New York, in the company of our brothers. In the meantime, I have been entertaining my charming Anglo-Scottish correspondent from London. To my disagreeable surprise, she did not arrive alone. She brought along a rather peculiar fellow who introduced himself as Mr. Wynfield Grant. I confess the selfish masculine part of me was a bit disappointed to see Miss Stuart in the company of another man, even if he is a Crimean veteran. Thus far, I am not particularly impressed. Except for his scars on his face and his mangled right arm, he has next nothing to show for himself. A pitiable ruin of a man at twenty-six! I doubt that he believes in or even completely understands our cause, but his devotion to Miss Stuart—soon to be Mrs. Grant—is unquestionable. He shall follow her wherever she directs him. I forgot to mention, they have a boy with them, a most vexatious little creature that I must praise and indulge. Alas, Johnny, I do not have the luxury of alienating our charming Anglo-Scottish lady friend. It would pain me to see her waste her fortune on some other cause. There are so bloody

425

many noble causes and so few persons willing to fund them. We must not allow trivial nuisances distract us from the vision of our triumph. After seven years of exile, I shall be able to return to Ireland and meet the comrades of '48. In my mind, I refer to the forthcoming pilgrimage as my three thousand mile walk. Until then, keep me in your prayers.

Yours in the spirit of Fenian brotherhood,
Jim Stephens

About the Author

___

Marina Julia Neary

Marina Julia Neary is an award-winning historical essayist, novelist, playwright, poet and multilingual arts & entertainment journalist. Her specialties include French Romanticism, Neo-Victorianism and Irish nationalism.

Her dramatic works include historical tragicomedies *Hugo in London* (Heuer Publishing) and *Lady with a Lamp: an Untold Story of Florence Nightingale* (Fireship Press). Her poetry and speculative fiction have appeared in numerous print and online magazines such as *The Recorder, Bewildering Stories, Other Voices* and *ResAliens*. Irish history enthusiasts will enjoy her short novel *Brendan Malone: the Last Fenian* (2011, All Things That Matter Press). *Wynfield's War*, a tale of the Crimean campaign, is a sequel to *Wynfield's Kingdom*, a tale of London slums, and was featured on the cover of the *First Edition Magazine* in the UK. Both books were published in 2010 by Fireship Press.

If you enjoyed this book you'll love the first book in *Marina Julia Neary's* Wynfield Series

Wynfield's Kingdom

A Tale of the London Slums.

Welcome to 1830s Bermondsey, London's most notorious slum, a land of gang wars, freak shows, and home to every depravity known to man.

Dr. Thomas Grant, a disgraced physician, adopts Wynfield, a ten-year old thief savagely battered by a gang leader for insubordination. The boy grows up to be a slender, idealistic opium addict who worships Victor Hugo. By day he steals and resells guns from a weapons factory. By night he amuses filthy crowds with his adolescent girlfriend—a fragile witch with wolfish eyes.

Wynfield senses that he has a purpose outside of his rat-infested kingdom; but he never guesses that he had been selected at birth to topple the British aristocracy.

www.FireshipPress.com

LaVergne, TN USA
21 March 2011
220967LV00002B/4/P

9 781611 790665